HEYERWOOD: A Novel

Lauren Gilbert

authorHOUSE®

AuthorHouse™
1663 Liberty Drive
Bloomington, IN 47403
www.authorhouse.com
Phone: 1-800-839-8640

© *2011 Lauren Gilbert. All rights reserved.*

No part of this book may be reproduced, stored in a retrieval system, or transmitted by any means without the written permission of the author.

First published by AuthorHouse   5/23/2011

ISBN: 978-1-4634-0250-1 (e)
ISBN: 978-1-4634-0251-8 (dj)
ISBN: 978-1-4634-0252-5 (sc)

Library of Congress Control Number: 2011908279

Printed in the United States of America

Any people depicted in stock imagery provided by Thinkstock are models, and such images are being used for illustrative purposes only.
Certain stock imagery © Thinkstock.

This book is printed on acid-free paper.

Because of the dynamic nature of the Internet, any web addresses or links contained in this book may have changed since publication and may no longer be valid. The views expressed in this work are solely those of the author and do not necessarily reflect the views of the publisher, and the publisher hereby disclaims any responsibility for them.

DISCLAIMER
This book is a work of fiction. The names, characters, events and places are the result of the author's imagination, or are used as fiction, and are not to be considered factual. Any resemblance to persons, places or other entities either living or dead is completely coincidental.

Dedication

To my husband, Ed Gilbert.
I deeply appreciate all of the patience, encouragement and support you
have given me during this long process. Thank you, Hon!

With grateful thanks to my mentors, John Di Lemme and Michelle
Prince, who helped push me to the finish line.

Chapter 1

Swathed in deepest black mourning, Catherine stared out of the window with unseeing eyes. If she had seen it, she would have felt the drab grey day to be appropriate for the occasion. Due to the recent death of her husband, the Earl of Heyerwood, she could not go out into her own garden without draping herself in black veils, so the absence of sunshine relieved her of any desire to leave the shelter of her house. "My house," she thought fiercely, "MINE!" Curled in a chair by the window, she brooded about the chain of events leading her to her present circumstances, events in which she herself had had little or no input. The only thing she had to do was get through the next few days with her resolve unshaken. She had already taken steps to ensure support in the event her strength faltered.

Catherine read again the letter from her solicitor. Her husband's will was quite clear, if unusual. Since he had died childless, had no male heir to succeed him, and no entail to consider, his property was entirely his to do with as he chose. He had chosen to leave everything to her outright, to do with as she pleased. More than that, he had even taken steps to bestow his title on her, to pass on to her heirs, should she have any. A most unusual step, it had taken him a great deal of work, including obtaining a special remainder from the king, but he had succeeded. She had not looked for such consideration; indeed she would not have been surprised had she been left with the merest competence. The solicitor indicated that he would be with her, to discuss the estate in detail, within a few days. In fact, she expected him to arrive this day. His presence would make the interview she anticipated with dread much easier. There was no one whose presence she desired less than the man she had to see tomorrow: her father.

The door opened and the smiling face of Mary, her aunt and companion, peeped around the door. "There you are, my dear. I am come to tell you that tea is ready. I am sure you must be dying of thirst. It is such a cold, gloomy day, and tea will be just the thing. Shall you come to the drawing room, or would you prefer that it be served here, in your boudoir?" "I will join you in the drawing room. I was just coming anyway; I find I've had enough of my own company for one day. I hope you are comfortably settled. Do you need anything?" "Oh my dear!" exclaimed Mary. "That beautiful room is so cozy, and I could not possibly want for anything. When I consider where I was, and my circumstances, just a few months ago, I dare swear I could weep for joy! Never was anything so timely as your request for my company. I only hope I can be of use to you in your time of need." Catherine smiled affectionately and replied, "Aunt Mary, I am the fortunate one. I have such urgent need for your presence and support. You, of all people know my circumstances and my present need. You, my father's sister!" The smile vanished from Mary's pleasant countenance, and, as she and Catherine entered the drawing room, she said with gravity, "Indeed, yes. While one must always be respectful of the head of one's family, there is no denying that Gerard is most.... unnatural in his lack of feeling. While I had hoped, I really did not expect him to exert himself for me, but his treatment of you! His callous disregard for .... but enough of that. I will help you in any way I can. When do you expect my brother's arrival?" "Sometime tomorrow. Hopefully, he will not want to stay when he sees that his errand is fruitless, but I know he will not give up tamely."

As the ladies sat before the fire and sipped their tea, a gig pulled up before the door. A loud knock proclaimed a visitor. As Catherine and Mary looked toward the door, the butler announced, "Mr. Stuart has arrived, Lady Heyerwood." "Please show him in immediately, Howard, and see that his room is ready. Mr. Stuart will be with us for a few days, I hope." They continued their tea, discussing the weather idly. Mr. Stuart approached, bowed deeply, and said "Lady Heyerwood, Madam St. Clair, I hope I find you well." Catherine inclined her head and said, "Mr. Stuart, pray be seated and do have some tea. It is so cold today, is it not? I hope your journey was not too uncomfortable." "Fortunately, there was no snow or ice on the roads, and few other travelers. I have brought copies of your late husband's will, the estate accounts, and the investiture of your title to go over with you at your leisure." "I trust, Mr. Stuart, that the original documents are safely bestowed?" "Indeed, my lady, everything is safely locked in a vault."

"Thank you, Mr. Stuart. I have no wish to start our business discussions with you so newly arrived. However, I must tell you that your presence and support will be of the greatest necessity to me tomorrow. A most painful interview will take place, and I hope I can count on your loyalty to my late husband's wishes." "How is this, my lady? I particularly desired any creditors or persons with affairs to settle to contact me directly, not to trouble your ladyship! I do not understand…"

Catherine said desperately, "My father is coming tomorrow, and will expect to be placed in charge of my person and property. This must and will not be! I am of age, and my late husband's intent and desires are clear. However, my father will try to browbeat me or trick me into giving him control. I rely on my dear aunt Mary's presence, and yours, to help me withstand his machinations for the first time in my life. Painful as it is to acknowledge, I have never been anything to my father but a commodity he could use for gain. You, of all people, you who drew up my marriage contract, know how little care and concern he has for me. I will not return to that…that state of bondage again!" Appalled, Mr. Stuart responded, "My dear Lady Heyerwood, you may rely on me completely. If you wish, I can send him to the right-about without your seeing him at all. After all, he received a generous settlement at your marriage. He has no valid right to expect anything further. You are of legal age, and your husband's will establishes your complete control over your property. Your father cannot reasonably demand…." "Reasonably! My father concerns himself only with his own needs and desires. Reason has no bearing. For my own self-respect, I must needs deal with this situation myself, so far as I am able. Having the support of my aunt and you, a well-respected solicitor, will be of the greatest value to me. And now, sir, I am persuaded you would like to get settled and to rest after your journey. We dine at seven o'clock. The butler, Howard, shall be at your disposal if you need anything." Mr. Stuart rose, bowed and said "Thank you for your consideration, Lady Heyerwood. Until later." Quietly, he left the room.

Catherine rose herself, and walked to the window. "Aunt Mary, I beg you will not leave my side tomorrow, until my father leaves this house. I do not, under any circumstance, wish to be alone with him. "Indeed not, my dear. I shall not leave you unattended." "Thank you! I must go to my room now, to make ready for dinner." With that, Catherine gathered her skirts and fled to her boudoir.

Chapter 2

Five years previously, the Honorable Catherine St John, daughter of Gerald, Viscount Stanton and his wife Mathilde, was five-and-twenty, and considered herself upon the shelf. Although she had been out since making her curtsey to the queen at age eighteen, and had had many offers, her father had refused them all. He made no secret of the fact that she was, in fact, for sale to the highest bidder and, so far, either the funds or the status had been inadequate to tempt him to approve a match. She did not fully understand what her father wanted; she only knew that her own feelings were not to be considered. She had, in fact, received an offer of marriage a few years earlier from a young man for whom she had felt a decided *tendre*. Her father had refused the offer. Violently angered by her tears and pleading, he had struck her several times and locked her in her room for a month. Since that time, she had taken care to stay out of her father's way as much as possible. His cold grey eyes, eyes that showed no emotion but calculation, horrified her.

Small, slender yet rounded in the appropriate places, Catherine's appearance was considered pleasing. She wore her shining brown hair in the feathery curls made popular by Lady Caroline Lamb, and delicate muslins became her slim figure admirably. After her first season, she was able to leave off white and pastel colours and wear the deep greens and yellows that set off her green eyes and creamy complexion to admiration. While not an accredited beauty, Catherine was held to be very taking. Being well born, with a decent marriage portion, she attracted a great deal of attention on the Marriage Mart. She met David Lovell, Earl of Heyerwood, at a ball at Lady Sefton's house. He skillfully detached her from a group of young people and swept her into a dance. She did not know what to make of him. He did not actually look at her; his eyes were busily gazing around the room. His shirt points were so high and so stiffly starched, he could scarcely bend his head, which made conversation difficult as he was quite tall. The top of her head barely cleared his shoulder. When the dance ended, the earl thanked her and abandoned her where she stood. Flushed with mortification, Catherine left the floor and went at once to her mother's side.

The next day, her father informed her that he had received an offer of marriage for her from the Earl of Heyerwood, and that he had accepted it. The contract was already being drawn. Stunned, she said, "The Earl of ....? The man who abandoned me on the floor last night? I was ready to sink! Why would he make an offer for me? I don't know him, and he certainly didn't seem interested in me at all." Lord Stanton roared, "WHY is none of your business, miss! He made the offer, I'm satisfied, and you'll marry him if I have to drag you to the altar myself! Go to your room. Soon enough for you to appear when the engagement is announced, and there's an end to it!" Trembling in fear and in sudden rage, she stood her ground. "Father, I am of age. I don't want to marry a stranger, and a forced marriage isn't legal! At least, let me be acquainted with him before a final decision is made." Enraged, her father grabbed her and struck her full in the mouth, splitting her lip and knocking her to the floor. As her head hit a chair leg, she heard him screaming in incoherent rage. Then she blacked out. She woke up in her bed, with a pounding headache. She rang for her maid. After several minutes, she heard someone in the hall, and a key turned in the lock. She had been locked in! Catherine was shocked. The housekeeper, accompanied by her mother, came in with a tea tray. "That's all, Martha." said the viscountess. The housekeeper left, locking the door behind her. "Am I a prisoner now, Mama?" asked Catherine. Her mother looked at her blankly from strangely faded eyes. "Catherine, you know your father will not tolerate question. I'm afraid you have no real alternative but to marry where your father chooses." "Mama, please, please help me!" "Help you? How can I, when I've never been able to help myself?" replied her mother hopelessly. "Marriage will at least get you out of your father's control." "Yes, but it will put me in the hands of strangers." Catherine said bitterly. "Have I no rights? Forced marriages are not legal!" "No, Catherine, you have no rights. If you refuse, your father can legally cast you out without a penny or imprison you in your room or even send you to a hospital for the insane. You know your father, Catherine." Appalled and terrified,

5

Catherine agreed to the engagement. To her dismay, the wedding was to be held quietly, within a few days.

The Earl of Heyerwood called at the house. Bowing over her hand, he said "Your servant, ma'am. Deeply grateful you accepted. Do my best to make you happy." He dropped her hand and, after tossing a small box into her lap, took a seat without waiting for an invitation. Taken aback, she opened the box and, to her surprise and dismay, found a betrothal ring of some magnificence. Set in heavy gold, the center stone, a topaz of glowing honey color, was surrounded by diamonds. She slid it onto her finger and was surprised to find that it fit her perfectly. "Thank you, sir. I neither expected nor desired such a token from you. Surely it seems a bit unnecessary?" He glanced at her with indifference, and replied "Family tradition. The ring is always presented to the bride-to-be. At least, topaz suits you." She sat across from him and attempted to engage him in conversation to no avail. He did not look at her again, just sat staring into the fire. She took the opportunity to study him. An extremely tall, thin man, his face was worn and his dark eyes deeply shadowed, as if exhausted. He was again dressed in an extreme fashion, with outlandishly high shirt points and a brightly-patterned waistcoat, and with what appeared to be paint on his face.

They did not meet again until their wedding, which was held in a side chapel at St. George's. She wore a satin gown of deep ivory trimmed with pearls, enhanced by the pearl necklace and earrings given to her by her mother on the way to the church, the only touch of colour being the glowing topaz on her finger. With tears in her eyes, the viscountess said, "Try to make your own happiness, Catherine." All of a sudden, the wedding was over, and she was almost running down the isle, her hand on her new husband's arm, trying to keep pace with his long stride. They got into his carriage and drove away, not even staying for the wedding breakfast, for which Catherine could only be grateful, as she had neither the heart nor the stomach for such a public display. As they rode along, the earl either stared out the window or slept. Catherine was, for all intents and purposes, alone with her thoughts. "Make your own happiness." Mathilde had said. "How could one do that with no control of one's own destiny?" she thought bitterly. On the second day of the journey, still having no idea of their destination, she turned desperately to the earl. "My lord, please talk to me. We are husband and wife now. I would ask some questions. Pray, my lord, do me the courtesy of answering them!" David opened his eyes and looked at her with some surprise, saying with indifference, "By all means, madam, ask and, if I can, I will answer."

"Where are we going?" asked Catherine. "Why, to my country seat in Somerset, Heyerwood Manor. Pretty enough place, between Bath and Bridgewater, near the water. Nothing nearby except the village, but close enough to the main road." Emboldened by his civil response, she asked, "Why did you ask for me, sir? I am passable but not an accredited beauty, and my portion is at best adequate." He leaned back in his seat and looked at her with boredom. "Frankly, ma'am, you are the only respectable female I could get, and I was the only one with a title grand enough who was willing to meet your father's price." Shocked, she could only stare at him for a moment. "Why were you driven to buy the first respectable female you could?" she finally whispered. Sardonically, he looked at her. "In a nutshell, you are lending me countenance in exchange for my title and money. Your father gained a title for his daughter that he thinks he can boast of and a tidy fortune of his own. You need not worry that I will bother you in any way; you will be free to make Heyerwood Manor your own, and to spend as much blunt as you wish. I neither expect nor wish an heir; some families should die out, and mine is one of them. We all gain, even you. From what I've seen of your father, you will be better off with me, such as I am. I will visit you often enough to satisfy convention. Otherwise, I will pursue … ah, my own amusements, as usual. You may do as you wish, as long as you do not foist a brat on me. It'll be good to have someone at hand, to see to the estate." Silenced, she withdrew her gaze and stared out the window as the continued to drive on.

After three days of travel, the carriage pulled up in front of the house, a huge stone manor obviously aged and built of many styles, as different generations had added on. Since the façade had been modernized, it presented a pleasing enough picture. The front gardens were well maintained and gay with flowers, even on a rainy day. The door was opened by the butler, who introduced himself to her, "I'm Howard, my lady, at your service. I hope you will find Heyerwood Manor comfortable." Her first confused gaze fell upon what appeared to be hundreds of servants but soon sorted out to a manageable number. Her husband bowed punctiliously and kissed her hand, saying, "Hope you'll be comfortable. Ask Howard for anything you want. May want to hire a companion or some such. Send any bills to Stuart; he'll pay 'em." With that, he went up the stairs to his own rooms. She did not see him again for a week.

Much to her relief, the house was well maintained, and the staff well trained and obliging. Within a few days, she felt comfortable meeting with the housekeeper and supervising the running of a large household. She had also met the agent and begun exploring the estate itself. Her own rooms were beautifully furnished with a cherry bedroom suite, and included a dressing room and a boudoir with a dainty desk, bookshelves, comfortable chaise longue and a few cozy armchairs. Her possessions had arrived, her grandmother's worktable already in place. She fell immediately in love with her rooms, with their soft ivory walls and delicately embroidered curtains and bed hangings with flowers and leaves in soft yellows, greens and peach tones. At least she had one place to call her own. Near the bay window overlooking the garden, she placed a chair next to the worktable and placed her embroidery frame where it would best catch the natural light. She then unpacked her books and bric-a-brac items, and felt herself at home. She would be able to read, write and embroider in comfort and privacy for the first time in her adult life. She admired the view while the maids unpacked her clothes in the dressing room, and then went in to place the miniatures of her mother and grandmother on her bedroom fireplace mantle.

She and David did not talk privately. They met only at dinner and in the drawing room after dinner, where their conversation was general and desultory, at best. Catherine was somewhat afraid to ask about his family and his life; David was obviously indifferent to her. At the end of the second week, David left and she did not see him again for six months. The next visit took much the same form; a week confined to his room, a second week seeing him only at dinner and he departed again, with no word of when she would see him again. For something to do, she began taking an interest in the operations of the estate and occasionally visited the village. She also engaged in desultory correspondence with a few of her friends. Although she attended church from time to time, she could never get accustomed to the curious looks she received. In the second year of their marriage, Catherine asked him if she could come to London for some part of the season, to see friends and to shop. He looked at her with surprise and said, "Don't think you should; might prove to be embarrassing for you. Most of London knows my story, and won't hesitate to cut your acquaintance. Better not expose yourself. Try Bath or one of the other such places. I don't go there, so you'll be able to make your own way. You'll need a companion though. Respectable females your age don't go jauntering about alone, even if married." She dropped the subject and contented herself with occasional visits to the village shops and ordering what she could not obtain locally by writing to various shops in London. She was mystified by her husband's frank statements about his reputation, puzzled as to what could be so bad that would result in her being cut upon showing her face in town. A letter from her father soon left her no illusions.

On the occasion of her twenty-seventh birthday, a gift from her mother came accompanied by letters from both parents. Her mother sent her a novel and some new embroidery silks, with a brief, warm letter extending her best wishes for Catherine's birthday and fond hopes for Catherine's contentment. The viscount's letter might have been written with acid-he was enraged by the poor bargain she had made. The first time he mentioned his son-in-law at his club, he found out about the earl's scandalous escapades; he couldn't hold his head up in town, thanks to the uproar created by the earl. If he'd known about Heyerwood's abominable reputation and the scandals he delighted in creating, he would never have agreed to the marriage. The letter went on and on, outlining Catherine's disgrace and its effect on her own family in brutal detail. Sold by her father into a sham marriage with a man apparently deep in all vices, then blamed by that same father who had made it impossible to refuse. Shattered by her father's revelations and obvious contempt for her, she stayed in her rooms for days, too humiliated to show her face. She did not hear from her parents again.

In the fourth year of their marriage, David came for one of his usual repairing leases. Thinner than ever and coughing painfully, he retired to his rooms immediately. She did not see or hear from him for several days. Finally, he sent for her. As she walked into the state chambers, into which she had never ventured previously, he said, "Sit by the window in the light, where I can see you, but don't come too close. I have things I must say to you before it's too late." She sat quietly, and looked at him enquiringly. "We have managed better than I thought. Just hope you haven't been too lonely here. I realize this hasn't been fair to you, cutting you off from society. Too late now, though." He coughed rackingly, and panted for breath. "Wanted you too know that I appreciate the way you've managed the house and estate, as well as the circumstances. Going to Italy for my health, and probably won't be coming back. Just want you to know that I am leaving you fixed up, all right and tight. I've got all the paperwork in train with my solicitor, Stuart. All the information is in my estate room downstairs-just contact him when the time comes. You still need to get a companion. Shouldn't be alone." Coughing, he lay back on his pillows, panting for breath, and looked directly at her for possibly the first time in their marriage. "You know, had I desired a conventional marriage, you would have been the female I would have chosen. You deserve better than a degenerate ruin and, after I'm gone, I hope you find someone with whom you'll be happy. Just don't let your father in the door!" Closing his eyes, he waved his hand weakly toward the door. "Got to rest now. I'll see you before I leave." Curtseying, Catherine left silently.

That was her last visit from her husband. After he left, Catherine did not hear from David again. Several months later, she received the letter advising her of his death in Italy, in the seaside town of San Benedetto. There was little information about the circumstances and none about his life there, for which she was grateful. His body was shipped back for burial in the family vault. The note from the solicitor, Mr. Stuart, advising her of her husband's will and his actions concerning the title, left her dazed. Earlier, she had remembered David's urgings for her to obtain a companion and thought of her father's sister, Mary. Older than her brother, Mary St Clair was a widow with a small competence who lived retired in Bath. She remembered seeing her Aunt Mary occasionally, when she came to town to shop and visit, but had not seen her in years. She did not know what had happened, but Aunt Mary had been in tears and her father enraged when Mary left, and Mary never came again. Catherine had written to her aunt, begging her to come to Heyerwood Manor, and Mary had been with her for a few months now. With the arrival of Mr. Stuart today, she had more company in the house than she had had since arriving at Heyerwood Manor five years before. Catherine felt deeply grateful for their presence as she contemplated the future.

Chapter 3

Gerard St. John, Viscount Stanton, pounded on the door. When Howard opened it, the viscount brushed by him. "No need to announce me. I'm her ladyship's father. I'll find my way; just take a look around first." Firmly blocking the way, Howard said, "I'm sorry, my lord, but I have my orders. You are expected. I will announce you to my lady. If you will wait here, please, my lord." Howard opened the door of the drawing room and announced "Viscount Stanton" as he was pushed aside by her irate father. "What the devil do you mean, keeping me kicking my heels while your butler announces me?" Catherine looked at him coolly. "This is my house, sir, not yours. I prefer that visitors be announced so that I can decide whether or not I am at home. Please be good enough to allow me to present to you my solicitor, Mr. Stuart. As you may know, Aunt Mary is kind enough to companion me." Forced by the presence of witnesses to exhibit at least a surface civility, he curtly acknowledged the introduction to Mr. Stuart and his sister's presence. From there, the atmosphere deteriorated, as her father demanded that Catherine return to the shelter of his roof and let him take over the burden of her affairs, becoming enraged when she refused. "I am thirty years old, mistress of my own affairs. Why should I return to your household, to be bullied, abused and used for your advancement? The fact that my circumstances allow me a choice is only to my good, and I choose to stay here!" The viscount's icy grey eyes bulged in disbelief at her defiance, and he advanced upon her threateningly. "You'll come freely, my girl, or I'll drag you! Without a husband, you belong to the head of your family, and I will decide where you'll live and how from now on!"

Clearing his throat delicately, Mr. Stuart said, apologetically, "I regret to inform you, my lord, that, strictly speaking, you are not the head of Lady Catherine's family. Upon her marriage, she became a member of the Lovell family and, in point of fact, she is now the head of that family, his late lordship having left her the entire estate in her own control and investing the title in her as well. You, as her father, are certainly entitled to give her advice, but you have no right or control over her or her property. While this is somewhat unusual, his lordship was most emphatic that his widow be left fully independent and emancipated from any interference or control. You will find the documents most clear on this score." Silenced, her father glared at the solicitor, then at Catherine. "You'll pay!" he screeched, "You at least owe me the return of your dowry!" Mr. Stuart interjected, "As to that, my lord, the dowry was paid to his grace, the Earl of Heyerwood, and was more than repaid in the marriage settlements. You have no claim on the estate at all." Purpling with fury, Gerald spun on his heel and stormed out of the room. "You aren't finished with this. I'll stay until you see sense, by God!"

Encountering Howard in the hall, Gerard shouted, "Have my things brought in and prepare a room. I'm staying until my business is resolved!" Howard looked past him icily and said, "I take my orders from the Countess of Heyerwood, sir. I shall desire her to make her wishes known." Leaving Gerard standing in the hall, Howard entered the drawing room and asked, "Shall a room be prepared for Viscount Stanton, my lady?" In tones audible to the hall, Catherine said, "No, my father will not be staying. If necessary, be good enough to have the footman assist him into his carriage. Do not admit him, should he call again." Howard returned to the hall, closing the door to the drawing room behind him. He looked enquiringly at Gerard and asked, "Must I repeat my lady's wishes, sir? I will be happy to render any assistance possible to ease your departure." Pale with rage, Gerard looked at Howard. "Tell HER LADYSHIP that she is not out of this yet and, if she has any regard for her mother's health, she'll keep a civil tongue in her head. I'm leaving now, but she hasn't heard the last of this!" Shrugging into his overcoat and hat, Gerard flung himself into his carriage and began the long journey back to town.

Shaken, Catherine turned to her aunt and her solicitor, with eyes blinded by tears. "Thank you for your support. I must...must go to my room for a little." Picking up her skirts, she fled to her room as if pursued by demons. Watching her depart, Mr. Stuart turned to Mary. "I was never so shocked, Mrs. St. Clair. Is her ladyship's father quite mad?" Perplexedly, Mary replied, "I begin to think he must be, sir. Gerard has ever been cold, unfeeling and greedy, but I have never seen him so lost to propriety before persons outside the family. I can only suppose that the late Earl's fortune to be larger than we thought, for Gerard to be so enraged." "As to that, ma'am, Lady Heyerwood will not need to be concerned about expenditures. Despite his best efforts, the Earl was not able to dissipate more than a tithe of his inheritance." Faintly, Mary said, "Oh, my. And Catherine is in complete control. I quite see, now, why Gerard was beside himself. But how wonderful! Now Catherine will truly be able to have a life while she is still young enough to enjoy it, if only her father will resign himself." "He will have to resign himself, ma'am, as there is no legal means that will allow him access to her funds. Even were she to become incompetent, all estate business would then revert to a trust for administration on her behalf. His late lordship started making the arrangements as soon as the betrothal was arranged, and thought of all contingencies. I must presume that he came to know her ladyship's father only too well in the course of the marriage negotiations and afterward." Mary repeated, "Oh, my. Gerard will be even more furious. Thank heaven we are here, out of London."

The next day, Catherine came downstairs, calm and again in control of her emotions. She and Mr. Stuart closeted themselves in the estate room, reviewing the will, the estate accounts and all of the other papers Mr. Stuart had brought for her perusal. Dazed, she looked at Mr. Stuart. "I never knew that it was so large. The Earl's family must have been of tremendous power and influence, yet I never heard of them until I met David at that dance. How is this?" Mr. Stuart coughed, and replied, "As to that, my lady, they had been of great power and held much influence at court. The earldom has been in existence for centuries, and has always possessed much wealth. Unfortunately, his late lordship's grandfather became…peculiar in his tastes, and withdrew from polite society as well as his duties in the House of Lords. This peculiarity was only magnified in the next two generations. I fear that your husband was right to discourage you from visiting London during his lifetime. Sadly, there was no sin or folly he did not commit, and he cared nothing for public opinion, so the scandals were great. However, since he left the country and subsequently died, the talk died quite soon. I would venture to say that it may be possible for you to take your place in London society, should you wish it, if some advance preparation is made. It would be of the greatest help to renew contacts with any friends or acquaintances before venturing to town. Catherine frowned thoughtfully. "Somehow, it seems ungrateful or disloyal to David, to toady for acceptance in London. Though we had no love for each other, indeed scarcely knew each other, he took such care for my future that I feel I owe him some loyalty and respect. Indeed, I feel he cannot have been as wicked at heart as he seemed to want people to think. However, I have missed London so. I must consider this. After all, there is no real hurry. I may even remove to Bath first. If I can venture into Society in Bath, quietly, that may smooth the way to London for the following season. However, it is too soon now. I cannot go into Society anywhere until I am out of black. How shocking to attend parties, trailing yards of black crape!"

The next few days passed quietly. Catherine spent a few hours each day with Mr. Stuart and Tom Jones, the bailiff, reviewing the rent rolls, discussing the improvements already in hand as well as those needed, funds needed for the next quarter day, and so on. "There is so much more to learn!" she signed wearily. "Thank goodness I have you and Mr. Jones to help me, sir!" she said to Mr. Stuart. "I only hope I can keep things running smoothly." Mr. Stuart replied, "The business of a great estate such as Heyerwood requires a concerned and attentive master or mistress, and will function well as long as each person knows and performs his duties. You need not supervise each level, madam; just be aware that each is there. Mr. Jones and I can manage the business and keep you informed of what needs doing. Your responsibility is to authorize needed expenditures, make sure that orders are given for things to be done when necessary and so forth. The most important thing is to be sure that you have competent people in place. Once established, the best thing is to let them do their work. You need not be physically present to stay informed. Fortunately, his late lordship retained a sense of responsibility about his estate and made sure he had an excellent, and loyal, staff. Indeed, many are of families who have served the Heyerwood estate for generations."

Chapter 4

Catherine and Mary went for a stroll around the gardens after a light luncheon. "Have you heard from your dear mother, my love?" asked Mary. "Not since the letter she wrote at my twenty-seventh birthday," replied Catherine. "I am certain that my father will not allow her to write, out of his anger and spite towards me. I wish she had the courage, and the means, to escape him. If she could come to me, I would shelter her from him gladly. How happy she could be here! She ever had a love of flowers and gardens, which my father seemed to take pleasure in thwarting. He seldom removed from town, and the town house garden was planted shrubberies at his order. I fear for her health, staying in that gloomy house and dealing with my father's temper." The walled garden was a riot of color and bloom, mostly from rose bushes. Still wet with rain, the flowers glowed in the late afternoon sun as if lit from within. Catherine sighed. "I do love it here. It is so peaceful and beautiful." They returned to the house and went to the drawing room. Catherine looked around. "I do believe it is time to redecorate, Mary. This room is handsome, but I would prefer something lighter, more colourful." Mary said nervously, "But my dear! Recollect that this is your late husband's country seat. Surely..." Firmly, Catherine replied, "I am aware, dear Mary. However, my husband is gone. I may make few changes to the library or, for that matter, the state apartments, but I want to feel that this is now *my* home. The drawing room and dining room require attention. I would also like to brighten the hall." Thoughtfully, she looked around. "We must explore the attics and all of the rooms before ordering furniture, as there must be a wide selection of furnishings already here. However, paint and fabric for curtains and cushions must be ordered immediately. We must discuss colours and make lists."

The next few weeks were a blur of activity. Tapestries were removed for cleaning, walls and ceilings freshly painted in a soft cream colour, and heavy curtains removed. She had found a complete suite of furniture for the drawing room in an attic. From the reign of Queen Anne, the graceful lines were exactly what Catherine wanted, and the cherry wood glowed when polished with a mixture of beeswax and lavender. The heavy dark red velvet draperies were replaced with jonquil satin embroidered with delicate flowers and leaves, and the cushions were remade in a soft green velvet that exactly matched the green of the leaves in the embroidered draperies. The heavy dark tapestry depicting a hunting scene that once hung on the drawing room wall was banished to the attic and was replaced with an equally old and valuable tapestry depicting a garden scene. Now clean and fresh, the lighter background and brighter colours, as well as the more cheerful subject matter, suited the room.

The dining room was similarly refreshed. Here, she had left the dark red velvet drapes and the dark oriental carpet. The fresh cream paint brightened the room, and she removed the depressing still life from over the mantel. ("I scarcely think that dead birds improve one's appetite! I have wanted to remove them for ages." Catherine said merrily as the painting was removed to the gallery.) She replaced it with a portrait of the late earl's mother, with David as a very small boy. The portrait showed a lovely young woman with dark hair and eyes, seated in the garden with her small son at her feet. All in white, she was surrounded by riotous blooms. Only when one studied her eyes did one wonder, as the artist could not disguise their sorrow. The portrait glowed in the light from the windows by day, and from the crystal candle sconces on either side at night. A delicate crystal chandelier, which had been found in a trunk in the attic, had been cleaned and hung over the table. When the candles where lit, it sparkled like diamonds.

The library was thoroughly dusted and polished, and the walls painted. Although the gleaming leather bindings showed to advantage with the heavy dark furniture and dark rugs and draperies, the cream paint brightened the walls, and the shining brass reflected the firelight. Even the great hall was lightened. Catherine had moved the heavy suit of armor from its place by the grand staircase to a corner, and replaced a massive oak table with heavy lion's paw feet with a beautifully carved cherry table and matching side chest. On the side chest, she had placed a pair of silver candlesticks and a heavy silver tray for cards. On the large table, placed in the center of the hall, a large, silver candelabra provided a warm, welcoming glow. The hall contained a huge fireplace, over which had hung a dark tapestry depicting a dying stag. She had the gloomy tapestry removed and replaced it with an ancient, beautifully painted shield with the Lovell arms. Another dark oriental carpet was left in place, for warmth and to muffle the sounds of people crossing the space. The guest rooms were all freshly painted and similarly brightened. When all was finished, each room was lighter and brighter and, somehow, appeared more spacious yet warmer.

Catherine visited the state apartments, the rooms belonging to her late husband and his father and forebears before him, one time. Large, high ceiling rooms filled with massive furniture, the suite consisted of a bedroom, dressing room, sitting room and small library, which was crammed with books. As she perused the shelves, pulling down books at random and glancing through the pages, she found herself blushing painfully. This was obviously a very private library. However delicate the etchings, and beautifully printed the pages, she was acutely embarrassed by the very presence of these particular volumes. She instructed the footman accompanying her, "Remove these books from the shelves and seal them securely into cartons. They must be removed to the small room at the back of the farthest attic." Catherine thought, "They really should be burnt, but I can't bring myself to destroy them." Closing the double doors behind her, she ordered that the rooms be thoroughly cleaned and the walls and ceilings repainted in the warm cream used elsewhere in the house, but that the rooms be otherwise unchanged for the present time. When asked about his lordship's clothes, she said, "Give the things that can be used to anyone in need. Consult the vicar if you need guidance. Anything that is too worn or shabby to be used should be torn up for rags. If there are items not practical for daily use but in good repair, they should be packed and stored." After all was done, the doors were locked.

Having been done recently especially for them, Catherine's and Mary's rooms required only their regular cleaning. Walking through the fresh, bright rooms, Catherine sighed deeply and said "All done! Now I feel it's truly mine. There isn't a room I haven't explored and made to my liking. Everything is clean and fresh. I dare swear that the house feels happier. What say you, Aunt?" Mary replied, "It is all beautiful. I could only marvel at that beautiful Queen Anne furniture being so hidden away and neglected, while that heavy gloomy stuff was cluttering up every room. No wonder your husband and his family had such crotchets, my dear! I was afraid you would sweep all out, but you have shown the utmost delicacy of taste in using your family heirlooms." "As I had hoped, it was really more a matter of rearrangement than replacing. It's amazing what some paint and polish and new curtains can do!"

Catherine found her feet with full control of the estate management as well. Thanks to her gradual involvement during her marriage as well as Mr. Stuart's careful guidance, she discovered she was able to deal with the needs of her tenants and employees. To her relief, she found that Mr. Stuart was right – the key was to let competent people do their work. She made sure, however to talk to her tenants personally as she walked, rode or drove around the estate, to hear directly from her people what was going on. To her gratitude, she found she was able to continue to entrust matters to the hands of Mr. Jones, her bailiff, as her late husband had done. Howard and Mrs. Davis had household matters in hand. She thought fervently, "Oh, David, thank you for your care of me and for entrusting Heyerwood to me. I am so deeply grateful." Now that all was in hand, she was astonished to realize that it was almost ten months since she had buried her husband. In two more months, she could put off her blacks! To be sure, she then should go into half mourning (greys, lilacs and lavenders which were even less becoming than black), but at least she could show her face in public without the heavy black veils she so detested.

Catherine hurried into the drawing room to find her aunt. "Aunt Mary, I find that I will be in need of clothes soon. I plan to write to a *modiste* in London for fashion plates and fabric swatches, to see what is in the fashion now. Do you need anything?" Mary looked at her in surprise. "Why, Catherine, I scarcely know. It has been so long since I even thought about new clothes." Remorsefully, Catherine hugged her aunt and said, "Oh, how selfish of me! I never thought …. And I knew how slender your means had been! Well, Aunt, you will have to resign yourself to a new wardrobe. We will both become fashion plates!" Her aunt fluttered breathlessly, "Now, Niece, you know you cannot …. I mean you can wear lavender and other such colours, proper for half mourning, but you cannot mean to dress me as well!" "Why not, Aunt? Such care as you take of me, too. I think it past time that we both were brightened up, now that the house is fresh. Can you not like the scheme?" "*Like* it?" breathed Mary. "My dear, if you mean it, I'm ecstatic! You cannot know how tired I am become of turning dresses and cleaning gloves. I would love new things!" "Well, then, we must write immediately for those plates and swatches! What fun we will have!"

Chapter 5

Catherine reviewed her post with pleasure. Only that morning, a large package of fashion plates, fabric swatches, and samples of various trims and laces suitable for half mourning, as well as two letters, were placed on her desk in the estate room by the footman. Putting the letters aside, she opened the parcel to examine the swatches and plates. She had been resigned to looking a dowd as her warm colouring was not flattered by lavender and grey, but was pleasantly surprised by the selection. In addition to the expected drab colours, there was a warm plum, a deep burgundy and a dark forest green that would become her to a nicety. To be sure, she would have to be careful with the trim and the design. Utmost simplicity would be needed, since the colours were at the very least unconventional for half mourning, but they were so much more becoming than the black she had worn for so long. There was a midnight blue velvet that caught her fancy, as well as a chocolate brown that would be perfect for a riding habit. Since autumn was approaching, she could order the heavier fabrics that such deep colours demanded. Although high-waisted, gauzy gowns were still being worn, she was delighted to see some drawings of less extreme styles in the package. She would have to call Aunt Mary, so they could both examine the samples and drawings and make selections.

As she put the package aside, the letters caught her eye. Picking up the first letter, she noted it was from Mr. Stuart, who addressed some of her late husband's expenses that had recently surfaced as well as some political events from the last several months. The second letter slipped to the floor. Stooping to retrieve it, she glanced at the direction and recognized, to her shock, her mother's elegant script. Fingers shaking, she tore open the letter and sat down to read.

"My dear Catherine, It has been many more years than I care to remember since I last wrote to you. I am from home at this moment, so have taken the opportunity to send you my love and care. I would warn you also, daughter. Your father is beside himself with rage. He has visited several solicitors and even the Prime Minister himself, to see if there is some means to set your late husband's wishes regarding your independence aside. Thank God, for your sake, he has not been successful. However, be warned, my love. Your father is your enemy, and I fear he is no longer fully rational. I do not fear for myself, but, were you to fall into your father's power, I could not answer for your well-being. If the chance arises, I will come to you. I must stop now so this can go by the Mail. Your loving mother"

Still holding the letter, she let her hands drop to her lap, tears blurring her sight. How unutterably sad, and at the same time, terrifying it was to think of her father as such an implacable enemy. Here, in the wilds of Somerset, out of the way, she felt safe, in her own home and surrounded by her own people; however, elsewhere it could be different. She would have to think carefully, consult Mr. Stuart, and be very cautious before venturing away from home. Rising, she carefully folded her mother's letter and went to her own room to put it among her personal papers. As she mounted the stairs, another thought struck her. Her mother's letter had indicated she was "from home." To Catherine's knowledge, her mother had never left her home in London without her husband's escort, moving from the town house to the country and back again. Her mother had never been allowed to leave on her own before. What could have happened? Suddenly overcome with concern for her mother, she sat down at her little desk in her boudoir and wrote to Mr. Stuart, asking him to discreetly enquire about Viscountess Stanton's health and whereabouts, as well as her father's current location, and the viability of a scheme to spend some time in Bath. Sealing her letter with a wafer, she rose and went in search of Howard, resolving not to think of such things again until she had her answer from the solicitor. Entrusting her letter to Howard to have it sent as quickly as possible, preferably as an Express, she went to find Aunt Mary.

The next day, she and Mary pored over the fashion plates, carefully drawn copies of plates in *LA BELLE ASSEMBLY*. She was somewhat relieved to see that she wasn't a complete Antidote, but knew she needed more than a touch to bring her up to snuff. She sketched out a design for a day dress, based on the plate but more simple in design and trim. Instead of the vivid red of the plate, Catherine thought it would do very well in the soft, deep plum wool. Since it was for cooler weather, the plum wool, trimmed with black velvet cording would be warm and practical, as well as becoming. She drew the sleeves long, with a fullness caught by the cording trim, and tapering down to the wrist. The neck came high to the base of the throat, trimmed with black velvet ribbon and a delicate ecru lace ruffle which echoed the lace ruffles at the wrists that finished the sleeves. A similar dress in the dark green, trimmed with a ruching of matching ribbon in a double row around the hem and around the fullness of the sleeves, with a touch of ivory lace at neck and cuffs, filled her with satisfaction.

Fired with inspiration, Catherine sketched out a redingote, to be of the chocolate brown wool, a heavier wool fabric than that used in the dress. Preferring a simpler design to the double breasted, heavily-frogged garment in the plate, she drew a single breasted design, with soft brown fur edging the collar and cuffs. For warmth, she requested that a quilted silk lining in matching chocolate silk be included. The fit would not be as slender and form-fitting as that in the plate, but she valued comfort above being in the first stare. She also designed the garment to come to her ankles, even if it meant covering her skirt. For evening, Catherine selected a deep violet velvet. This she drew lower over her bosom, though still sufficiently modest for a young widow. The sleeves were of tiered shirring, and finished with black lace that would fall gracefully over her hands. The bodice was embroidered with black silk in a delicate lacy design of flowers, discreetly accented with sparkling onyx and amethyst beads in their centers. The skirt was plain and flowed to a short train in the back, but the front revealed the dainty black silk slippers. She sighed with pleasure, thinking how long it had been since she had had new clothes, and in colours!

Catherine also made a selection of fine muslins, lawns and linens for chemises and handkerchiefs; a beautiful warm Norwich shawl in soft shades of plum, forest and fawn; a muff, pelerine and close bonnet of the same soft brown fur as the trim of the redingote; and fichus of delicate lace in ivory and ecru, just because they were so pretty. The plate of the riding habit, full-skirted yet almost masculine in its severity, she marked as it was, to be made up in dark blue wool. Guiltily, she thought she had stretched the convention of half-mourning to the breaking point, selecting colours so much more vital than the conventional lavenders, lilacs and greys, but could not resist the warmer, richer colours she knew would become herself to a nicety. She consoled herself with the thought that, though different, the colours were at least dark and discreet. Catherine also had the uncomfortable thought that the whole issue of mourning was difficult, and somewhat hypocritical, given the nature of her marriage and of her husband's reputation. Resolutely, she selected a couple of simple house dresses to be made up in a deep, dark burgundy crepe, and a warm brown sarcenet. By keeping the designs simple, and the trim minimal, she felt she had successfully satisfied her desire for colour, style and discretion. Completing her list of necessities with the required gloves, stockings, petticoats and so forth took little time.

Frowning at a sudden thought, Catherine turned to her aunt. "Must I have caps, Aunt? I know that it is customary for married women to wear something of the sort and that, as a widow, I might be expected to wear them. I never thought about them, being in the country and out of society as I am." Mary looked startled, and pondered the issue. "Well, dear, as you know, I never leave my room without my cap. However, I must say, I never thought about your needing such things. I still think of you as a child, you see. What about these trifles of lace, dear, just as a compromise?" They pondered the plates earnestly. "Well, I will order an ecru and an ivory lace, one of each, just to try. However, I cannot and will not wear a mob cap! Aunt Mary, is your list complete?" "Oh, yes, my dear. Such luxury to choose new things. Are you sure….?" Catherine said, firmly, "Not another word, my dear. It is a pleasure to be able to share this with someone. What think you of my designs?" Mary turned the sketches over, studying each in turn. "Are they too daring?" asked Catherine anxiously. "Do you think them shocking for someone in half-mourning?" "My dear, I believe you have struck the perfect note. The colours are suitably dark, even if not conventional, and the simplicity of the designs cannot be improved upon."

Flushed with pleasure, Catherine kissed her aunt. "Now we must order the fabrics and find a mantua maker as soon as possible. I am awaiting a reply from Mr. Stuart regarding … family affairs to see if a trip to Bath or even Taunton is feasible. If not, we will make do with a local seamstress." "Do not forget, dear, boots and slippers, too." Catherine replied gaily, "Don't worry, Aunt, my list is complete, from half boots for walking and riding boots, all the way to evening slippers! We shall be as fine as fivepence from top to toe, you'll see!" Sending the list of fabrics, trimmings, furs and so on needed for outfitting two ladies to Grantham's in London took but a moment more. "Done!" she said with deep satisfaction, as the footman rode to the village with her letter for the Mail. "Shall we have tea, Aunt?" Mary replied, "I vow, I'm ready for a cup. We have been busy today."

Chapter 6

A few weeks later, Catherine was crossing the hall to the drawing room, when she was startled by a thunderous knocking on the door. "Howard," she called, "pray see to the door!" as she whisked into the drawing room. Peering through the partially opened door, Catherine watched Howard make his stately way across the hall, refusing to be hurried by another round of bangs at the door. Howard opened the door to see a messenger standing in the cold autumn rain. "Tradesmen are to call at the rear door," said Howard reprovingly. "What is your business here?" "Express from London for the Countess of Heyerwood," gasped the messenger. "Let the man in, Howard," called Catherine, "He must be half dead with cold." "Yes, my lady," said Howard disapprovingly. Taking the letter from the messenger, Howard carried it to the drawing room and presented it to Catherine. "Take him to the kitchen for a hot drink, while I read this. A reply may be needed, and he can carry it with him as he returns." Howard bowed without comment and withdrew, pausing in the hall to instruct the messenger to accompany him to the kitchen. Catherine sat down in her favorite chair by the fire.

As she had hoped, the Express was a reply from Mr. Stuart. As she read, she frowned in some consternation. Mr. Stuart gave her a summary of recent political events before discussing more personal matters. It appeared that matters with her parents had worsened. Her mother apparently was in hiding. The Viscount's search for legal recourse against his daughter had kept him from home longer than anticipated, and his wife took advantage of the opportunity to flee. Making the excuse of a morning call and business with a mantua maker, Viscountess Stanton had left her home with three bandboxes and never returned. Upon his return to London, Viscount Stanton ransacked his wife's rooms and discovered that she had left with all her jewels, night gear and fresh linens, and at least two day dresses. Beside himself with rage, he had stormed around London searching for her without success. His boorish, threatening behavior, displayed to the *Ton* for the first time publicly, had resulted in social ostracism. Even those who considered him a friend hoped that Viscountess Stanton had made good her escape from such a brute. In the meantime, it was assumed that she was on her way to her daughter for shelter. Mr. Stuart wrote that it was only a matter of time before her father reached the same conclusion and pursued her there. On no account, he wrote, should Catherine leave her home until her father had either regained control or had been restrained. He had taken the liberty of sending his Express by a messenger he trusted, who could stay to provide additional support to her staff. He had also taken the liberty of informing the local magistrate of the situation, requesting that he have the area patrolled to be sure of Catherine's security. Catherine fled from the room, clutching the letter, calling for Howard and her aunt.

Having sent for the bailiff, she met with Howard and Mr. Jones in the bookroom, and requested that Mr. Jones meet with the tenant farmers and their helpers and warn them of the her father's apparent state of mind. "It is of first importance that no one be injured. I could not bear to have any one hurt or killed in this affair. However, should my father appear, if he could be convinced to leave quietly, I would be eternally grateful. I would also be deeply grateful if all could be on the watch for my mother, and any assistance possible be given her in reaching me safely, with all discretion. The less attention garnered by her arrival, the better. At this point, I am sure she would value safety above any consideration of her consequence," Catherine said, trying to smile. Howard bowed. "All is already in hand, Lady Heyerwood," he said with affection. "Your efforts over the years have won the loyalty of your people and, I venture to say, they will spare no effort to ensure your tranquility. Your father's ways have become common knowledge, and no one will stand by and see him try to usurp your position quietly. May I suggest that Mrs. Davis have rooms prepared for Viscountess Stanton's arrival?" Relieved, Catherine said, "Yes, thank you, Howard. I believe the rose rooms overlooking the garden would be suitable. She will be near me and Aunt Mary, and there is plenty of room. We must also be thinking about engaging a suitable lady's maid for her, unless she has succeeded in bringing her old dresser with her. I know that Miss Potter would die for her; she has been with my mother since my mother made her come out."

Bowing, Howard made his way to the servants' parlor to have Mrs. Davis give the necessary orders for the rooms to be prepared and to send for the bailiff, and as many tenants as could be located quickly. In the meantime, Catherine took the letter to her aunt's sitting room, as Mary had not appeared in the drawing room. She found Mary staring listlessly out of the window at the rain. "My dear, whatever is the matter?" asked Catherine in concern. "I heard the messenger arrive, and your conversation with Howard. My own brother! I am too distressed to show my face. Your poor, dear mother. I only hope she is safe in shelter. Dare I hope she has family somewhere? It would be encouraging to know if she had someone to whom she could go. I know Mathilde would not wish to bring Gerard down upon you if she could avoid it." Catherine said slowly, "Do you know, Aunt, I am not sure. May father so limited my mother's contact with people outside his own circle, I do not recall ever meeting any of my mother's relatives. I know her parents died shortly before she married my father, but I believe she had a brother and a sister, as well as cousins. Mother never spoke of her family. I vaguely recall hearing that my aunt married a man of property near York and that other family members lived in Bath and in Salisbury. I was never allowed to meet any of my mother's family or to have contact with them. I have no idea if my mother maintained contact with anyone in her family; if she did, she did not mention it, as my father would have taken steps to stop it. Oh, Aunt Mary, I do hope you are right. Having no choice is so lowering, and she would so dislike having to look to me, her child, for shelter and protection! If only she would write again!" Mary replied, "Take heart, child. The hard part for Mathilde was deciding to leave Gerard. She has been so oppressed and watched, since their marriage day, that all initiative and decisiveness was drained out of her. Taking the opportunity to leave was the biggest step. I know her well enough to believe that, having taken that step, she will waste no time in contacting family and friends on whose loyalty she can count, as well as you. Why, she may be here in time for Christmas!" Embracing her aunt, Catherine said, "Thank you, Aunt Mary, you are always so good to me, and so supportive. You always make me feel hopeful. Do not allow my father to sink your spirits. You have no part or blame in his actions and behavior, and I rely on you for your good cheer and good sense. This situation will be resolved soon enough, and we shall be free to get on with our lives."

Chapter 7

A few weeks later, as a cold and stormy November was drawing to a close, the delivery of the fabrics and other items that Catherine and Mary had ordered from Grantham's arrived from London. Catherine had visited Mistress Anderson, the village seamstress, and had been reassured that she would be able to handle their needs; after several years sewing as a *modiste* in London, marriage and widowhood, she had returned to her family home. She could enlist the help of a village woman who had trained with a seamstress in Bath, and another seamstress in Taunton if need be. Local women able to assist with cutting and basting could also be employed and would be pleased to earn money by assisting her. Mrs. Anderson took the necessary measurements and made a few suggestions about the designs that reassured Catherine about her taste and skill. She took the bulky parcels and the plates away with her, to begin work on Catherine's and Mary's new wardrobes immediately.

Catherine prowled the house restlessly. The weather was too bad to go out into the garden, and she could not settle to a book or her embroidery. She had heard nothing further from Mr. Stuart, and was beside herself with anxiety about her mother's safety and worry over her father's next move. It would almost be a relief if he appeared at her door; at least she would know what was happening! Heavy-hearted, she decided to explore that back attic room. During the refurbishment of the house, she had gone through all of the attics, but there were several small rooms that she had had no opportunity to have thoroughly turned out. The little room was filled with boxes, trunks and parcels that almost obscured the window. She put on her oldest and warmest black wool day dress, and directed one of the maids to accompany her with some rags and some candles for light.

They climbed the stairs to the attics. Howard opened the heavy baize door which he propped open. As Catherine and the maid proceeded on to the back attic, Howard said, "I will call you for tea, my lady. Pray be careful, and let the maid assist you as much as possible." Shaking his head in disapproval, Howard made his way back downstairs.

Insensibly, Catherine felt her spirits rise somewhat. The lure of hidden treasure was strong. The maid did a cursory dusting of the tops of the boxes and trunks and a more thorough wipe-down of the window, which allowed more light into the little room. They began opening boxes and trunks. As she sorted old silk and brocade gowns, moth-eaten woolen shawls, and yellowed linens, she realized that she had found more of David's mother's things. Propped against the wall, she found another portrait of her, this time clad in black with visible sorrow in her pale face. At the bottom of a trunk, Catherine discovered a small box and a book. The book was bound in leather with a delicate design stamped with gold on the cover. Glancing through its handwritten pages, she discovered it was a collection of poetry and a diary. The box contained a jumbled assortment of jewelry: earrings, bracelets, chains, cameos, necklaces, all slung together as if a child had been playing with them. She set the book and box aside, to take downstairs with her.

Catherine spent several hours sorting the clothing items. They had found some men's clothing, in addition to the late countess's wardrobe. She found several brocade gowns that would cut up into cushion covers nicely, and a large pile of shifts and night rails that wanted only washing to restore them to a useful state. There were also some warm woolen stockings and shawls that had escaped the moth's tooth. These linens and woolens would be distributed to the wives and daughters of her tenants and the women of the village, to use as they chose. Items too badly warn or damaged would be used as rags or discarded. A similar pile of men's shirts and linens would be similarly washed and distributed to the men. Catherine also found sketchbooks, filled with sketches and water colour pictures done by David's mother. She had had an unconventional taste and some talent, demonstrated by illustrations of storm clouds and dead trees as well as the more common-place flower studies. When the huge pile of usable garments were carried down for cleaning and distribution, and the equally huge pile of trash hauled away, the room was dusted and swept. Now brighter, and emptier, the room was noticeably improved. The maid packed the brocades and sketchbooks away for future consideration, and carefully covered the portrait. Just as they started back downstairs,

Howard appeared. "Tea will be ready to serve shortly, Lady Heyerwood. Where would you prefer to take it?" "In my boudoir, Howard, as I am too tired to dress for the drawing room. Pray ask Aunt Mary to join me in a quarter of an hour or so. I must wash and change. I have not been this dirty in my life, I think," said Catherine, ruefully. Howard noticed the small box and the book. "May I carry those to your boudoir for you, my lady?" "No, thank you, Howard. I can manage." "Yes, my lady. Tea will be brought to your boudoir in one half hour. Will that be all?" "Yes, thank you, Howard," replied Catherine with a smile, dismissing the butler. Relieved, she watched him bow and make his stately way below stairs, and made her escape to her rooms.

Catching her reflection in the mirror, she was overcome with giggles. What a ragamuffin! Dirt streaks on her face, cobwebs in her hair, and smudges all over her dress! No wonder Howard had looked so disapproving. Catherine hurriedly shed the filthy black dress, washed thoroughly and brushed her hair. She put on a warm velvet dressing gown with a lace fichu, tied her hair back with a ribbon and sat down next to the fire. Just then, there was a discreet tap on the door, and Aunt Mary peeped in. "How have you occupied yourself this dreary afternoon, my dear niece?" enquired her aunt affectionately. "I vow, it was so cold and rainy, I had all to do to keep from pulling the blanket over my head and staying in my bed!" Looking up with a smile, Catherine said, "I have explored the attic room in the back, Aunt, and found some useful things. I may also have found some treasure. See, Aunt Mary, I believe I have found some of David's mother's jewelry." Heads together, they opened the small box. Inside, on a faded satin lining, were heaped pins, earrings, bracelets and the like. Emptying the box's contents on the tea table, Catherine was struck by the simplicity of the items-no jewels of great value or antiquity here. She stirred the heap gently with a finger, finding delicate earrings, a double strand of pearls which were sadly dulled from lack of wear, an amethyst chain. "Aunt, these must be her personal jewels, not estate pieces. David specifically told me of an emerald parure, a diamond necklace with matching bracelets, and a set of rubies-you can see them in the portraits in the gallery. How glad I am to find these. It's an opportunity to know something of her at last!" They set to work, patiently matching earrings in pairs, and locating matching pins, bracelets or necklaces.

All in all, there were six pairs of earrings, including a pair of pearl drops to match the necklace; a cameo set with brooch and bracelet to match, of a soft coral shade with ivory figures; a lovely topaz set which was set in gold with a matching necklace, the clusters of topazes strung on gold chains, pearls in the centers; a delicate frost work of diamonds dangling from silver settings with a matching hair ornament; and two pair of heavy earbobs, one pair set with garnets and the others in sapphires, both in gold. Also in the box was a gold locket on a chain, and a pair of carved ivory bracelets. "How lovely," sighed Catherine. "I much prefer these to the heavy, ornate jewels in the portraits. These will be a delight to wear. I will have Jane clean them. What say you, aunt? Which would you prefer?" "Prefer?" asked Mary, blankly. "Why, what do you mean?" "I mean you to share in this find, aunt. You live here too, and you need pretty things as much as do I. Take your choice!" "Oh, dear, I cannot! It would not be fitting, your late husband's mother's things." "Well, then," said Catherine mischievously. "I will choose for you! I think the amethyst chain will suit you, and the diamond earrings with the hair ornament will be most becoming with your black lace gown." Gathering the items, she put them into Aunt Mary's hands with a smile. "We will consider the other items later, although, I must say, I have a weakness for the pearls and the topazes."

Just then, Howard and a maid entered with tea. "Oh, Howard, I am sorry. Is there another table? We have cluttered the tea table so, and I cannot wait for my tea." "To be sure, my lady, there is no reason for concern." The tray was placed, and the tea poured before Howard glanced at the items scattered across the table. "Oh, my lady, you found them. My late mistress would be so pleased. Where were they?" Catherine looked up at Howard, startled. "You recognize these jewels, Howard?" "Oh, yes, Lady Heyerwood, my late mistress wore them before her marriage and as a young bride. After his late lordship's father began to decline, he bade her throw them away, as he ordered her to wear only those things he had given her. Many of her things were lost or destroyed. These were gifts from her mother and father, and her favorite pieces. I had hoped she succeeded in hiding them. She would be delighted to know you were wearing them, as they had brought her much pleasure."

Stunned, Catherine looked at Mary. "I now understand why my husband was so mindful of my security! It seems I am not alone in having a surfeit of fathers. I vow, I will have to look at her diary. She may have some useful suggestions for me in coping with my situation." Saying nothing, Howard bowed and left the room. The two ladies looked into the fire, sipping their tea and thinking of the former mistress of the house. Now wonder she had looked so sorrowful in her portraits.

29

Chapter 8

A few days later, the seamstress and her helpers delivered the first of the new clothes ordered by Catherine and Mary. The redingote with matching close fur bonnet were as elegant, yet as warm as Catherine had hoped, and she appreciated the speed with which they were delivered as the December weather was icy cold. This winter had shown promise of being as severe as the one some years before when the Thames froze solid, and none of her old things were warm enough. The seamstress had also furnished a supply of undergarments, the dark green day dress, and the warm brown house dress. The boots, slippers, stockings and so forth had been delivered from London a few weeks before, and Catherine was ecstatic at having new things to divert her attention. Aunt Mary had also received new under things, a wool cloak with a fur-lined hood, and a dove grey day dress as well. The seamstress promised completion of their order within a few more weeks. Both ladies spent the rest of the afternoon trying on and putting away their new things.

At tea time, Catherine came down wearing the dark green day dress, matching dark green slippers, and the warm Norwich shawl about her shoulders. In her ears, she wore the heavy gold earbobs set with garnets, that had belonged to the late countess. "Aunt Mary, I vow I feel as fine as five pence! What do you think?" She pirouetted before her aunt, who was seated near the fire in the drawing room. Catherine's face glowed with pleasure, and her aunt smiled fondly. "You look lovely, my dear. The garnets are perfect with that dark green, and I never saw you look so becoming." "As do you, Aunt. That dove grey sets off your blue eyes and fair skin to a nicety." Both ladies smiled complacently, and enjoyed their tea. As they lingered before the fire, it grew dark. "How early the light fades now," mused Catherine. "It is, of all things, that which makes winter so long and dark." "I know, dear, but at least, when winter is over, spring follows." Amused, Catherine said, "You are always looking for the bright side, Aunt! You absolutely refuse to allow me to enjoy my doldrums!"

Just then, they heard horses in the drive, then a knock at the door. Wide-eyed, the ladies looked at each other, waiting for Howard to announce...whom? Hearing his footsteps approaching the door of the drawing room, Catherine could not prevent herself from looking anxiously toward the door. Howard opened the door, bowed, and announced with a smile, "My lady, the Viscountess Stanton!" As her mother entered the room quietly, Catherine sat frozen in shock. "Catherine?" said her mother hesitantly. "Oh, Mother, Mother, where have you been? I've been so afraid for you! Pray, come in by the fire-you must be frozen!" Mary had also risen and made as if to leave the room. "Stay, Mary, I would thank you for your kindness to my daughter," said Mathilde with a wan smile. All three ladies sat down, Catherine holding her mother's hand tightly. "Pray, won't you welcome my cousin's son? It is he who escorted me to you, and I would have you know some of your family as soon as possible."

Catherine tugged the bell rope and, when Howard answered, said, "Please admit my cousin at once, and have a room prepared for him. He must stay at least a night or two, so that we may show our gratitude." Quietly, the gentleman walked into the room and bowed. "A pleasure to make your acquaintance at last, my lady," he said quietly. Catherine looked at him curiously. Tall, with black hair and dark eyes, he had a commanding presence. Not handsome, but by no means ill-favored. "I am Michael Amory. Your mother is my mother's cousin." Mathilde smiled. "Properly speaking, my love, he is the Viscount Chatellerault." Catherine curtseyed, "I am honored, my lord. Pray accept my deepest gratitude for your kindness to my mother." "It was my privilege to serve her, my lady." Mathilde, amused, broke in again, "Children, may we not dispense with such formality? We are, after all, family. Michael, I would have you know my sister-in-law, Mary St. Clair, who companions my daughter." "Your servant, ma'am." He bowed as Mary also curtseyed, blushed at such courtesy.

"Mother, I have been so worried. Where have you been? What has been happening? Is there any word of my father?" asked Catherine fearfully. Mathilde patted her hand gently. "Patience, daughter, I will tell the whole. Some months ago, after your father visited you here, he returned in such a rage. Even after all these years, I was quite shocked for I have never seen him so …. uncontrolled. He left to confer with solicitors and to whomever he could talk about gaining control of your inheritance. When he left, he told me he would return within a week and to hold myself ready for a journey. His face …. I think I have never seen such anger and hatred in a human before. I knew you were safe here, so I was not terribly worried about you but, for the first time, I began to think about my own situation. I could not sit there, waiting for heaven knows what."

Mathilde paused, and took a reviving sip of sherry. "I thought about my choices because, of all things, I was most reluctant to cast myself upon you right away. I feared your father would immediately turn to the law to fetch me home, and drag you into such a hideous scene I could not bear to do! I have lost touch with so many old friends, but still maintained a correspondence with my cousin and her family." Pausing to refresh herself again, she held out her hand to Michael. "I have been so deeply grateful to you and your family, my dear Michael!" she said, smiling affectionately at the young man. "I can never express the whole of my gratitude!" "Pray, madam, do not." Michael said, deprecatingly. "We did no more than anyone might." Turning to Catherine, Mathilde continued. "I fled with my dear Potter, with all we could carry without being obviously in flight, to the town house of an old friend. We made our come-out together. She had the misfortune to marry one of your father's bosom-bows, but her husband had died some years ago. I had been allowed to maintain contact with her. I stayed long enough to write to you, and to send an Express to my cousin and her husband. They sent Michael to fetch me away. The family estate is in Cheshire, near Chester, so I was well out of London in a twinkling. I must tell you that my poor Potter suffered miserably from the motion, but I was so ecstatic to be away, I enjoyed the journey immensely!" Pausing again, she looked at Catherine, stricken. "I forgot my poor Potter. Oh, Catherine, have you room? I never thought…." Smiling in sympathy, Catherine replied soothingly, "Pray, mama, do not disturb yourself. I had rooms prepared for you immediately upon receiving your letter, and of course made a place for Miss Potter. I knew nothing short of her death could separate her from you. All is in readiness. She is probably unpacking for you even now." Pale with relief and exhaustion, Mathilde replied "Oh, the relief! Pray, Catherine, may I go to my room? I…I am suddenly sorely fatigued!" "Of course, my love, Aunt Mary and I will escort you." Turning to Viscount Chatellerault, she said, "Pray excuse me for a little, sir. If you would like, there is a tolerable fire in the library, and I will have Howard fetch you more suitable refreshment." Bowing slightly, Michael smiled and said, "Thank you, ma'am. That sounds delightful. Pray do not concern yourself for me." Pausing only to give Howard the necessary instruction to provide for Viscount Chatellerault's comfort, Catherine and Mary swept Mathilde out of the room and up the stairs.

Walking into the rose rooms, Mathilde looked around in a daze. "Oh, how lovely, Catherine. These rooms are delightful." Walking to the window, she looked out into the cold, rain-swept night for a moment. "My dear, I am so delighted to see you, yet so mortified as to the cause! If only I had stood up to your father years ago! You do not know the anguish, especially when he made *such* arrangements for your marriage. I can only pray that someday you will be able to forgive me." Mathilde began to weep and buried her face in her hands. Catherine embraced her gently and said, "Pray, Mama, do not! You could not have withstood him. We both must face the fact that my father cannot be fully rational. Be at peace, my love. We are both out of his power now. I can provide for all of our needs. I will not pretend that my marriage is what I would have chosen, but you must know that I am amply provided for. We need look to no one for assistance. I think you must be more tired than you know, Mama. I will have hot water for a bath brought up, and you shall get between sheets as soon as possible. You shall have your dinner in bed. Please, do not think about it anymore; just look forward to the fun we shall have!" Just then, Miss Potter entered the room from the dressing room. "Oh, Miss Potter, shall I send a maid to attend my mother tonight? You must be exhausted from the travelling." Shaking her head, Miss Potter said severely, "Never you mind, your ladyship, no one will care for my lady but me, not while I can draw breath. Just you leave her to me. She'll be as right as a trivet with some rest and some food taken in peace and quiet. Do you send a maid with the bath water I heard you mention, and a light little supper, and I'll take care of the rest!" "It shall be as you say, Miss Potter. I trust you found your room next to the dressing room, and that you have all you need. Pray do not hesitate to tell Howard, Mrs. Davis or any of the maids if ought is necessary. I shall be sure to order supper for you both, so that you can retire as early as may be." Curtseying slightly, Miss Potter said, "Thank you kindly, your ladyship. Now, *if* you will be so kind, the sooner you go back down stairs, the sooner I can get your mama to her rest."

As Catherine and Mary made their way back down the stairs, Catherine began to laugh. "Miss Potter was ever a tartar. I do not know why I feared for my mother. I do believe Miss Potter could put Napoleon himself to route if she thought he posed a threat to Mama." Aunt Mary chuckled.

"I vow, I had forgot how plain spoken she is. She will take good care of your mother, you may be sure." On the way to the library, in the Hall, she stopped and spoke to Howard giving order for a nice little supper to be served in the rose rooms for her mother and Miss Potter, as well as a more substantial meal in the dining room for herself, Aunt Mary and her cousin in an hour's time. "Pray, Howard, have Mrs. Davis give the cook my apologies for any distress this causes. I am well aware how disconcerting such a change in plans can be. If she needs more time, tell her to do whatever is necessary. I will rely on you to announce when all is ready." Howard bowed, and thanked her for her consideration but "I venture to mention that Cook will be ready as desired, Lady Heyerwood, as she has been making preparations since the carriage arrived. All will be as you desire, never fear, my lady!" Smiling gratefully, Catherine said, "Such good care as you all take of us, Howard! Please let Mrs. Davis and the cook know how their efforts are appreciated." Howard bowed the ladies into the library.

Chapter 9

Michael rose from the comfortable chair before the fire, in which he had been sitting. Making his bow, he said, "May I offer you ladies some refreshment? As you see, Howard has thoughtfully provided sherry in addition to the brandy I am sure you requested for me." Sinking onto the sofa placed on the other side of the fireplace, Catherine said, "Sherry would be delightful, I thank you, my lord. Would you care for some, Aunt Mary? I vow, we could all use a restorative after such excitement!" Sipping their wine, Michael looked up and said, "My mother wishes me to extend her greetings to you, cousin. I need hardly say, it has been through no desire of my family that we were so estranged from your mother, and from you. My mother is hoping you will visit our home in Cheshire one day. She is all eagerness to meet the daughter of her favorite cousin."

Catherine smiled and replied, "Your mother is all goodness. I am ashamed to say that I know nothing of the connection. I am sure that my mother was only able to maintain occasional contact with her family by practicing extreme discretion. I'm certain my father never allowed her to tell me of her family. I hope that you can spend some days with us, so that we may get to know you. I know my mother would wish to have you here with us for a while." Michael returned her smile and said, "As to that, cousin, I would be honoured to spend a few days, but must return within the week, to reassure my mother of her cousin's safe arrival and to complete some business affairs. Possibly, a return visit may be made within a short time, if that would be agreeable? The journey is somewhat lengthy, I fear, or I would suggest you return with me for a few days. I believe your mother will require some days of rest, and it would be too cruel to deprive her of your company so soon." Catherine was somewhat taken aback;

the suggestion of family intimacy coming so soon on the heels of first acquaintance seemed somehow premature.

Just then, Howard announced that dinner was served. They rose and went to the dining room. Catherine said, as they were seated, "I hope you are not accustomed to multiple courses, my lord. I fear my aunt and I dine more lightly than a man, and have formed the habit of some informality as well, as it has just been the two of us for so long." Michael surveyed the laden table, which included a roast duck with apples, a fish pie and some ham removed with assorted vegetables, a pupton of pears and some Chantilly cream, somewhat ruefully. "I believe I can be satisfied by what I see, my lady. They do say that hunger is the best sauce, after all." The three of them laughed and were seated. They enjoyed a merry meal, sitting over the last glasses of wine, instead of the ladies leaving the gentleman to his port.

As the clock struck eleven o'clock, Catherine said remorsefully, "My lord, forgive me for keeping you at table so late. You must be greatly fatigued, after such a journey in such conditions. Pray, allow Howard to show you to your room. I hope you rest well. Do not hesitate to ring if there is aught you need." Michael replied, "It has been a delightful evening. However, I own, a very long day. Don't worry, cousin, a good sleep will set all to rights. At what time is breakfast served?" "Well, as to that, my aunt and I generally have tea and something light in our rooms between eight o'clock and nine o'clock. At what time would you like breakfast? I shall order it brought to your room." "I must confess to being an early riser. Would seven thirty be too much for your household? If only a cup of coffee and a roll…" Beaming, Catherine said, "That is not trouble at all, sir. I shall have your breakfast brought to your room at seven thirty. Rest well." Rising, she and Aunt Mary curtsied and made for the door. Michael rose, saying "Thank you, and good night, my lady. Until tomorrow."

While one of the footmen escorted Viscount Chatellerault to his room, Catherine gave orders to Mrs. Davis for a full breakfast to be prepared and served to his lordship in his room at seven thirty, as well as a light breakfast taken to her mother and Miss Potter at the same time as her own and Aunt Mary's. On her way up the stairs, Aunt Mary remarked, "What a very pleasant evening! Your cousin seems a delightful young man. It is wonderful to have guests after all this time. We must have become very dull." Catherine agreed, "Indeed yes, Aunt. I had forgot about courses for dinner, not to mention conversation. We need to broaden our outlook. I haven't even invited the vicar or the squire to call. Of course, while David was living, no one called here and I felt too uncomfortable to call on them myself. At least, we do get to church occasionally. Maybe, this Sunday, we will prevail on my mother to join us and we will all go to a service. At least, it will make a start."

Catherine retired to her dainty rooms. As she prepared for bed, she mused about the isolation in which she had become accustomed to live. She had grown used to being buried in the country, left to her own devices. Circumstances surrounding her husband and his activities had made society distasteful for her; then she had been immured in mourning, and in concern for her mother. Now, all was changed. She bethought herself of her old, dear friends from school. She had continued an irregular correspondence with a few of them. Although it had been some time, she felt sure that she could rely on them to respond to fresh overtures. Her two dearest friends had married in their first season, and she was sure letters would reach them without difficulty. "I will write tomorrow!" she thought. "I will return to London one day, and I want to have some friends with whom I can share my pleasures."

Her thoughts turned to her cousin. A handsome and pleasant young man, she reminded herself that he was still, in fact, a stranger. "He seems rather impetuous," thought Catherine, "repeatedly, calling me 'cousin', whilst I am still calling him, and thinking of him as 'my lord'!" He seemed to make himself so completely at home. After a while, she chided herself-he was obviously accustomed to being in company, while she hadn't been away from Heyerwood in many years, never mind mingling with new people!

After brushing and braiding her hair, she tied on her lacy nightcap, and got into bed. She read by candlelight for a time, then blew out her candle. On impulse, she got out of bed and went to the French doors opening onto the balcony and stared through the glass. The clouds and rain had blown away, and the stars were shining in the cold night sky. "Thank you for bringing my mother safely to me!" she said softly, staring out at the night. She returned to her bed, pulled the covers to her chin, and fell deeply asleep.

In his room in the guests' wing, Michael loosened his neckcloth as he stared into the fire. Even though his mother had told him of his cousin's fortune and title, he had not expected such evidence of wealth. It seemed apparent that his cousin had control of her fortune, but he knew there would be a man of business lurking in the background somewhere. Still, he mused, he had some address and a family connection must surely provide some leverage. The next few days would give him a chance to prepare the ground. He seated himself in a comfortable chair before the fire, and poured out a glass of brandy from the decanter conveniently found on the small table next to the chair. He gazed unseeingly into the fire, the glass of brandy cupped in his hand, and lost himself in thought.

Chapter 10

Catherine woke the next morning to bright sunshine streaming through the window. Next to the bed, her breakfast tray sat on the table, obviously there for some time. "It's late! I must hurry." She leaped from the bed and rang for her maid. While she waited, she sipped some cold tea and nibbled at a muffin. Catching sight of the clock, she gasped and rang again. "Ten o'clock! How could I oversleep on such a morning? What will my cousin say?" When Jane appeared, she assisted Catherine in dressing in the warm, brown sarcenet house frock, with matching slippers. Slipping the topaz earbobs into her ears, and picking up her Norwich shawl, she hastily made her way down the stairs. As she reached the main floor, she saw Howard making his way from the parlor. "Howard, have you seen my mother or my cousin yet this morning? I'm shockingly late." Howard bowed, saying "Viscountess Stanton, my lady, is still in her room, attended by Miss Potter. She sent word by Miss Potter that a quiet day would suit her of all things, and asked that you visit her about one o'clock this afternoon, if quite convenient. Lord Chatellerault breakfasted in his room, and went for a ride an hour or so ago. He left a message that he would return in time for luncheon. Madam St. Clair, I believe, is walking in the main garden. She went out a few moments ago, saying she wanted a breath of air. May I bring you some tea, my lady?" Catherine said gratefully, "Oh, Howard, what would I do without you? If you could bring me some tea in the library, I would love it. I have a few items of correspondence requiring attention, and can get them out of the way now, since everyone is occupied. Thank you!"

Catherine went to the bookroom and seated herself and her desk, intending to write to her school friends in London immediately. She also wanted to send an Express to Mr. Stuart, to advise him of her mother's arrival with her cousin and to request information about her father's whereabouts. She opened a drawer to get her stationery and ink. She looked into the drawer and frowned. Surely, she had not left her stationery so untidy the last time she had used it. Shrugging, she pulled out a few sheets, and engrossed herself in her letters. Folding and addressing each, she reached for her supply of sealing wax and her seal, but it was out of place. Another oddity. Unfolding the letter to Mr. Stuart, she added a brief request that she find out about her cousin and his family. Blushing and feeling guilty, she none the less felt it would be prudent to get an objective report, especially since her mother had been out of touch with her family for many years, and was now looking forward to renewing a family intimacy. She sealed and franked her letters and took them to the main hall. She rang for a footman to carry them to the village for delivery by the Mail. As she put her letters into the young man's hand, she casually asked, "Did you see the Viscount Chatellerault this morning? Did he find all he needed?" He bowed and said, "Oh, yes, my lady. I showed him all over the house so he could find his way about. He was most complimentary, my lady, especially about the quality of the library." "Was he, indeed?" queried Catherine. "Oh yes, my lady. He mentioned how unexpected it was to find a business-like desk in a woman's home." "How flattering!" said Catherine drily. "Thank you for taking care of him. You may go now."

As the footman hurried to the stables, Catherine returned to her bookroom and stared sightlessly out the window. So her cousin had been all over the house and in her desk. She wondered if he had been responsible for the disorder of her desk drawers. Had he been looking for something specific? If so, what? Pondering these unanswerable questions, she was glad she had requested that Mr. Stuart investigate for her. Such musings made her acutely uncomfortable, but she had to look out for her own, as well as her mother's, security. Painful experience had taught her to be cautious.

She turned as her aunt came into the hall, her cheeks glowing from the cold air. "Oh, my dear, isn't it wonderful that your mother is with us at last? And in time for Christmas, too! It is just a few weeks away. Should we not make some plans? At least a Yule log, and some carols and, of course, a few gifts!" Smiling, Catherine hugged her aunt and said gaily, "Of course, Aunt. Make all the plans you wish. I shall leave it all in your capable hands! This shall be our merriest Christmas in years, I do believe!"

Later in her mother's rooms, Catherine mentioned her aunt's excitement. "Mama, Aunt Mary desires to make plans for Christmas. Just think, it's only a few weeks from now. We will have our first Christmas together for years! How wonderful it will be, here in our own home!" Mathilde, ensconced on a chaise near the fire, smiled. "Yes, my dear, it will be delightful. How have you spent the morning?" Blushing, Catherine replied, "Well, I'm afraid I overslept, but I did get my correspondence done. I believe my cousin is riding, but should be in anytime for luncheon. I ordered luncheon for two o'clock. Will you join us, or would you prefer a tray? Mathilde leaned back against the pillows and sighed, "Frankly, my dear, I should prefer a tray. I think I am more tired that I knew. Since leaving London, I have been so tense and now, it is as if my nerves have given way. I hope you don't mind." Hugging her mother gently, Catherine said, "I do understand. I believe you just need time to recover from the strain. Pray, consider this your home and do as you please, Mama. There is no rush or reason to push yourself. Take your time and rest fully. I shall order that all of your meals be brought up until you feel more the thing."

Catherine decided to speak with Cook directly, as the preparation of trays in addition to guests in the house could definitely overset domestic arrangements. As she approached the kitchen, the housekeeper joined her. "Have you instructions, my lady? Such a treat to have company, and with Christmas coming, too!" "As to that, Mrs. Davis, we must make some plans. Madam St. Clair is going to take care of planning for Christmas, so you must confer with her. I know she will appreciate any suggestions, especially if the late earl's mother had any special traditions that you can recall. At this moment, I wish to confer with Cook about my mother's meals, and the meals for the household in general. As you may know, my mother has had a difficult journey and does not yet feel up to coming down to dine." Mrs. Davis responded, "To be sure, my lady, we had heard she was knocked up, poor soul. I know Cook will appreciate your coming, but we can manage easily enough."

As Catherine and Mrs. Davis entered the kitchen, Cook looked up from the pastry she was rolling. "My lady," said Cook as she curtseyed deeply, "What can I do for you? Luncheon is ready to serve in the dining room. Is there something wrong?" "No, no, your meals are always delicious. It is just that my mother feels unwell and would prefer a tray. I know it can be inconvenient, so I wanted to confer with you myself, and be sure that you have all you need in supplies and help. Is there anything you require?" "Now, my lady, there was no need for you to worry your head," said Cook reprovingly. "We're well enough stocked to feed an army, and I can manage trays for your ladyship's mother easily. Would she like a nice custard, do you think, my lady?" "I'm sure whatever you provide will be delightful. My mother will want all her meals on a tray for the present. She eats lightly in the morning, and prefers a light supper before retiring, such as soup and fruit, or some such thing. I think the mid-day meal should be more substantial, some chicken or something similar. Do you try to tempt her appetite, as you know so well how to do! I'll leave it to your judgement, Cook." Pleased, Cook replied, "I'm sure we all do our best, my lady. Let me know if her ladyship has a taste for something special." "Thank you, Cook, I shall, and my aunt and Mrs. Davis will be planning for some special treats for Christmas, too. They shall make their plans known to you directly. You, and they, have a free hand for the holiday." "Oh, my lady, how splendid! It's been years since we had a proper celebration."

Catherine made her way back up to the dining room, just as the clock struck the hour. Her aunt and cousin were about to take their seats as she hurried in. "I feared I was late. I am so sorry!" she exclaimed. "Pray be seated, and tell me about your morning." The three enjoyed a leisurely luncheon, as Michael described his tour of his cousin's estate, and Aunt Mary discussed her plans for a proper Christmas celebration. Smiling slightly, Catherine turned to Michael and said "I trust you found all you required? The footman told me he had taken you over the house." "Yes, cousin, he was most helpful, and I no longer fear losing myself in the corridors." Catherine persisted, "Pray let me know if you need anything, or have correspondence to attend to. My desk in the library is fully stocked, and my late husband obtained franking privileges for me." "As to that, cousin, I have no pressing matters," said Michael.

After luncheon, she and Michael went into the garden. "It seems like days since I've been out in the fresh air. So much as happened in the last few days," said Catherine. "Have you received any news yet, cousin?" asked Michael. "News? From whom? Should I be expecting anything?" asked Catherine, brows slightly raised. "Your mother was so concerned about your father's whereabouts, and I merely wondered if you had heard anything." "Not at present, but I have sent to my solicitor for some information. As it happens, one of the footmen went to the village for me this morning, with correspondence to Town to go by the Mail. Mayhap, he will bring something back," she replied.

Chapter 11

Left to his own devices later in the afternoon, Michael stared moodily out of the library window. His cousin was not the naïve, inexperienced miss he had expected. True, she was thirty years old, but her circumscribed life with her parents, and then her exile from society during her marriage, had prepared him to expect a nonentity wanting nothing more than someone to take care of her. Catherine was clearly an intelligent woman, well able to manage her own affairs, who enjoyed being in full control of her household and property. This was not a woman who would turn over that control lightly to anyone, not even a husband. Clearly, he had overlooked the effect that having power would have on someone who had previously no control over her circumstances. He would have to consult with his father.

He thought about his conversation with his father, Hugh Amory, Earl of Aldersey, before he left to bring his mother's cousin to Somerset. "Family connection, money and a title. One couldn't ask for more, really. All the better that she's been out of society. Can't miss what you've never had, now, can you? She shouldn't mind being here. I'd be pleased to make her my daughter, if you find that it answers. I don't want to make it a command, but it's time you were setting up your nursery, and the family fortunes could always do with an addition. From what I've heard, Heyerwood was a regular 'Golden' Ball, without a smell of the shop. Of course, her father is a problem, but shouldn't be beyond resolution. No, no, my boy, take your mother's cousin to her daughter and see what you think. It wouldn't hurt to ... keep an eye on things at that end, for a while." Sighing, Michael turned back to the fire. Having no desire to change his life to accommodate a wife, he had thought to bring home a little mouse who would be grateful enough to be treated with consideration, who was accustomed to being buried in the country, away from society. He really had no interest in a nursery or domesticity at this juncture, but his father seemed set on it. Sardonically, he thought of taking home a wife the social equal of his mother. "Which countess takes precedence, a countess by warrant or a countess by marriage?" His mother was accustomed to ruling the family with an iron fist in that velvet glove, despite her cozy appearance and genuine affection for her husband and children. He had not known of his mother's attachment to her cousin; his mother had never mentioned her except for the rare instances of receiving a note. He knew, however, that the idea of his marriage to Catherine had been planted in his father's head by his mother, and was more or less a command. Michael poured out a glass of brandy, and slumped into a chair to think.

Meanwhile, Catherine was in the library with her bailiff, Mrs. Davis, and Howard. "I wish to tell you myself how pleased I am with all the arrangements made. I realize that it has been some time since company was entertained in this house, yet you have managed all most satisfactorily. Is there anything needed? Have we sufficient staff?" Howard said, "Thank you, my lady. We are glad that all is satisfactory. Since your ladyship's mother has her dresser, we have not troubled to bring in another maid. Unless you deem an additional person useful, I believe our existing staff will be sufficient. Mrs. Davis has taken the liberty of preparing a list of supplies needed, including some special items for the Christmas celebration." "I will review it, and may make some additions. Would it be possible for a footman or two to go into the village for what is needed, or will it be necessary to send to London? "I fancy all that is needed may be found locally, either in the village or in Taunton, unless your ladyship desires something not readily available." "Good, then. You are all dismissed."

Catherine was left alone in her library. She had received some post, including a letter from Mr. Stuart that she wished to read, and wanted to complete some estate business before dinner at eight o'clock. Opening the letter from Mr. Stuart first, she began to read. As requested, he had made discreet enquiries about her mother's cousin and her family. "Your mother's cousin, Maria Charles, married Hugh Amory, now the Earl of Aldersey, before your mother married Viscount Stanton. The title is a very old one, and there have been Amory's in Cheshire for generations. The family fortune seems quite respectable, due largely to their prudent marriages. They seldom visit London, and have the reputation for being recluses. The connection between your family and that of the Earl of

Aldersey is not one they have ever been known to mention, and there is no indication that the Countess of Aldersey had been overly concerned about her cousin's interests, until after your marriage to the Earl of Heyerwood. There is a hint that your father was somehow influenced in this choice by the Earl or Countess of Aldersey. However, the Countess of Aldersey welcomed the Viscountess Stanton warmly and without question, and seems to be delighted to renew the old family tie. It may be that time and distance had caused an unintentional rift. I have enquired in several quarters, including amongst my colleagues and in the business community. I have heard nothing to their discredit, but there is a look I can't define. Definitely something odd. I will continue to investigate, and will provide more information when I get a reply from envoys I dispatched to Chester, where the Amory's have a town house and conduct their business."

"I have also kept my eye out for any report concerning your father. The word amongst his creditors is that he has not been paying his debts, and may be facing action if he does not surface soon and make some effort to allay their concerns. Viscount Stanton has not been seen in London society or his clubs for some weeks now, but no one seems to know, or care, where he may be. I have found that he has hired a carriage and driver, and mentioned plans to leave town, but no one knows if he has done so. I fear, my lady, that he may be planning to visit you in the near future, so have a care."

Carefully folding Mr. Stuart's letter, Catherine started to put it with her other papers, but checked. "If he has already searched my papers once, he may do so again. I do not want him to discover that I am having his family investigated; I will take this to my room. I must also have a word with Howard and the bailiff regarding my father, to keep them on the alert." Putting the letter aside, she completed her business, checking her personal accounts and the estate accounts, arranging payment of some bills. "The dressmaker, and all of the seamstresses, must be paid in full, with bonuses for their efforts, immediately," she thought, preferring to clear her accounts promptly. With her father's example ever before her, she would have no debts accrue!

Catherine left the library, after carefully tidying and closing her desk, and putting her letter in her reticule. She was crossing the hall when she became aware of Michael standing in the doorway to the drawing room. "Will you join me for a glass of sherry, cousin?" he asked. "I vow, you need something to warm you, after dealing with business on such a gloomy day." Smiling, she joined him before the fire. "Sherry sounds delightful; I will enjoy a glass before I go up to change for dinner." Accepting the delicate glass he handed her, Catherine took a sip and set the glass down on the table next to her. "I hope you have not been too bored, cousin. We have been buried in the country so long, we have forgot society ways. I vow, when my family's affairs are more settled, I plan to go to London for a long visit." Frowning, Michael asked, "Is living in the country distasteful to you? I did not know that you had connections in London. Do you plan to remove there?" Catherine looked at him with surprise and said, with some reserve, "I have more reason than many to love my home here, and will not abandon it. However, I did have a few seasons in London, after leaving school, and still have some friends there. I enjoyed my seasons, and would like to be able to visit London. I may even want to acquire a town house. However, I have made no plans. How you take one up, cousin!" Rising, she went to the window and looked out to the garden.

To her dismay, she saw that the afternoon had grown dark and threatening, with heavy clouds massing overhead. "Oh, dear," she said with dismay. "I fear a storm of some sort. Look how dark it has become, and how the wind is rising!" Mathilde and Mary walked into the room just then. "I hope you do not object, my love, but I have ordered tea to be served before the fire. It is such a gloomy afternoon, and there is nothing like tea before the fire to make one feel cozy," said Mary. "Good afternoon, my dears. I fear I picked a dreary day to come down, but I was thoroughly tired of my own company, and could not resist when Mary suggested tea by the fire," said Mathilde with a smile. "Why, Mother, I am so delighted to see you up and about, we could have tea on the roof if you choose!" exclaimed Catherine, running across the room to hug her mother and aunt.

Just then, Howard came with the maid, bearing the tea tray. Pulling forward a carved table, Howard watched the maid set down the tray, and then made sure all was in order. Catherine turned to her mother and asked, "Will you pour out, Mother? It has been so long since I had tea with you, and I remember that you always served it so gracefully." Smiling with pleasure, Mathilde filled the cups and passed them. "As a child, tea was the one thing I could count on you to attend happily," said Mathilde. "You always seemed to enjoy it so." Sipping her tea, Catherine reflected that her enjoyment of tea in the afternoon had as much to do with her father's unfailing absence at the tea table as her mother's refreshments, but kept that observation to herself.

Suddenly, conversation was interrupted by a loud crack of thunder.

Icy rain and hail cascaded in sheets driven by the wind. Even though the windows were closed, the intensity of the wind was sufficient to cause a draft, stirring the delicate curtains. Shivering, Mary pulled her shawl closer, and went to pull the heavy drapes over the windows closely. "Such a storm! I vow, I can't recall so much wind and rain in the winter. I pity anyone out on the road on such an afternoon." Unconsciously, they all pulled their chairs a bit closer to the fire. Resuming her seat, Mary turned to Michael and said, "We know so little about you and your family. Will you tell us a bit about your home?" Michael responded, "We have a country seat at Aldersey, which is about fifteen miles from Chester. For convenience, we also keep a town house in Chester. Since all of our family's interests are in Cheshire, we seldom have had occasion to go to London. I did attend Oxford, and take the Tour, of course, but somehow have always returned directly to Cheshire. My father has never cared for London, so we simply never went unless in response to a specific invitation, or a business or political matter required my father's presence."

"What of your family, my dear Michael? Have you brothers or sisters?" Quietly, Michael said, "I am the only son. I do have a sister, Rosalie, but her marriage displeased my parents, and we do not see much of her. She is younger than I by several years." "Oh, oh dear," said Mary, flustered. "I do apologize. Not for the world would I have brought up a painful subject!" Coolly, Michael said, "Not painful, ma'am. My sister and I were close, but I agreed with my parents regarding her choice of a husband. We do see them occasionally, but find it easier to minimize contact since her husband is … so out-of-place." Somewhat shocked by his coolness, Mary and Mathilde glanced at each other. Catherine was not shocked, but felt some distaste. What was the cause of this disdain for his brother-at-law? Was there a valid reason, or mere snobbery?

She looked at the clock and rose. "Dinner is at eight o'clock. I have some matters requiring my attention, and must change. Mother, Aunt Mary, do you wish to accompany me?" Eagerly, Mathilde and Mary rose. Catherine glanced at Michael. "Well, sir, I hope you can entertain yourself for a few hours. As you see, I am endeavoring to get back to more sophisticated standards!" Curtseying slightly, she swept her mother and her aunt from the room and up the stairs. Michael stood still before the fire, after rising to bow the ladies from the room. Cursing himself for his clumsiness, he remembered the distaste he had seen on Catherine's face, and the dismay on her mother's face, when he spoke of his family situation. While he was by no means set on a course, there was no sense in setting his cousin on her guard. Replacing his cup and saucer on the tray, he decided to return to his own room. Some time to himself, and a change of raiment, would help him focus his thoughts.

Chapter 12

The next day, Michael was descending the stairs for breakfast, when he heard a knock at the front door. Howard opened the door, and found a footman wearing Aldersey livery. "A message for Viscount Chatellerault, sir. A matter of some urgency, if you please!" Michael crossed the hall, and said, "I am the viscount. Pray give me the message and explain the urgency, if you would be so good." The footman bowed hastily, and Howard suggested, with a slight bow, "My lord, if you would be private, the library is not in use at present." Leading the way, Howard bowed Michael and the footman into the library, and shut the door behind them. Frowning, Michael opened the message. Recognizing his father's hand, he started to read. "Damn! What a coil." Glancing at the footman, he asked, "What do you know of this?" "Nothing, my lord. Only that his lordship said to send for you at once, and wrote that letter," the footman replied. "No one has seen her ladyship in some days, except his lordship and her maid. His lordship wants to see you before any decisions are made. He charged me to be of any assistance possible in your getting home as soon as may be, my lord." Michael smiled, without mirth. "Well, then, I will have Howard show you to my room, and you may pack my things while I take leave of the ladies and have the carriage brought around."

Michael returned to the hall, had a word with Howard regarding his packing and the carriage, and discovered Catherine had come down for an early breakfast. Breathing a sigh of relief at not having to do the pretty with the older ladies, he went hastily into the breakfast room and bowed to Catherine. "Good morning, cousin. I hope the storm last night did not disturb your rest." Catherine replied, "I thank you, Michael, I slept tolerably well. And you, sir?" "I'm quite well, I thank you for asking. I must apologize for the abruptness, but I must take my leave today. I've received a message from my father, and there is family business of great urgency that requires my presence." Concerned, Catherine said warmly, "Pray, Michael, don't apologize. How can we assist you? Your packing…" "As to that, the footman who brought my father's message is already packing, and I have already spoken to Howard about the carriage. I have only to take my leave of you, your mother and aunt. Pray give your mother and aunt my compliments, and my apologies for having to take my leave so suddenly." "I hope it is nothing too serious, Michael. I hope it is not illness or injury. Your sister…?" Evasively, Michael said, "No, no, cousin, my sister is well, so far as I know. I will let you know, so soon as I may, what the situation is. I don't really know myself what's to do, only that my father writes urgently for my return. May I hope to see you soon? I would like you to visit my home one day, so that you may meet my parents, and get to know us." Catherine flushed slightly, and stammered, "Why…thank you, Michael. Maybe, when the weather is more conducive for travelling, after the holidays, and your family is more settled…we'll see. Do let me know as soon as possible how things are. Have a safe journey."

Just then, Howard opened the door, and announced, "Your carriage is at the door, my lord, and your man has brought down your luggage. At your convenience, my lord…" Turning back to Catherine, Michael lifted her hand to his lips, and said "Farewell, cousin. I look forward to seeing you again." Turning, he strode across the hall to the door, down the front steps and into his carriage. As the carriage trundled down the drive, he reread his father's message. "Come at once, my boy. Your mother is in a taking such as I have never seen, and I am at a loss. Your assistance is essential." Staring sightlessly out the window at the gloomy day, Michael pondered the question of his mother. There had been something odd for many years. He had been most surprised by her professed attachment for her cousin Mathilde, and her insistence that he bring her to their home. Sighing, he shook his head; so many contradictions. She would be calmly in charge of the household, managing with an almost masculine competence and lack of sentimentality for months. Then, a fit of screaming hysterics over a minor inconvenience or annoyance would set her back for weeks. Appearing to be a motherly, warm-hearted creature, she would occasionally take an intense, irrational dislike to someone. Witness Rosalie's husband… Wincing, Michael pushed the memory aside.

After several changes of horses, Michael's carriage stopped at the great doors of Aldersey Manor. As he stiffly descended the steps to the ground, the doors were flung open and his father appeared with both hands outstretched. Thank God, you are come. I have been beside myself with worry." Putting an arm around his father's shoulders, Michael gently turned him toward the hall. "I'm here now, sir. What's to do?" Side by side, the two men went straight into the library. Waving Michael into a chair, the earl slumped into his seat behind the great desk.

"Obviously, it's your mother, my boy. After you left, she went into a decline, decided you were never coming back. I don't understand it at all. She was the one who said Mathilde was her dearest friend, who thought Catherine would be perfect for you. Now, to hear her talk, you'd think Mathilde had stolen something from her, and that Catherine was scheming to take you away forever. She keeps talking about London, like she was a prisoner here. Hell's bells, son, you know we've never spent time there. I hate the place, and have too much to do here. When we were younger, your mother mentioned the season a few times, but never seemed to mind that we didn't go. I'm afraid to leave her alone now. By chance, did you happen to hear if Catherine had had any strange correspondence?"

Flushing deeply, Michael said, "My God, sir, I didn't know... No, I'm sure that Catherine received nothing out of the way. I had occasion to see her library, and I was in the hall each time messages were delivered. I think I would know had she received anything untoward. Be frank, sir. Has my mother lost her reason? "Honestly, son, I don't know. She has always been somewhat high strung, had spells of unwellness. However, she has always recovered, and would go months, even years, without an episode. Would that I knew what triggers it!" Sighing deeply, he said, "The decision for which I need guidance is how to help her. I want to have some special attendants for her, who can be with her and do what is needed. Her maid simply cannot cope with her twenty-four hours a day. The question is, where do we find them? How can we do this discreetly? I do not want her harassed or humiliated by having the world at large thinking her mad. Do we look for trained professionals, or hire more domestics and hope for the best?"

Michael sat in silence for a few moments. "Father, I will stay here a few days, to see my mother and to try to calm her fears. I believe the best course is to confer with a physician. Frankly, I know nothing about illness of any kind, and this is beyond anything in my experience. I think the best thing would be to go to London to confer with Dr. Knighton. You may recall, he is one of the Prince's doctors and is noted for his good sense, as well as his professional manner. He may have suggestions for us, and put us in the way of hiring someone appropriate. I met him a few years ago, at Brighton. What think you of this?" The earl nodded slowly. "I'm at my wits' end, and would welcome any assistance. Do as you think best, my son. I'm too tired to go on as we are."

Chapter 13

After Michael's departure, Cather, her mother, and her aunt became absorbed in more feminine interests. With no male in the house requiring attention and feeding, meals went back to the lighter fare favored by Catherine and Aunt Mary and, now, Mathilde. Evenings were spent embroidering in the drawing room as they took turns reading aloud from a new novel. Other than the few hours a day Catherine spent in the library with her estate business, the days passed with the three ladies always together. As Christmas approached, there were preparations made and early bedtimes allowed all three ladies to work on surprises in their chambers. On Sundays, Catherine and her aunt ventured to church in the village. Mathilde chose not to venture out due to the cold, but Catherine's silk-lined redingote, fur bonnet, and matching pelerine and muff kept her warm as toast, while Mary swathed herself in her warm cloak. Having met many of the villagers in prior visits, Catherine nodded and smiled as she escorted her aunt to her pew. After the service, Catherine and Mary stopped for a word with the vicar and his wife.

"I am so glad to see you again, my lady. I had intended to call before now, but hesitated to intrude on your privacy, especially now that her ladyship has joined you," said Mr. Lamb, the vicar warmly. "I am so glad to have seen you today, sir. You and your wife must join us for tea. We are making plans for Christmas, and cannot imagine celebrating this most cherished festival without attending church and contributing to any plans or projects." Eagerly, the Vicar and his wife assured her of their intent to call soon, and suggestions for her consideration. "His late lordship's mother was most active in local affairs before her death, and we have missed her sadly. Your participation would go a long way toward filling that gap."

Cordially, Catherine extended an invitation for tea to the Vicar and his wife for the very next day.

That evening, Catherine was telling her mother about the church, the service and the Vicar's kindness. "The church is of stone, of course, quite small, and very old. There is a beautiful stained glass rose window behind the altar. The vicar and his wife will be joining us for tea tomorrow, Mother. I hope you do not mind. He will be bringing me information about special needs and wishes for the parish, with which I can assist for Christmas. I want to do something special, but privately. I don't want to seem ...pushing." Smiling at her daughter with affection, Mathilde said, "My dear, this is your house. You certainly do not need to consult me before inviting guests. Besides, it will be good to have company for tea; we have been rather dull since Michael's departure, and it will do us good. I would relish a chance to speak with the Vicar quietly."

Catherine looked at her mother in some surprise, and decided to change the subject. "Mama, what would you say to a visit to town after Christmas? Aunt Mary has not been to London for many years, and you know how long it has been since I've been there. I would love to see the shops, visit the opera, and meet with some dear friends. Could you enjoy the scheme?" Taken aback, Mathilde faltered, "Town? In the New Year? But what about your father? Where would we stay?" Catherine smiled mischievously, "We can dare do as we choose. My father has not been seen for some weeks, and is supposedly hiding somewhere from his creditors. As to where we would stay, I will never set foot in my father's house again. I will have Mr. Stuart hire us a house for a month or so." Taking her mother's hand comfortingly, Catherine said quietly, "Don't fear, Mother. We will not venture to London without considering our safe journey, and our situation there. Frankly, I don't know what kind of a welcome to expect. I have been away so long, and you know about the late earl's reputation. I only know that I must go sometime, and I want to visit the shops in any case. A few weeks are the sum of my desire at present. If it passes well, I may return for future visits. If it is not successful, at least I will know where I stand. In any event, you and Aunt Mary have some old friends, too. We have done nothing, and have no reason to hide. I have already written to Caroline, Julia and Maria. Caroline and Julia have assured me that they will see me when I care to come. Cannot you like the scheme, Mama?"

Staring into the fire, Mathilde frowned in thought. Straightening her back, she held her head up proudly and looked at Catherine. "You are right, my love. We must go sometime. I have ever enjoyed Society, especially when your father was least in sight. I am so accustomed to bowing to his wishes that I have forgotten myself, and you. We will go after the new year, and see what we will see. Have you made any arrangements, my dear?" Just then, Mary entered the room. "As to that, Mathilde, before ever you arrived, Catherine had writ to Mr. Stuart about finding a house of some sort, I believe. We had hoped, if the weather is favorable, to go near the end of January. I hope that is agreeable?" Mathilde replied, "It couldn't be better; Parliament will be in session, so there will be plenty of company and entertainments, but the Season will not be in full swing. I couldn't bear to make this first attempt at the height of the Season. Maybe next year, in the spring, if this visit goes well, we will be able to give a ball or route party. This year, I would like to visit quietly. Do you agree?" Both Catherine and Mary nodded.

The next day, the Vicar came alone, making apologies for his wife's absence. "A heavy cold, my lady, and she feared it turning to a putrid sore throat if she went out again in the cold. She begged me to extend her apologies for failing today." Smiling, Catherine extended her hand. "Pray, sir, assure her that we understand, and hope she will be feeling more the thing very soon. May I offer you some tea? We enjoy it in the library before the fire in this cold weather." Leading the way, she escorted the Vicar to the library, where her mother and aunt were already seated at the laden table. At Catherine's request, Mathilde poured out. The conversation turned to the needs of the parish. "I fear, ladies, there are many households affected by loss of work, and the cold is contributing to illness. There is a great need for many things, as basic as food and firewood in some cases." Picking up a pen and paper she had at hand, Catherine took down the names and directions of several families severely in need. "I may be able to find work for some, and can provide some supplies for those in need now." They also discussed the need for a village school.

When tea was concluded, Catherine rose with Aunt Mary. "Pray, excuse us sir, for a few moments. My mother will entertain you until we return." Sweeping Mary out the door, Catherine left her mother with the Vicar. Ringing for Howard, she instructed him to have some bundles of firewood prepared, as well as some baskets with some stores, to be brought to the hall as quickly as possible. "And, Howard, remind Mrs. Davis of those woolens and linens we found in the attics some months ago. If there are any in good condition remaining, have those brought as well." She and Aunt Mary looked at each other. "Aunt, we just had our wardrobes replenished. Do not you still have some older items? I know I still have some black shawls and at least one cloak still in good condition. Let's see if we can find some things to add to the collection. If necessary, we can send it all in a wagon, if it won't fit in the Vicar's carriage." "What a good idea, my dear. I know I have some heavy woolen stockings and gloves, and at least a shawl or two." The ladies hurried upstairs to rummage through their wardrobes.

Some little time later, they returned to the hall, each laden with a bundle of warm items. Catherine looked about, pleased and touched. There were several baskets, each laden with preserved foods, small sacks of flour and dried peas, and some tea. There were several bundles of woolens, ranging from blankets to shawls to a couple of old cloaks. Howard bowed and said, "The firewood has already been tied to the roof of the Vicar's conveyance, my lady. I believe that these items can be safely bestowed within, and still leave him sufficient room to ride home in comfort." "Howard, pray tell the staff how pleased and touched I am by their efforts. Will there be sufficient room for these additional items Aunt Mary and I have found?" "Of course, my lady," said Howard with a bow.

Catherine and Mary turned to the library door. Just as Catherine reached for the knob, the door opened and the Vicar appeared, escorted by Mathilde. He turned to Mathilde, took her hand and said with a smile, "Now, remember, my lady, you are promised to us for the Christmas services." Turning back to the hall, he started in surprise at seeing Catherine and Mary so close at hand. He said with another bow, "I must take my leave of you, ladies, but I hope I will be welcomed for another visit in the near future, and that we will see you again at services?" Catherine and Mary both curtseyed, and Mary said, "Of course, sir, we will be most happy." Catherine said, "Please, sir, distribute these items to those most in need. We will send more shortly, now that we know what is needed." Looking about the hall, the Vicar saw the remaining baskets and woolens. Hurrying to the door, he surveyed his laden coach and the footmen busily finishing the loading. Turning back, he took Catherine's hand and bowed low. "My lady, this will help several of our neediest families through the next week or so, and give us time to work out longer-term solutions. I did not expect such kindness at such short notice." Catherine replied, "Pray, sir, forgive my tardiness. This is a responsibility I should have addressed sooner." They parted at the doorway, mutually pleased.

Chapter 14

With Christmas approaching rapidly, preparations reached a fever pitch. The ladies were occupied with embroidering handkerchiefs and lavender bags, sewing dainty trifles of silk and lace, and pleasurably occupied in contriving gifts for each other and the household. The party for the tenants and villagers was well in hand, with specially chosen gift baskets for each household and a toy for each child. Mr. Stuart had sent a letter outlining the arrangements for the house in town, and agreeing to come for the Christmas holiday. Catherine was pleasurably engaged in sorting through the late countess's jewels yet again, hoping to find something special for her mother and her aunt for Christmas. Taking up the carved ivory bracelets, she studied them. Not a pair, as she had originally thought. Though the same size, the carving on each was totally different, and each was accented with inlay, one with gold, and the other with silver. She studied them carefully, and gave them a careful cleaning. The ivory glowed warmly, accenting the delicate carvings and the now-shining metallic inlay. She determined to give the gold-inlaid bracelet to her mother, and the silver to her aunt. Smiling with pleasure, she tied and labeled the two parcels, and put them with her little hoard of gifts in the drawer of the table by the window.

She had determined on a truly handsome shawl for Mrs. Davis, and a bottle of fine cognac for Howard, to accompany their annual bonuses. The footmen and maids were each to receive a gold sovereign. For Jane, she had ordered a beautifully bound Bible and a new reticule, in which she had placed five gold sovereigns. With the embroidered handkerchiefs and lavender bags and the bracelets for her mother and aunt, there was indeed a fine show. She eagerly anticipated the happiest Christmas in several years.

Idly looking out the window at yet another dreary evening, she thought suddenly of her cousin Michael. As much as she loved her aunt and mother, there was no denying that she had enjoyed Michael's presence. She wondered what the family crisis had been, if it was resolved, what he was doing for Christmas... Calling her thoughts to order, she turned back to her dressing table. Lighting the candles, she studied her reflection in the mirror. All ready for dinner except jewelry, she was wearing a midnight blue velvet gown, made high to the throat and long-sleeved for warmth, trimmed with a wealth of ivory lace and sapphire blue satin ribbon at the neck and sleeves. There was also a ruching of the ribbon in three rows at the hemline. She had never worn this gown, and felt it was appropriate for the holiday spirit in the air. She slipped the late countess's sapphire earbobs into the holes in her ears, and looked at her reflection with satisfaction. Her hair, grown long, was pulled high up to the crown of her head except for a few curls that spilled down the back, and tendrils curling around her face. Laughing, she swept a curtsey to the mirror, blew out the candles, and hurried down the stairs.

In the drawing room, she found her mother and Aunt Mary sitting with Mr. Stuart, who had arrived earlier than expected. All three were sipping sherry and laughing as they turned toward her. She smiled and held out her hand to Mr. Stuart. "My dear sir, how delightful to see you. You are so kind to spend this holiday with us, and we are so glad to have you here." Mr. Stuart bowed over her hand. "I am grateful to you for this opportunity to spend time with you, ladies." As he rose, his eyes went involuntarily to Aunt Mary, who blushed slightly. Catherine, taken aback, turned to her mother. "I trust I see you well this evening, Mother? You look delightfully." Mathilde smiled, pleased at the compliment, and smoothed the skirt of her violet silk. "I felt festive tonight, daughter. You also look lovely. Surely, that is a new gown?" Aunt Mary was also looking her best in black velvet with the diamond earrings and hair ornament that Catherine had bestowed on her glittering like frostwork. Catherine accepted a glass of sherry from Howard and turned to her three companions. "A toast, I vow, is appropriate tonight. May we have many more merry evenings like this one!" They all laughed, and gently clinked the delicate glasses. When Howard announced that dinner was served, the four rose with alacrity, and went to the dining room.

Warm with a blazing fire and the light of the candle sconces and candelabra, the room glowed. Seating themselves around the table, the little group enjoyed Mrs. Davis' carefully chosen menu, which included a roasted chicken and oyster pie, and concluded with a delicate pudding and champagne. The ladies, each sipping a little sherry, lingered with Mr. Stuart as he sipped his port and enjoyed the hothouse grapes and walnuts. They sat late into the evening, laughing and chatting, rising only when the clock in the hall struck midnight.

"Ladies, I don't know when I've enjoyed an evening more," said Mr. Stuart. "The food, the wine, the company-all delightful! I hate to see it end. My lady, I beg you, could we continue our evening with a little music in the drawing room? I recall seeing a piano-forte. Surely one of you ladies can play?" Laughing, the ladies rose, and Catherine led the way to the drawing room, to find the fire and candles already lit, the piano-forte opened and a pile of music ready. Playing by turns the ladies played their personal favorites, while Mr. Stuart stood gallantly by to turn the pages of the music. Mary was playing an old favorite by Mozart, which the clock suddenly struck one-thirty. Catherine, observing the shy glances exchanged by Aunt Mary and Mr. Stuart, turned to her mother and surprised her in a yawn. "Mother, I had no idea it was so late. I dare swear you are exhausted, and I, too, am ready to retire." Helping Mathilde to her feet, Catherine turned to the other two, who were engrossed in the music. "Pray continue, Aunt Mary, Mr. Stuart. I will escort my mother to her room." The two ladies left the room and went upstairs, while the strains of Mozart continued.

The gaiety continued the next day, unabated. After attending church for the Christmas service, and a delicious breakfast was consumed, gifts were exchanged and everyone was delighted. Below stairs, the servants had had a special breakfast after receiving their gifts from Catherine. Above stairs, Mr. Stuart was enthralled with his gift. "The most beautiful edition of *Dr. Johnson's Dictionary*, both volumes so beautifully bound. A treasure, indeed!" Mathilde and Mary were trying on their ivory bracelets, enjoying the warm ivory glow in contrast with the glints of the precious metal inlay. Catherine was very pleased with her own gifts. Her mother had given her a beautiful ruby cross on a gold chain, and some beautifully embroidered handkerchiefs. Aunt Mary had given her an antique brooch of gold set with topaz. "It was your great-grandmother's brooch. It is just the thing to wear in the lace at the throat of your brown gown." Catherine was touched and pleased to receive such family treasure. Mr. Stuart had brought the latest novels for each of the ladies, which were received with delight. The ladies took turns playing carols while all sang. Catherine reveled in the warmth of the atmosphere of peace and contentment. Truly, the happiest Christmas of her life!

Chapter 15

Glancing at her nodding companions, Catherine turned back to the window, looking out that the cold grey landscape rolling by the coach windows. After the celebrations at Christmas, they had gone to services for Twelfth Night, supervised the cleaning of the house for the new year, and finalized plans for their visit to London. Catherine at first had waited for word from Michael, but as the days passed with no sign, forgot about it. Now she, her mother and Aunt Mary were bowling along the highway on the final leg of their journey to London, with Jane and the indefatigable Miss Potter riding behind with the luggage. Opening her reticule, she removed the letters from Caroline and Julia to reread. Caroline, now married and happily awaiting the birth of her first child, was effusively welcoming. "I am so glad you are coming now. I still have a few weeks in which I can still show myself abroad, and we will have such fun. Since the Season has not really begun, we can shop and visit to our hearts' content. We must go to the Adelphi Theater at least once. They are showing a tragedy I am dying to see, and my dear Tom positively loathes plays!" Married to a well-off younger son since her first season, Caroline had almost despaired of producing a child and was ecstatic now. "If it is a girl, you must be her god-mother. A boy, I'm afraid, will have to make due with Tom's brother and sister-in-law for sponsors!" Smiling as she read, she reflected that Caroline was obviously overflowing with joy.

The letter from Julia was…different. Julia was also married, to Jean-Paul DeGryce, *Comte* DeBeaumonte. A French nobleman, whose family had escaped the Terror, he had been in England a short time when he had met and married Julia, the granddaughter of a powerful and wealthy house. His family had managed to salvage some of their fortune, but he had made no secret of his desire to wed a well-born, and very rich, young woman. Julia had been deeply in love with her Jean-Paul at the time of their wedding. Julia wrote, "So pleased to hear from you after these many years. I will be honored to receive you. Pray write to me when you have arrived, to give me your direction. You must come to tea." The letter went on to discuss her social schedule, the duties she shared with "*Chere Maman*", the dowager *Comtesse*, and her position at court. There was no word of her husband or any children, and the letter seemed tepid. Still, Julia had said she would receive her, which was what she had hoped. She turned back to the letter from Caroline, as a chilled man would hold his hands out to a blazing fire.

The house Mr. Stuart had hired was in a quiet neighborhood just off Grosvenor Place. A well-kept grey stone townhouse of three stories, the entry was immaculately clean and welcoming, with warm light shining from the windows. As the ladies mounted the steps, the door swung open as if by magic, and a dignified butler bowed, "Welcome, my ladies, to London. I am Morrow." Catherine blinked in the brightly-lit foyer. A graceful staircase rose to the first floor, and a vividly patterned oriental carpet glowed on the floor. As the footman took their wraps, Morrow said, "If you will follow me, Lady Heyerwood, Lady Stanton, Madam St. Clair, I will show you to the drawing room. You must be ready for tea after your long journey." Gratefully, Catherine smiled and replied, "Oh, Morrow, you must have read my mind. A cup of tea would be lovely. Will you have Miss Potter shown to my mother's rooms, and Miss Thomas to mine? Some tea for them as well, if you please." Morrow bowed, and signaled to a footman. "Of course, my lady. This way, if you please." Mounting the gently-curving stair, they entered a small but tastefully-furnished drawing room, where a laden tea tray waited before the tire. A comfortable sofa on one side of the table faced two comfortable armchairs, all placed cozily before the carved fireplace. Carefully assisting the ladies to their seats, Morrow bowed and walked to the door. "My lady, be pleased to ring when you are ready to be shown over the house or to your rooms. I will send the housekeeper to you." Morrow bowed again, and closed the door behind him.

Catherine her mother and Aunt Mary sank gratefully into their seats. As she poured out the tea and passed the cups, Catherine said, "How delightful this is! I was positively chilled to the bone, and don't care if I see that coach again. We may have to stay for the whole season, if going home means freezing one's nose off in a carriage in the dead of winter!" Lady Stanton said faintly, "My love, pray let me get my breath and thaw my toes before we even speak of going out again." Aunt Mary pulled her shawl closer and sipped her tea in silence, looking around the pleasant room. "What a delightful welcome!" she said suddenly. "One would think Morrow knew to the moment when we would arrive. How well Mr. Stuart has chosen." "As to that, Aunt," teased Catherine, "I believe Mr. Stuart to be more concerned for your comfort than anything else!" Mary blushed rosily, and hid behind her teacup. "Frankly, I am longing to retire," sighed Mathilde wearily. "I had forgotten how uncomfortable even the best-sprung carriage becomes after a while." Catherine jumped up and rang for Morrow. When he appeared and bowed, she said, "Morrow, pray have my mother shown to her rooms, as she is quite tired." Morrow bowed again, saying, "Yes, my lady, and before I forget, some messages have been delivered in anticipation of your arrival." She took several sealed missives from the salver he presented. "Thank you, Morrow." Her mother followed the butler out of the room.

"By your leave, Aunt," said Catherine, as she broke the seal on the first letter. "I am still hoping to hear from Maria, and there may be a message from Mr. Stuart." "Certainly, my dear." Catherine glanced at the first letter, pleased to see that it was from Caroline. She read hastily, smiling at Caroline's overjoyed welcome. Her marriage to the Honorable Thomas Berkley, younger brother of Baron Lyle, and her anticipated blessed event filled her with a happiness brought to a peak by the arrival of her dearest friend. "Let me hear from you as soon as you arrive, so that we may lay our heads together and make plans! I am *determined* to see the shops and at least one play with you, before I must retire to the country." Catherine opened another missive. A brief note from Mr. Stuart was disclosed, hoping all was to her liking and promising to look in on Wednesday. Staring into the fire, she had to think for a moment before realizing that it was Monday evening. Opening the next letter, Catherine hastily skimmed to the signature. When she saw the sprawling "Maria Harwood, Baroness Fortescue" at the bottom, her brows drew together slightly. Such formality did not bode well.

She went back to the beginning. Addressed formally to Lady Catherine Lovell, Countess of Heyerwood, and couched in the most frigid terms, Maria made it clear that she would unfortunately be engaged for the entire length of Catherine's visit to town, however long it might last. In terms of the iciest disdain, she regretted that she would be unable to meet Catherine, even privately, and that, while holding the memory of their girlhood friendship in affection, she had no desire to renew her acquaintance. With tears in her eyes, Catherine crumpled the letter in her hand, and jumped to her feet. Aunt Mary looked up in surprise. "My dear, what…?" she began. Catherine strode to the fireplace, and threw the letter into the heart of the blaze. "That was my long-awaited response from my 'dearest friend', Maria," she said in a trembling voice. "Maria makes it quite clear that she is unwilling to risk contaminating herself by continuing an acquaintance with me!" "Oh, my love, don't be hurt! You have not seen or heard from her in so long. It may even be that she was constrained to respond so." "Hurt? I am furious! I could accept that she did not wish to resume the acquaintance-we all grow and change. It was the icy contempt of her letter that so offends me. How dare she take that tone with me?" She paced the hearthrug, shaken by fury. "Does she think that I need her approval, or anyone else's? I am not a young girl, making my first curtsey, to be thrown into despair by *her* disdain!" Resuming her seat, she picked up the rest of the letters and put them carefully on the table. "I believe I have had all of the 'good news' I can take for one day. I'll read these later. Aunt, let us ring for Morrow to bring the housekeeper. I think we should see over our new home."

The next day, Catherine answered her letters. In the briefest, curtest tone she could muster, she was pleased to reassure Baroness Fortescue that she could dispense with her company. She sent Mr. Stuart a friendly note that they would look forward to seeing him on Wednesday, and that they were totally charmed with their new home. She also sent Caroline a warm invitation to tea that afternoon, and requested the housekeeper to have a footman deliver it and wait for a reply. Then she read the remaining letters. To her surprise, the last was a note from Michael, indicating he had just discovered her expected arrival, and asking permission to call when convenient, as he was also in town on business. Remembering his dislike of London, she was puzzled as he had not mentioned any need to visit London before his hasty departure from Heyerwood. Shrugging, she wrote a friendly note welcoming him any time. Hastily sealing her letters, she took them down to the hall.

Chapter 16

Thanks to the footman's prompt return with a note accepting her invitation, Catherine ordered an elegant tea. Looking over her wardrobe, she decided to wear the forest green dress and slippers, with the Norwich shawl and the topaz earbobs. Her mother and aunt were still resting, so she would be able to see Caroline alone. Suddenly nervous, she dressed carefully, and studied herself in the mirror. She dressed her hair simply, leaving a few curls around her face. Should she wear something on her head? She pinned on a delicate trifle of ivory lace, complimenting the lace at her throat and wrists. Not bad. Was the green too bold? She changed to the plum gown with black slippers and pearl earrings. Oh dear, the ivory lace didn't suit, as the plum had ecru lace. She changed her headgear to that of ecru lace, and nodded in satisfaction. Adding a dainty pearl pin to the lace at her throat, she stood before the long mirror. Catherine was pleased with her appearance. She picked up the Norwich shawl, and hurried down the stairs.

She was sitting before the fire in the drawing room, when Morrow announced, "The Honorable Madame Berkley." She rose and turned toward the door. Caroline appeared unchanged, a mop of short, silky black curls and sparkling grey eyes, dimples in both cheeks. She held out both hands to Catherine, and said, with a giggle, "How glad I am to see you! You look just as I remember. Oh, but I have missed you so!" Catherine caught her hands, and led her to the sofa before the fire. "Pray be comfortable! We have so much to catch up on. I am so glad you are here!" Seated before the fire, with cups of tea in hand, the two began to talk.

Catherine told Caroline of her letters from Maria and Julia. "Pray, think nothing of it," said Caroline earnestly. "After I married Tom, a mere younger son, she cooled towards me and, once she married her baron, she sent me a similar letter. I never bothered to respond. You must recall that Maria had ever a … STRONG conviction of her own worth, matched only by a sense of everyone else's inferiority. If anything, your title probably galls her as you will have precedence if you ever attend a function at which she is present! I am glad you heard from Julia. Although she and I are not in the same circles, she and I still see each other at least once a week. Her husband is very formal, and selects their social functions with a view to prestige. Unfortunately, she has only one child, a daughter, which does not suit the *comte* or his mother, so Julia has had much to bear. The child is lovely, with Julia's red-gold curls and big blue eyes. Her name is Juliana, and Julia adores her. She has been allowed full charge of Juliana's upbringing since the child is only a girl. Neither the *comte* nor his mother show any interest in Juliana. However, Julia is still hopeful of bearing the necessary heir. I am sure you will meet Julia's family while you are in town." "What of Julia's own family?" "Oh, my dear, she is not allowed to spend much time with them. Even though the *comte* values their fortune and their connections, they do not live in the pomp and circumstance that he requires. She sees them during the day, when they are in town, and is allowed to take Juliana to visit them in the country for a few weeks during the summer, but that is all."

Catherine looked at Caroline. "How long ago school seems! The four of us were inseparable then, and I feel that you and I have never been out of touch in spite of the years. But Maria and Julia seem to have gone beyond us, out of reach, somehow." Briskly, Caroline replied, "Well, that is true in some respects, although I think you will find that Julia will do her best-she wants friends so badly. However, my dear, as we grow up and marry, we do change and move on. Look at you, so dignified and a grand lady now! When I think what a sad romp you were at school!" Laughing the two finished the last cakes, and the conversation turned to shopping and clothes. "Your dress is lovely, Catherine, but wools are not widely worn in town these days, in spite of the cold. You need not completely redo your wardrobe, unless you wish to do so, but a few gowns for Town wear would not be amiss. Sarcenet and silk are stylish, and a fine silk or wool crepe is also modish. I will take you to Grantham's and the Pantheon Bazaar. They are so much fun! If you like, we will pay a visit to my *modiste*. She has exquisite taste, just like yours."

Catherine asked, "Caroline, must I wear half-mourning? I hate lilac and grey. I don't want to be stared at or cause tattle, but I don't wish to be a dowd, after a whole year in black!" Caroline looked at her squarely. "Catherine, your circumstances are such that I honestly don't think anyone, except the highest sticklers, would say anything were you to burst upon the *Ton* in scarlet. I think that you may safely trust your own taste and discretion. If the gown you are wearing is any indication, your appearance will be unexceptionable and becoming." Pleased, Catherine relaxed and smiled. The two went up to Catherine's room, and Caroline looked over the wardrobe Catherine had brought to town. "A gown or two for balls, a few more silks and velvets, and you will be completely up to snuff!" The young ladies made plans to start their shopping later in the week, and debated earnestly whether to attend a concert or a play. Just then the clock on the mantel chimed, and Caroline looked up, startled. "My dear, I must fly! Tom gets worried if I'm out late just now," she said with a blush and a smile. "I am so glad you are here. We will have such fun." Catherine and Caroline descended the stairs, and Catherine ordered a chair for Caroline. After a fond embrace, she watched Caroline depart, and returned to her rooms.

Since Caroline had approved her taste, she would take sketches with her when they visited the modiste. Catherine took fresh paper and sketched out an evening gown, suitable for a ball, similar to her violet velvet but in a lighter silk of a different colour. She made the neckline a bit lower, and the sleeves short. Dark green silk, with delicate gold embroidery around the neck, the edge of the sleeves, over a golden underdress? Gold lace? Gold slippers and fan? A second drawing was for an afternoon dress, similar to her dark green wool, to be made up in a deep burgundy velvet and a golden brown wool crepe as well. Privately, she resolved that she would wear wool if she chose. She had forgot the *Ton*'s slavish devotion to fashion, even at the cost of comfort and health. Well, she refused to freeze. As long as her gowns were becoming and within the current style, that should be sufficient. She debated about a second ball gown. Since she had not considered attending balls before her arrival to town, she had not given serious thought to having several. She sketched out another gown for the evening, this time to be made up in a pattern-weave silk, with a lower rounded neckline. She again chose short sleeves, and decided that velvet ribbon matching a colour in the pattern could be used to trim the sleeves and hem, and possibly some delicate beadwork around the neckline. A bronze and gold would be lovely, with a small train and bronze slippers or sandals. Gold beads? Since she was not using lace this time, perhaps the sleeves should be trimmed with beads as well? She decided to see what fabrics she could find before planning further. Rising, she rang the bell for Jane, and went to dress for the evening.

The next day, after a nuncheon, Catherine was in the library dealing with correspondence. She had received a letter from the bailiff, outlining some needed repairs at Heyerwood Manor, and some items needed for spring planting. She wrote back, authorizing the repairs and suggesting that he speak to the vicar about using local men in need of work for extra help if needed. She also wrote to Mr. Stuart, authorizing the expenditures, and to the vicar, advising him of the work in hand, asking him to keep in mind the names of some likely men who needed the extra work. She also asked the vicar to advise her what things were needed in the way of staples, cloth for clothing and other necessities, so she could order them and have them sent from town. She wrote to Howard and to Mrs. Davis, advising them of the safe arrival in London, suggesting that they send her lists of any goods or supplies needed from London, so that she could see to their procurement. As she was sealing the last of her letters, a footman brought her some post. A note from Julia, whose hand she could recognize, a letter from Mr. Stuart, and a letter in a hand she did not recognize.

The letter from Mr. Stuart was very short, advising her that her father had, in fact, been seen in town and had settled some of his debts, but was avoiding his old haunts. He did not know if Viscount Stanton was aware that his wife and daughter were visiting town, and he urged caution especially in going about after dusk. For the rest, he addressed some minor business, and asked if he might call for tea sometime next week. She responded with pleasure, inviting Mr. Stuart to call at his leisure, assuring him that he would always find a welcome at tea. She made no response to his warning about her father; after all, what was there to say? The note from Julia was next, welcoming her to town and asking her to call the next morning at ten o'clock. Julia indicated that no reply was needed unless she was unable to call. Puzzled, she thought, "Why so early?" A call that early in the day was highly irregular. Fortunately, she kept the same hours she had at Heyerwood Manor, preferring to walk early in the day for exercise.

She opened the last envelope. The handwriting was feminine, but scrawled across the page, as if the letter were written in a hurry or in the dark. She could make nothing of it. The scrawl was virtually illegible. Shrugging, Catherine threw it on the fire. She filed away the letters from Mr. Stuart and her bailiff, with the notes she had kept regarding her suggestions to the bailiff and the vicar. Gathering her letters to be mailed,

Catherine left the library and paused in the hall, leaving her letters in the tray for a footman to take to the post. She went up the stairs, to her room, to change her dress. She and Caroline were going to visit the Pantheon Bazaar and Grantham's that afternoon.

Wandering around the stalls and tables at the Pantheon Bazaar, Caroline was stunned at the amount of goods available. She found the golden brown wool crepe, the burgundy velvet, and the deep green silk for her ball gown, as well as the trimmings she had wanted. She was unable to find a pattern-weave silk to her taste, but did find a most unusual oriental silk that shifted colour from bronze to gold as the light played upon it. She also found a delicate golden *crepe lisse* to make the underdress for her ball gown. She even found the golden slippers and bronze sandals that were exactly what she wanted. As she browsed, Catherine found a length of silver-grey velvet that would make a lovely overdress or dressing gown for her mother, with silver lace to trim, and a length of amethyst satin for Aunt Mary. In another department, she found lengths of heavy muslin and cotton, black and brown woolen broadcloth, and Turkish toweling, of which she ordered yards to be bundled up and shipped to Heyerwood Manor. Dazed, she turned to Caroline, "I can't believe it! I have never seen such a place. I've found all the goods I'd planned to purchase, in a fraction of the time and for far less than I'd expected to pay. Are you sure that we need go on to Grantham's?"

Mischievously, Caroline smiled and said, "Of course, silly, we've just gotten a good start!" With the dress fabrics and trims dispatched to the *modiste*'s address, and the gifts for her mother and Aunt Mary directed to the townhouse, Catherine continued with Caroline to Grantham's. There, she bought delicate Brussels lace, blonde lace, and a beautiful Kashmir shawl in a soft buta design of gold, brown and bronze with a touch of deep blue on a cream ground. Catherine also found a pattern-weave silk in a deep chocolate brown woven with gold that she could not resist. Caroline looked at baby things, and bought a selection of soft, light woolens, suitable for country wear, as she would be retiring to the country in a few weeks. Both ladies purchased a selection of embroidery silks, fabrics and needles. As they left, Catherine turned to Caroline and said, coaxingly, "You must be exhausted; I know I am, but please may we stop at Hatchard's Bookshop? I have dreamed of buying some new books, especially now that I have a library. Please say we may?" "Of course we will stop there! I wouldn't mind a book or two myself. 'Twill keep my mind busy whilst I'm buried in the country." Catherine beamed with delight.

As with her previous shopping, once started, Catherine could barely tear herself away. Picking up Southey's *LIFE OF NELSON*, and a beautifully bound volume of Shakespeare's Sonnets, she browsed the aisles. She chanced upon a novel called *SENSE AND SENSIBILITY* that sounded interesting, as well as Richardson's *CLARISSA.* The clerk noted her choices and mentioned that they had a copy of a newer novel, called *PRIDE AND PREJUDICE* by the same author as *SENSE AND SENSIBILITY*, which was very well thought of. "I'll take it," said Catherine, and she continued to browse. She noticed a small pamphlet by Hannah Moore, "Strictures on the Modern System of Female Education," and picked it up. "This may be useful, given our plans for a school," she thought, and put it on her stack. The clerk offered to have the books delivered, but Catherine did not want to let the precious volumes out of her sight. Caroline had also picked up a couple of books. "Byron," she sighed, "So romantic, is he not?" Caroline had also picked up one of Fanny Burney's novels.

Returning to Caroline's carriage, laden with their parcels, the ladies leaned wearily against the velvet squabs and looked at each other. "Now where?" asked Catherine. "Home for tea, as it's almost five o'clock," said Caroline. "I vow, you are the fastest shopper I have ever seen. We have accomplished more today than I expected to do in a week! I am too exhausted for anything more than tea, my feet most of all!" Remorsefully, Catherine replied, "Since I am nearer, let us go to my house for tea, then you can go straight home to rest without having to send the carriage out again." Pulling up outside the door, the footman helped Catherine and Caroline down. Morrow directed the footman to take Catherine's parcel of books to the library, and bowed the ladies into the drawing room, where Mathilde and Mary were already seated before the fire with teacups in hand. "Well, my dears, was your shopping successful?" smiled Mathilde. "Indeed yes, Madam," said Caroline, "Your daughter is most efficient and decisive." Aunt Mary chimed in, "Parcels have been appearing all day, and have been left in your sitting room, Catherine, except the two with our names on them; so thoughtful of you, my love!" After a pleasant half hour, toasting her toes and sipping tea, Caroline rose and took her leave. "Tomorrow, Madame Claire, the *modiste!*" she said over her shoulder, with a twinkle.

Chapter 17

Sipping her morning chocolate, Catherine mulled over her wardrobe. What should she wear to call on Julia? She did not want to be uncomfortable, but did want to look her best. The formality of Julia's letter, combined with the snub from Maria, left her feeling the need of moral support, and looking elegant would be a comfort. Of course, a call so early would be private; few, if any, Society ladies would be out and about at such a time. She settled on the forest green day dress and slippers, pinned the ivory lace confection on to her head, and slipped the topaz earbobs into her ears. She pinned the topaz brooch, Aunt Mary's Christmas gift, into the ivory lace at her throat, and wrapped herself in her chocolate brown redingote. After tying on her close fur bonnet, she draped the matching fur pelerine about her shoulders, picked up her gloves and fur muff, and ran lightly down the stairs. The footman helped her into the waiting carriage, and she was on her way.

Seated in Julia's drawing room, a vast and chilly apartment decorated in white and gold, Catherine looked at Julia in some dismay. Julia had ever been slender; now she appeared a wraith. She seemed restless, and her slim hands fluttered nervously as she talked. Catherine was surprised at the warmth of Julia's welcome. She handed Catherine a cup of tea, and said, "I was so glad to hear from you. Pray forgive the formality of my reply, but my husband expects me to be ever mindful of his status." "Does he read your correspondence, then?" asked Catherine, in shock. "Yes, indeed. I am somewhat careless, as you may recall," said Julia nervously, her eyes on the door. As the maid shut the door noiselessly behind her, Julia's hand shot out and grasped Catherine's. "Oh, Catherine, I have missed you and Caroline so! Caroline and I manage to meet fairly often, but I am not encouraged

71

to become intimate with others. I am so lonely. Jean-Pierre is so remote since I disappointed him with a daughter instead of a son, and his mother never wanted him to marry an Englishwoman in the first place. Your title, of course, makes you acceptable to them. I so hope you will let me call on you." Soothingly, Catherine replied that she would be delighted to spend as much time as possible with her friend. Regaining her composure, Julia sipped her tea, and the conversation changed to more cheerful matters. After a while, Julia asked, "Would you like to meet Juliana, my little girl?" Smiling, Catherine said, "Indeed, yes. I've heard she resembles you greatly." Julia rang the bell, and requested the maid to bring Miss Juliana to the drawing room. She smiled and said, "She is much prettier, and so bright and lively. She is my delight."

Just then, the little girl peeked around the door, and darted into the room. "*Maman, Maman,* may I please have a cake?" Leaning on her mother's knee, she suddenly noticed Catherine and ducked back shyly. "In a moment, love. Please make your curtsey, and say "How do you do?" to Aunt Catherine." The child bobbed her curtsey, and bounced back to Julia, saying "Now may I have a cake?" Julia laughed and nodded. Catherine studied the child. The curls were more golden than Julia's, and the eyes a darker shade of blue, but the likeness was striking in the delicate bones and graceful movements. She turned to Julia and said, "Caroline did not exaggerate. She is so much like you." The three put their heads together, and fell into a comfortable chat while enjoying the delicious refreshments. After an hour, spent far more pleasantly she had dared hope, Catherine rose and said, "Forgive me for staying so long. It has been delightful. I hope you will come to see me and, if I may, I will call again." Julia gave her a hug, and said, "Mornings are best for me. I don't have to worry about interruptions."

When the maid announced Catherine's coach was waiting, she donned her redingote and furs, hugged Julia again, and knelt down to Juliana's level. "I hope to see you again soon, my dear," she said gently and put out her hand. To her astonishment, Juliana leaned forward and kissed her cheek. "Thank you for making my mama laugh. I like you!" Catherine rose, smiled at the two, and went out to her carriage. To her astonishment, it was after eleven o'clock, so she gave the coachman directions to take her to Caroline's home, as they had planned to visit the *modiste*, Madame Claire, at noon. On the short ride, she mulled over her visit with Julia. There were definitely some disturbing undercurrents, and Julia was clearly unhappy. Well, at least she knew Julia was still her friend, and her heart warmed at the thought. She would try to spend as much time as possible with her.

Alighting from the carriage at Caroline's house, she looked about her. Smaller than her own town house, the brick-faced structure had a warm and inviting feel, with its wide, welcoming step and double doors. Seated in Caroline's small, cozy sitting room, she told Caroline of her time with Julia. Caroline said nothing until she had finished. "There *is* something wrong, but I don't know what. Frankly, I am astonished at Juliana; she is usually a rather reserved child. You must have won her heart. Poor Julia, we shall have to try to cheer her, maybe get her to go out occasionally." The conversation then turned to fashion. Drawing her sketches from her muff, Catherine and Caroline put their heads together to talk of clothes. Caroline was lavish in her praise of Catherine's ideas, and they chattered happily as they left the house.

Hours later, Catherine collapsed in her sitting room, exhausted. Clad in a warm velvet dressing gown and slippers, she decided she was too tired to dress for dinner. After ordering supper on a tray, she sat in her favorite chair next to the fire, with one of her new books at hand. Leaning her head back, she gazed into the fire, remembering the hours at the dressmaker's shop. After being measured, she rather shyly told Madame Claire that she had made some sketches she thought might clarify her desires for the *modiste*. After studying Catherine's drawing of the delicate gold underdress, Madame made some suggestions for trim, showing a short, delicate gold silk fringe randomly decorated with tiny gold beads. "Short sleeves edged with this fringe, just showing beneath the sleeves of the overdress." The overdress itself, dark green silk draped and decorated with fragile gold embroidery at the neck and hem, parted over the golden *crepe lisse* underdress. Madame Claire was quick to suggest that the chocolate and gold pattern-weave silk be made up as an overdress as well, in more of a half-robe design, to be worn with the golden underdress, and possibly over an ivory silk as well. The bronze-gold oriental silk required a design of the utmost simplicity to set off the beauty of the fabric. They agreed on a simple, high-waisted design, with short sleeves, a square neckline, and a slightly lower back. Madame Claire had a brocade ribbon in shades of bronze and gold with accents of yellow and deep green to trim the waist, and a narrow edging of gold lace for the neck and edges of the sleeves. She also had the ivory silk for the second underdress at hand. Madame Claire approved the golden brown wool crepe for day wear, and suggested three rows of *rouleaux* of velvet trim at the hem, with matching velvet ribbon edging the long sleeves. Instead of a contrasting colour, Madame Claire suggested that the trim match the golden brown of the gown itself, and to finish off with a deep collar of ivory lace. For the burgundy velvet, Madame approved Catherine's day dress design unchanged. She also suggested a deep blue wool crepe made in a similar style to the golden brown, changing only the neck to a higher line edged with creamy lace and matching lace edging the sleeves.

Madame Claire happened to have some gowns already made up, for another client who had failed to pick them up, requiring only slight alterations. One was a soft sea green sarcenet, trimmed with deeper green velvet ribbon and delicate flowers embroidered around the neckline and hem. There was also a soft rose wool crepe that she could not resist. The dressmaker also had some lovely lace fichus, and a warm Kashmir shawl in shades of pink, rose and seagreen that complimented both gowns. While Catherine and Madame Claire had their heads together, Caroline had a final fitting of a day gown and a quilted silk bed jacket to wear in the country, and looked over some baby clothes that the seamstress had completed. The two young women waited while the final adjustments were completed, sipping tea in Madame's comfortable office. Once their packages were ready, Caroline and Catherine settled their accounts for those items they were taking away, gathered their parcels and bandboxes together, and departed, with Madame promising to contact Catherine about her fittings.

Back in the carriage, the two friends burst into giggles. "Did you see the shocked look on Madame Claire's face when I asked for the bill for today's purchases?" Catherine asked Caroline. "Yes, and I saw how her eyes lit up when you counted the guineas into her hand. She must have been ecstatic to get those gowns off of her inventory. She should be delighted to have two customers who do not wait to be dunned to settle their accounts." After two strenuous days, Caroline was exhausted and decided not to come in for refreshments. Catherine dropped Caroline and her bundles off and went home, where she now sat, glad to be by her own fireside. She was pleased that her mother and Aunt Mary were having a few old friends in to dine, so gave instructions for her own supper on a tray, and wished them both a pleasant evening through Jane. Thanking Providence that she had no plans for the next few days, Catherine watched the dancing flames drowsily, her book forgotten.

Chapter 18

Keeping to her room the next morning, Catherine sipped her morning chocolate in bed. She contemplated her schedule for the next few weeks, including attending a play with Caroline and her husband, and an evening entertainment at Julia's home. She decided to meet with Mr. Stuart to discuss further plans for Heyerwood Manor estate, the possible purchase of a townhouse in London, and setting up some sort of entail for her estate. "Although I may never marry again, if the question should arise, I want to be sure I am being considered at least in part for myself, not just as a honeyfall. I don't ever want to be totally dependent again, either. I like have control of my own affairs." Rising she wrapped her dressing gown around her, and went to her writing table to make some notes of the business she wished to discuss with Mr. Stuart. Having decided to stay in for the day, Catherine impulsively selected the rose wool crepe. She thought, "No one will see me to be shocked, and I might as well enjoy it now." Jane brushed her hair into a soft knot at the nape of her neck, and she hooked pearl earbobs into her ears. Pleased with the gaily coloured gown, she picked up the coordinating shawl, went to her sitting room and sat down in the window with her embroidery. Moving her embroidery stand to capture the best possible light, she bent her head over her work, a profusion of flowers worked in silk on linen which she had designed herself. The warm fire and bright silks lifted her spirits. She worked contentedly for some time, until the light began to dim. Putting her work aside, she looked out the window and was astonished to see how late in the afternoon it was.

A few nights later, dressed in the violet gown she had designed for evening wear, Catherine dined with her mother before she was to leave for the play. This being her first public appearance, she decided to dress simply, and the violet had a simple elegance enhanced by the rich yet discreet colour. She wore her hair swept up high on her head in a simple knot, with a few curls around her face and neck. Her mother had loaned her a pair of amethyst earbobs, and a delicate pin of amethysts set in gold, which she wore pinned to a narrow violet velvet ribbon around her throat. Mathilde smiled fondly, and said, "Catherine, you look lovely, and quite perfect for the theatre. I'm glad you chose a gown with long sleeves; it's so cold, and theatres can be draughty." Catherine laughed and swept her mother a curtsey, thanking her for the compliment. Just then, Morrow announced, "The Honorable Thomas Berkley, and Mrs. Berkley, are here, my lady." Caroline flew to the door and said, "Tom, Caroline, pray come in by the fire, while I put on my things. Caroline, you recall my mother." Caroline and Tom stepped into the drawing room, and Caroline extended both hands to the Viscountess. "Indeed yes, my lady, I am so glad to renew our acquaintance. It is so delightful to see you again. May I present my husband, Thomas Berkley?" While the introductions were completed and a desultory conversation was carried on by the fire, Catherine put on her black silk gloves and caught up a warm black velvet evening cloak, trimmed around the hood and hem with black fur. "Let us be off!" she said, smiling. "I want to get there early, so I can see everything, and everyone! It has been so long since I have been to the theatre." Tom assisted the ladies into the carriage, and they chatted light-heartedly as they rumbled over the cobblestones. "I am so pleased to be on our way. I have been impatient to see this play since I read of it, and was afraid I would miss it. Caroline, do you remember when we went to see Kemble perform at the Drury Lane? He was so overly dramatic, it quite spoiled the play but was so funny to watch!" Caroline replied with a giggle, "I, too, remember Kemble. He pronounced things so strangely! Kean is supposed to be wonderful. I was so glad that they decided to do *Othello* again; I missed it when he and his company performed it at the Lane a few years ago."

Seated in the theatre box, Caroline and Catherine watched, entranced. During the interval, they decided to stay in the box, to observe and chat. Tom rose and went out, to stretch his legs and smoke, and promised to be back before the curtain went up again. Catherine admired Caroline's rose silk and diamonds. Caroline said, "You look most becoming, Catherine. Your gown is perfect, an excellent choice for your first appearance." They looked around, bowing and smiling to Julia, sitting in a nearby box with her husband and an older woman gowned in severe black. "Julia's mother-in-law...something of a martinet, I believe," whispered Caroline. "Oh, my, there is Maria!" Gazing across the crowed theatre, Catherine saw her former school friend, dressed in unbecoming puce satin, with her black hair pulled into fat bunches of curls, peering around the room through a glass. She glanced hastily away, in time to see Michael entering the box. He bowed over her hand, saying "Well met, cousin! I have been meaning to call." "Good evening, Michael, I hope you are enjoying the play. Caroline, may I present my cousin, Michael Amory, Viscount Chatellerault? Michael, this is my friend, Mrs. Caroline Berkley. Her husband Tom will return to us shortly. Do join us," said Catherine. "I would it were possible, but I'm engaged with a party. May I call on you tomorrow?" Catherine smiled and nodded. "My mother and aunt will be delighted to see you. Pray come for tea." Michael bowed, and withdrew, saying "Your servant, ladies." Caroline looked at Catherine, "I didn't know you had a cousin, never mind such an attractive one! When did you make his acquaintance?" Catherine explained, giving an abbreviated summary of her mother's relationship to the Countess of Aldersey, and Michael's escort of Mathilde to Catherine's home. Round-eyed, Caroline said, fanning herself, "How dramatic! I vow, the play is *nothing* to this! A veritable knight in shining armor!" Just then, Tom returned and the lights dimmed as the play resumed. Again, Catherine was mesmerized by the drama unfolding on stage.

When the play was over, Tom suggested they stop by the Piazza for a light supper. As a surprise for Caroline, he had reserved a table and bespoken some champagne. Delighted, the ladies agreed. Seated at a comfortable table, they enjoyed thinly sliced ham, salad and brimming glasses of iced champagne. Raising her glass to sip, Catherine smiled and said, "Such a lovely evening, my dear friends. I vow, I feel like a girl in her first season!" Caroline and Tom laughed and agreed that it was all delightful. As they laughed and chatted over the supper, they enjoyed the music in the background and watching all the fashionables coming and going. Unnoticed, a man sat a few tables away, staring with interest at Catherine and her party. Idly glancing in his direction, Catherine's eyes met his. Her father! She couldn't mistake those icy gray eyes. She let her eyes drift away without acknowledging him and, slightly pale, turned back to Caroline and Tom. Quietly, she said, "Caroline, Tom, pray forgive me, but I must leave as soon as possible without making a scene. My father is here, and I fear he may try to approach me, or make a scene. I am so sorry!" Tom said quietly, "Don't worry, Catherine, we are all finished, are we not? This is a perfectly natural time to take our leave. In a moment, I will summon the waiter, and you and Caroline can go for your wraps."

She smiled with relief, saying, "Thank you for understanding. That will be perfect." Deliberately, Catherine glanced back in her father's direction. He still sat, sipping his brandy and staring at her over the rim of his glass. She turned away and, as Tom called for the waiter, she and Caroline rose and left the dining room.

Tom helped them into the carriage, and he and Caroline made polite chat about the play and the excellence of the supper. Catherine shook off her brown study, and joined in. As the carriage slowed to a stop before her door, she said, "Thank you a thousand times for this evening! The play was truly magical, and the supper delightful. I hope you can forgive me for asking to leave so abruptly." After she and Caroline hugged affectionately, Tom helped her alight, and escorted her to her door, where Morrow and the footman waited. Tom squeezed her hand and said, "Don't worry Catherine. Caroline has told me something of your circumstances regarding your father. You were wise to leave. There is no need to apologize. Come and see Caroline soon. We'll be going into the country shortly, and she wants to spend as much time with you as possible." Gratefully, Catherine smiled and agreed, bidding him goodnight.

The next morning, she instructed Morrow to admit no one but Mr. Stuart, Viscount Chatellerault, and the Berkleys, should they call. She penned a hasty note to Mr. Stuart, and instructed the footman to deliver it without fail and wait for a response. Feeling more at ease, Catherine went to the dining room to join her mother and aunt for breakfast. She found the two ladies, sipping tea and chatting in a desultory fashion while they nibbled and read their post. Catherine found three letters by her plate. "How was the play, my love? Did you enjoy it?" asked Aunt Mary. "Indeed, yes, Aunt, the play was excellent. *Othello* has ever been a stirring drama, and Kean was truly excellent. Afterwards, we had a lovely supper at the Piazza. My cousin stopped by our box, by the way. He may call." Mathilde smiled and said, "I am so glad you had a pleasant evening, dear. What are your plans for today?" Catherine dropped her eyes and stirred her tea. "Why, I hardly know. As I said, Michael may call, and I do have some business to discuss with Mr. Stuart. I've sent him a note, asking him to call at his earliest convenience. I don't have any appointments, so I thought I'd stay at home." Mathilde looked at her with some concern. "Is something wrong, my dear? I quite thought you had some shopping to do and intended to stop by the *modiste*'s. Are you tired, or feeling not quite the thing?" Catherine felt her mother's eyes on her, and flushed slightly. She had never been good at hiding her feelings from her mother. Aunt

Mary looked up from her letter just then and said, "My dears, Gerald has been seen in town! An acquaintance saw him in a shop in Oxford Street yesterday! I wonder, what can it mean?"

Catherine looked up and said, "I know, aunt. I saw him last night at the Piazza. This is one reason I've requested Mr. Stuart to call. I was quite shocked to see him." Mathilde stirred her tea calmly, saying "I dare say he has been in Town all along. He ever had a distaste for the country, and I cannot imagine him being out of London at this time of year, even if he had to live retired. I'm sure we'll know soon enough his purpose." "Just then, the footman entered. "The reply from Mr. Stuart, as you requested, my lady." He bowed and left the room. "By your leave, ladies," said Catherine as she opened the note. Reading the brief missive, she looked up and said with relief, "Mr. Stuart was informed a few days ago of my father's presence in London. Apparently, he has been in the townhouse all along, with his valet and the housekeeper. It seems he's been quietly negotiating with his creditors. Mr. Stuart will join us for tea, and will bring more information then. He suggests we stay in if we are concerned, but feels that my father is too preoccupied to concern himself with us. I would that were true! If I hadn't seen him, and he me, I would feel more sanguine, I confess."

Mathilde smiled slightly. "Well, daughter, your father is not a young man, and has suffered a series of setbacks and reverses such as he has never before experienced. Instead of being in full control, he has been made to feel…unnecessary, shall we say? I have wondered if his health has been affected. This long silence is totally unlike him, unless he has been incapacitated in some way. I have been in touch with the wives of a few of his cronies, and from what they have said, and *not* said, I believe he has been confined with some sort of illness or breakdown. When Mr. Stuart comes, I will ask him to check with Dr. Baillie or Sir William Knighton. Your father would consult with one or the other of them if medical care were needed; they have both attended the Prince, you know, and Gerard sets great store by such things."

Catherine looked at her mother in some surprise. "Why, Mama, I was afraid to tell you I had seen him for fear of upsetting you. You are so calm. Are you not concerned that he will try to take you back to that house? I confess, the thought occurred to me that he might try something at the Piazza last night, so I had Tom and Caroline bring me home early." Mathilde smiled again, and shook her head. "No, my dear, I am not overly concerned. I am no longer afraid of him and his tantrums. The world knows too much about him now, after his behavior and the scenes

Lauren Gilbert

he caused. Besides, he is not concerned with me. Trying to compel me to return now would not change the past, and would diminish his standing even further in the eyes of the world. Imagine him publically admitting his difficulties in controlling his own wife!"

After breakfast, the ladies separated, Mathilde and Mary to discuss their plans for the day, and Catherine to her bookroom. Re-reading Mr. Stuart's reply to her note, she noticed his lack of urgency. That, with her mother's remarkable unconcern, calmed her and steadied her nerve. She reviewed the response from the bailiff-the repairs were set in motion. Extra hands had been needed, which gave a boost to the local men in need of work. She pondered some changes to make permanent employment possible. She knew there were some cattle grazed at Heyerwood Manor; what about a dairy? With all of the acreage at the estate, even with the countryman's dislike of enclosure, it might also be possible to set aside an area for sheep. The wool, at the very least, could be used locally, and the sheep's milk may be useful in the dairy as well. The need for additional herders, dairy workers, and maybe even spinners and weavers could give employment to a number of her people, including women. She made a note to have Mr. Stuart find out if the climate of Somerset were conducive to any of these activities, and the best way to set about making the changes. She wrote to the bailiff to plan to extend the home farm, increasing the planting of vegetables and fruits, and to see if any expansion of the apple and pear orchards could be considered. Increased produce would improve the diet of the local people, allow for increased canning, bottling and drying for storage for winter, and even for possible sales at market time. She asked the bailiff to make note of any need repairs or improvements needed for the house, stables, and other outbuildings, to keep all in the best condition.

80

Chapter 19

Just then, Mr. Stuart was announced. Catherine rose and extended her hand. "Mr. Stuart, how glad I am to see you! I have so many things to discuss that I scarce know where to start!" He bowed over her hand, and said "Lady Catherine, I am so pleased to be with you. Before we start our business, let me rectify a matter long neglected." She sat down and stared at him, mystified, while he, in turn, opened a valise. Removing a large, carved, wooden casket, he turned to her and said, "My lady, these are the jewels of the Countess of Heyerwood. You may recall from the portraits that the Lovell family acquired a truly remarkable collection over the centuries." He opened the casket, and began to unpack numerous smaller leather boxes, velvet bags, and rolls of cloth. Dazed, Catherine watched and asked, "Why, Mr. Stuart, where have all of these been?" He looked up and grimaced. "You may well ask, my lady. It has taken months to locate all of his late lordship's assets. Some have been in store at Hoare's Bank, and some at Drummond's. Some have been held for decades at Rundell and Bridge's or other jewelers after being left for cleaning or repairs and, apparently, forgotten. Fortunately, an inventory had been left with the estate papers. I have been writing and visiting all over London, but have finally located all of the pieces we know about."

The largest box contained the ornate ruby set, complete with diadem, heavy necklace and bracelet, glowing with sullen, red fire. A heavy emerald necklace next appeared. A small roll of fabric unfurled to reveal an ornately-wrought gold chain, from which dangled a large emerald drop. A velvet bag sheathed a delicate gold tiara, made up of fragile flower shapes, each with a small emerald at its heart. In a similar bag, silver tissue wrapped a dainty bracelet of similar flower shapes, also set with emeralds, and a pair of gold and emerald earbobs. "The tiara, bracelet and earbobs were purchased in Italy, for the late Countess, while she and his lordship's father were on their honeymoon. She wore them with the pendant, when she was presented at Court after their marriage." Numerous bags, boxes and rolls of fabric littered the table in front of Catherine, as yet unopened. Stunned, she stretched out a shaking hand. "I never knew it was so much! Whatever shall I do with these things? I could never wear all of this." She halted Mr. Stuart before he could open more boxes. "Pray, sir, let us clear as we go. I could never forgive myself if something were lost. Do we still have a vault or other safe storage?" When he answered in the affirmative, she said with decision, "Thank goodness! Most of these things can be placed there until we decide what to do with them." Looking up suddenly, she said, flushing, "Would it be unbecoming to wear any of these pieces now?" Amused, Mr. Stuart smiled and said, "These are yours, my lady. Who could criticize Lady Catherine Lovell, Countess of Heyerwood, for wearing her own jewelry? Unless, of course, you wore it all at once!" Catherine laughed. "Well, then, I would like to keep the emerald tiara, necklace and earbobs, and the pendant as well. Pray, pack up the ruby parure, and that massive necklace. I remember those from the portraits. Far too heavy and ostentatious for me." Mr. Stuart repacked the rejected pieces.

Next came a set she at first thought were topazes, but they gave a pale golden blaze, not the vivid golden glow she associated with the topaz. "Yellow diamonds, from India, my lady. Quite rare!" She gazed at a delicate golden necklace and matching earbobs, set with the fiery golden stones. She set those aside to be kept. A set of pink pearls appeared, a necklace with two matching bracelets. A thought struck her. "Mr. Stuart, may I give any of these things away? It seems such a shame to lock all of the items I will not wear away. These pearls would so become my aunt." Mr. Stuart considered the question. "My lady, were there any other heirs, the propriety of giving away family heirlooms might be an issue. Since you are, in effect, the sole remaining Lovell, and would be disposing of your own property, there really can be no question. I see no reason why you should not do what pleases you." Catherine smiled, and set the pearls aside as well. Another set of rubies appeared, with a matching hair ornament and ring. Like the others, they were set in gold, but much more delicately wrought. "These, I shall give to my mother," said Catherine firmly.

Business forgotten, she and Mr. Stuart engaged in examining an amazing treasure trove. Another parure appeared, this time of sapphires set in heavily carved gold, consisting of necklace, bracelets and an extremely ugly diadem. Catherine firmly bade Mr. Stuart to pack it back up. A brooch set with amethysts and pearls caught her eye. "Perfect with my violet gown!" Another dainty brooch, of pink pearls in gold, appeared. "This will be just the thing for Caroline! I believe it will be most becoming." From a heavy roll of black velvet, a blaze of diamonds glared. Three massive necklaces, heavy drop earbobs, a brooch, and two bracelets appeared, and were packed away again. "These give me a headache just to look at them! I remember these from another portrait." The last box, tiny and carved of wood, contained two silver lockets. They were almost identical, carved with delicate flowers and leaves set with tiny rubies and sapphires; however, one was smaller and hung from a shorter chain. "These look like something designed for a mother and her daughter," said Catherine softly. "How sweet! These will be ideal for Julia and Juliana." Mr. Stuart replaced the pieces to be stored in the chest, and replaced the chest in his valise. Catherine excused herself, taking the pieces she decided to wear or to give away to her room. Having found a concealed cubby in the floor next to her bed, she placed the packages in with her regular jewelry already hidden there, replaced the floor board, and covered it over with the rug.

Returning to the bookroom, she smiled at Mr. Stuart. "What fun that was! I daresay every woman dreams of such an experience. Now, sir, I do have some business to discuss." She outlined her concerns about setting up an estate and the possibilities of an entail. "I must make some provision for the future. Whether or not I marry, I must designate an heir, or heirs, and do my best to protect the estate and the people who depend on it, as well as myself. I do not know how to set about it. I am also concerned about the possibility that I might marry. I am not too old to marry and have children, and I would never want to find myself in the position of a chattel. I would also like to have some hope of being chosen for myself, not just my fortune." "As to that, my lady, since your husband managed to invest the title fully in you, you will have the right to designate an heir to the title, and to establish your property as you please. If you wish to entail a specific amount of money to be tied to the property, and the property to the title, you could certainly do so, even before you have designated a specific heir, or heiress. Generally, any unentailed property would be subject to your disposal in marriage settlements, should you remarry, as a dowry. We would have to be very clear to set up in the settlement agreements funds remaining specifically under your control and at your discretion, as well as the dowry. You know, of course, that, if a subsequent marriage ended in your husband's death, your dower rights would generally result in some sort of guaranteed income. The agreements made in the settlement would have to be quite specific, of course." He agreed to look into the issues of the title, property and entail for her.

Catherine asked him, hesitantly, how her husband had set about arranging her inheritance. "Especially the title; I cannot imagine how that came about." Mr. Stuart smiled slightly, and replied, "I was not directly involved with that aspect of the settlement. My expertise lies in wills, estates and trusts. As you may know, his late lordship kept company with many… interesting persons also known to the Prince of Wales, now the Regent. The prince has ever had a propensity for falling into debt. From what I understand, his lordship approached the king, before his most recent illness, of course, and the prime minister, offering a sizeable sum of money to apply to the prince's debt in exchange for their approval of his arrangement for the title. I believe there was a suggestion of even more interesting revelations regarding the prince's activities if the remainder for the title could not be settled. I do not know all of the details, but all parties involved were delighted with the agreements. Frankly, I believe that is why your father's efforts were so completely unsuccessful-no one wanted to rake any of the business up again, especially the Regent."

Catherine thanked him for satisfying her curiosity. "I believe, sir, I shall save the remaining items of business for our next meeting. I vow it is near time for dinner, and I hope you will join us. I know my mother and Aunt Mary will be delighted to see you. I hope you don't mind the informality." Mr. Stuart bowed. "Not at all, my lady. I would be honored." Just then, Morrow announced that dinner was ready to be served, and Mr. Stuart escorted Catherine to the dining room. As they dined, Catherine regaled her aunt and mother with descriptions of the afternoon's treasures. She hinted mysteriously about surprises, and had them laughing and protesting with impatience. Mr. Stuart was placed next to Aunt Mary, and they continued their previous conversation about the delights of music, Mozart in particular. Mathilde voiced a sentimental preference for Lully, as her French mother had taught her a few of his airs. As the last course was cleared, Catherine smiled mischievously at Mr. Stuart. "Since we are three to your one, Mr. Stuart, we shall *not* withdraw while you sip your port. I think a celebratory glass of champagne is called for, and beg you will all join me!" Laughing, they sipped the cool, frothy wine and continued their conversation.

After dinner, they adjourned to the drawing room, where Catherine played a ballad on the piano-forte. After Catherine finished playing, much to her surprise, Mathilde settled herself by the harp in the corner. Catherine had not really even noticed the harp, having no talent for it, and had forgotten her mother's fondness for playing a harp. Mathilde tested the strings, made a few adjustments, and played a delicate, rippling air. Catherine, Aunt Mary and Mr. Stuart sat, spell-bound, as the silvery notes poured forth. Mathilde's face bore a faint smiled as she played on, changing from one melody to another. Suddenly, she stopped and said, "Come, Catherine, surely you remember the duet we were used to play when you were a child!" Playing the first few notes enticingly, she smiled encouragement to Catherine. Catherine returned to the piano-forte, and, after a false start or two, they played the duet, a charming little piece, very simply arranged.

Mary then took her turn at the piano-forte, again playing a few of Mr. Mozart's airs and, smiling at Mathilde, a couple of Lully's pieces. Mr. Stuart watched, enthralled, and Mary's light touch produced the lovely melodies they both enjoyed. As the clock struck the hour, he rose hastily, appalled by the lateness of the evening. "Dear ladies, I fear I have overstayed my welcome. I cannot believe how late it has grown. May I saw how greatly I have enjoyed the evening, especially the music." All three ladies protested, but Mr. Stuart held firm in his decision to leave. Morrow assisted him into his greatcoat, and carried the valise containing the heavy casket to the carriage for him. When the door shut behind Mr. Stuart, the ladies went upstairs. Bidding her mother and aunt an affectionate goodnight, Catherine went to her room, where her maid waited to help her undress. Once clad in her lace-trimmed night rail and warm velvet dressing gown, she dismissed her maid and told her to go to bed. She sat at the dressing table, brushing her hair and thinking about the jewels so unexpectedly delivered. "The emeralds with the green silk, the yellow diamonds with the bronze. How wonderful to see such amazing treasures! I would not have ventured to purchase such things myself, but, I confess, I will feel more the thing, to go out in company wearing such beautiful pieces. Mother and Aunt Mary will be so delighted, as well!" Carrying the candle to her bedside table, she lighted the candelabra there. She settled herself against the pillows with her book, and read until she felt sleepy. She blew out the candles and snuggled down, relishing again the luxury of doing as she pleased in her own home.

Chapter 20

Catherine was preparing to out early the next afternoon for some shopping, when Jane entered the room, curtsied, and said, "If you please, my lady, Mr. Morrow wanted me to tell you that you have a visitor, a Lady Rosalie Ridley, who said she is my lady's cousin. Mr. Morrow wants to know, if you please, my lady, if you are at home to visitors." Surprised, Catherine turned and said, "My cousin, Rosalie? She must be Michael's sister. I am certainly at home. Please tell Morrow to show my cousin to the drawing room, and to order tea be served." Jane curtsied again, and hurried off. With some excitement, Catherine removed her bonnet and smoothed her hair. She was wearing the golden brown crepe, sent over by Madame Claire, with the topaz eardrops. She hastily changed her half boots for soft brown slippers, pinned a trifle of ivory lace on her hair, to match the lace at her throat and wrists, and snatched up her Norwich shawl. She hurried down the stairs and into the drawing room.

Seated before the fire, her back very straight, was a small young woman with black hair and very dark eyes, becomingly gowned in silver grey sarcenet. When she saw Catherine, she rose hastily and curtsied slightly. "I had heard you were visiting town, my lady, and wanted to meet you. Thank you for receiving me like this." Looking into the dark eyes, Catherine was surprised to see anxiety. Reaching out her hands, Catherine smiled and said, "But I am delighted to make the acquaintance of another cousin. Michael had mentioned you, but had not told me you would be in town at this time. How delightful of you to call!" Rosalie flushed and smiled. "I am amazed that my brother even mentioned me. I am not on terms of intimacy with my family, as you may know, my lady." Gently, Catherine said, "Pray, let us not be so formal, Cousin Rosalie. Michael did mention that you had been estranged since your marriage. However, these things cannot be considered my business, so I beg you to let us just be cousins." Rosalie smiled again and said, "How kind you are, cousin! John, my husband, encouraged me to call on you. It is so comfortable to feel that one has family, after all." Catherine laughed and agreed. "Tell, me where are you staying, Rosalie, and for how long?" "John and I have rooms at Fenton's Hotel. We are just in town to do some shopping and to visit some friends. When I heard you were here, I determined to meet you, if I could. Catherine's brows rose slightly. "I have heard that Fenton's is most comfortable and accommodating. Do you expect to make a long stay? "Just a few weeks. Not long enough to make renting a town house eligible. At Fenton's, our rooms include a private parlor, which is so convenient when I wish to invite friends for tea, or when John's friends wish to dine." "Pray, cousin, tell me about your husband. He sounds delightful."

Rosalie's small face lit up like a candle. "Oh, John is the dearest of men!" she said warmly. "He is the youngest son of the late Baron Ridley, who died two years past. His older brother James is now the baron, and the middle brother, Charles, is a captain in the Army. John is helping James on the estate, acting as his agent, you know. His father encouraged him to help with the estate business, and he studied law at Oxford, so that he would be ready. He is devoted to his family, and is the handsomest man. He takes such care of me, too! Always ready to partake of my sentiments," she laughed, "or at least to pretend he does. I do hope you will have a chance to meet him while we are in town." Blushing, she stopped talking abruptly. "I am sorry, cousin, rattling on in this...*besotted* way!" Catherine encouraged her to continue, asking "Where do you live, cousin?" "We live in a dear house between Ridley Hall and the town of Ridley, in Flint, which is near Cheshire. James, of course, has Ridley Hall. Our house is a small manor house near the edge of the estate. There is plenty of room for us all. There is another house, in the opposite direction, just waiting for Charles, if he should sell out." Catherine sat looking at Rosalie in some surprise, and thought "This makes no sense. Michael implied that a totally unsuitable alliance had been made, but it seems quite eligible." Rosalie looked back at her and said, acutely, "You are thinking of the estrangement between me and my family. It is a source of great pain to me, and to my father. He was great friends with the late baron, and while not terribly pleased with the match, was not angry. But my mother and my brother...full of my duty to our name, and my obligation to make a great alliance! I had been out three seasons, and never met any one I wished to marry but John. We were both of age. We were married quietly in church, here in London, by special license."

Catherine patted her hand and said, "It sounds like you and your John are quite ideally matched. It may not be the most ambitious alliance, but imminently suitable." Rosalie continued, bitterly, "You would think we had fled to the Border! I understand my mother's feelings; she had always had great plans for me to take a higher place in Society. But I do not understand why my brother is so unforgiving...we were used to be so close as children, and I had thought that my happiness would mean something to him. Unfortunately, I was wrong. I hear from my father at Christmas only, and from my mother and brother, never." Tears shone in Rosalie's eyes. "It is so unfair! No one in John's family has been other than kindness itself, to me, even when Father cut my portion in half. They never felt that the money was more important than John's happiness, and were pleased to welcome me for his sake. John has sufficient to keep us both in comfort; we are not destitute. He inherited a comfortable amount from both of his parents, and earns a living as his brother's agent, and by practicing law in Ridley. Why, we are almost *boringly* respectable. Yet my family treats us as outcasts. Michael has even cut off his friendship with James, as well as with John. They had been friends since boyhood, went to school together. Now, I believe, Michael is capable of giving James the cut direct. It is so mortifying."

Catherine patted Rosalie's hand again. "Come, cousin, let us have some tea, and talk of happier things. Mayhap, one day, the breach will be healed. In the meantime, we can get to know each other better." Just then, Morrow entered with the tea tray. "Pray, join me in some tea. I was getting ready to do some shopping. Would you care to join me? I need to go to the linen drapers shop for some fabrics, and I wish to look for some lace. As well, I was thinking of visiting the Pantheon Bazaar. I would also like to order some special nostrums and tinctures at the apothecary shop for my housekeeper. Please do come!" Rosalie smiled and replied, "I would love to join you. I have still some shopping to do myself." After they finished their tea, Catherine whisked upstairs, put on her half boots, bonnet and redingote, threw her pelerine about her shoulders and picked up her gloves and muff. She had ordered the carriage on her way upstairs, and found Rosalie ready and the carriage at the door when she descended the stairs. The footman handed them in, closed the door, and away they went, chattering happily about their prospective purchases.

After a busy few hours of shopping, Catherine asked Rosalie if she and John could come to dinner one evening before they returned home. Warmly, Rosalie accepted. "I know John shall be delighted, as am I. I would love to meet your mother. I know she is my mother's cousin, and have longed to know her." "We would love to have you both, and I will invite my solicitor, Mr. Stuart as well. He has become our dear friend, as well as my most trusted adviser." Rosalie laughed, and said, "You can do nothing more perfect to make John feel completely at home. John is justice of the peace at home, and will thoroughly enjoy a coze with another well versed in law." Catherine gathered up her shopping and got out of the carriage, leaving Rosalie with her packages to be driven home, after promising to send a note settling the date for their dinner engagement.

Upon her arrival at the townhouse, Morrow bowed her into the hall and said, "I have placed several letters in the bookroom for you, my lady, and Viscount Chatellerault called while you were out. He also left a note." "Thank you, Morrow, I'll attend to those things when I have made myself presentable and have spoken with my mother." She ran lightly up the stairs to her room, doffed her outerwear and smoothed her hair. She went down the hall to her mother's rooms, and tapped lightly on the sitting room door. "Mother, may I come in?" Mathilde called, "Come in, my dear! What have you been doing this dreary day?" Mathilde, reclining comfortably on chaise with a shawl over her feet and another around her shoulders, smiled as Catherine entered the room. Catherine answered, "I have been shopping with a new cousin. Michael's sister, Rosalie, is visiting town with her husband, and called today. She seems delightful, and we had a most enjoyable afternoon. I would like to have her and her husband to dine. She is eager to meet you, Mother, and I believe you would enjoy her company." "Rosalie?" said Mathilde slowly. "My dear, are you sure this is wise? My cousin seemed most unhappy about her connections, and cannot speak of her without coming very agitated." Catherine replied earnestly, "I know, Mother, Michael also spoke of Rosalie and her husband with distaste. I must say, I found her to be a lovely person and a delightful companion. Her husband, too, seems most respectable. He is the younger son of a baron, and has a comfortable house on the family estate. It wasn't a brilliant match, but it certainly seems to have been acceptable. She even said that her father had been friends with her late father-in-law. She was most eager to have some family ties, since her father and brother no longer accept her, and her father's contact with her is limited. I would like to have them to dine, so I can see for myself. Can you not like the scheme?" Mathilde responded, "My dear, of course you are right. I would love to meet Rosalie and her husband. Why, if you are correct, the poor girl probably feels like the veriest cast-off. After your experience, even though it ended for the best, I would not want to see any young woman with no family connection at her back." Catherine smiled and said, "I will send a note this afternoon."

Catherine went to the library after tea. She had letters from the vicar and her bailiff at Heyerwood advising her of the needs and situations there. She wrote her responses, and gave instructions for the delivery of the nostrums and fabrics she had purchased that day. She also wrote to Mr. Stuart, asking him to ascertain her father's current status, including the exact amount of his indebtedness, and to find out what he could about Baron Ridley, his brother John and their circumstances. She invited him to dinner, asking him to come earlier than the other guests and to bring the information she requested, if he could. She then opened Michael's note. As she read, her eyes narrowed with annoyance. "Cousin, I am sorry to have missed you. I have just discovered that my sister and her husband are in town. If she has the temerity to call, pray do not receive her until I can ascertain why she is come. I will advise you. I remain, cousin, yours, etc. etc." Catherine fumed, "How dare he presume to order my acquaintance, and with my own family? How does he dare assume that he can 'advise' me on who I will see? He takes too much upon himself!" Crumpling the note, she threw it into the fire, not deigning to write a response. She wrote two more notes, one to Rosalie and John, the other to Caroline and Tom, inviting them to dine as well. Thinking, "We will make a party of it!" she dispatched the three notes by the footman.

Chapter 21

The next day, Catherine opened a note from Julia, inviting her to tea that afternoon. "No reply is needed, if you can come. Pray, do join us; Juliana and I so enjoy your company!" Catherine smiled-a perfect opportunity to present the lockets! She looked at the clock, and was amazed to see that it was time to leave if she were going to arrive timely for tea. After ordering the carriage, she ran lightly up the stairs to her room. Removing the lockets from their hiding place, she wrapped them in silver paper and put them in her reticule. Hastily donning her redingote, bonnet and gloves, she went downstairs. While waiting for the carriage, Catherine wrote a hasty note for her mother, which she sent up with a maid. She got in, gave the direction for Julia's townhouse, and relaxed with a sigh, thinking "I vow, I'm almost ready to go home to Heyerwood. I really miss the peace and quiet."

Admitted by the footman, who took her wraps, Catherine entered Julia's private parlor. Juliana ran to her for a hug, while Julia smiled and said, "We had almost given you up! We are so glad to see you." Embracing her friend, Catherine returned the smile and said, "I have been busy! Before I tell you of my doings, I have a surprise for you both." Reaching into her reticule, she pulled out the silver-wrapped parcels, and gave Julia and Juliana each one. Juliana exclaimed, "A present, *Maman*, she has brought us each a present! May I open it? Please?" Julia smiled and said, "We will open them together!" The silver paper was duly torn away, and the little boxes opened. "Oooh, *Maman*, a locket! It's so pretty and my very first necklace! Put it on me, *Tante* Catherine! Please, put it on me!" Julia looked at her own locket, then her daughter's. With tears in her eyes, she said, "Oh, Catherine, they are lovely. What a sweet idea! I even have miniatures to have set in them. You should not have done it, but, oh, I do thank you!" We will treasure them always." Catherine smiled and replied, "You are most welcome, but you are wrong – it is exactly what I should have done. The lockets are perfect for you and Juliana, and it makes me happy to think of you wearing them. Why should I deny myself so much pleasure?" The friends embraced. Then all three ladies sat down by the fire, and enjoyed their tea, chattering happily.

Arriving home, late in the evening, Catherine started up the stairs, somewhat wearily, when Morrow stopped her. "Oh, Morrow, I hope I am not late for dinner. We lost all track of time. Pray, give my mother and aunt my excuses, but I will be down as quickly as I can get changed."

Morrow bowed, and said, "Viscountess Stanton had dinner moved back an hour, my lady, so you have plenty of time. I just wanted to advise you the Viscount Chatellerault has called again. He insisted on waiting, and is in the drawing room with the ladies." Catherine sighed, and said, "Please, Morrow, advise my cousin that I will be down shortly. I will be happy to discuss his business with him, but not until after we have dined. If he wishes to stay for dinner, he is most welcome. "As you wish, Lady Heyerwood." Morrow bowed again, and Catherine went on up the stairs.

Once in her own rooms, she decided to wear the sapphire blue velvet. It was warm and becoming. Instead of the sapphire earbobs she had worn last time with the gown, she chose to wear the yellow diamond drops. Catherine left the necklace in the box, deciding that it did not suit the high neckline of the dress. Replacing the box in the cubby, she set the earrings on the dressing table, and then called her maid. "Pray, Jane, bring me some warm water so I may wash, and help me change as quickly as possible. I am so late!" After she removed her jewelry and gown, she washed and Jane quickly took her hair down, brushed it thoroughly, then twistd it into a simple knot high on her head. She then picked out a few curls around Catherine's temples and forehead, and helped Catherine into the blue velvet gown. Catherine thanked her and picked up the yellow diamond earbobs. Again, the pale golden fire caught her eyes. Pleased with the look of the delicate golden drops with the velvet, she picked up her velvet reticule, and dismissed Jane with a smile. "Thank you for your help, Jane. Now, do not wait up for me. My cousin is here to discuss business, and it could take some time. You need your rest, too."

Catherine entered the hall just in time to meet up with her mother, aunt and cousin on their way to the dining room. "Forgive me for being so tardy. Mother, Aunt Mary, I hope you had a pleasant day. Cousin Michael, how nice to see you. Pray, let us be seated at once. I vow, I could eat a horse!" Chuckling at her remark, they took their places at table. Catherine determinedly kept the conversation light and general throughout the meal, ignoring Michael's meaningful glances. After the meal, when the ladies rose, Michael said, "Cousin, I have some business to discuss that cannot wait. May we discuss it now?" Catherine, sighing inwardly with resignation, said courteously, "Of course, cousin. Morrow, please bring some brandy for my cousin, and sherry for me, to the library. We will join you in the drawing room as soon as may be, Mama, Aunt Mary."

Entering the library, Catherine took her seat behind her desk, and waved Michael to a chair. Morrow brought in the wine, bowed and left the room. As she poured out the brandy and sherry, Catherine said, with a lift of her brows, "Pray, cousin, what business brings you here today? It seems of some urgency." Michael leaned forward and said, "Catherine, as I said in my note, my sister is come to town. I have not yet had speech with her, but must beg you to avoid her acquaintance until I ascertain why she is here." Catherine said coolly, "Frankly, cousin, I find your assumption of authority somewhat surprising and, I may say, rather offensive. I have given you no leave to order my acquaintance. To be blunt, sir, I do not intend to be told whom I might see by anyone. I am above thirty years of age, and am an independent person." Looking at Catherine's flushed, indignant face, Michael fought back irritation. "As a near male relative, I meant only your good, cousin. Living secluded as you have for so long, I thought only to guide you...." Rising hastily, Catherine strode from behind the desk. "Pray, disabuse your mind that I went into the country as an ignorant child. I had more than one season in London. Once in the country, I ran my home, and subsequently my estate, without let or hindrance. I will not accept unwarranted, unsolicited interference now! I know that your sister and her husband are in town. What, pray tell, can you tell me that would warrant my cutting the connection? And please stop beating about the bush! Tell me to my head what this mystery is, or leave the subject before we come to cuffs!"

Michael replied, choosing his words with care, "My sister was groomed by my mother to be worthy of the highest in the land. As the only daughter of the Earl of Aldersey, my mother felt it was Rosalie's duty to make a suitable match of at least equal rank and fortune. When Rosalie refused her opportunities, it affected our mother's health and cut up her peace. Knowing this, Rosalie, stubbornly insisted on going her own way. Even when my mother prevailed upon my father to order Rosalie to obey, or face having her portion reduced, Rosalie refused to listen. She went through with her plan to marry an untitled younger son with a mere competence. They married by special license in London. My parents found out by seeing the announcement in the *Times*. My mother suffered a severe breakdown in her health resulting from the shock, and insisted that my father and I cut the connection. My father was most distressed, as Rosalie was ever his favorite child, and the young man the son of an old friend. His fondness causes him to send her greetings every Christmas, but my mother will not hear Rosalie's name spoken and considers her as dead. Can you wonder that I would be concerned at her presence in London now, while you are here? Who knows what mischief she may be plotting, hoping to embroil you in a scheme to force us to recognize her again? Cousin, I must insist...."

Catherine looked at him with disgust. "You would cut your own sister for the great 'sin' of marrying a respectable young man, known to your family, because she loved him? The fact that she had multiple seasons without meeting any one for whom she felt more strongly means nothing to you and your family? I cannot believe you would rather see a beloved sister sold to the highest bidder than happy in a respectable marriage!" Michael flushed and replied angrily, "The sin was that of disobedience to her parents! Does it mean nothing that she broke her mother's heart, and disappointed her father? Should she expect to be welcomed and congratulated for her disobedience? I am now in the position that I must be even more circumscribed in my choice for a bride and my way of life, to make up for her selfishness! How can we be expected to reward her for such behavior? She totally disregarded the best interests of her family."

Looking Michael squarely in the eye, Catherine felt she was looking at a stranger. "If a happy marriage to a respectable man is Rosalie's 'crime', I find I must disappoint you, my lord. I must honor Rosalie for possessing greater courage and resolution than I possessed. Having allowed myself to be forced into a marriage for the 'best interest' of my family, I have a keener understanding for her situation than you can possibly know. If my willingness to be acquainted with your sister and her husband distresses you and your parents, I am sorry, but I see no reason to refuse her acquaintance. The reason for your concern seems to be nothing more than vindictiveness, because she had the courage to make her choice herself and you, apparently, do not! I would not have believed you capable of such pettiness or cruelty, and feel every sympathy for Rosalie. I will, of course, understand if you and your parents are no longer eager to know me, unless my title and fortune make my heinous conduct tolerable!"

Now deeply flushed with anger, Michael also rose and said through gritted teeth, "You would do better to be guided by me in this, madam! You would be responsible for more harm than you could possibly know if you interfere in this matter. It would affect not only you, but your mother's relations wit her cousin. You have no right....!" Paling with rage, Catherine strode the door and opened it. "Pray, sir, let us say good night before we say any more. I have no wish to offend you further. I would only remind you that, although we are related, I have given you no reason to assume you could order my conduct. I will also remind you that I am in no way dependent on you for anything. If you wish to meet again, after you have had time to reflect, please send me a note. I would hope to be always on cordial terms with family members. Now, my lord, good night!"

Sweeping out to the hall, Catherine saw Morrow and ordered, "Call his lordship's carriage and assist him with his hat and coat, Morrow. He will be departing immediately." She vanished up the stairs, leaving Michael standing in the door of the library, staring after her in impotent fury. Morrow bowed and said, "Your coat, my lord." Saying nothing, Michel donned coat and hat, and waited in the hall until his carriage arrived. The footman assisted him into the carriage, and shut the door.

Chapter 22

It seemed to Catherine that she flew up the stairs. "How dare he!" she seethed. She went into her own rooms and shut the door. She paced up and down before the fire, thinking of Rosalie's tear-filled eyes as she spoke of her parents and brother with wistfulness, and comparing it to Michael's coldness. "If that is what they value, I am better off without the connection. I am sorry to give my mother pain, but it is clear that Rosalie is the best of her family. I knew there was something odd, but I never dreamed that Michael was capable of such callousness. And his mother! She must be beyond anything!" Just then, there was a discreet knock at the door. Catherine opened it to find Miss Potter there. "Excuse me, Lady Catherine, but your lady mother couldn't help hearing that you and his lordship were having words. She's that concerned. Will you come to her, my lady? She's in the drawing room." "Thank you, Miss Potter. Please tell my mother that I am fine, and will be down in a moment." Miss Potter retreated back down the stairs. Catherine splashed her flushed face with cool water, smoothed her hair, and followed her.

Catherine entered the drawing room to see her mother and Aunt Mary at the fire, with a tea tray and their embroidery. Her mother looked at her anxiously. "We could tell that your conversation with Michael did not have a pleasant outcome, my dear. Pray, what sent him off in a temper? Morrow indicated that he left without a word." Catherine kissed her mother's cheek. "I know this will pain you, dear one, as you were so pleased to resume a relationship with your cousin. However, I must tell you the issue involving Rosalie is solely her marriage. Her mother and brother have cast her totally aside for failing to fall out of love with a respectable man, and for not being willing to be sold to the highest bidder. I do not know what offended me more – Michael's assumption that he could order my conduct, or his assumption that I would share his and his mother's feelings in this matter. I pity the earl; Rosalie was apparently his favorite child, and it pains him to have no contact with her, especially since her husband is the son of his old friend. Michael's primary concern was that he would now have to be even more particular in his choice of a bride, to make up for Rosalie's failure! I'm afraid we had words, Mama, and he did indicate that his mother may not be willing to recognize me and, because of me, you anymore if we are known to accept Rosalie and her husband. I'm sorry if it causes you pain. Pray forgive me if this imbroglio rebounds upon you, but I can't be sorry for refusing to knuckle down to them, especially having been in such a position myself!"

Mathilde sat staring into the fire. Sighing, she said softly, "Maria was ever ambitious. I never realized… When we were in our first season, she had a *tendre* for a young man. My uncle, her father, checked his family and discovered that his prospects were respectable, at best. The next thing I knew, Maria gave him his *conge'*. The next year, Aldersey made an offer for her and she accepted him. It was one of *the* weddings, of course. St. George's and all the rest. Then she retired with him to the estate in Cheshire, and I never saw her again. She wrote to me when I married Stanton, of course, but we never maintained a steady correspondence. How sad to think she would cut her only daughter, and what a strain on Michael, to be the sole object of her ambitions now! I heard she was having some health problems. I can see why – such bitterness must eat at the soul. I should be sorry to anger Maria, but it has been many years since we were bosom-bows. My gratitude for her help, I hope, will not blind me to fairness and common decency. I will be happy to meet Rosalie and her husband. When do they dine?" Catherine hugged her mother. "I knew I could count on you, Mother! I have asked them to dine tomorrow. I have also asked Caroline and Tom, and Mr. Stuart. We shall make an occasion of it! How do you feel, Aunt Mary?" Mary looked up, blinking away tears. "My dear, had I a tiny bit of your cousin Rosalie's resolution, my life would be different today! Of course, she will be most welcome, and her young man! How harsh, to disown her for a respectable marriage to the son of a family friend! It's to be hoped that, one day, her father, at least, will soften." The three ladies put their heads together, making plans for the next evening's party. Having written the menu, selected the wines, and decided what flowers to order in the morning, the ladies bade each other good night and retired to their rooms.

Catherine rose early, sipping her chocolate while seated at her writing table. She rang for Jane, having selected the sea-green sarcenet with the rose and green Kashmir shawl for morning wear. She then selected pearl earbobs, and a pearl pin for the lace at her throat, and soft black leather slippers. She dressed hastily, with Jane's assistance, and Jane brushed her hair into a soft, braided coronet for the day. Somewhat surprised, Catherine surveyed the style. "Thank you, Jane. This is quite different, is it not? Very elegant. I like it very much." Flushing with pleasure, Jane curtseyed, and said, "I'm pleased that you like it, my lady. I saw a picture in a fashion plate, and thought it would become you. I have been practicing, my lady." "I am most satisfied, Jane. Please tell the housekeeper that I will meet with her in an hour. We're having guests this evening, and I want to discuss arrangements, and see if she has any shopping that I can do for her. Pray, when you have time, look out my violet velvet. I would like to wear it tonight."

Seating herself at the breakfast table, she enjoyed a heartier breakfast than usual. Her mother and aunt preferring to breakfast in their rooms, she brought her lists with her to review while at table. On her way to the library, Morrow bowed and said, "Some notes delivered this morning, my lady. I was just on the way to place them on your desk." Taking the missives in hand, Catherine smiled mischievously, and replied, "Well, Morrow, I will take them with me now. I will be meeting with the housekeeper shortly, to discuss plans for dinner. Pray join us. Your suggestions, I know, must be of great help, especially regarding the wines." Morrow opened the door, and followed her into the library. Taking her seat behind the desk, she invited Morrow and the housekeeper to sit down as well. They reviewed the menu, and decided on *service a la russe,* so that there would be fewer courses, allowing the servants to have their own meal after the last course was served. "A clear soup to start, I think, with some *filet de soles* and some lobster *rissoles,* some oyster patties, and some carrots. Possibly another vegetable? For the main course, a roast quarter of lamb, and some ham, removed with peas and some of your mushroom fritters, with some sautéed apples. Some quail with grapes, as well. To finish, a compote of cherries and a chocolate cream for sweets, some grilled mushrooms and cheese and nuts for savory." The housekeeper had a few suggestions about service, especially since Catherine's desire was to maintain a level of informality. The housekeeper also had suggestions about flowers, suggesting low arrangements with more greenery, so that eye contact and conversation would be more general and convivial than at a more formal dinner. Satisfied with the arrangements, Catherine smiled and said, "I leave it all in your hands. I know everything will be more than satisfactory." She dismissed the butler and housekeeper to their duties and turned to her letters.

A hastily written letter from Rosalie asked if it would be possible to include her brother-in-law, James, Baron Ridley, in the evening's plans. "I would not be so forward, but he is here unexpectedly, and your mother could meet us all at once. I would be so pleased to introduce you, if it would not overset your arrangements. Pray, do not feel compelled – we would all understand if it is not convenient." Dashing off a note cordially welcoming James, Catherine reflected that one more could not hurt. Caroline had also written a note, accepting Catherine's invitation for that evening. A brief missive from Mr. Stuart indicated that he had obtained the information she had requested regarding her father and other issues, and would visit her at six o'clock, as that should give them plenty of time for review before dinner. Opening the last letter she saw a confused, almost illegible, scrawl, with no signature or direction to indicate who had written it. She thought of the previous anonymous letters; probably, this was the same author. Shrugging, Catherine started to put it on the fire, then stopped. Changing her mind, she put it aside to show Mr. Stuart. The last item was a formal invitation card for an evening party with dancing, to be held by *le Comte* and *Comtesse* DeBeaumont the next week. A hand-written note by Julia warmly pressed her to accept. She wrote her response immediately, expressing her pleased acceptance.

Catherine then wrote out a list of some shopping for that evening's dinner party. She made a second list of some books and sheet music. The idea of returning to Heyerwood was becoming more and more appealing, and some new books and music would be welcome diversions. Thoughtfully, she added a harp to the list. The drawing room at Heyerwood contained a piano-forte, but no harp, and Catherine wanted to encourage her mother in her renewed pleasure in music. She had heard that wonderful harps, made by Erard, could be ordered from the factory in Great Marlborough Street. A third list of special items for the pantry at Heyerwood was written up, to be left at Fortnum and Mason; special seasonings, tea, preserves and dried fruits not readily available out of London, ordered for shipment directly to Mrs. Davis. Catherine pondered; if she bought the London townhouse, she would have to consider the advisability of fully staffing each house, or bringing key staff members back and forth with her. She hoped to entice Morrow into entering her service permanently, but was not certain about keeping the London cook and housekeeper. "I know Mrs. Davis and her ways so well," she thought.

Catherine decided to call in at Madame Claire's to order another redingote, similarly styled to her brown one, in deep green wool, again with a quilted silk lining. Her brown fur bonnet, pelerine and muff would be suitable with either, and she decided to order a matching deep green velvet bonnet and muff. Deep green velvet bands could trim the redingote, and would match the bonnet and muff to a nicety. Although still good, she was getting a bit tired of the chocolate brown wool, and there were still some months before she could expect to be comfortable with just a spencer or shawl. Catherine ran her errands, leaving her orders at the harp factory and Fortnum and Mason's. Everything was to be shipped to Heyerwood, except the items wanted for that evening's dinner, which were to be delivered to the town house shortly. She went on to the Pantheon Bazaar, where she found the dark green wool, silk and velvet that she wanted, as well as some intriguing frog fasteners she could not resist. At Madame Claire's establishment, she was fortunate enough to find Madame herself available. They discussed the design of the redingote, and, though Madame pleaded for a more extreme designed, Catherine held firm to her plan. She did agree to a slightly lower waistline, and a bit of fullness in the back, gathered into a half-belt of velvet. She also agreed to a cockade of bronze and gold feathers with green velvet ribbon to trim the bonnet.

Her last stop was at Hatchard's Bookstore. Catherine went into the shop with her list. Smiling at the clerk, she said, "Sir, I am contemplating removal to the country, and wish to take some new books with me. May I place a list with you, and arrange for shipping to my home?" The clerk, recognizing her from her previous visits, bowed and said, "Certainly, my lady, I will be happy to assist." Catherine went over her list with the young man, and all of the items she wanted were available. Diffidently, he also suggested, "We have another book by an author you seemed to enjoy. It is called *Mansfield Park*, and was written by the same author as *Pride and Prejudice*. She approved his suggestion, along with *Pamela*, by Richardson. On impulse, she also requested *A Vindication of the Rights of Women* by Mary Wollstonecraft. She included Walter Scott's *Marmion* and *The Lady of the Lake,* which she knew her mother and aunt would enjoy. Catherine provided the direction for shipping to Heyerwood, paid for her purchases, and returned home, well-pleased with her errands.

She was in time for tea, which she enjoyed in the library, as her mother and aunt had already gone upstairs to rest before dressing. After tea, she ran upstairs to dress for dinner herself. The violet velvet gown lay read, and the washing water steamed gently in the pitcher. Before ringing for Jane, Catherine opened the cubby, removed the pearl and amethyst pin and a pair of pearl and diamond drops. Replacing the rug, she removed the sea-green dress and the pearl earbobs. Jane came in as Catherine finished washing, in time to help her into the violet velvet and to do her hair. Jane elected to allow curls to fall from an intricate knot on the crown of Catherine's head. Catherine pinned the amethyst and pearl brooch to a violet velvet ribbon, which she tied around her throat, and slipped the hooks of the diamond and pearl drops in her ears. The clock struck six o'clock as she glided down the stairs, to find Mr. Stuart already waiting in the bookroom.

Chapter 23

Catherine held out her hand. "Mr. Stuart, it is so kind of you to come early! Shall we get our tiresome business out of the way?" Mr. Stuart bowed over her hand. "It is my pleasure to serve, you, my lady, and may I say how delightfully you look this evening? Our business will soon be finished, and I am definitely looking forward to the rest of the evening." Catherine seated herself behind her desk. "Well, Mr. Stuart, what have you to tell me about my father?" "It appears, my lady, the Viscountess was correct; no one knows the nature of his illness, exactly, but Doctor Knighton has called on him at his townhouse several times since December. It also appears that he has been quietly selling off unentailed properties and assets. Apparently, he has been compounding with his creditors, because there are no writs against him at present. He still has significant outstanding accounts with various tradesmen and merchants, but there is no indication of any large gaming debts..."

Making a *moue* of distaste, Catherine said, "I never understood the principle of letting honest persons wait for their just due in order to pay a 'debt of honor' – what 'honor' is it to deprive one person of his livelihood to repay a foolish debt to someone who usually has more than he needs?" She sighed heavily. "Well, no matter. What are his current debts?" Mr. Stuart named the figure. Catherine responded, "So little? I expected much worse. Well, then, Mr. Stuart, pray settle them. Please see that all of the balances are cleared immediately, but do not let his creditors know who has paid them. I do not wish to be dunned in future." "Do you wish Viscount Stanton to be advised that the debts have been paid, my lady?" "No, Mr. Stuart, he will discover it soon enough, and I do not wish to give him an excuse to call here. Hopefully, he will not discover who has done the deed.

It will be enough that the debts are paid. Pray, keep track of the balances and the dates paid; if he tries again to approach me for funds, I will be able to tell him he has had all there will ever be from me." She tried to smile. "A soft touch, am I not? However, I cannot forget that he is my father. If he is disgraced, does it not affect my mother and me? I will not see her subject to such humiliation, if I can prevent it." Mr. Stuart inclined his head. "I will carry out your instructions, my lady. The arrangements will be easy enough to make. There is no reason why anyone, including your father, should discover how or by whom, the settlements were made. Now, before I give you the information about the Ridleys, I do have some additional information about your cousin's family."

He continued, "I discovered that Viscount Chatellerault came to London specifically to consult with a physician. It seems his mother has had some disturbing symptoms. Apparently she is given to periods of hysteria and delusions. There is a rumor that she was writing very upsetting letters to persons she feels have wronged her." "Letters?" Catherine asked, thoughtfully. "Do you mean anonymous letters?" "Why, yes, my lady. How did you know that?" Catherine replied, slowly, "Why, I have received a few letters, illegible, written in a strange scrawling hand. I burnt the previous, but saved this last one to show you." Mr. Stuart took the letter, and looked it over with distaste. "Most distressing, Lady Heyerwood. I can scarce make out a word. When did you receive the first of these letters?" "Right after my cousin brought my mother to me. While he was with us, he received an urgent express from his father requesting his immediate return." Catherine and Mr. Stuart Looked at each other. "Is it possible that my mother's cousin has written these letters?" she asked. "But, why? I have never met her. What harm could she possibly think I could do?" Mr. Stuart looked uncomfortable. "Have you any feeling that the Viscount is bent on fixing an interest with you, my lady? It may be she is unready to share her son's attention, especially being so estranged from her daughter." "I have had no indication of a...romantic issue," she said, blushing, but he has been trying to become involved in my affairs in a way I found most annoying. We had words about that, and I made it plain that he had no right to order my affairs or my acquaintance. I do not know why his mother should fear an attachment to me, unless.... Oh, Mr. Stuart, do you think it possible that Michael was deliberately setting out to fix an interest, when he brought my mother to me? That his family discussed this before ever he met me?"

Mr. Stuart thought of her title, her lands and fortune, and thought to himself, "They would have been mad not to make at least a push in that direction. Heiresses are few and far between as it is, and seldom with your endowments of birth and charm combined with wealth." Aloud, choosing his words with care, he replied, "Well, my lady, it would only be natural for a young man of marriageable age to consider possibilities. There is no great family that does not consider the practical aspect of such an alliance." Catherine considered the issue dispassionately, and said, "Unfortunately, you are correct. How unfortunate for Michael that I am not a young miss in her father's care. I am sure my father would have been only too happy to consider his suit. However, I am delighted to say that I need not concern myself with this matter. I am sorry for my mother's cousin; her illness must be painful indeed for herself, and deeply distressing for her family. I'll wager they are searching for medical advice for her care." Mr. Stuart replied, "I'm sure you are right, my lady. The Viscount has consulted with Dr. Knighton several times, and has also spoken to Dr. Baillie as well."

"Now, to the rest of your business. I have found that Baron Ridley and his family are from a comfortably-fixed and respected family in Flint County, just south of Cheshire. The barony is an ancient title, and the family seat is Ridley Manor. The estate is large, containing sufficient acreage to allow for comfortable country homes for the baron's brothers, in addition to the main holding. The baron also owns a small townhouse in London, which has been leased for this season. The baron's younger brother is married to your cousin Rosalie, the Viscount's younger sister, which has, strangely, led to a breach between her and her family. I could not find a logical reason for this estrangement, as the Ridley family is solid and respected, and the Earl was a good friend of the old baron. At any rate, Rosalie's husband, John Ridley, was educated in the law at Cambridge, and acts as the baron's man of business and estate agent. He also handles certain legal matters for clients in Ridley and Malpas, the nearest city of any size, and is a Justice of the Peace. James, the current baron, is unmarried and childless at this present. He had married very young, but his wife died, sadly, soon after the marriage. I could not determine the extent of the family fortunes, but they are comfortable, and there is sufficient to allow James to travel extensively, and to buy the middle brother a pair of colours as a captain in the Army, where he serves with some distinction. His house is maintained in readiness against his selling out or retiring. All in all, a good connection, one would say, my lady."

Catherine smiled. "You are most efficient, Mr. Stuart. I cannot believe you found all this out so quickly! I am very happy to know Rosalie is so well settled." Her smile faded a bit. "How sad to have to check up on one's family and acquaintance so," she said softly. "A nasty, suspicious character, am I not?" Mr. Stuart said staunchly, "Indeed, my lady, no one could fault you for taking sensible precautions. If you were still married, or were living in the care of a parent, these questions would be answered for your husband or guardian. Since you are fully emancipated, you must take up these responsibilities for yourself. Not all duties can be…pleasant. A certain amount of caution is necessary, if only to prevent unnecessary suspicions."

After a slight pause, Mr. Stuart continued, "Now the last of your inquiries concerned an entail and trusts. I have researched the matter most thoroughly in English common law, and Scottish common law as well (since Scottish common law does not bar females from inheriting property or title), and structured an entail that ties one third of your fortune to the estate of Heyerwood Manor itself, a trust for another third, and the remaining third in your direct control. That portion would be the only part of your fortune available for consideration in any marriage settlement, should you consider remarrying. That third and the trust could be left by you to whomever and in whatever shares you desire. The heir you designate for the title and Heyerwood estate would, of necessity, receive the income from the third of your fortune entailed to the estate. The entail allows you, during your lifetime, and your heir in future, the use of the income only, which is sufficient to maintain the estate and live quite comfortably, without considering the rest of your fortune. Please look over these papers, my lady; I think you will find that, between the entail and the trust, your future well-being and financial status are secured."

Catherine reviewed the papers carefully. "Mr. Stuart, I am amazed again at how much David left me, and at his goodness in his arrangements for me. Do you think he would approve of these arrangements?" Mr. Stuart replied, "My lady, had he been in better health, his intention had been to secure these matters for you so that you would not have to concern yourself. Unfortunately, his health was failing, and it took all of his energy to push through the matter of the title, and make sure that your father could not overset the will. I believe that he would consider these arrangements a suitable solution." Catherine nodded. "I agree. What must I do, sign before witnesses? Pray, call Morrow, if you please. You and Morrow will be acceptable witnesses, will you not? Then we can put this seriousness aside, and have a gay time at dinner. You will meet my cousin Rosalie, her husband and her brother-at-law, the baron!" Catherine signed her name clearly, and watched as Morrow and Mr. Stuart both fixed their signatures below hers. Then Mr. Stuart fixed the seal, rolled the papers into a scroll which he tied up and placed in his pouch. "These shall be placed in the vault with the rest of the estate papers, and I will file the record of the entail and trust myself, my lady." Catherine dismissed Morrow with a smile, and held out her hand to Mr. Stuart. "Thank you for your care and concern for my interests, Mr. Stuart. You must know that all of my dependence is upon you. I vow, I do not think I could manage without you!"

Mr. Stuart smiled and bowed. "It is my pleasure to serve your ladyship." To Catherine's surprise, he was blushing. "My lady, now that the business matters have been concluded, dare I ask your assistance on a personal matter?" "Of course, Mr. Stuart, I would be happy to assist in any way I can. What is it?" Mr. Stuart turned, and strode to the window and back. "It cannot have escaped your attention, Lady Catherine, that I have had no common pleasure in the company to be found under your roof. Forgive my boldness, but I must ask your ladyship...may I have the privilege of asking your aunt for her hand in marriage? I thought it proper to ask your permission first, my lady. Could you approve of such an alliance for a near family member?" Speechless, Catherine stared at Mr. Stuart and sank back into her seat at the writing table. She remembered the musical evening, and Aunt Mary's smiles and blushes. She smiled and replied, "Mr. Stuart, I am touched and honored that you would ask my permission. If Aunt Mary accepts your offer, I would be delighted to welcome you to my family. I just hope you can find someone to take care of my affairs with your diligence!" "As to that, your ladyship, I intend to continue my practice, you see. I hope you understand that I must continue my work to support a wife, as well as my own dignity." Catherine, understanding, said gently, "Of course, I understand, and will be only too happy to have my affairs in such trusted hands. By all means, sir, make my aunt an offer! I will be pleased to wish you happy!" Speechless, Mr. Stuart grasped her hand again. Rising, Catherine asked, "Shall we join my mother and aunt in the drawing room? I believe we have time for a glass of sherry before dinner. All this press of affairs is thirsty work!"

Chapter 24

Over her shoulder, as they left the bookroom, Catherine said roguishly, "If you are to be my uncle-in-law, I believe it's time we were on a first name basis. You know that mine is Catherine; I am ashamed to admit that I do not know your given name, sir! Pray, enlighten me!" Mr. Stuart smiled and said, "I hope to become your Uncle Miles, my lady. However, I feel it is a bit…premature to take advantage of your invitation just yet." "I understand, sir, and it shall be as you wish. By the by, I still need to make a will, do I not?" "Yes, my lady, but you must consider whom you would wish to appoint your heir, should you die without issue, as well as any bequests you may wish to leave." Catherine stopped short. "Mr. Stuart, if I were to die without a will, what would happen to my estate?" "Well, my lady, given the unusual nature of your investiture, and the fact that you have set up an entail, the title, estate and the portion of the fortune entailed to the estate would automatically revert to the Crown. I am not sure about the remaining two-thirds, but I believe that would also revert to the Crown." "Well, I must give this some thought. Pray, sir, can you visit me again in a day or two, so that I may make a will based on my current situation? I may revise it later, if circumstances change, may I not?" Mr. Stuart replied, "Indeed, my lady, I believe it would be wise, if only for your own peace of mind. And a will may be revised and updated as it becomes prudent."

They entered the drawing room together, to find Mathilde and Mary seated before a blazing fire, enjoying a desultory conversation with Caroline and Tom. "Caroline, Tom, may I present Mr. Miles Stuart, my man of business and dear friend?" said Catherine, glancing at Mr. Stuart with a mischievous glint. "Mama, Aunt Mary, how lovely you both look! Have you ordered refreshments for yourselves and our guests?" Mathilde smiled and replied, "Indeed, Catherine, Morrow is fetching the sherry, some ratafia and some brandy even now! Have you finished your business, my dear?" "Indeed yes, Mama, and now I am ready for some pleasant conversation!" Just then, Morrow entered with the decanters and glasses. Caroline accepted a small glass of ratafia, while the other ladies preferred the sherry. Tom and Mr. Stuart elected a glass of brandy. "Catherine, that violet shades so becomes you!" said Caroline. "It seems an age since our last visit. What have you been doing?" "Well, I have been finishing up the shopping I needed to do for Heyerwood. I have been indulging in buying some books and other pleasurable items, as I am contemplating removing to the country before long. I have so enjoyed our stay here, but there are issues at home that need my attention, and I will frankly be glad of some peace and quiet for a change! Are you going to Julia's evening party next week?" "Yes, indeed. Tom and I are looking forward to it, as it will probably be my last social engagement. I am barely fit to be seen, but I refuse to retire to the country without one last waltz!" laughed Caroline, glowing with happiness. "I have everything prepared and packed for the journey to the country, and I vow that Tom would leave tonight if I would let him." Tom smiled and said, "Well, you madcap, you are right about that. If you had your way, our child would be born in the middle of a dance floor!" Caroline turned scarlet, but laughed with the others anyway.

Just then, Morrow announced the Mr. John and Mrs. Ridley, and Baron Ridley. Catherine rose to greet her guests. "Rosalie, John, how delightful to see you again. May I present you to my mother and Aunt Mary? And to my dear friends, Thomas and Caroline Berkley, and Mr. Miles Stuart? Rosalie curtseyed and John bowed, and, upon rising, Rosalie said,"Catherine, I would make you known to my brother-in-law James, Baron Ridley." Gracefully, Catherine extended her hand and curtseyed slightly, while the baron bowed punctiliously over her hand. "My lady, I thank you for including me in your gracious invitation, especially on such short notice." Catherined smiled and said, "Sir, I must always welcome my cousin Rosalie's family. We are delighted to make your acquaintance." Catherine looked up at James and added, "Pray sir, join us for some refreshment and conversation before we dine. I hope you do not object to an informal, chattery evening?" "Indeed no, my lady. Good company and a good meal are a superb combination, and, I am persuaded, no evening could be anything else in your home." Blushing slightly at the unexpected compliment, Catherine led the baron to the couch where her mother and aunt were seated, chatting with Mr. Stuart, and introduced him. Detaching herself from the company, she privately instructed Morrow to pass the decanters again, and to serve dinner in thirty minutes.

Moving from the drawing room to the dining room, the conversation continued unabated. At table, Rosalie and Mathilde complimented Catherine on the flowers, and all praised the menu that Catherine and her housekeeper so carefully selected. At length, when dinner was over, Catherine rose and led the ladies to the drawing room for tea, while Tom, Mr. Stuart, John, and the baron sat with some port and walnuts. As they took their seats by the fire, Caroline whispered hastily, "Your cousin Rosalie is lovely, and I could tell that Tom took a liking to her husband. A delightful couple!" Catherine smiled and nodded. "Indeed, I like them both so much. One feels so...at home with them." Just then Mathilde poured out, and conversation was interrupted for the passing of tea cups. "Rosalie said, with a shy smile, "Aunt Mathilde, I am so grateful that you have received my husband and myself this evening. It means so very much, to be with family again." Mathilde patted Rosalie's hand, and said, "Don't despair, my dear. Time heals many wounds. Your parents may come about. In the meantime, you have us and your husband's family. Your brother-in-law seems a delightful young man." "Indeed, he is most kind. James is not with us as often as we could wish, as he travels extensively, but we are excessively glad when he is at home. He and John are very close."

The conversation became general again, and turned to the subject of poetry. Not being fond of poetry, Catherine went to the piano-forte, and began to play softly, as a background to the chat by the fire. Just then, the gentlemen rejoined the ladies. Tom, John and Mr. Stuart made a beeline for seats by the fire, and joined in the conversation. The baron strolled over to the piano-forte, and said, "Not fond of poetry, my lady?" "Not terribly, I'm afraid, Lord Ridley. Byron gave me something of a distaste for the genre some time ago. I have found Scott enjoyable, but generally prefer novels or history. Is poetry to your taste, sir?" James grimaced, and said, "I have little time for reading for pleasure, but, when I do, I generally do not waste my time with poetry!" Catherine laughed and said, "How interesting to share, not a taste, but a DIStaste for something so popular! It is rather refreshing not to have to pretend an interest while someone rhapsodizes over the latest rhymes!" She looked up at James, and noticed, with some surprise, that he was as dark as his brother John was fair, but with the same deep blue eyes. He, too, was tall and broad shouldered. However, he was darkly tanned, and dressed with neatness and propriety, without the a la modality favored by his younger brother. His appearance suggested an indifference to matters of mode, and a tendency to go his own way regardless of others' opinions.

Catherine and James continued a light conversation, as she played. The conversations around the fire also continued. Finally, the clock ponderously struck midnight. Mr. Stuart looked up, startled. "So late! My lady, ladies and gentlemen, I do apologize for being the first to leave, but I have business engagements in the morning." Rising, he went to Catherine and bowed. "My thanks for a lovely evening, my lady. I will be seeing you soon." Aunt Mary rose and said, "I will see you out, sir." As Mary and Mr. Stuart left the drawing room, Mathilde rose and said with her sweet smile, "Well, my dears, I must retire as well. I fatigue more easily than I was used to. It has been a delightful evening." The gentlemen bowed and the young ladies curtseyed, as Mathilde left the drawing room and mounted the stairs, her back straight as always. Catherine rose from the piano-forte, and joined Caroline and Rosalie and their escorts near the fire. The Baron remained standing in the background, watching the group as they chatted pleasantly.

He had been surprised by Catherine. Aware of the unusual arrangement made by her late husband, he had expected to see someone older and very much on her dignity. He was pleased by the warmth of Catherine's welcome of Rosalie into her circle as a family member. He had been disappointed in Rosalie's treatment by her own immediate family, and the severance of his own close friendship with her brother Michael, when she married his brother. He also had not expected her unusual attractiveness and gaiety. Unpretentious himself, he had expected to be bored by a display of pomp and circumstance. He had very much enjoyed being proved wrong by the lack of ceremony displayed and by the make-up of the company, obviously selected more for conviviality and affection than by rank or fortune. He was amused to find himself rethinking his position that Rosalie was well out of her family's drama and was in danger of new injury in pursuing the new acquaintance.

Tom and Caroline were the next to depart, with Tom telling Caroline, "I know you are fatigued, and you must get your rest. If you racket about too much, you will not enjoy Julia's party next week, and you will be too knocked-up to enjoy the journey home." John and Rosalie rose also. The Baron joined them as Rosalie hugged Catherine and said, "Thank you a thousand times, dear cousin. A truly lovely evening. I hope you will come to us as well, you and your mother and aunt." John bowed and kissed

Catherine's hand. "You have made Rosalie very happy, ma'am, and I too thoroughly enjoyed the company, the conversation, and, of course, the meal. A perfect evening, in short!"

As Rosalie and John donned their wraps, James bowed over Catherine's hand. "At the risk of being repetitive, I too found the evening most enjoyable." He straightened and, without letting go of her hand, held Catherine's eyes as he said, "I hope you will permit me to call on you, ma'am." Catherine returned his gaze, seemingly unaware that he had retained his grip on her hand, and blushed. "I am delighted that you were able to join us, sir. We would be happy to see you when your schedule permits." As Morrow cleared his throat, she started and pulled her hand away. "Pray, sir, allow Morrow to assist you with your coat. It is too cold to keep Rosalie and John waiting." James smiled, shrugged himself into his coat and hat, and bowed again. "Good night, my lady, and many thanks." Catherine stood in the hall, and watched the door close behind him. Then she turned, lost in thought, and went slowly up the stairs.

Chapter 25

A few days later, Catherine paid a morning call on Julia. Julia received her from a chaise in her dainty morning room. "The party is tomorrow night, and I've been run off my feet with preparations. I finally have everything planned, the shopping ordered, and the decorations decided, and thought I'd relax today. How are you, my dear?" Catherine bent and hugged Julia gently. "I am quite well, and so looking forward to your evening party! Will there be dancing?" Julia laughed, "By all means! Caroline is so looking forward to one last waltz. She would never forgive me if I failed!" Catherine laughed, too. "Indeed, she said as much to me as well. She does love to gad about so! However, I think she is secretly glad to be going home. She fatigues more easily now. Are you planning a full ball?" "Nothing so formal. However, I will have musicians on the harp and piano-forte in the drawing room, and decided to use the ballroom with a scattering of small tables in bowers of flowers and plants. Putting a small orchestra in that room seemed like a pleasant plan, and there will be plenty of floor space for dancing. The refreshments will be laid out in a buffet on the dining room table, and I thought it would be kind of a foretaste of alfresco parties if people could enjoy them among flowers and music. The dancing just fell into place, as it were. You must tell me what you think. I flatter myself that it will be something of a hit." Catherine said, "It sounds delightful! Bowers in the corners and along the walls, with banks of flowers outlining the dancing area would be completely out of the common way. I do look forward to it! What are you planning to wear?"

Julia hesitated. "Well, the gown I had originally chosen had a train, as I was not planning to dance. I believe I'm going to wear a figured lace robe over an peach satin slip. It will be perfect for an evening party, and I will be able to dance if the opportunity arises. And you?" Catherine smiled. "I have a gown I've been saving for a special occasion. It is a deep green overdress to be worn over a gold *crepe lisse* under dress with gold sandals. I designed it myself, and I am so excited about it!" She told Julia about the embroidery and the beaded fringe edging. "It sounds lovely, and green is so becoming to you. I look forward to seeing it. I remember that, in school, you had an eye for colour. By the by, will your mother and aunt be joining us? I sent them invitations." Catherine replied regretfully, "No, I am afraid not. They will be writing to you today, I believe. My mother retires early these days, and I believe Aunt Mary to have made other plans. I know they were so pleased to be asked. It was most thoughtful of you, Julia."

Just then, Juliana came into the room with her nurse. "*Maman*, must I wear my heavy cloak today? The sun is shining, and I'm sure it is not cold! I'm so tired of that heavy thing. Please say I can wear my blue pelisse." Julia smiled, but said reprovingly, "Juliana, your manners! Pray, make your curtsey and say 'Good morning' to Lady Catherine." Juliana turned her head, saw Catherine, and blushed. "I am sorry, *Maman*, I did not know you had a guest. Good morning, Lady Catherine. Is it not a lovely day?" Catherine laughed and held out her hand. "Indeed it is! So good to see the sun for a change! Are you going out, my dear?" "Yes, my lady, we go to walk in the park every morning if it is not raining. Do you think any flowers are out yet?" "I hardly think so, dear, it isn't quite spring yet, you know." Juliana looked at her mother coaxingly. "Please, *Maman*, say I don't have to wear the heavy old cloak today!' Julia smiled, but shook her head. "I am sorry, my love, but it is still too cold, even if the sun is shining. You do not want to catch a chill and be too ill to stay up to see the ladies' gowns tomorrow night, I'm sure." Brightening at the prospect of the treat, Juliana agreed to the hated cloak, curtseyed and went off, chattering happily, with her nurse.

Julia shook her head as she and Catherine both laughed. Sobering suddenly, Julia looked at Catherine and said, "I want you to know that, if something happens to me, I would like you to be Juliana's guardian and look after her for me." Startled, Catherine opened her mouth, then shut it. Julia flushed painfully and said, "It is no secret that Jean-Paul does not concern himself with Juliana; nor does his mother. If something were to happen to me, I would want her to be cared for by someone who has feelings for her, and would be concerned for her well-being. Jean-Paul and his mother would simply pack her off to school." Catherine leaned forward, and took Julia's hand. "I would be happy to look after Juliana if the need arises. Whatever has put this into your mind now?" she asked. Julia looked away. "Well, I have not been robust of health since my confinement with Juliana, and I have just discovered that I am increasing again." Julia looked back at Catherine. "Needless to say, I am delighted as I have always wanted several children, but I cannot but be somewhat nervous, too. Jean-Paul and his mother are sure that, this time, the child will be a boy and the heir, and that the outcome will be happy. You and I, however, know that risk is always present."

Catherine smiled and congratulated her friend. "I know that you have yearned for this and, indeed, I feel sure that the outcome will be happy. If it will make you feel more comfortable, by all means be sure that Juliana will be cared for as if she were my own if the need arises. Does Jean-Paul know your feelings on this matter?" "Indeed, Catherine, I have discussed it with him. He believes my fears are morbid; however, he has agreed that Juliana may come to you if needs must." Julia looked at Catherine sadly, and said, with some bitterness, "I have loved Jean-Paul since I met him, but discovering the depth of his indifference to Juliana has almost been a death-blow to that feeling. He has been so aloof since her birth and, for some time, I felt that it must have been my fault somehow. Now, in his pleasure in this news, his feelings for me have miraculously revived, but he still has no interest in our daughter and pretends none. If he cannot love her for herself, one would think that, if he loved me, he would have some feeling for her as being part of me. I feel betrayed. What if this child is a girl, too? What if something happens? These are circumstances I cannot control, and I cannot feel any real security in Jean-Paul's feelings for me now. I am trying to make some peace for myself. Can you understand that?" Tears thickening her throat, Catherine managed to nod. "Be sure, Julia, that Juliana will become my daughter if anything happens to you. Pray send her to me at any time you desire. Be sure to contact your man-of-business and set out your instructions in writing. I think you would feel more at peace, if you know that your desires are clearly outlined."

Rising, Catherine hugged Julia again. "Pray, rest and gather your strength, my dear. We have to be in our best looks for your party tomorrow!" "Indeed, I look forward to it now more than ever. Thank you, dear friend." As Catherine was walking to the foyer, she was surprised when a door opened. Jean-Paul DeGryce, *Comte* De Beaumonte, appeared. Startled, she swept a curtsey. "My lord." The *Comte* bowed. "Pray, my lady, join me for a moment if you would be so good. "Certainly, my lord."

Catherine preceded him into the room, which turned out to be an elegant library. The *Comte* seemed startled and somewhat ill-at-ease. "I know you are my wife's good friend. Has she told you her good news?" Coolly, Catherine replied, "If you are referring to the fact she is increasing, indeed she has. I know that she has looked forward to this event, and is indeed delighted. I am happy for her, and for you, of course." The *Comte* bowed and said, "I appreciate your good wishes. I am concerned for Julia's health. She is not strong, and I wish to take every care of her. I cannot seem to reassure her as much as I could wish. Has she told you of her wishes for Juliana?" Looking at the *Comte* directly, Catherine replied, "She has asked me to be Juliana's guardian in the event of her death or inability to care for the child, if that is what you mean. I have, of course, agreed to this. Juliana is a delightful child." The *Comte* flushed painfully, and his faint French accent became more pronounced. "I see that you are direct. Julia has expressed this desire, and I have agreed to it. What would you? I would agree to anything she asked, if it would give her any peace. I hope you were able to reassure her."

Raising her brows, Catherine said, "My dear sir, I have assured Julia that I expect the outcome to be happy, but that, if the need arises, I will take Juliana and raise her as my own. She assures me that you and your mother are indifferent to the child, and that you have agreed to this plan. Frankly, sir, she would be immeasurably happier if she could believe that you had any feelings for your daughter at all. Forgive me if I am impertinent, but I would expect you, her husband, would be the best person to reassure Julia." Taken aback, the *Comte* stared at Catherine. "No feelings for Juliana? You would say, she thinks I dislike the child?"

Equally taken aback, Catherine said, "My lord, she thinks that your feelings for her dwindled when she presented you with a girl, instead of a son to be the heir that you and your mother crave, and that you've no interest in Juliana at all. Is she wrong?" He turned and stared into the fire. "What do I know about the needs of a girl-child?" he asked. "I was raised in France, in a large *chateau*. My parents were occupied at Court, and I saw very little of them. When the Terror came, my father did not survive, and my mother brought me here. I have never had a brother or sister to share my youth, and I know nothing of how English family life is conducted. My mother has ever been on her dignity, as she raised me to be. You are saying that Julia sees this as indifference? She thinks I have withdrawn from her? My God, I never knew...I was trying to protect her! She was so ill, so fragile after Juliana's birth. I would give anything to protect her. I left Juliana to her care, because that was the only thing that seemed to give her pleasure." Catherine approached him, and put her hand on his arm. "My dear *Comte*, you must tell Julia these things. It would be your greatest gift to her. She has loved you so long, and needs to know that you love her and Juliana, too. That would be her greatest security." He put his hand over hers, and said, "I do not know if I can find the words, but I shall surely try. I cannot thank you…!" Catherine gently drew her hand away, and said, "Sir, I must go now, but shall look forward to seeing you and Julia tomorrow." Silently, he bowed while she curtseyed and left the room.

Chapter 26

The next evening, just before Catherine retired to dress for Julia's party, Aunt Mary peeped around the sitting room door. "My dear niece, may I have a moment?" she asked. Catherine smiled and said, "As many as you please, Aunt! Pray, come in and join me by the fire." Mary glided into the room, and took a small chair. Blushing slightly, she said, "I wish to discuss something with you, my dear. I'm really not sure how you may take my news." Catherine patted Mary's hand. "Indeed, Aunt, tell me anything you wish. I hope your news is pleasant?" Blushing furiously, Aunt Mary said, "Well, I hardly know if I'm on my head or on my heels. My dear, I've received an offer of marriage. At my age!" Catherine grasped Mary's hand and said, "How delightful, my dear! From Mr. Stuart, of course?" Mary, taken aback, said, "Of course! How could you know?" Catherine laughed, and replied, "My dear, he did me the honor of asking me for your hand! Have you accepted him?" Mary smiled and said, "Not yet. I told him that I was deeply honored and grateful, but that I must discuss it with my family. I'm not a flighty girl, to act heedlessly."

Catherine, sobered, said, "My dear, can you not like the idea? I know that you have been widowed many years. If you do not wish to marry, you need hardly feel constrained. Your home here is always available. I hope you do not feel obliged to stay with us, however." Mary shook her head. "My dear niece, these months with you have been amongst the most pleasant I have ever spent, and I am delighted to know that I have a home with you. The idea of marriage, however, is very pleasant, and I find Mr. Stuart to be most … acceptable. However, would such an alliance be acceptable to you and to your mother? He *is* your man of business, after all, and some might consider my marriage to him something of a … a misalliance." Looking at her aunt squarely, while retaining her grasp on Mary's hand, Catherine said emphatically, "Aunt Mary, if that is the only thing concerning you, pray forget the thought immediately. Mr. Stuart is a gentleman, and is highly respected. He has firm principals and is as great a gentleman as any I know. I consider him a dear friend, as well as a man of business on whom I place the greatest dependence. If you care for him enough, I would be delighted to see you his wife. The fact that he is a solicitor and plans to continue his work is certainly no dishonour; to my mind, it is rather otherwise. He is a man of honour and dignity, and wishes to hang on no one's sleeve! My mother and I both think most highly of him. I would welcome him into the family." Smiling mischievously, Catherine added with a twinkle, "He has already indicated that he would not object to my calling him 'Uncle Miles'!" Scarlet now, Mary laughed and said, "Well! I could hardly refuse him now. I suspect you would not forgive me!" Laughing, the two ladies exchanged a warm embrace.

Retiring to her room, Catherine sat in a warm, scented bath, smiling as she thought of her aunt's engagement to Mr. Stuart. Musing as she dried herself, applied scent, and slipped into her shift, she found herself hoping she could convince Aunt Mary and Mr. Stuart to make their home under her roof. A separate suite, even a separate entrance would be easy enough to arrange. She allowed Jane to assist her into the golden underdress, and sat down at the dressing table. With the emerald pendant, earrings, bracelet and the delicate golden tiara with emerald flowers lying ready, she watched Jane dress her brown curls high on her head, leaving a few wispy ringlets at her temples and the nape of her neck, with a few long shining curls disposed on one shoulder. "Thank you, Jane, that is delightful." Leaning forward, she touched her lips with a little colour, and slipped the hooks of the earrings into her earlobes. After clasping the heavy gold chain around her neck, she observed the pendant resting on her bosom just above the neckline of the delicate underdress. "I believe this will do nicely," she said.

Jane assisted her with the deep green overdress, settling the sleeves so that the delicate beaded fringe showed, complementing the golden embroidery on the edges of the sleeves of the overdress. The golden underdress showed slightly at the neckline, and where the skirt of the overdress parted in the front. Catherine looked at herself in the pier glass mirror, a vision in green and gold. She was pleased with the way the emeralds in their gold settings complimented her gown. Slipping the bracelet on her wrist, she picked up her champagne kid evening gloves, her deep green silk reticule and her fan. Nodding to Jane, she left her room and descended the stairs. Flushed with excitement, she went into the drawing room where her mother and aunt sat by the fire. "Well, my dears, what do you think? I believe my design made up well, do not you?" Twirling before them, she swept a deep, formal curtsey with a saucy smile. Mathilde, smiling tenderly, said, "Oh, Catherine, my love, never have I seen you look so becoming! Your dress is lovely, and not just in the common style. Most elegant! And the green sets off your colouring delightfully." Aunt Mary agreed, "Quite so! You will be setting a style, I daresay, my dear niece." Just then, Morrow announced the coach was at the door. Kissing her mother and aunt, Catherine went to the hall, where Jane carefully assisted her with her gloves and folded her black velvet evening cloak around her.

Arriving at Julia's door, she was taken aback by the number of guests she glimpsed entering the already-crowded hall. Obviously, Julia's evening party was going to be the ultimate success, a fashionable squeeze. Descending with the assistance of a footman, she mounted the steps and entered the house. After being divested of her cloak, she found her way to her hostess. Julia, a radiant vision in peach satin under lace, embraced her friend. Glowing with happiness, Julia said, "How lovely you look, my dear! Pray, let us try to talk later. You will find Caroline and Tom in the conservatory. Your cousin Rosalie and her husband and brother-in-law are also here somewhere. I must tell you, although this isn't the best time, I am so happy! Jean-Paul and I have had the most wonderful reconciliation. I know not what prompted it, but I can't tell you how wonderful it is! Come to me tomorrow, so we can have a comfortable coze."

Catherine made her way through the crush to the conservatory. Feeling rather shy, she kept her head up and a mile on her face. She nodded to acquaintances as she picked her way through the crowd. As she proceeded, she came face to face with Lady Castlereigh, one of the patronesses of Almack's. "Oh, lord!" she thought nervously. "I haven't seen any of the great ladies since before my marriage!" Her head held high, she curtsied gracefully and murmured, "Good evening, my lady. A sad crush, is it not?" To Catherine's surprise, Lady Castlereigh nodded regally and extended her hand. "A crush indeed, Catherine. It has been too long, child. Is your dear mother here? Mathilde and I were friends in our younger days, you know." Catherine clasped the extended hand briefly, and said regretfully, "I am afraid that my mother was not able to attend this evening. She finds evening parties too tiring these days." Lady Castlereigh smiled slightly and said, "I understand. Pray tell her I asked for her. You must bring her to call one afternoon next week." Taken aback, Catherine said, "I would be honored, my lady. Thank you for your condescension. My mother will be pleased to be remembered." Nodding graciously, Lady Castlereigh swept on. Stunned, yet vastly relieved, Catherine watched her on her way, then continued on. Somewhat to her amusement, the welcome extended her became positively lavish. A bit cynically, she thought, "I must assume that Lady Castlereigh's approval is still hard to win. I had forgot she was a bosom-bow of Mama's. How David would laugh!" She was vastly entertained to receive a nod and smile from her former friend Maria, the Baroness Fortescue. Slightly inclining her head without a smile, Catherine swept on her way.

Caroline hailed her just then. "Catherine, how sumptuous your gown is! You have such a flair. You must join us!" Catching Catherine's hand, Caroline whispered, "I saw Lady Castlereigh speak to you just now. My dear, you clearly need not fear taking your place in Society! Everyone is terrified of her, and, with THAT greeting, she has assured you of a welcome anywhere. I had forgot that you knew her!" Catherine smiled and shook her head, "No, my dear Caroline, I must confess that I owe Lady Castlereigh's kindness to her friendship with my mother. I must say that I was never so terrified in my life! I was prepared for a cool nod at best, if not the cut direct. I was ready to sink. She was so very kind to me-she even asked me to bring my mother to call next week. I did not look for any such attention." Extending her hand to Tom, she greeted him warmly. Joining the group in the conservatory, Catherine smiled and chatted happily, the conversation becoming general and light-hearted.

Strains of music were heard from the ballroom, and Caroline turned to Tom. "I hold you to your word, my lord!" she said with mock severity. "I insist on *all* the waltzes." As the group made their way to the ballroom, Catherine was pleased to see Rosalie and John. Clasping Rosalie's hand warmly, Catherine said, "Is this not delightful? Pray join us! We are going to the ballroom, and I am agog to see Julia's decorations!" Laughing, the group proceeded to the large, elegant ballroom. The banks of flowers, the bowers in the corners of the room, and the myriad shades of the ladies' gowns created a kaleidoscope of colours. Sets were being formed for the first quadrille. Just then, James loomed up behind her. "Dare I hope you are free for this dance, my lady?" he asked as he bowed over her hand. Taken aback, Catherine blushed and smiled. Putting her hand in his, she curtsied and rose. "Sir, I would be honored." He swept her into a set with Rosalie and John, and Caroline and Tom. As they stepped and twirled lightly through the figures, Catherine's thoughts were initially on her feet. As they came together briefly, she looked up at James and smiled wryly. "Pray forgive my lack of conversation, sir. I must mind my steps, like a schoolgirl!"

After the quadrille, the party stood together, near one of the bowers, the ladies fanning themselves after their exertion. As the musicians began the first strains of the next dance, a country dance, a touch on her elbow caused Catherine to turn. To her surprise, her host bowed and asked her to dance. She curtsied briefly, and was swept into a set. To her relief, Jean-Paul made no effort to engage her in conversation as they came together and parted again in the steps of the dance. She relaxed and let herself enjoy the music and the evening. Only when the dance ended did her host say something. As he bowed over her hand, Jean-Paul looked up at her and said quietly, "Accept my gratitude, madam. Your words were timely and effective. It saddens me to think what I might never have known was mine without your honesty. My wife is fortunate to have such a loyal friend." Catherine smile, and pressed his hand.

After that dance, the evening sped by in a whirl of music and colour, scented with flowers. Finding herself alone, she slipped into the conservatory and sat down on one of the benches, near a fountain. Fanning herself, Catherine relaxed and enjoyed the cool stillness. A voice behind her said, "I had hoped to catch you alone, my lady." She turned her head and saw James standing there. "Pray, sir, be seated and join me. I was taking advantage of an opportunity to catch my breath. I have not been to such a squeeze in years, and find it all a bit overwhelming. Are you enjoying the party, sir?" Seating himself, he pondered the question. "Frankly, I find a gathering of this type to be more fatiguing than anything. One seldom enjoys any meaningful conversation. Such evenings are more for the purpose of seeing and being seen, and I have never really cared for such things. However, if one is with a congenial party, and the music is good, it can be quite pleasurable." She laughed and said, "Sir, I must tell you that you have answered my question with a riddle!" James smiled and said, "I believe the next dance is the supper dance. May I hope that you will dance it with me, and go into supper? Caroline, Tom, Rosalie and John will be saving seats for us, in the hope that I am successful." Catherine smiled back at him, and said "Sir, you did not need to bribe me with the lure of additional pleasant company; I would be delighted to dance and to have supper with you." Rising, they made their way back to the ballroom.

To her surprise, the supper dance was a waltz. James bowed and she curtsied, then he swept her into the maelstrom of dancers. Catherine was grateful for his arm and guidance, as she concentrated on her steps through the first few measures. Looking up, she found his eyes on her face, and he was smiling. "You look like a young girl, given permission to waltz in public for the first time! Are you counting your steps?" Blushing, she laughed. "Sir, I distinctly remember telling you earlier that I had to mind them. You will have no one but yourself to blame if I tread on your toes!" Relaxing, she laughed and chatted lightly through the rest of the dance. As he led her into the supper room, she saw Caroline and Rosalie at a table in the corner, waving to her. James steered her to the table, seated her and said, "I will fetch some refreshments. Pray, save my seat." The young women sat, chatting and looking around at the other guests. Caroline said, "Pray, don't tell Tom, but my feet are exhausted! I just can't sit out a dance. I will be in need of a rest in the country by the time this night is over. Julia has certainly outdone herself. The decorations are truly exquisite, and the music delightful." She looked at Catherine with a twinkle. "You seem to be having a most delightful time, my dear! I think you need have no fear regarding being snubbed by Society after tonight." Rosalie laughed, and added, "Even James seems to be enjoying the party, and, I must tell you, he seldom graces us with his presence at these affairs when he is in England." Just then, Tom, John and James returned with refreshments. The party laughed and talked and ate, one of the merriest in the room.

After supper, they returned to the ballroom. Tom swept Caroline into another waltz, and James made his bow to Rosalie. Catherine and John had just taken seats, content to sit out, when Michael stalked up. Nodding curtly to John, he held out his hand to Catherine, saying imperiously, "Pray, cousin, give me this waltz, if you please." Flushed with mortification, Catherine greeted Michael coolly, and replied, "As you see, cousin, I am not dancing this…" Interrupting her, Michael took her hand and said, "I must and will speak with you immediately, and this dance is as good an opportunity as any other time." Sweeping her out onto floor, they danced a few moments in silence, Catherine struggling to master her outrage. Michael cleared his throat, and said, "I have observed you this evening, cousin, and have seen you encourage my sister and her connections to hang on your sleeve. Is there nothing I can say to you, to convince you to respect her parents', and my, wishes in this matter?" Affronted and incredulous, Catherine said icily, "This is neither the time nor the place for this discussion. Nevertheless, Viscount Chatellerault, I will say this. You will always have my gratitude for your kindness to my mother. However,

I must tell you, sir, I have never given you reason to believe that you have any rights or responsibility to order my conduct or my friendships. We have nothing to discuss on this head, and I will not indulge in a vulgar brawl with a family member in public. Pray, sir, let us leave this subject and try to enjoy the remainder of this dance like civilized persons!" Silently, Catherine and Michael finished the waltz. When the music ended, she swept him a formal curtsey and walked away without a word.

Catherine did not see any of her friends immediately at hand, and suddenly felt tired. Making her way to Julia, she congratulated her on the success of her party, and bid her a fond good night, promising to call tomorrow. A footman helped her on with her cloak and into her carriage. As the carriage rolled through the silent streets, she reviewed the evening. It had been totally delightful, except for the awkward exchange with Michael. She decided that, if she encountered him in public, she would give no more acknowledgement than a formal, unsmiling nod, and would no longer receive him. Dismissing him, she pondered Lady Castlereagh's kindness, and Maria's discomfiture. All in all, a most satisfactory evening! She did not dwell on the fact that dancing and having supper with James contributed significantly to the pleasures of the ball.

Chapter 27

Catherine awoke late the next morning. While sipping her chocolate in bed, she decided that she would plan to return to Heyerwood within the next few weeks. She considered that that would give her time for any last minute shopping, to take her mother to call on Lady Castlereagh, and to take leave of her friends. She wanted to discuss the family issues with her mother, to be certain that Mathilde would not be upset or offended if Catherine did not extend further courtesies to Michael. She also wanted to talk to her aunt and Mr. Stuart about their plans and see if they would be willing to share her household. While she would miss the convenience of the London shops and entertainment, she wanted to be at home, to be sure that the estate repairs and expansions were well under way. Catherine reflected, "It is as if, after a few weeks of nothing but cakes and confections, I suddenly awoke craving solid food."

The day proving cold, dreary and rainy, Catherine dressed in the golden brown wool crepe day dress, with topaz earbobs and soft brown slippers. She went to her mother's rooms and tapped on the door. When Miss Potter answered, she smiled and said "Good morning, Miss Potter! Is my mother awake yet?" Miss Potter bobbed a brief curtsey, and said, "Yes, my lady, your lady mother is awake and having her morning tea. She's still in her bed, but I know she'd like to see you, to hear about the ball and everything." Stepping aside, she bade Catherine enter. Seated on the foot of her mother's bed, Catherine regaled her with all the details of the decorations, the excellence of the refreshments, and the beautiful gowns worn by the ladies in attendance. Mathilde was particularly gratified to hear of Lady Castlereagh's kindness to Catherine. "Fancy her remembering me! You must know, I was older than Amelia-even though we became very close, I don't think we were in school together at the same time for more than a year, and it has been several years since I ventured into Society. I would be delighted if you would accompany me to call on her."

As Catherine continued her story of the evening, she mentioned spending the bulk of the evening with her friends, including Rosalie and John and his brother. "I am delighted that you are seeing so much of her. She is a delightful young lady, and reminds me a bit of her mother when we were very young." Uncomfortably, Catherine told Mathilde of her miserable dance with Michael. "I must tell you, Mother, that I cannot and will not accept his unreasonable interference. I have told him repeatedly, and he continues to push. I would hate to cause you pain, but I can no longer be comfortable in his company, and do not plan to receive him. If he calls upon you, please do not let me prevent you from seeing him, but I cannot subject myself to further annoyance!" Mathilde patted her hand, and said, "My dear, I *must* receive him out of kindness for the great service that he and his mother did me, and for his mother's sake, but I perfectly understand your feelings. I do not ask that you subject yourself to such discomfort, nor will I discuss you with him. If he is so improper as to press the issue with me...well, we shall have to see."

Much relieved, Catherine outlined her plans for the next few weeks. "Shall you return to the country with me, Mother? If you prefer, you may remain in town. As you may know, I have written Mr. Stuart about purchasing this house, and I believe all is proceeding well. We still have a few weeks on the lease as it is. You may join me at Heyerwood later, at your convenience." Mathilde smiled and said, "My dear, this visit has passed much more easily and enjoyably than I ever anticipated, and I have relished this visit to town. However, I am ready for the peace and quiet of the countryside. I must say, though, we may have a job to convince your aunt!"

Catherine descended to the bookroom, to make some lists and attend to some correspondence. She wrote first to Lady Castlereagh, thanking her again for her kindness and asking if a day in the next week would be acceptable for Catherine to bring her mother to call. She also wrote to Caroline, bidding her a fond farewell and wishing her a safe journey home. She reminded Caroline that she expected to be notified of the outcome of Caroline's lying-in as soon as may be. Enclosing a small, gaily-wrapped parcel containing the pink pearl pin with the note to Caroline, she sent a footman off to deliver the notes to Caroline and Lady Castlereagh. Catherine then reviewed her ledger of purchases for Heyerwood, noted a few omissions and made a list of final purchases needed. She wrote a note to Mrs. Davis, and another to Mr. Jones, the bailiff, advising them of her return within the next few weeks. She set those notes aside to be sent by the Mail. Checking her accounts, she made sure that all were paid and correct. Finally, she sent a note to Mr. Stuart, asking him to join them for dinner in two days' time and to bring any information he may have on the status of her offer to buy the town-house. "I will ask him at that time, about him and Aunt Mary living here after their marriage. If she does not wish to return to Heyerwood with us presently, I will see about a companion for her. She does not need a chaperone, but it would not do for her to be lonely." Dispatching that note by another footman, she instructed him to wait for an answer.

Satisfied with the state of her books and business matters, she went upstairs to prepare for her morning call on Julia. Checking her gown and earbobs, Catherine decided not to change. She pinned over her curls a trifle of ivory lace, complimenting the deep lace collar of her dress, and added the topaz and pearl necklace to compliment her earbobs. Changing her slippers for brown leather half boots, she decided to wear the new green velvet redingote and bonnet, using the brown fur pelerine and muff for added warmth. As she left the house, Catherine gave the coachman Julia's direction, then got into the barouche and rolled away. Arriving at Julia's door, she climbed down from the carriage with the footman's help. Noticing the increasing coldness and cloudiness of the day, she dismissed her coach, saying "Pray, return for me in two hours. It is too cold for you to sit her waiting." Touching his hat, the coachman thanked her and drove away. Catherine mounted the steps and was admitted.

Climbing the stairs to Julia's morning room, she noted the hall tray piled high with notes and cards, and the side tables gay with flowers. Entering the room, she saw Julia, reclining elegantly on the *chaise longue* near the fire. Extending her hand, Julia exclaimed, "My dear, come into the warm! It is so bitterly cold out today, I was afraid you might not choose to leave your fireside!" Clasping Julia's hand warmly, Catherine chuckled and said, "After promising to call without fail? Dear friend, you should know better! Besides, my people take such care of me, even to a hot brick for my feet for just a few squares' ride. You look fully recovered from last night's raking. Such a squeeze! Julia, your party was delightful." As Catherine seated herself in the chair near the fire, Julia smiled proudly and said, "It did go well, did it not? I was most pleased with the music, and the refreshments. I gave our chef and his helpers all of the compliments I could recall, and a bonus besides for all of their efforts. Oh, Catherine, I saw Lady Castlereagh speak to you, and cannot tell you how pleased I was. I was not certain she would be able to attend, and she did not stay long, but she was so kind. And did you see Maria's face...?!" Catherine smiled mischievously. "Indeed I did. She was suddenly so very ... cordial! I had all to do not to laugh – I merely nodded politely, and continued on my way. I didn't want to strain her feelings too much." Sobering, Catherine said, "I must tell you, I dread the possibility that she may seek me out, try to renew our friendship. I really could not bear her to try to resume our old intimacy because of Lady Castlereagh's favor. If I was not worth Maria's loyalty before, I am not a different person now. It would be too shallow and self-serving for Maria to try to return to the old intimacy now." Julia nodded, and replied, "Indeed, Catherine, I do understand your feelings. However, you underestimate Maria's self-consequence. I don't think her pride would allow her to show such a *volte face*. I think she will be more pleasant in public; that is all, at least for now."

Catherine laughed and said, "Well, that should create no difficulty. I am returning to Heyerwood soon, in any case, and have much to do to prepare, so I shan't be making many public appearances between now and then. I understand that you and Jean-Paul have cleared the air between you, have you not? So I may leave you with a clear conscience!" Julia blushed. "Indeed we have! After your last call, when we discussed Juliana's guardianship, I was in a very low state. Later in the day, he came to my room and found me in tears. Catherine, he was so concerned and considerate. We have not had such a talk since the early days of our marriage. He explained so many things that I had not understood, and I was able to share my fears for the first time. I feel that so much of our...estrangement was of my own doing! I should have pressed him to listen to me before. I am the happiest of women. We, too, shall be retiring to the country soon, to await my confinement. This time, however, it will be the two of us and Juliana. *Chere Maman* will be spending time here in Town until closer to time. It will give us a chance to get to know ourselves as a family."

Chapter 28

After bidding Julia an affectionate farewell, Catherine decided to attend to some shopping. Directing her coachman to the warehouse district, Catherine ordered some additional spices, candied and bottled fruits, and preserved items for shipment directly to Heyerwood. She also visited a stationer's shop where she ordered items suitable for a schoolroom, again for shipment directly home. She made a last stop at Hatchard's where she picked up a dictionary, some globes, and some histories, as well as a copy of Culpepper's herbal, to be sent directly to the Vicar for the village school. She resolutely forbore a browse through the novels, and returned home. Crossing the shopping trip of her list, and entering the purchases into the ledger gave her great pleasure. Setting up a proper school in the village would give her much satisfaction. Hopefully, her tenants and the villagers would allow their children to attend! Checking the list of household supplies, she felt the estate was well stocked, and able to withstand a siege, if needs be.

Just then, a footman brought Catherine a reply from Mr. Stuart, accepting her invitation to dine and indicating that he expected to have good news regarding the purchase of the house. Smiling with anticipation, she debated the wisdom of putting her proposal regarding the couple residing with her to Mr. Stuart first, or to make her suggestion to her aunt and Mr. Stuart together. Not wanting to offend him or to damage his pride, Catherine decided to make her proposal to Mr. Stuart alone, during their meeting before dinner. Setting his note aside, she continued reviewing her ledgers.

As she sat, reviewing her lists and thinking about her coming interview with Mr. Stuart, Morrow came to the bookroom door. "Pardon me, my lady. Viscount Chatellerault is here. I explained that you were not at home, but he insisted that I check again. Do you have other instructions?" "Thank you, Morrow, but I am not at home to the Viscount today, or at any other time. Should he wish to call on my mother, tomorrow morning after eleven o'clock will be convenient." Morrow bowed slightly, and silently left the room. Catherine returned to her lists, annoyed that her cousin had questioned her butler. A few moments later, Morrow reappeared. "The Viscount has departed, my lady. He expressed his intent on making a call upon Viscountess Stanton in the morning, and left this note for you. Have you any further instructions, my lady?" "None, thank you, Morrow. I trust there was no...unpleasantness?" Morrow replied, "The young gentleman was not best pleased, ma'am, but I had had the forethought to have a footman available to escort him to his carriage, so he did not press the issue." Catherine smiled, and said, "Accept my thanks, Morrow. You are never at a loss." Impulsively, she added, "Morrow, I am in negotiations to purchase this house, for my use and the use of my family. If I am successful at acquiring a town house, would you be interested in accepting permanent employment with us?" Morrow bowed and replied, "I would be honoured, my lady. I was in hopes that, should you acquire a town residence, you would consider me. I need not assure you that I will endeavor to give complete satisfaction." "I am sure you will, Morrow. Thank you for your willingness to stay on." Nodding dismissal, Catherine returned to her lists, relieved. If she would retain the housekeeper as well, whether she acquired this house or another, her primary town staff would be made up of loyal and trustworthy people she knew.

Sighing, she opened the note from Michael. As she read, Catherine noted that it was a jumble of apology, recrimination and insistence. She crumpled it and through it on the fire. She found it entirely consistent with their last few conversations, and not worthy of response. He was still determined to interfere and dominate. Catherine felt a mixture of annoyance and regret. She reflected, "How sad that my first new acquaintance in years, and a relative, has turned out so unhappily." Just then, a footman entered with the post. Shrugging, she dismissed Michael from her mind, and turned to the rest of her correspondence.

The next day, Catherine made it a point to be up, dressed, and out of the house before ten thirty in the morning. Too early for conventional calls, she decided to visit the Pantheon Bazaar to see if there were any new fabrics, laces or trimmings of interest. As the barouche rolled through town, she observed Baron Ridley striding down Bond Street. Tapping on the glass, she instructed her coachman to pull up. Seeing her, the baron removed his hat and bowed, stepping up to the window. Extending her hand, Catherine smiled and said, "I am delighted to see you, my lord. A lovely party the other evening, was it not?" "A lovely party, indeed, my lady, but one that ended too soon. I finished my dance with Rosalie, only to find you had vanished." Somewhat embarrassed, Catherine said, "I found my last dance to be...fatiguing. It seemed best to take my leave." Raising her eyes, she said, "I did regret not having the opportunity to take my leave of Rosalie and John, and of you, my lord." James smiled slightly and said, "I had observed your partner in the dance; you did not look to be enjoying it excessively."

Flushing, Catherine said, "Indeed, I find you to be a master of understatement! As you know the situation as well as I, there is no point in trying to wrap it in clean linen. I found my cousin to be quite presumptuous, and let him know it. Rather than deal with a scene, or subject myself to further annoyance, it seemed best to take my leave." She held out her hand. "I mustn't keep you standing in the cold. Pray, give John and Rosalie my greetings." She smiled, and added, "We will be in town for the next few weeks. You are all welcome to join us for tea at any time, and I hope that an invitation to dine sometime next week will be welcomed. I hope it is not too bold to say that I hope we will see you soon?" James took her hand and held it tightly. "Indeed not, my lady, and I can assure you that you will see us, individually or collectively, quite soon. As to dining next week, I do not know John's or Rosalie's plans, but I will certainly look forward to it." Bowing, he replaced his hat on his head and stepped back up on the curb. She smiled as she put up the window, giving a little wave.

Catherine entered the Pantheon Bazaar, and wandered from booth to booth. She found some lovely Norwich shawls, one in violet and shades of lavender, and the other in soft silvery tones, that would be perfect for Mother and Aunt Mary. She found some lengths of Chantilly lace in soft ivory that would be a perfect overdress, come the spring. She also found some delicate, soft woolens, perfect for baby garments, in lovely pale yellows, blues and pinks. Buying several lengths, she determined to send them to Caroline's and Julia's country homes for their use. She also discovered some new embroidery silks in clear, soft colours that she did not have. Waiting for her parcels to be wrapped, she browsed a table of silk stockings. Hearing her name called, Catherine looked up to see Baroness Fortescue bearing down on her, followed by a maid and a fubsy-faced, overdressed young girl with thick black hair who was obviously her daughter.

"My dear Catherine," gushed Maria, "How lovely to see you again! I had hoped to have a chat with you at dear Julia's party, but it was such a sad crush! I trust you and your dear mother are both well?" Bowing slightly, Catherine said, "Baroness Fortescue, such a surprise! I trust I see you in health?" Laughing to cover the awkwardness of the meeting, Maria said, "Never better, my dear. Lydia, my pet, pray make your curtsey to the Countess of Heyerwood. You must know that she is one of my oldest friends. This is my daughter Lydia, Catherine. She is just the age we were when first we met. Oh, dear, how long it seems since our school days! What times we had, did we not, Catherine?" Coolly, Catherine returned Lydia's curtsey, and said, "As to that, Baroness, I have learned to put the memory of those times into perspective. It was delightful meeting your daughter. Now I find I must go. Good afternoon, Baroness!" Another slight bow, and Catherine turned on her heel and swept away without looking back. Finding her carriage awaiting her, she instructed the waiting footman to bring her parcels. As she drove away from the Pantheon Bazaar, she hoped she did not look like she was fleeing. Realizing that it was two-thirty in the afternoon, she decided to make a couple of calls before returning home for tea. Perhaps some rational conversation would help get the bad taste out of her mouth!

Chapter 29

Catherine left a card at the home of Lady Castlereagh, not wanting to look a courtesy, and stopped at Fenton's Hotel, to see if Rosalie was at home to callers. She was escorted immediately to Rosalie's parlour. "How delightful, cousin!" exclaimed Rosalie, as she hugged Catherine. I was getting quite bored with my own company on such a dreary day, but didn't want to leave my fireside. John and I talk of returning home soon. Catherine smiled and said, as they took seats near the blazing fire, "I, too, am planning to return home. I have enjoyed this visit to Town more than I thought possible, but must get home to Heyerwood. I vow, it seems a twelve-month since I was there, and there is all to do! I just finished some shopping, and thought I would call to invite you, John and Baron Ridley to dinner sometime next week. Have you plans? What night would be best for you?" Rosalie answered, "I believe we have no plans at all for the evenings next week. However, I must confer with John, as he is completing some business, and may have a dinner engagement that I am not aware of. As far as James is concerned, I do not know his plans, but…" with a twinkle "…I suspect he will be available whenever you choose!" Catherine blushed rosily. "As to that, Baron Ridley and I spoke earlier today, and he seemed to find the idea pleasing enough."

The two women laughed and chatted over tea brought by the waiter. Hearing the mantle clock chime, Catherine looked up guiltily and started. "So late! My dear, I did not mean to stay so long. I will send you a note as soon as I may. Do you let me know if John has any plans that might interfere with your evening with us, so we can pick the best time." Back in the carriage, Catherine decided to return home. She wanted to enter her last purchases in the ledger and relax in her rooms before dressing for dinner. Even though she was planning to dine quietly at home with her mother and aunt, she suddenly felt the desire for a chance to rest. As the footman helped her out of the carriage, she directed him to carry the parcels from the Pantheon Bazaar up to her sitting room. Morrow bowed as he opened the door for her. "Welcome home, my lady. A few notes have come and are in the library. Viscountess Stanton and Madam St. Clair are entertaining visitors for tea in the drawing room." "Thank you, Morrow. I will attend to the notes later. I would appreciate some tea in my sitting room upstairs. Pray, do not interrupt my mother and aunt. I will see them at dinner."

Catherine mounted the stairs, and entered her sitting room. She was pleased to see the parcels on the table near the window. She unwrapped the shawls and took them to each lady's room. Returning to her own rooms, she removed her earbobs, slippers and gown. Slipping into a warm velvet dressing gown and slippers, she sat down near the fire, and leaned her head back. Sighing wearily, she stared into the dancing flames. Ideas for the dinner menu for next week, thoughts about what she would wear and how she would have the lace overdress made up, and plans for the school at Heyerwood all swirled through her mind. She closed her eyes, and within seconds was fast asleep.

She awoke an hour later, feeling much refreshed. Since she was dining at home, Catherine decided to wear the midnight blue velvet – it was pretty, but, more to the point, warm. Ringing for Jane, she washed quickly and took down her hair. As Jane entered, Catherine was slipping the sapphire earbobs into her earlobes. "Good evening, Jane, I'm all ready except for my dress and my hair. Something simple will be sufficient. I'm dining in, and expecting no visitors this evening." Seated before the dressing table, she sat lost in her plans for the dinner party next week, enjoying the gentle, yet thorough brushing that Jane gave her hair. Jane expertly twisted Catherine's hair into a simple knot at the nape of her neck. Catherine thanked her, saying "Very nicely done, as always, Jane. Now the dress." After hooking the back of the blue velvet gown, Jane hastily brushed the skirt. "Thank you, Jane. You needn't wait up for me this evening. I expect an early night, in any event."

As Catherine descended the stairs, she remembered the notes, and went directly to the library. The first was a thank-you note from Caroline, expressing her pleasure with the pink pearl pin, her regret at not getting to see Catherine before leaving for the country, and her hope that Catherine would write often. A letter from the bailiff outlined the matters he had in hand, which projects were completed, and suggestions for improvements to be done when the weather was warmer. The vicar wrote about the progress made in preparing the school, and provided a list of the neediest families in the district. Mrs. Davis sent a brief note, advising that all was in hand for Catherine's return, and providing a list of last-minute purchases needed. Reviewing Mrs. Davis' list, Catherine was pleased to see several items she had purchased that day. Recording that day's purchases into her ledger, she placed the ledger and notes in her desk, and closed it.

Entering the drawing room, she discovered her mother and aunt, sitting placidly near the fire. Mathilde was engaged in knotting a fringe, while Mary read aloud. Both ladies looked up with pleasure as Catherine entered the room, Mary putting her book aside and Mathilde stretching out her hand affectionately. As Catherine kissed her mother's cheek, her aunt exclaimed, "How lovely you look, my dear. That dress has ever been a favorite, and so practical for such a chilly evening!" Mathilde smiled and said, "Thank you for the lovely shawl, dear. As you see, it is perfect with this gown." Catherine smiled, and sat down. "Well, my dears, how was your day? I know you had callers for tea." Mathilde said quietly, "Michael came this morning just after you had gone. He was quite disappointed to have missed you, and I did not tell him it was purposeful. He seems to quite regret your estrangement, and cannot comprehend your feelings." Catherine replied, "Indeed, I am also disappointed in our falling out, but I cannot share his opinions, and will not accept his dictum that I avoid Rosalie. I cannot and will not accept his mother's viewpoint, and do not understand why Michael and his father acquiesce." Turning to her aunt, she said, "Aunt Mary, were there other visitors? I could hear voices when I came in, but was too fatigued for conversation."

The ladies became animated, discussing their afternoon callers. It seemed that, after Catherine's success at Julia's evening party, several ladies called to tell Mathilde and Mary about the evening. Catherine described Julia's decorations more fully, and the refreshments. When Morrow came in, Catherine suggested some sherry, with which the two older ladies concurred. Conversation became desultory as they sipped, relaxing by the fire. They took their glasses in to dinner with them. As they chatted while they dined, the ladies discussed a few novels, and the latest fashions. As they rose from the table, they could hear a knocking at the door. Passing from the dining room to the drawing room, they could hear voices in the hall. Just then, Morrow appeared in the drawing room door. "Mr. Stuart has called, my lady, and would like a word with you in the library, if quite convenient." "I will join him immediately, Morrow. Bring the brandy decanter and a glass for Mr. Stuart, and another glass of sherry for me, if you please." She turned to Mathilde and Mary. "Pray excuse me, Mother, Aunt Mary. Hopefully, I shall return shortly with Mr. Stuart."

Catherine entered her library to find Mr. Stuart standing by the fire. She extended her hand, and greeted him. "Please be seated, sir. How kind of you to call on such a bitter evening! What news have you?" Mr. Stuart beamed at Catherine. "My lady, I have such good news and could not wait to share it with you. Our efforts to purchase this house have been successful, even to the furnishings. This means you can take possession with minimal upheaval." "I am so pleased, Mr. Stuart! I have already asked Morrow if he would stay on, and he has accepted. If I can persuade the housekeeper, we will be splendidly served!" Catherine beamed back at Mr. Stuart as she continued, "And now sir, I have a proposition for you! I am hoping that, when you and my aunt are wed, you will take residence here. You will be doing me a great favor, as a house is always best kept occupied, and I believe we can make this a suitable place for you to use as a...a center for you. It is near enough to your offices, and is certainly an eligible address; we could certainly arrange a library and even a private entrance for your use, if you would prefer. This way, we can see much of each other when in town, and you and Aunt Mary will, of course, be welcome at Heyerwood any time your business and your inclinations permit. After several years on my own at Heyerwood, I am relishing having my family about me. What are your feelings, sir? Can you like my scheme?"

Mr. Stuart, slightly stunned, sat silently for a moment. "There is no doubt that your aunt and I have discussed a suitable residence, and were even considering this neighborhood." He continued, with dignity, "My situation is such that we can well afford to look about this area, and wanted to be near you and your mother. Have you discussed this plan with your mother and your aunt?" "No, dear sir, I wanted to discuss it with you first. If you found the idea inconvenient, for any reason, I did not want you to feel any awkwardness in refusing. However, I know my mother would be most pleased, as she is very close to my aunt, and has mentioned her pleasure at being able to be much with her." Mr. Stuart said slowly, "I would not want to be dependent on your generosity. However, if we can work out the expenses, speaking for myself, I could wish for nothing better. I have come to feel a great regard for you, and I know your aunt would be happy to remain a unit with you and your mother. Also, having our housing situation settled, your aunt and I could move up our marriage date." Beaming again, Catherine held out her hand and said, "Delightful! Have we arrived at a suitable moment, *Uncle* Miles?" Mr. Stuart laughed and took her hand. "I believe we have, my dear Catherine!"

Rising, they returned to the drawing room, where Mathilde and Mary were seated by the fire. Mr. Stuart bowed to Mathilde, and kissed Mary's hand. "Good evening, my lady. My dear, I must share with you your niece's scheme. If you approve, we can start to make our plans in earnest." Taking a seat next to Mary, he outlined Catherine's suggestion for their taking up residence in the townhouse. Mary glowed with delight, and said, "My dear, I would like it of all things. This house is so comfortable, and the location so convenient for Miles. We would be able to see so much of you both. Mathilde, you could stay in town as you chose, and you, Catherine, could come and go as you pleased, without having to worry about opening or closing the house." Mr. Stuart said, "I agree, my love, that the arrangement would be most pleasing. However, I want it clear that we will contribute our share to housekeeping costs and, if any alterations are required for our needs, we will pay for them. I cannot agree to hang on your niece's sleeve!" Mary looked at him with pride and said, "My dear Miles, I quite agree. Our taking residence here will allow me to be of more service to Catherine, as well as resolving our housing issues." Mathilde smiled warmly. "Allow me to say, sir, that I can think of nothing more delightful. My sister and I have so enjoyed spending our time together. I can only add that I am delighted our family is being increased so unexceptionably!"

Rising, Catherine rang the bell. When Morrow appeared, she said merrily, "Morrow, we are celebrating. A bottle of champagne and some glasses, if you please!" When the glasses were filled with the frothy wine, Catherine said, "I give you a toast…To Aunt Mary and Uncle Miles! Long may they live in peace and contentment." As they raised their glasses and toasted, Mathilde added, "To my dear sister and my new brother!" Seating themselves cozily before the fire, Catherine suggested that Mary and Miles take a tour of the house, to select rooms most suitable for their use. She also invited Mary and Miles to visit Heyerwood for the summer, so that any alterations in their chosen rooms could be done with little inconvenience. The talk then turned to general matters. They sat late before the fire, sipping their wine and chatting gaily.

Chapter 30

Catherine awoke exceptionally early the next morning. Irritatingly wide-awake, she rose, slipped on her cozy velvet robe and a pair of warm slippers, and went over to the windows. Pulling aside the heavy draperies, she looked out. It was just before dawn, and the darkness was just starting to lighten, a few faint streaks of lavender and rose at the edge of the horizon. Staring out, she mused over her future. There was no doubt that coming to town had given her greater pleasure than she had expected, and widened her acquaintance in ways she had not thought possible. Her deepening friendships with Caroline and Julia, and their families, was deeply satisfying and filled with the promise of future intimacy. Her acquaintance with her cousin Rosalie and her husband was an unexpected joy. After years of being controlled and confined, first by her father, then by her late husband's neglect and shocking reputation, Catherine felt like she had freedom and opportunities in plenty, with her country estate and the town house in London as anchors. Not even a year ago, she would have considered her cup overflowing.

Now, however, Catherine wondered about her purpose in life. Women her age, she found, were involved in their own families, their children. Bleakly, she remembered planning for children, especially a daughter. She recalled the schoolgirl plans she had made with Caroline, Julia and Maria: they would all marry in the first season, have several children and bring them up to be friends as their mothers had been. She had always assumed a happy marriage and children would be in her life. Although her friendship with Maria had ended, disappointingly, her friendships with Caroline and Julia were stronger than ever. She enjoyed her new relationship with Juliana, and hoped to be in the nature of an aunt to

Caroline's baby, and to Rosalie's children if she had any. She stared out the window, deep in thought. "I'm not too old to think of marrying and having a child. Women older than I am have children and survive. I'm only a year or so older than Caroline. I am approaching my thirty-first birthday, not my fiftieth!" Thoughts of Michael and James flashed through her mind. "I'm not completely old-cattish, or too long in the tooth. Two men have seemed to enjoy my company; it's not impossible that something more may come about."

She thought about Heyerwood. "Who will care for it when I'm gone?" she pondered. "I am responsible for so much. I must consider the future of the estate and its people." She thought about her plans for the school, the expansion of the orchard, and the new possibilities with sheep, wool, the dairy. "I must have a plan for continuity. I must be responsible; I can't just enjoy the pleasures of my rank and fortune without considering my duties." She remembered the scandals of the *Ton*, great families and their estates thrown into disarray because the irresponsibility of one individual, sometimes gambling, sometimes general profligacy. She had never wondered about the servants and tenants, dependent relations. How did they manage; where did they go after a great estate collapsed? Dejected, she felt unprepared, inadequate. "I was not brought up to handle these issues. I am so ignorant!" Mentally, she shook herself, remembering that, since her marriage to the late Earl, she had in fact managed the estate, made decisions and improvements. With the guidance of Mr. Stuart and her bailiff, she had made Heyerwood more secure and set it on a path of even more improvements.

Catherine watched the sky as the early dawn clouded over. Having a child, she thought, would give her a certain stability of purpose, a focus for creating a solid, stable home and estate, with someone to continue after her. Since her late husband had made it possible to name her own heir, and she had set up her own entail, she had the freedom to decide on an heir, or heiress. Struck, she though, "What about adoption? If I don't have a child of my own, I could adopt a child." She also considered that her cousin Rosalie was expecting a child, a relation of her own, who would not have a large expectation of his or her own. She could even consider Juliana as, if Julia's next child were a boy, he would be the heir, and Juliana could not expect more than her dowry and other possible settlements. Heartened, Catherine realized that, even though she did not yet know how she would resolve the issues, she had options to consider to ensure continuity to Heyerwood.

Suddenly, conscious of the chill, she went over to the fire, which had died down, and added some wood. She also lit the candles on the mantle and the lamp next to her bed. Crawling back under the quilts, Catherine reached for her book. Reading a few pages of the novel, she still felt restless, unable to concentrate. Placing the embroidered bookmark in the pages, she put the novel aside, and picked up her drawing pad and pencil. Catherine decided to sketch out a new design for embroidery, something larger to mount on a screen for the fireplace. "Spring is coming, and then summer. This will be something useful and pretty as well. Perhaps a wedding gift for Aunt Mary and Mr. Stuart to use in their rooms?" Absorbed, she sketched on, noting colour choices for the design on the margins. Suddenly, she was distracted by the rumble of thunder and a bolt of lightening. The new day dawning was a stormy one. She glanced at the mantle clock, and was shocked to see that it was already nine o'clock. More than a reasonable hour for her chocolate! Tugging the bell pull, she returned to her sketch, a large urn filled with her favorite flowers. Since it was to be mounted in a frame, a border of some type would look well, she thought.

Just then, Jane entered the room with her tray of chocolate. "My lady, it is a dreadful morning out. It is raining so hard, and the damp just creeps into your bones because it's still cold. I hope you do not have to go out this morning!" Smiling mischievously, Catherine sipped her chocolate. "Thank you, Jane, you know exactly how I like it. Fortunately, I have no engagements today, and expect no callers. Frankly, I have no intention of leaving my fireside today! I see no reason to even get out of my dressing gown at present." Jane noted the novel and the drawing pad. "I see you have been awake for some time, my lady. You should have rung." Distressed, Jane moved to the windows to fling back the other draperies. Catherine could see the heavy grey clouds, and the rain splashing in torrents onto the balcony. "I could not sleep, so I occupied myself. Why should I deprive you of your rest? You take such care of me, Jane. I do appreciate your hard work." Jane crimsoned, and curtsied briefly. "My lady, it is a pleasure to work for you. You always notice the efforts made, and remember the feelings of those whom you employ." Catherine, touched, replied, "Why, Jane, how could I not notice? You and the others work so hard. I could not manage without you all."

Catherine stared out at the dull day. Impulsively, she said, "Jane, since I have no immediate plans to get up, and certainly no plans to go out, why do not you take some time for yourself? Write to your family, sew, whatever you wish. Of course, it would not replace your regular day; it would just be some time to occupy as you choose. Go out if you wish; be sure to wrap up well if you do." Flushed with pleasure and surprise, Jane dropped a curtsey and said, "Thank you, my lady! A few hours would be lovely. May I...may I borrow a book from the library? I would take the greatest care of it, my lady. I saw a copy of *THE RECESS* by Mistress Sophia Lee on a bottom shelf. It's ever so exciting. My sister once read me a chapter of it, but my father took the book away before we could finish it." Catherine smiled, and said, "By all means, finish your novel, Jane. It is a bit out of date, is it not?" Earnestly, Jane said, "I don't care for that, my lady. I will be most careful, and return it as soon as possible." She hurried from the room, smiling.

Catherine relaxed against her pillows again, sipping her chocolate and watching the rain cascade over the balcony rail. Putting her pad and pencils aside, she took up her book again. This time, she lost herself in the story and read on for a few hours. She was startled by a tap on the door. Aunt Mary peeped in and said, "May I come in, dear?" "By all means, Aunt. Pray do." Mary closed the door and sat down in a small armchair by the fire. "You look quite cozy and comfortable, my dear. You have chosen a sensible place to spend such a dreary day!" Catherine chuckled and said, "At least, you did not call me a lazy bones! I feel quite decadent lounging in bed like this, but, in truth, the weather is so dreadful, I could not bear to get up." Mary leaned forward, asking, "Are you feeling quite the thing, dear? If you are coming down with an epidemic cold or putrid sore throat..." Catherine smiled and replied, "No, nothing like that, Aunt. I am just taking advantage of the opportunity to do nothing. I have even given Jane the day to herself. I am in the coziest place I can imagine, and, with my books and embroidery, can entertain myself without cold toes. If I desire, I may even nap!" Mary laughed and said, "Well, I daresay there is one thing you have forgot, which is food!"

Conscience-stricken, Catherine stared at her aunt. "My dear Aunt Mary, forgive me! I have not ordered a single meal for today! No, nor even thought of it! What must you and Mother think of me?" Mary chuckled and said, "Well, my dear, as to that, I myself spoke with the housekeeper and ordered breakfast for Mathilde and myself. If I may suggest, I will be delighted to order luncheon, tea and dinner as well. If you agree, I will be happy to have your meals brought on a tray if it pleases you." Catherine smiled gratefully and said, "Pray do take charge, my love. All shall be as you wish! I must say that luncheon and tea before my own fire sound delightful, but I will join you and Mother for dinner. If you wish to invite guests, please do so." Roguishly, she suggested, "You may wish to send a note to Mr. Stuart. If he is willing to leave his own fireside to dine informally, he is always a delightful companion. He may as well have the opportunity to get to know us!" Blushing slightly, Mary smiled and replied, "Happily, Mr. Stuart has sent a note asking if he might impose on us this evening. I ventured to respond that it would be considered no imposition, but a welcome diversion from such a gloomy downpour." Mary rose and kissed Catherine's cheek. "You shall have a lovely luncheon in a trice, my love." Catherine got out of bed and spread up the covers. She put on the slippers matching her warm robe, and sat down in the chair by the fire. Staring into the flames, she mused over her wardrobe drying to decide what to wear for dinner. Dining *en famille* as they were, she would not wear an evening gown, but the warmest velvet gown she possessed. Torn between the midnight blue with the high neck and the violet, she considered. Both gowns were long-sleeved and appropriate. She settled on the violet, with her pearl earbobs. Just then, there was a tap on the door, and the housemaid entered with a tray. Her luncheon already!

Chapter 31

That evening, as Catherine, Mathilde, Aunt Mary and Mr. Stuart lingered over their last course, Morrow entered the room. Bowing slightly, he said, "My lady, Baron Ridley, and Mr. and Lady Ridley have called. I've taken the liberty of putting them in the drawing room. What message may I give?" Flushing with pleasure, Catherine said, "Oh, Morrow, bid them most welcome and provide some refreshment...tea or sherry for Rosalie, as she chooses, and brandy for the gentlemen. Pray assure them we will be with them in a trice!" As Morrow left the room, Mathilde said, "How delightful this is, to have family calling on such a dreary evening! With Mr. Stuart and ourselves, we will have a merry group indeed!" They hastily finished, and rose from the table.

James and John rose from their seats by the fire as the ladies and Mr. Stuart entered the room. Smiling mischievously, Rosalie said, "You did indicate that you would be at home to callers, cousin!" Catherine laughed and said, "Indeed I did, and am delighted you took me up so promptly! Good company is just what we need this evening. You were so brave to venture out into such a dreary, rainy night." She curtsied slightly to James and John. "I stand on no ceremony tonight, gentlemen. You must resign yourselves to a family party!" As the rest of the group greeted each other and chatted comfortably, James took Catherine slightly aside. "I am delighted not to be a ceremonial visitor, ma'am. Being treated as...family is just what I had in mind." Blushing, Catherine looked up at him, unsure what to say. His deep blue eyes gazed directly into hers. She smiled slightly, and withdrew her hand, annoyed at her own tongue-tiedness. Looking over her shoulder, she saw that Mary and Mr. Stuart were seated on a sofa near the fire, with Rosalie and John in armchairs nearby. Mathilde was seated in a chair next to the fire, with her netting in hand. "A cozy group, indeed," said James, softly. Flustered, Catherine moved to the piano-forte. Seating herself, she began to play a simple air, just to busy herself. "This is foolish!" she scolded herself. "You are almost one-and-thirty, and have been out for years. A widow, in truth! A little, mild flirtation should not be such a shock." Catherine smiled up at James as he stood near the piano-forte. "And how have you occupied yourself today, sir? Surely such inclement weather prevented you from the amusements in town!" James replied with a grin, "Frankly, ma'am, I stayed in the sitting room, pretending to read, while I pondered how long I must wait to make a call on you. The weather, in truth, became my excuse – I thought that, after a day inside, you might welcome a little leavening! Rosalie and John were ready for a change of scene, and were delighted for the opportunity to spend a little more time with you and your relations before we all adjourn to the country, so the thing was done quite easily."

Blushing again, Catherine smiled and said, "Indeed, pleasant company is always a delight. Mother and Aunt Mary are so pleased to spend as much time as possible with my cousin and her family." "And is it a pleasure for you, ma'am?" he said softly, so the group by the fire could not hear. "To be plain, my lady, I did not give a fig if Rosalie or John accompanied me. I was determined to see you this evening." Speechless, Catherine looked up at him, her hands still on the keyboard. She saw the warmth in his eyes. Withdrawing imperceptibly, she faltered, "My lord, indeed, you are always..." Leaning closer, James said, "My dear Catherine, do not hide behind empty platitudes. You must know I have no uncommon pleasure in spending time with you. I tolerate missishness from my friends' daughters, but not from you! To be clear, I desire to court you, to get to know you properly. I do not wish to embarrass or distress you, but I must know if this would be distasteful or unwelcome to you. You are not a debutante in her first season; you are a woman, fully in charge of her own life. I hope you can plainly tell me your feelings." Her poise in tatters and her cheeks scarlet, Catherine rose precipitously and walked to the window, James behind her. "It is not missishness, but surprise, my lord, that affects me! You must know that I had no expectation of...of such a topic of conversation this evening! I had not thought... James took her hand firmly and interrupted, "Well, think on it now! You are planning to return to your estate, and I have business that requires my presence abroad. If you cannot like the idea, say so; we can go our separate ways and, if we meet in future, need feel no awkwardness. However, if you do not object to my courtship, I must consider how best to conclude my business and call on you in the countryside." Deliberately moving away from her, toward the fire, James entered the general conversation.

Speechless, Catherine reseated herself at the piano-forte. Playing one simple tune after another, she thought about James' words. She felt distinctly outraged at having this sprung at her in such a way, but was undeniably flattered. She remembered their first meeting, and the evening of Julia's party. Mr. Stuart had checked his credentials thoroughly, at her own request. She also, uncomfortably, remembered their conversation in the street. Considering everything honestly, she had to admit to herself, at least, that the idea of being courted was…pleasing. Lifting her eyes to gaze at the group around the fire laughing and chatting, she caught his gaze fixed on her with warmth and a question in its depths. Blushing deeply, she lowered her gaze to her hands and finished the last melody. Catherine rose in response to a question from her mother, and joined the group by the fire. The rest of the evening passed merrily, with James making no further attempt at private conversation. A game of lottery tickets left them laughing helplessly. As the clock struck the hour, Rosalie said guiltily, "My dear cousin, I never meant to stay so late! I vow, I have not so enjoyed an evening in an age. It is a shame we are leaving town so soon. There is all to do, and I must rise early." John rose and helped Rosalie to her feet. Mr. Stuart also rose. "I, too, must take my leave, as I must be in chambers tomorrow." As the group entered the hall, making their farewells, Morrow and a footman appeared to help the guests into their wraps. Catherine turned, to find James at her elbow. Before she could speak, he took her hand and kissed it as he bowed. Looking at her intently, he asked, "Will I find you at home tomorrow, Catherine, in the afternoon?" Blushing slightly, she replied, "Of course, sir, I am always at home to my friends."

As the door shut behind her guests, Catherine found herself alone in the hall. Climbing the stairs to her own rooms, she pondered James' words at the piano-forte again. Seating herself at her dressing table, she stared into her own eyes as she removed her earbobs and took down her hair. "What do I *really* want?" she mused. "I have total independence and control of my own affairs now. If I marry, of necessity, I will lose some of that as the law will consider what is mine to be my husband's, even though Mr. Stuart has helped me arranged things to prevent a total reversion. And marriage will help me try to achieve an heir of my own, to ensure the future as much as is possible. James is…very attractive and intelligent. But he moves so fast! Mayhap, too fast for my peace of mind. I must not be pushed, or coerced.

I must be allowed to know my own mind and heart. Can he respect that?" She shivered as she thought of the way her father had brutally thrust her into marriage with the Earl of Heyerwood, and the years of isolation it had brought her. "Never again will I allow any man to ride roughshod over me. Even though he may be offended or disappointed, I will have to have the time I need to make a decision. This is not just about James. I must consider my own wishes, and the welfare of my people at Heyerwood. Will James be willing to spend time there, and let me continue to manage my property, or will he expect his estate to take precedence, to profit at the expense of mine? It has happened before, that assets from one property were drained to improve another, resulting in ruin. I must know him better, and I must know my own mind!"

As Jane helped her out of her gown and into her night rail, Catherine pushed all thoughts of James and courtship aside. As she cleaned her teeth, she resolved to read a bit more of her novel before blowing her lamp out to sleep; *PRIDE AND PREJUDICE* was an intriguing title, and she was finding the story very much to her taste. "Let tomorrow take care of itself. If he wants frankness, he shall have it in full measure!" Settling herself amongst her pillows, she lost herself in her novel.

Chapter 32

Catherine rose early, and dressed warmly in the brown sarcenet day dress. She selected the coral cameo earbobs and brooch. Her brown hair braided into a coronet, she descended for breakfast. Her mother and aunt were breakfasting in their rooms, as usual, so she looked over a variety of notes, letters, and advertisements that had been delivered. After finishing her morning coffee, she went to the library to answer her correspondence. She wrote notes to Howard and Mrs. Davis at Heyerwood, telling them when she planned to return, and giving some instructions for turning the former state apartments into a suite for her aunt and Mr. Stuart to use after their marriage. "The small library and sitting room will give them privacy and a place for him to read and work when they are in residence. Their warmth and happiness will exorcise the past from those rooms better than anything else!" Catherine also wrote to the vicar, advising him of her impending return and asking him to let her know of any necessary last-minute purchases needed for the tenants, the school, or anyone else in the parish. She then wrote brief notes for Caroline and Julia, letting them know when she was departing from town, to be sent to their country estates. Next, she prepared instructions for the housekeeper and Morrow for packing, closing rooms, and other preparations for the departure. She prepared menus for the next few days' meals. All she had left to decide was which gowns to take with her, and which to leave. Busily making notes, Catherine did not hear the butler until he coughed discreetly. "My lady, you have a caller. Viscount Stanton has requested a few moments. I have asked him to wait in the drawing room. What would you have me tell him, Lady Heyerwood?" For a moment, Catherine sat, rigid with shock. Her father, here! What could he want? Her thoughts in a whirl, she said calmly,

146

"Thank you, Morrow. Pray tell him I will join him in a few moments, and offer him refreshments-tea or coffee, I think, will be sufficient. And Morrow...pray, have a footman within call." Morrow bowed silently and left the room. Catherine sat, breathing deeply, gathering control. When she had mastered herself, she rose and walked slowly and deliberately to the drawing room.

Her father stood before the fire, a cup of tea poured, but untasted, on a table near him. As she entered the room, he swung around to face her. "So nice of you to join me, my lady!" he sneered. "What do you mean, keeping me waiting like this?" Seating herself without haste near the tea tray, Catherine poured out a cup and took a sip. "As to that, Father, I might ask you to what I owe this...unlooked for attention? I was not expecting to see you this morning." Looking at him calmly and deliberately, she was shocked to see how thin, pale and...*old* her father looked. "Come, sir," she said quietly, "surely, you have a reason for calling? I find it hard to believe you have sought me out for the pleasure of my company." His eyes glared angrily, and he made an uncontrolled motion with his hand, but she refused to flinch and met his gaze directly. Visibly swallowing his spleen, he forced himself to sit down. "Well, Catherine," he said icily, "you are no more dutiful a daughter than you were when last we met. However, you are correct in assuming that I have a reason for calling. I have discovered through my man of business that you were the party who paid off my debts. I wanted to discuss a business matter with you...." "Stop, Father, not a word more! I am sorry that that was disclosed to you. I must make it clear that I have no intention of franking you! You should have more than enough remaining to live comfortably if you refrain from excessive gambling and speculation. Between the marriage settlements and the satisfaction of these last debts, you have more than realized a return on my dowry. Let that be an end to it." she said coldly.

Shocked, her father stared at her. Catherine looked at him calmly, and said, "If there is nothing else, Father, will you not have some more tea? I am sure yours must be cold by now." Swallowing, he said softly, "You jade, how dare you speak to me so? I am your father and demand your respect...." Cutting him off, she said, "I would give you respect had you given me reason. You have cared nothing for my mother or for me; all you have done or thought of is for your own comfort, your own advancement. Fortunately, sir, I am not dependent on your...generosity or good will, for you have none! Now, sir, I repeat, if there is nothing else, we can have tea like civilized beings, or I will wish you good morning. The choice is yours."

His face deeply flushed and engorged, and his eyes glittering with wrath, her father rose slowly. Through gritted teeth, he said, "Take care, my girl. If you have a care for your mother, you'd best take care…!" Clenching his fists, he started toward her. She rose and pulled the bell pull. As the door opened behind him, Viscount Stanton started and turned. Clutching his throat, he gasped and reeled. "Morrow," said Catherine, "Pray stay here while I send the footman for…" Just then, her father, his face purple, gasped again and collapsed. Stunned, Catherine and the butler stared down at him. Gathering her wits, Catherine grasped a cushion and slipped it under her father's head, as she instructed Morrow to send the footman for a doctor and return immediately. "Under no circumstances should my mother or my aunt be allowed to enter this room without being told that my father is here and taken ill. I would not have them shocked for the world." After covering the viscount with a rug, she rose and, when Morrow returned, requested him to bring some brandy. Pouring out a glass, she took a small sip, made a face, and took another. Feeling steadier, she picked up the glass again, and knelt down. "Father, pray sip some of this. You will feel more the thing." When he did not respond, she held the glass to his lips, but the brandy trickled out of the corner of his mouth and he neither choked nor swallowed.

Just then, Mathilde and Mary entered the room. Both women stared in horror at the viscount lying on the floor. Mathilde shook Mary's hand from her arm, and came forward. "Catherine, my dear, what has happened here? Is your father…?" "Pray, Mama, will you and Aunt Mary not go to the morning room? I have sent for a doctor, but I fear it may be too late… he is so still and I cannot tell if he is even breathing!" Mathilde stood looking at her husband silently, then knelt beside him. "Gerard," she said firmly, "if you can hear me, you must make a sign!" The swollen, purple face did not change for a moment, then the eyelids flickered. Putting her hand on his shoulder, she said quietly to Catherine, "My dear, it is my duty to be here with your father. I am his wife, after all." The eyes opened, and the viscount looked at her, struggling to speak. As he gasped for breath, a tear formed and rolled won his cheek. Still looking at Mathilde, he struggled for a moment, then collapsed. After a moment, Mathilde put out her hand, and closed the staring eyes. Rising to her feet, she said quietly, "My dear, I am afraid your father is dead." Mary, Catherine and Mathilde all stood uncertainly, looking at the body at their feet. The door opened again. Morrow came in and said anxiously, "My lady, the doctor and Mr. Stuart are both here…I hope…?" Stepping carefully around the remains of the man she had feared and hated for so long, Catherine said, "Morrow, please show them in immediately, although I fear it is too late for the doctor to be of help to Viscount Stanton. My mother or my aunt may need his services." She sat down rather heavily in her chair, and said, "Mother, Aunt, pray sit down."

Mr. Stuart hurried in and went straight to Mary. Putting his arm around her, he led her away from the fire to a seat near the window, saying tenderly, "Sit here, quietly, my love. All will be well." Mathilde, in the meantime, had seated herself on the settee, and was sipping a small glass of brandy, calmly. The doctor knelt by the viscount, loosening his neckcloth and feeling for a pulse. Finding none, he held a mirror before the viscount's nose and mouth with no result. "I fear, Lady Heyerwood, that your honored parent is no more. What has happened here?" Steadily, Catherine said, "We were discussing a matter of business, and Viscount Stanton became... enraged. His face turned purple and swollen, he couldn't breathe, and he... collapsed. It was so quick!" Her eyes filled with tears, which she blinked away. "Doctor, Mr. Stuart, what must we do?" The doctor and Mr. Stuart conferred in low tones. The doctor went to Mathilde, bowed, and asked, "Lady Stanton, do you know aught of this? What of your late husband's health?" Mathilde looked at Mr. Stuart and the doctor. "Gentlemen, you must know that my husband's health of late has not been good, and he has ever had a choleric temper. This...could have happened anytime these last few years."

Mr. Stuart asked, "My lady, what arrangements would you prefer?" Mathilde replied, "Gerard must be given the respect due his position. I know he would want to be laid out in his home, and buried in the family vault here in town. Pray contact the vicar of our parish, and arrange for the funeral. I wish it to be held with all dignity, but as quickly and as quietly as possible. Gerard had...few friends, so there is no reason to prolong matters." Looking at Mr. Stuart, she added, "You know his man of business, I believe. He will have any will that Gerard may have made, and will be aware of how his business matters stand." Rising, Mathilde said with dignity. "I am going to my room to rest, and to gather my thoughts. Catherine, pray send word to the Viscount's housekeeper and butler to start preparations, and advise them that I will be returning tomorrow." She left the room, walking slowing but steadily, her head high. Mr. Stuart gave Morrow and the footmen low-voiced instructions, and said firmly, "Mary, Catherine, this is not fit for you. Please allow me to see to the removal of the Viscount and the necessary arrangements. You may wait in the morning room, if you do not wish to retire to your rooms to recover a little." The two ladies rose and, clasping each other's hands, started for the door. Looking over her shoulder, Catherine said, with gratitude and affection, "Thank you for your kindness, sir. I know I should not take such advantage of you, but I believe I must!" With a wavering smile, she led Mary from the room and closed the door.

Chapter 33

Ten days later, Catherine was in her coach, on her journey back to Heyerwood. Staring out the window at the grey landscape, she pondered recent events. The announcement of her father's death in the *Times*, the funeral arrangements, the funeral itself were all resolved so quickly. Neither she, nor her mother, nor her aunt, attended the funeral, of course. Mr. Stuart and her father's man of business had attended to all arrangements. After a quiet funeral, her father had been interred in the family vault with due respect, if little mourning. The day after the funeral, her father's will was read and entered into probate. Viscountess Stanton had been left her jointure, an additional sum of money, and some jewels that were unentailed. Neither Catherine nor Aunt Mary had been mentioned. The title and the entailed properties were left to a distant cousin, of whom Catherine had never heard. This cousin was, even now, making his way to London in a leisurely fashion. Her mother was staying in town, to give proper recognition to the new head of the family, with Mary's support, but both ladies would follow her to Heyerwood as soon as the necessary formalities were concluded. "Your presence is not necessary, my dear. It is not as if Gerard's heir had ever shown interest in the family. Of course, Gerard never mentioned him, either. It's to be hoped that the new viscount's branch of the family is of a more…equable temper!"

Mr. Stuart and Jane were accompanying Catherine to Heyerwood, with Mr. Stuart planning an immediate return to town. Hopefully, the journey would not require more than two nights on the road. Catherine closed her eyes, suddenly longing for her room and the peace of the garden. After an uneventful and rather tedious journey, enlivened only by brief stops to change horses, snatch a hasty meal, and to rest for the night, the coach finally rumbled up the last length of the drive, and halted before the door. Howard and the footman appeared before the coach had fully stopped. "Your ladyship, I hope your journey was pleasant. Welcome home!" said Howard, as the footman assisted the passengers from the coach. Catherine smiled, and replied, "Well enough. We had only two nights on the road, as I had desired. I am so glad to be here! It seems like an age since we left. How are you, Howard, and Mrs. Davis?" "We are all well, my lady, and delighted to have you with us again. All of the rooms are prepared." A few hours later, after a rest, a bath and changing to her violet velvet, Catherine descended the stairs, and entered the drawing room, to find Mr. Stuart awaiting her.

Catherine came up to the fire and seated herself in her favorite chair. "Mr. Stuart, will you join me in a glass of sherry before dinner, or would you prefer something else?" Turning from the window, he smiled and replied, "Frankly, my dear, I would prefer a glass of brandy. The coach was comfortable enough, but travelling in this raw weather, between winter and spring, makes me feel cold to my toes. Your aunt desired me to make her apologies; she would have preferred to accompany you, but felt that your mother was correct in wishing to greet the new viscount and wanted to support her in what may be a difficult time. You and I can enjoy a comfortable coze. If you are agreeable, I thought I would spend tomorrow conferring with the bailiff and reviewing the estate books. I have no need, and, indeed, no desire to rush back quite immediately!" Catherine laughed and said, "Frankly, 'Uncle Miles,' I am delighted that you will spend a few days with me! I am sorry Aunt Mary did not come with us, but I quite understand her feelings. I, too, offered my support to my mother, but she was quite adamant that I return home, and I am not sorry that I did so." Mr. Stuart nodded his appreciation to Howard for the glass and decanter, and poured out a glass of brandy for himself, while Howard served sherry to Catherine. Sipping silently, they sat comfortably by the fire. "How pleasant this is!" observed Catherine, "And tonight, we will be able to enjoy a delicious dinner ordered by Mrs. Davis, and retire without concerns. I did enjoy my visit to London, but I find traveling to be exhausting, even with careful planning and arrangements." Mr. Stuart agreed. "I, too, find coaching inns to be somewhat lacking. They always seem cold and, when crowded, accommodation is not what one could wish."

As they dined, Mr. Stuart suddenly asked, "Were you shocked by your father's will, my dear? Is there some item you were expecting…?" Catherine shook her head. "No, dear sir, there is nothing I expected from my father.

I would have been surprised had he remembered me in his will. Frankly, I was pleased and somewhat astonished that he had had such care for my mother. Before I left, Mother and I discussed this, and I could think of nothing that I want. Upon my marriage, my personal effects were shipped here, including my late grandmother's worktable, which was a bequest, and a few other items my mother wanted me to have. Any jewels that had been given to me, I brought with me. It is sad, is it not, to think how little my father thought of me, or, at the end, I of him? I am glad to have been spared the funeral arrangements, and meeting the new viscount. I believe my mother is finding some comfort in this business, but I know she is looking forward to returning here. There is no dower house, but she will not have to accept any offer of housing or other assistance from the heir, unless she chooses. Have you had any contact with him, Mr. Stuart? I do not even know his name!"

Mr. Stuart nodded, "Yes, I did get a response to my letter. His name is Mr. Martin St. Clair St. John Stanton. I believe his mother was distantly related to your aunt's deceased husband. He has been living in family holdings in the north. I know little of him, but understand that the holdings are considerable. Your late parent's man of business mentioned that he had approached them on the Viscount's behalf many years ago, and their refusal to frank him resulted in the breach with your aunt. He and his family have not spent much time in London, preferring to sojourn in Bath when not at home on their estates. The new Viscount Stanton is married, but, as yet, has no children." "Indeed!" said Catherine, somewhat staggered. "I seem to have numerous relatives who prefer anywhere to London, of whom I have never heard until recently! First, Michael and his family on my mother's side, now Martin and his on my father's! How odd, to be so unconnected all of my life, and now to find all of these new relations." They finished their dinner quietly, and then, both fatigued from the long journey, retired to their respective rooms.

Catherine changed into her night rail and a warm robe, and sat before the fire in her sitting room. Her novel in her lap, she gazed drowsily into the flames. Her thoughts slipped to her mother, hoping that the new viscount was kind and well mannered, able to appreciate her mother's thoughtfulness. Then thoughts of James surfaced. Unconsciously, she had expected to hear from him, at least when the notice of her father's death was published. She was somewhat piqued that she had not heard received any word at all. So much for his protestations of interest in her! Resolutely, she opened her novel and read a few pages before deciding to retire to sleep.

Awakening early in the morning, Catherine faced a small dilemma. What to do about mourning? The death of a parent usually required at least six months of black, preferably nine months, and then half mourning for the rest of the year. Not surprisingly, Catherine found herself unwilling to don the heavy blacks she had put aside just months ago. Rebelliously, she thought, "I will not go into black for him! At least, David was kind, and I was able to regret his death. My father thought even less of me than I of him, and black would be almost blasphemous! My father was almost as unacceptable to Society as my husband."

As Catherine pondered her wardrobe, Jane came in with her morning tea. "Jane, what can I do? I should go into mourning, but I CAN'T go back into black again!" Jane stood beside her mistress, perusing the gowns in the wardrobe. "If I might suggest, my lady, for this morning, the plum wool would be suitable for day wear. It is close enough to the lavenders and purples of half-mourning to be discreet, and the colour is vastly becoming," she said with a twinkle. "You also have the burgundy crepe, the dark forest green, and the brown sarcenet for day. If your ladyship feels the need, I could use some black velvet ribbon to change the trimmings, and you could wear your pearl earbobs with no necklace or brooch. For evening, you have the violet velvet, the midnight blue velvet, and the violet silk. If you desire, my lady, we could send for some black lace to change the ruffles, and to make a cap or two, for the conventions. However, as you are in the country, at present, you may think it unnecessary. If you plan to return to town within the next six months or so, however, you may wish to consider the need for more formalized mourning attire, my lady." After Catherine finished her tea, Jane helped her into the suggested plum wool day dress. With a trifle of ecru lace on her hair, and no jewels but her pearl earbobs and her wedding ring, Catherine was satisfied with her appearance. "Thank you, Jane, you were absolutely right. This is the perfect compromise. Hopefully, no one will be shocked at my lack of filial respect at this time." She dismissed Jane, and descended to the dining room for breakfast.

Chapter 34

Catherine was seated in the drawing room by the window, working on the embroidery she had designed, when Howard announced that the vicar and his wife had called. Putting her work aside, she rose and said, "Show them in, Howard and ask Mrs. Davis to send up some tea and refreshments, if you please." As Howard bowed the Vicar and Mrs. Lamb into the room, she went to them, extending her hand in welcome. "How good of you to call! Pray, sit here by the fire and get warm. I hope you will join me in some tea presently." Shaking hands with the Vicar and his wife, she guided them to the settee by the fire, and seated herself in an armchair opposite. Mrs. Lamb leaned forward with a smile, "We are so glad you have returned, my lady, but were so sorry to hear of your father's death. It must have been such a shock for you and your family. I hope Viscountess Stanton and Madam St. Clair are well." Catherine smiled back, and said, "Thank you for your concern. My mother and aunt are quite well. They are staying in town, to show the new Viscount over the house. Then, my mother and aunt will be returning here. We will be spending the next few months here, quietly. The situation has been quite…exhausting."

Eager to change the subject, Catherine turned to the vicar and said, "I ordered quantities of supplies for the school and for the apothecary while I was in London, sir. I hope the deliveries have not inconvenienced you?" "Indeed, no, ma'am. Such 'inconvenience' is delightful, as everything is needed and will be used with appreciation. I venture to say, we are ready for almost anything now." He looked at his wife, and said, "My dear, you must tell Lady Heyerwood what plans have been made for the school." Catherine said, "Yes, indeed, Mrs. Lamb. Pray, tell me, when do you expect the school to open?" "As to that, your ladyship, I am not quite sure, and was hoping you could advise me. As you know, spring is fast approaching, and many of the children will be required to help with the spring planting, the lambing season, and so forth. They will be needed through the summer and the harvest. Many of the parents do not see the value of education, and fear it will put the wrong ideas into their children's heads, make them discontented. However, I hate to have the school sit idle until after harvest." Pondering the issue, Catherine asked, "Are there any older children with a desire to learn, or, for that matter, any adults, who would be willing to spend time in the evening? It would be a simple matter to provide a few lamps and, if we had a willing schoolmaster or mistress, we could open the school for those students during the summer evenings. Then we could start the regular classes in the fall and winter for the rest of the children. If there are any young people seeking advancement or a profession, this might be appealing because adults may feel foolish or uncomfortable, sharing lessons with young children."

Warming to the idea, Mrs. Lamb took up the suggestion. "We could offer some handwork classes, such as mending and darning of fine linen, and embroidery. With basic reading, writing and arithmetic, such lessons would fit a person for any station in life, but would not place them too high above their families. Even if they only come to two or three evenings a week, they could reap such benefit! Do you think a schoolmaster would be willing to work on such a basis, though? It is not the usual routine." Catherine frowned, "Indeed, that could be a problem. However, if we make it part of the terms, and offer a good wage with comfortable living quarters, I should think a schoolmaster or schoolmistress would be willing at least to try. If necessary, we could offer a period of trial before signing a contract. I would think a true educationist would be delighted to have willing and interested students, would not you? Vicar, you could help by stressing the importance of reading the Bible for oneself!" The Vicar laughed and said, "As to that, I have already had a few adults ask for some help. Many of the villagers do know their letters and can read a little, as well as sign their names. I also know a few of the older girls want to go into service, and would be eager for just such lessons as you have discussed. If we could recruit a sympathetic schoolmaster or mistress, one who could approach older students without condescension, who is willing to work with them at times convenient for them, we may actually have more students than we expect!"

Catherine asked, "Have we any candidates for teaching the school as of yet? I did not want to advertise myself, until I could discuss it with you. Are there any local candidates, or would it be better to bring in a complete stranger?" As they sipped tea, and discussed the selection of a suitable teacher, the Vicar caught sight of the waning daylight. "My dear Lady Heyerwood, forgive our taking so much of your time," he said remorsefully. "We can pursue this matter another day. I am persuaded we have delayed you." He rose, and helped Mrs. Lamb to her feet. Catherine rose also. "Pray, Mr. Lamb, do not apologize. It has been a delightful afternoon, and I have so enjoyed discussing these issues with you both." Turning to Mrs. Lamb, she said impulsively, "I hope you will let me assist in other areas as well. I would appreciate your advice and guidance. I am still learning some of my duties, and would be so grateful." Obviously, this was the right thing to say, as Mrs. Lamb beamed and pressed her hand. "My dear Lady Heyerwood, I have several projects I was only waiting for the right moment to lay before you! However, Mr. Lamb is right; we have imposed enough for one day." Howard opened the door to the hall and bowed, "Your carriage is at the door, sir." The Vicar said, "That's right, Howard, awake on every suit as always!" The Vicar bowed, and the ladies curtsied slightly. "Good afternoon, Mr. and Mrs. Lamb. We will discuss these matters further very soon," said Catherine as they left the drawing room.

Thinking of this conversation as she worked, Catherine was seated in the drawing room a few days later, occupied with her embroidery again. The urn and flowers had progressed, the colours bright and glowing. Attired in the sherry brown sarcenet, with ivory lace covering her hair, and her pearl earbobs shimmering in the late morning sunshine, she was startled to hear a coach on the drive. She laid aside her work, and rose. Hearing voices in the hall, she started toward the door, just as Howard entered and announced, "Lady Stanton and Madam St. Clair have arrived, my lady. I will have Mrs. Davis see that their rooms are prepared immediately." Catherine stepped forward to embrace her mother and aunt. "Mother, Aunt Mary, how delightful to see you! Why did you not send me word, so we could have all in readiness? I am so glad you are come home!" Flushed and smiling, the three ladies took seats near the fire. "How delightful this is!" sighed Mathilde, stretching her hands to the blaze. "It is not near so cold now, but somehow the coach always seems so damp and chilly. The fireside is most welcome." Mary agreed, and took a sip of tea, saying, "I must confess that this chair feels like air after all those hours on the road." Catherine leaned back in her chair, and asked, "What of the new Viscount? I hope he appreciated your staying to welcome him. What did you think of my cousin Martin?" The two older ladies looked at each other significantly. "Well, my dear," said Mathilde, "he was all condescension. Would you not agree, Mary?" "Indeed, yes," replied Aunt Mary. Tartly, she added, "If he had held himself any higher, he would have fallen over backward. Apparently, he assumed we were going to cast ourselves at his feet!" Amused, Catherine looked at her mother. "What, did he fear he was going to have to shelter us from the stormy blast?" Mathilde smiled and said blandly, "Let us say, rather, that he was prepared to shoulder more responsibility than required. I vow, he was disappointed when he realized that, so far from being our savior, we were only there to make him acquainted with his new dignity."

Catherine raised her eyebrows, and asked, "Ah? And just why did he think you and Aunt Mary would require such...assistance?" Mary replied, "Well, my love, apparently Gerard had not kept Martin apprised of our family circumstances. It appears that he assumed all three of us were in need of guidance and support. I quite enjoyed telling him of your situation, generosity and kindness, of my impending marriage, and, of course, that Gerard had provided for Mathilde. I vow, he looked quite chagrined to think that we had no need of his patronage!" "He did say that he intended to visit you here in the country, to be certain you stood in no need of his guidance. I assured him that, with us, and, of course, Mr. Stuart and your excellent bailiff, you managed quite well. I ventured to suggest that he send a letter advising of his intention before departing town, in the event you might be from home. My dear, I dare swear that the thought you wouldn't be awaiting his convenience never entered his head!" Catherine shrugged slightly, and dismissed all thought of her cousin, with the remark that she would be happy to make his acquaintance, as long as he did not try to interfere with her affairs.

Catherine then turned to a far more interesting topic of conversation, her conversation with Mr. and Mrs. Lamb regarding the plans for the school. "The Vicar has placed advertisements in the London and Bath newspapers. With so many seminaries in Bath, we may be able to attract an experienced teacher wanting to make a change," she concluded. Just then, Miss Potter appeared at the drawing room door. After a brief curtsey, she addressed Lady Stanton, "My lady, you said you would be right up. Your bath water is getting cold, and you need to rest if you are thinking of coming down to dinner...." Remorsefully, Catherine gave her mother a quick hug, and said, "Dear Mother, pray, go up and be cozy for a little. We can talk more at dinner." She directed a laughing glance at Miss Potter, and said, "I forgot myself, Miss Potter. Please don't let her overdo!" Miss Potter curtsied again, and replied gruffly, "No fear of that, your ladyship." Miss Potter then swept Mathilde out of the room and up the stairs, scolding audibly all the way. Catherine and Mary looked at each other blankly, then burst into amused giggles. When she could talk, Catherine chortled, "I could enjoy seeing my cousin Martin face down Miss Potter. He would not stand a chance of imposing on Mother!" Mary agreed, saying, "Indeed, my dear, I am certain she would put the Prince Regent himself in his place if he dared annoy Mathilde."

They returned to their seats by the fire, and Catherine asked, "Have you and Mr. Stuart discussed your wedding, Aunt?" Mary replied, "Indeed we have, and I must tell you at once that, since we want a quiet wedding anyway, we have decided not to delay our plans." Lifting a troubled gaze to Catherine's face, she went on, "I would not wish you to think that I am unmindful of your father's death, or the period of mourning. I would not disrespect your father's memory. He was my brother, indeed, my only living besides yourself. However, matters between us were not such that contribute to a sincere depth of grief. Miles and I have discussed it in detail, and do not feel that a small, quiet family affair would be… irreverent." Catherine leaned forward to hug her aunt, and responded, "My dear, I quite agree. I, too, have had difficulty with the concept of traditional mourning in respect to my father. I have been hoping that you and Mr. Stuart would have your wedding here. It will be spring in a few weeks. The garden is already stirring, and the church would be lovely. What do you think of the idea? If you and Mr. Stuart would not dislike it, I would enjoy it above all things. We could plan a spring fete for the village to celebrate. Can you like the scheme?" Mary beamed. "My dear niece, it sounds like the very thing! A few friends, this lovely house, and the church…who could require more? I don't even need to ask Miles. Thank you, my dear. It sounds quite perfect. What date were you considering?" With a roguish smile, Catherine twinkled, "That is rather a matter for you and Mr. Stuart to decide, don't you think? However, Easter is a few weeks away. If we planned on the Saturday after Easter, we should have time enough to invite any friends you desire. There is ample room here; we could plan a house party. A relaxed, cozy week, with dinners, maybe some dancing. We can confer with the vicar as soon as you have a chance to write to Mr. Stuart. We also need to think about your gown, a possible trousseau." Mary laughed and said, "Trousseau! My dear, do you forget how recently my wardrobe was completely replaced? I already know what I wish to wear. I need nothing more. As to the date, it is exactly the date we had discussed. We had thought to have you and Mathilde come to town, but your idea is even more perfect! Oh, Catherine, let us talk to the vicar tomorrow, so that I may write to Miles that all is settled!" "We will call on him first thing tomorrow, and send an Express to Mr. Stuart later in the afternoon! Now, we should start preparing our lists. Who would you like to invite?"

Mary said seriously, "Our family party in town was so congenial. If you do not object, I would like to invite your cousin Rosalie and her husband. I realize she is increasing, but the event is some months away. If she can make the journey, I would be so pleased. I think we must invite the new Viscount Stanton and his wife, because it is the polite thing to do. They probably won't find it convenient to come here at such short notice. You, your dear mother, Rosalie and John, Miles and myself-a comfortable family party, just to my taste! Mayhap, John's brother, the baron, should be invited as well?" Catherine said casually, "We could certainly extend the invitation. I daresay he is occupied with business. I would love to invite Julia and Caroline and their husbands as well, but Caroline is too near her time, and I would not disturb Julia for worlds right now. It sounds like you and Mr. Stuart have indeed given this thought, my dear. It shall be as you wish. If the vicar agrees, and you are certain that Mr. Stuart will approve of these plans, we can write the invitations and have them out this week. We will also confer with Mrs. Davis to plan menus and rooms." With a sparkle in her eyes, Catherine added, "By all means, make a list of Mr. Stuart's favorite dishes so we can include them!" Observing the time, the ladies parted to dress for dinner.

Chapter 35

Some days later, Catherine laid down her pen and stretched. "All done, I will dispatch them today, so that Rosalie's invitation can go by the Mail. It was so obliging of Mr. Stuart to respond so quickly, Aunt Mary. Obviously, he is an eager bridegroom!" Mary pinkened, and replied with dignity, "We are both eager, dear, after so many years alone…. Delay seems so pointless now." Catherine smiled at her aunt. "By the way, my dear, I would like to show you something. As you will see, I have been plotting and planning for you. I am so hoping that your and Mr. Stuart's willingness to share the house in town betokens a willingness to spend time here as well. Tell me what you think of this…" Rising, she led her aunt up the stairs, but, instead of turning toward her own boudoir, she led her aunt to the former state apartments Mary said, with some astonishment, "Why, Catherine, what…?" Just then, Catherine threw open the door. The rooms had been brightened with new paint and paper, new softly coloured drapes, and comfortable furniture. Mary and Catherine went around the vast, canopied bed to the door of the private library. This room had also been repainted and freshly curtained. The bookshelves had been polished, and a big beautiful desk placed before the large window, with a beautiful globe standing next to it. Mary turned to Catherine, bewildered, what does this mean?" "My dear aunt, I have prepared this apartment for you and your husband. I want you to feel totally at home and independent, and, since these rooms were empty, it seemed to be just the thing. Here, you will have some privacy, and Mr. Stuart can work or read without feeling confined, or as if he is imposing. Frankly, I am using this to entice you and Mr. Stuart to spend as much time as possible here. We are family, are we not?"

Mary looked at Catherine in silence for a moment. "But, my dear niece, these rooms are the state apartments; they are a noted part of a famous estate. What if you marry? Your husband could reasonably expect to share the State Apartments with you. Frankly, I would find it hard to shift around; you have made these rooms so lovely..." Catherine broke in, "Dear Aunt Mary, IF I should marry, there are plenty of rooms for my husband and me to share. In fact, I've already made alterations to my suite, incorporating some additional rooms and putting a door to the corridor that have made a complete set of apartments. If 'State Apartments' are required, I have them. There is no reason anyone should know which apartments were what. If that is your only objection, may I consider this settled? Unless you think Mr. Stuart might object to these rooms...?" Mary smiled affectionately at her niece. "Indeed you may, dear girl. I must tell you that Miles is extremely fond of you, and was so touched by your request that we make your home with you. Of course, I have been most content with you, and am delighted to continue the arrangement. However, I must insist that you allow me to help with the household business and, of course, Miles wishes to continue handling your business affairs if that is your wish." "Indeed, Aunt, I will only be too happy to have your and Mr. Stuart's continued assistance. I can think of nothing I'd like more!" The two ladies embraced, then left the suite, shutting the door behind them.

Catherine sat on a bench in the garden, clutching Rosalie's reply in her hand. Warmly wrapped in a clock with the hood pulled up over her hear, she sat in the sun. Having waited more than a fortnight for a reply to her invitation, she was a little afraid to open it. What if Rosalie's heath would not permit her attendance? Mary would be so disappointed, as would her mother. Mathilde had warmly approved of the plans made by Catherine and Mary, and the vicar had agreed to perform the ceremony on the Saturday after Easter as requested. Mr. Stuart had written an enthusiastic letter, giving his delighted consent to all of the arrangements as well. In her heart, Catherine knew that some of her nervous flutters were actually qualms about James. What if he accompanied Rosalie and John? What if he didn't? Finally, she tore open the missive. Rosalie was in glowing health, she wrote, and had never felt better. Since the weather had improved, she would see no reason why she and John could not come for a visit, especially since they did not have to rush back to Ridley immediately. Catherine chuckled, seeing Rosalie's mischievous smile in her mind's eye. As for James, he was from home, so she could not answer for him; she suggested that a room be prepared as they were expecting him any day and, to her knowledge, he had no immediate plans to leave again soon. If time allowed, she would send a note to advise Catherine how many their party would be. In the meantime, she was affectionately hers, cousin and friend. Catherine felt a warm glow, and was pleased for Aunt Mary to be able to plan on such a delightful party for her wedding. Rising, she walked on to the rose garden. Green leaves were starting to slowly unfurl. Unfortunately, it did not seem likely that roses would be blooming in time for the wedding. However, other flowers would be available from the hot houses, and the church was small anyway. As she strolled on through the gardens, the path took her up the side of the house towards the front. She was just in time to see a large carriage halt in front of the door. Startled, she hurried back the way she had come.

Catherine fled up the stairs to her room, and flung the enveloping cloak onto a chair. Her hair was untidy, and she was out of breath. She walked to the window, and forced herself to take a deep breath. "Who was it?" she wondered. "Could it be...?" When her breathing had steadied, she rang the bell for Jane. When Jane entered the room, Catherine said casually, "I walked further than I intended, and muddied my boots and hem. I must tidy my hair and change." She had already laid out the plum wool day dress, with the ecru lace for her hair, and the pearl earbobs lay ready on her dressing table. Jane looked somewhat startled, but said only, "Of course, my lady." It was after her outdoor dress was removed, and Catherine was seated at the dressing table wearing a warm robe while Jane brushed her hair, that Jane mentioned the new arrival. "Lady Heyerwood, while you were out walking, a guest arrived. I believe he said he was your cousin, and that he had come early for the wedding...." Gaping, Catherine turned and looked up at Jane. "My cousin...you mean, the new Viscount Stanton is *here*? Without warning? The wedding is still weeks away!" She closed her mouth with a snap, and turned back to the mirror. "Pray, braid up my hair quickly, Jane, and help me on with my dress." Within minutes, Catherine was tidy, dressed, and hooking the pearl earbobs in her ears. She shut her door briskly, and went down the stairs.

She met Howard in the hall. He was looking harassed as he conferred with Mrs. Davis. "Lady Heyerwood, Viscount and Viscountess Stanton are in the drawing room. They have come to stay, my lady, in advance of the wedding. He has asked that their luggage be placed in the State Apartments, my lady. What would you have me do?" "How dare he?" she fumed to herself. "Well, Howard, as you know, those rooms are occupied. Place the Viscount and Viscountess in the west wing in the green suite.

Those rooms are pleasant and roomy, and should suffice." She smiled at Mrs. Davis, and added, "I know that you have been cleaning and refurbishing these last several days, so have no doubt that the rooms are ready for guests." Mrs. Davis bridled and said, "To be sure, my lady, we have never had to ask a guest to wait for a room to be made up." "Well, then, have their luggage carried up. Did my cousin and his wife bring their valet and maid?" Upon Howard's nod, she said, "Good, they can take care of the unpacking. As I recall there is a small chamber on the next floor that will do for the maid; the valet can use the dressing room attached adjacent to the green suite. Pray, Howard, bring some refreshments; sherry, brandy and some wine will suffice. Thank you both for your efficiency." Catherine turned toward the drawing room door, and paused, drawing a deep breath. Opening the door, she went into the room. Her mother and aunt were already there, painstakingly conversing with their guests. She saw a small, pale and rather expressionless woman sitting next to the fire. On the hearth, a gentleman racked from heel to toe as he held forth to the ladies. His rather loud, insistent tones were clearly audible as he lectured. Catherine approached the hearth, held out her hand, and said carryingly, "Cousin Martin, I believe? How do you do? I am delighted you have decided not to stand on ceremony. Please introduce me to your wife."

Viscount Stanton spun so quickly to face her that he almost stumbled. He bowed awkwardly, and took her hand. "Cousin Catherine, how do you do? We came as quickly as we could, knowing you needed support in this time of bereavement. My wife, Alethea, Viscountess Stanton." The ladies curtsied slightly, then both took their seats. Viscount Stanton continued, "I have come to offer not only my condolences, but my assistance. Since the death of your esteemed father, I am sure you have felt the want of male guidance and protection. It could hardly be otherwise. I insist on...." In order to stem his flow of eloquence, Catherine lifted her hand and spoke. "My dear cousin, I have felt no want of guidance or protection as you suggest. My father was not in a position to provide such care for me for some years before his death, and I have no need of such...support... from you. I am well served by my man of business, who is so soon to be my uncle, my bailiff and my staff. Indeed, I may say quite freely that you have no duty here, but to be at ease and get to know us. Now, sir, may I offer you and your wife some refreshment?" Howard entered with the tray, which he placed on a small table next to Catherine. As she dispensed sherry to the ladies and a glass of brandy to the viscount, she kept her mouth shut as her mind fulminated at his effrontery. His wife was engaged in painstaking conversation about the inconveniences of the London house, and the difficulty of hiring servants. Viscount Stanton turned to Catherine, and said, "My dear cousin, you are a sheltered young female. I must protest! You can know nothing of business....!" "My dear sir," said Catherine icily. "You and I have just met. You have had no contact with me or my family prior to my father's death. You know nothing of me or my circumstances, and it hardly behooves you to make any assumptions. Neither my title, nor my estate, is derived from Stanton holdings , and you need not concern yourself with my affairs. This is plain speaking indeed, but I would have you labor under no misapprehensions. The invitation to which you responded so...immediately...was strictly a social one. I would have you and your charming wife as my guests. Anything more is quite unnecessary." Catherine smiled at the red-faced Viscount.

Just then, the door opened and Howard appeared. "Ah, Howard, your timing is perfect, as always," she said. "Are my cousins' rooms ready, and their luggage cared for?" Howard bowed and answered, "Yes, my lady, if the Viscount and Viscountess would care to follow me, their rooms are ready." Turning to her cousin, she held out her hand in dismissal, and said, "Cousin, I hope you and your wife will be comfortable. We stand on no ceremony, so, please make yourselves completely at home, and rest from your journey. We keep country hours for dinner." The Viscount bowed over her hand, and left the room silently, his wife in tow. Silence reigned in the drawing room for a moment. Then, gravely, Mathilde said, "Don't you think you were harsh, my dear? I'm sure he meant well...." "All I can say, Mother, is that I am not so certain. Given the slightest encouragement, I feel sure that my dear cousin would be only too happy to take over everything for me, whether I willed or no. I *was* quite direct, but I was afraid that, if I were too subtle, he would not take my meaning!" Catherine strode impetuously about the room. "You would think he could at least wait long enough to be introduced before thinking to manage my inheritance, would you not? I would wager he has plans to discuss my situation with Mr. Stuart as soon as ever he can!" Mathilde and Mary looked at Catherine with some surprise. Stopping before the fire, Catherine drew a deep breath, and then began to laugh in spite of herself. "What an absurdity! I am become too sensitive, I think. This whole situation is almost farcical, don't you think?" Resuming her seat, she poured herself another sherry. "More wine, my dears? Let us drink the health of Viscount Stanton!" Turning the subject, the ladies enjoyed a comfortable conversation over their needlework.

As they dined on the delicious meal, the Viscount held forth on his plans for the Stanton estate, the remodeling of the London house, and the preparations he was making for his speech, when he took his seat in Parliament. Patronizingly, he extended an offer to frank letters for her. Catherine smiled slightly, and said, "That is indeed gracious of you, cousin." Turning to his wife, who sat silently on her left, Catherine said, "I hope you found your rooms to your taste, Alethea." Alethea looked up fleetingly, and said expressionlessly, "Most pleasant, I assure you , my lady." Refocusing on her plate she continued eating. Viscount Stanton took up the conversation. "Indeed, cousin, the rooms are quite adequate. However, I had hoped to be placed in the 'state apartments'. As your senior male family member, I felt it appropriate, and the guidebooks say they are quite luxurious." Holding her temper, Catherine replied, "Unfortunately, I occupy the master apartments in the house, cousin. After my husband's unfortunate death, I replanned the family apartments to suit my own desires. I am sorry that you find your suite…inadequate to your consequence. However, as your stay is to be fairly brief, I can only hope you will not be too uncomfortable." Unexpectedly, Alethea remarked, "Indeed, my lady, the rooms are most pleasant and comfortable. Our home in the north is not nearly as cozy. The night winds are chilly, are they not? I vow, we will not feel the cold tonight." Catherine smiled and replied, "I am delighted you are so comfortable, but please call me Catherine. After all, we are marriage relatives, and this is a family party." To her surprise, Alethea smiled back fleetingly again, and said, "Thank you, Catherine. I am delighted to be considered family." Catherine was taken aback. Just then, Mathilde and Mary began a discussion of Mary's wedding plans. "Since our party is so small, I would like to have a simple breakfast early, and then a luncheon party afterwards," said Mary. "I have already spoken to our good Mrs. Davis, and she assures me that that arrangement would be quite easy for the staff, and most convenient for our guests." Catherine replied, "That sounds delightful. What about supper and some dancing in the evening, as well? Not a set ball, perhaps, but some country dances and a few waltzes, perhaps. I could arrange for some musicians from Taunton or from Bath, if that sounds agreeable." Mary beamed and said, "That would be wonderful, my dear! It all comes together so delightfully!" The ladies rose and left the dining room, leaving the Viscount to sip a glass of port in solitary state.

Chapter 36

The days passed quickly. Catherine and Mary conferred with the gardener about the flowers, and the vicar about the arrangements for the decoration of the church and the service. Some daffodils, hyacinths and narcissus forced in pots would provide spring colour and delicious scent, while some early lilies would be perfect for Mary to carry. With the wedding on a Saturday still a few weeks away, Catherine conferred with the vicar's wife about musicians, and subsequently sent an express by footman to Taunton, with instructions to wait for a reply. Upon receipt of an acceptance from a quartet to provide music at the wedding luncheon, and to play for entertainment, and possibly dancing, that evening, Catherine gave instructions to Mrs. Davis to prepare quarters and arrange for refreshments for the musicians; another task completed! Alethea, though quiet, proved to be an efficient member of the household and a pleasant addition to the tea table. She was engaged in her own delicate handwork, and contributed her quiet insight to the conversation. Mathilde and Mary spent a lot of time looking over their wardrobes, debating the all-important matter of the wedding costumes. Mary selected a gown of soft grey silk, with silver lace, for her wedding, to be worn with the diamond earrings and hair ornament given her by Catherine as her only jewelry. Over her hair, she planned to wear a delicate veiling of silver lace. Mathilde planned to wear a delicate black lace overdress, over shimmering lavender silk, with a black lace cap on her silver hair. Pearl earbobs and a pearl cross completed Mathilde's *ensemble*. Catherine herself had given little thought to her apparel for the festivities during the day. For the evening, she planned to wear the chocolate silk overdress, with the ivory underdress. Although she would have preferred the golden underdress and the canary diamonds, she decided the ivory would be in better taste, and that she would wear the double strand of pearls with matching earbobs, given her by her parents at her marriage, and would have Jane weave a strand of pearls into her hair. While not actually mourning, the colours were sufficiently discreet, and the pearls always acceptable. After due consideration, for the wedding and the wedding luncheon, Catherine decided on a gown she had had made in London but had not yet worn. A deep plum silk, it had long sleeves, slightly puffed at the shoulder with embroidered ribbon at the shirring and the wrist. The scooped neck and high waist were trimmed with the same embroidered ribbon, and the hem was trimmed with three rows of wider ribbon embroidered to match. The embroidery was a delicate tracery of gold, lavender, rose and green on a black background. With this gown, she decided to wear a single strand of pearls, and her pearl and topaz earbobs. A trifle of ivory lace on her head would be sufficient covering, and she could carry her Norwich shawl for warmth, in case the church were cold.

The next day, Catherine, her mother, aunt and her cousin's wife went to church. After the service, the ladies greeted Vicar and Mrs. Lamb with pleasure. Catherine invited the vicar and his wife to tea that afternoon, so that they could finalize the plans for Mary's wedding and discuss the school. Mr. Lamb disclosed that he had received some replies to his solicitation for school master or mistress to discuss with her. Making their way home, Catherine explained their plans for reaching older students as well as children to Alethea. Unexpectedly, Alethea showed great interest, and even offered some suggestions for possible courses in embroidery, if students showed interest and sufficient skill. "There is always a need for skilled embroiderers, not only for gowns, waistcoats and the like, but for repair of tapestries and similar textiles," she explained. Catherine looked at Alethea with respect, and said, "I had not even considered that area of education, but will certainly do so. Thank you for the suggestion." Alethea blushed and smiled, saying, "I have ever been interested in such matters, being considered something of a bluestocking as a girl, and fond of needlework as well. I am hoping to interest Martin in a similar project at our country home." Over the next few days, Catherine and Alethea spent more time discussing the school and their needlework, comparing designs and current projects. Catherine felt her interest in, and liking for, this new cousin growing, and looked forward to introducing her to Rosalie. Unfortunately, her cousin Martin did *not* improve on acquaintance. He was unfailingly pompous and prosy. When told of his cousin's and his wife's conversation about the school, he patronizingly said, "It's good of you to have an interest, and to keep busy, as long as it doesn't disrupt the work on the estate." Turning the conversation to the Stanton estates, he prosed on about his plans to enlarge the staff and redecorate the London house. Catherine and Alethea looked at one another. Alethea looked down into her teacup; Catherine quietly excused herself.

Catherine, the Vicar and Mrs. Lamb met to discuss the applicants for the teaching position at the school. Catherine said thoughtfully, "Vicar, do you think one teacher will be sufficient? I am thinking that we may need two, and that it might be as well to have a school master *and* a schoolmistress. A vacant cottage in the village would be appropriate housing for a schoolmaster; we could even consider a husband and wife together if both had the appropriate education and skills. It seems to me that the villagers would be more comfortable at the idea of the small children, and especially their daughters being taught by a woman, whereas the older pupils, especially the boys, would benefit from instruction by a man. Having a woman available to teach certain domestic skills, such as knitting, sewing and embroidery, would allow us to expand our offerings. Such useful skills might also encourage parents to let their girls acquire other knowledge as well. What do you think?" The vicar rubbed his forehead thoughtfully. "My lady, you may be right. As it happens, one of the applicants was a schoolmaster in Birmingham, a Mr. Berkeley, who is married. If I recall aright, his response included the information that he was married, and that his wife had previously been a governess. He also included references. He may be the very man!" Mrs. Lamb added, "If his wife was in fact a governess, it would be most helpful to know her qualifications, and if she would be willing to work in the school. Would it be too impertinent, do you think, to write to him requesting more information about his wife, as well as his own specific qualifications? If I might be so bold, if we tell him what we are considering, and what remuneration he and his wife could expect if the position were to be offered, it would give him the opportunity to confer with his wife and see if the situation would be one they could consider."

Catherine thought deeply. "I would, of course, provide and maintain the cottage, and provide firewood. I had thought that a schoolmaster's salary would reasonably fifty pounds per year to start. I had assumed that a schoolmistress's salary would be thirty pounds per year, but was going to have to discuss with the candidate the living arrangement, whether the cottage or boarding with a local family would be better. If Mrs. Berkeley is going to be an adjunct to her husband, with less involvement,

I think that seventy pounds per year for them to start, with the cottage for quarters, would be reasonable. What to you think, Vicar?" "I think that is most reasonable, my lady, considering that a curate is paid thirty pounds per year! Mr. Berkeley may indeed consider himself fortunate! How did you plan to handle the matter of paying their wages, Lady Heyerwood?" Catherine said slowly, "I have heard that people tend to lack appreciation of something given away, but do not want anyone prevented from attending. I had thought to see how much interest we had, and how many students return subsequently, and then determine some sort of remuneration, whether in cash or in kind, for the parents to provide. I could then make up the difference. However, I think this is important enough to engage myself to guarantee the wages regardless of the villagers' input, if necessary. I have no experience in matters of this nature. I would not want any child prevented from attending by a parent unwilling or unable to pay, but I do think that some contribution by the parents must be made at some point. In time, we may even find ourselves having students from nearby villages or the surrounding area requiring boarding who could cover some part of the expenses. I believe, Vicar, that I will have to guarantee the wages for at least the first year, until we can see where we are."

Mrs. Lamb interjected, "Mayhap we could write to someone who has had experience with a similar endeavor? I know others are interested in starting school such as ours. Mrs. Hannah Moore, the author, and her sister have done something along those lines, I believe." Somewhat shamefacedly, Catherine replied, "An excellent suggestion! I have one of her books on education, but have yet to read it. I will ask Mr. Stuart if he can suggest a way to contact her, and how to find out if there is someone else he can recommend." Coming out of a brown study, the Vicar suggested that he write to the incumbent of St. John's Church in Gloucester. "The previous rector, Thomas Stock, was an acquaintance of mine. He and a newspaper owner started a Sunday school, which I believe is still in operation. They taught reading and spelling to poor children, as well as Bible lessons. Although he died some years ago, the current rector should be able to give us some information that may prove useful to our effort. I fear that some parents would be reluctant to send their children if a fee were required. Mayhap, as we offer specific courses of instruction in certain skills, we could set fees for those, as the benefits will be more apparent." Catherine said, "Well, then, Mr. Lamb, I will leave it to you to correspond with the Berkeleys, to see if they are both willing, and qualified, to undertake the situation we have, and to communicate with the rector at the church in

Gloucester for any information or suggestions." At that point, Howard brought in the tea tray, and the conversation became more general. After tea, Mr. and Mrs. Lamb took their leave. Pondering the issues at hand, Catherine suddenly realized she had no idea what the vicar's stipend was or how frequently it was paid. She made a note to herself to discuss the matter with Mr. Stuart when he arrived.

After dinner, Catherine retired to her rooms. As she walked through the door into her suite, she reflected that the remodeling done at the same time work was done on her aunt's new quarters was definitely a success. Because her existing suite was at one end of the hall with another, larger room at the far end, and another room with an attached dressing room across the hall, it had occurred to her to create a formal suite simply by installing a formal doorway separating these rooms from the rest of the corridor. It had worked surprisingly well. The room at the end of the hall was decorated comfortably to be a private sitting room, less formal than the drawing room, and liberally supplied with comfortable chairs near the fire, a built-in bookcase, and seating on the balcony overlooking the garden. As in her own room, the sitting room was brightened with warm paint, this time in a pale yellow, and soft cream brocade draperies framed the window. The bedroom and dressing room across the hall had been furnished simply with heavy walnut furnishings, and darker draperies of warm, deep, golden brocade hung on the bed and windows. A shaving stand and a massive walnut wardrobe she had found in the attic were placed in the dressing room. A rich oriental carpet covered the bedroom floor, and set off the golden draperies, as did the rich deep green velvet covering the settee and chair by the fireplace. That the room was admirably suited for a masculine inhabitant, she refused to consider. Passing into the sitting room, she sat down before the fire, relaxing gratefully in its warmth. She had moved her needlework frame and supplies from her boudoir into the room, and a few of her previously-completed pieces had been framed and hung on the walls. She relished the additional space and privacy the remodeling had enabled her to enjoy. Catherine reflected, "I should have done this before, when we were first refurbishing the house." Definitely, in truth, anyone could declare that she occupied the 'State Apartments' herself!

Chapter 37

A few evenings later, Catherine, Mary and Mathilde were seated in the drawing room, awaiting Viscount Stanton and his lady for a glass of sherry before dinner, when the bustle of an arrival was audible. They glanced at toward the door, just as Howard opened it. "Mr. John and Lady Rosalie Ridgley have arrived, Lady Heyerwood." He stood aside as Rosalie and John entered. A babble of welcome broke out, as Rosalie swooped upon the three ladies, dispensing hugs and kisses. Catherine rose and instructed Howard to tell Mrs. Davis to have set back dinner, and to advise Martin and Alethea of the delay. She also instructed him to place John and Rosalie in the blue suite, near her and her mother. He bowed and left the room, as a footman entered with the tray of refreshments. "Rosalie, will you have sherry or ratafia, or would you prefer tea after that cold drive?" asked Catherine. Smiling, Rosalie replied, "A small sherry would be delightful." Pouring sherry for the ladies and brandy for John, she resumed her seat by the fire and joined in the conversation. Having become fast friends with Julia and Caroline since Julia's ball, Rosalie had heard from Julia just before leaving home for Heyerwood. "She is well, and enjoying herself with Jean-Pierre and Juliana in the country. Even though the weather has been cold and rainy, they have occupied themselves, with (of all things!) nursery games, like lottery tickets, with Juliana, and reading by the fire in the evenings. Did you ever imagine such a complete change, Catherine? They lived so very formally, and spent so little time together before." "I suspect her mother-in-law's continued residence in London may have allowed them to ... relax...a bit," said Catherine, with a mischievous smile.

Rosalie also indicated that Julia had received a note from her old schoolmate Maria, effusive with compliments for Julia and her ball, and overflowing with delight at encountering their dear friend Catherine. "She wanted to know when you might be returning to town, and your plans for entertaining. Apparently she has discovered that you have purchased a townhouse at an unexceptionable address, and has decided to cultivate your acquaintance. You may thank Lady Castlereagh for that, according to Julia's letter! Julia informed Maria that she would have to write to you directly." Meeting Rosalie's eyes, dancing with glee, Catherine wavered between annoyance and humor, and ended up laughing at the foolishness of it all. "Poor Maria! She was ever concerned with appearance, and in a hurry to advance her own interests! And she *does* have that rather plain daughter to launch. Well, I will worry about it if ever I hear from her. I did get a letter from Caroline not long ago. She is also doing well, but is looking forward to getting back to town already. Tom has had a great deal of business, requiring his attendance, and the rain has turned the garden into a bog, according to Caroline. She says Tom is fussing like a hen with one chick so she can't get out much." Rosalie smiled in sympathy.

Just then, Mathilde claimed their attention, to introduce the new Viscount and his wife, who had entered the room. Alethea joined Rosalie and Catherine by the fire, and the conversation turned to talk of embroidery. "Did you finish the fire screen for your aunt's wedding gift?" asked Rosalie, in a low tone. "Indeed, and found a local woodcarver who mounted it beautifully. I have placed it at their fireplace upstairs. It will be a surprise for them on that day, as it was not in place when the rooms were completed. Would you like to see it?" Alethea asked about the screen, and Catherine explained that she had designed and embroidered the fabric for the fireplace screen. "May I join you? I would so like to see it. I am always looking for new ideas." The three ladies rose, excused themselves to the rest of the company, and went upstairs. Opening the door, Catherine led Rosalie and Alethea to the small study, next to the bright sitting room. The screen was placed to the side of the fireplace. The cherry frame had been carved with leaves and vines, and charmingly set off the flowers so carefully embroidered by Catherine. Both ladies were impressed with the design, and the way it came together in the frame. "How well it will look, before the hearth in summer or when they are away, and the fire isn't lit. It's charming as a purely decorative addition, and useful as well. Why, it could even block a draught from the window, I believe," said Alethea. Rosalie admired the colours Catherine had chosen, and the delicate carving on the frame. "You said the frame was made by a local woodcarver. Does he have a shop in the village?" Catherine replied, "No. He is the son of one of tenants, who carves as a hobby. I happened to notice a frame on a portrait at the vicarage, and the vicar referred me to him. He is still working with his father on the farm, but, I believe, could bring in much-needed funds with his carving. I showed him my embroidery, told him what I wanted. He designed and carved this piece himself, and mounted the embroidery for me as well. He does beautiful work, does he not? I hope to talk to him and his father, to see if he would be interested in pursuing this kind of work for a living. There is a cabinet maker in Taunton and another in Bath, I know, if he does not want to go to London. I don't want to meddle, but such artistic skill is unusual, and I would love to help him if he desires to pursue it."

A few days later, Catherine was in the library, catching up with much-needed paperwork and answering some letters. She was reading a missive from the vicar, who had heard from Mr. Berkley regarding the school, when Howard opened the door and coughed apologetically. "My lady, I am sorry to disturb you. However, we have another arrival. Baron Ridgley apologizes for not responding to your invitation more promptly. Mrs. Davis and I were not sure in which rooms we should place him." Surprised, Catherine said, "Why, I hardly know; that is, I had assumed…." She thought for a moment, and asked, "Has he a valet or other attendant with him?" Yes, Lady Heyerwood, his man is waiting with the luggage. Lord Ridgley has joined the ladies and Viscount Stanton in the drawing room." Taken aback, Catherine said, "Well, Howard, I'm not sure…. Is the Tapestry Room ready? As I recall, it has its own dressing room, and a small room next door that would do for Lord Ridgley's man. It's in the same corridor as the green suite." Howard bowed slightly. "Yes, my lady, I venture to say the rooms are quite suitable. I'll see that a truckle bed is set up in the small room." "Thank you, Howard," said Catherine with relief. "Pray, have one of the footmen assist Lord Ridgley's valet with the luggage, and let my mother know I will be joining her shortly." As Howard left the room, Catherine swung round to stare sightlessly out of the window, the vicar's note crumpled, forgotten, in her fist. "How like him to just appear without a word!" she fumed. "It would have served him right if I had denied him." She strode over to the fireplace, and was about to hurl the crushed note into the fire, when she mastered herself. "After all, what did I expect? He comes and goes at will, according to Rosalie. Well, at least his brother and sister-in-law will be pleased." She smoothed out the crumpled letter, and a sentence caught her attention.

Resuming her seat, Catherine finished reading the missive, and was pleased to discover that Mrs. Berkley had been a most superior governess, skilled with the globes, an excellent command of French and Italian, and something of a musician as well. Mr. Lamb indicated that Mr. and Mrs. Berkley were pleased to accept the positions offered, and were quite satisfied with the cottage and stipend. It remained only to decide the date for their arrival, and the opening day for the school itself. She decided to suggest to the vicar that they come as soon as convenient, so that Mr. and Mrs. Berkley could get settled in their home, have a hand in the final arrangements and furnishing of the school, and be introduced to the village. They could determine the best day to open the school together. She put the Mr. Lamb's note away in the drawer, and picked up a letter from Mr. Stuart. He brought her up to date on certain business issues, suggested a couple of business ventures to consider for investment, let her know who was in town, and finally mentioned the vicar's stipend. "The living has ever been in the gift of the Earl of Heyerwood. Mr. Lamb has held the living since the late earl's father appointed him. Mr. Lamb's stipend is three hundred pounds *per annum*, and he retains all of the tithes collected for use in the parish. Mr. and Mrs. Lamb own the rectory in which they live, plus about five acres of land on which they maintain a kitchen garden and small dairy. He is distantly connected to Lord Melbourne, and has a small but secure personal fortune as well. In addition, his lady is well connected and brought a respectable portion to the marriage. He has never indicated a need for any change in these arrangements, but would undoubtedly appreciate an increase, as their adult daughter is a widow with young children living on her late husband's estate in the north, and their son is in orders himself. They assist both of their children with their expenses."

Catherine took pen in hand, and wrote out an update to the Vicar's appointment. She increased his stipend to four hundred pounds *per annum*, to be paid quarterly. She also established that ten per cent of any school fees collected were to be paid to the vicar, as he would be overseeing the school operations, as well as teaching the Bible and catechism classes. She reflected that the remainder of the fees could be applied to keeping the school supplied. She herself could supplement as needed. She also established that, in the event the vicar decided to retire, or if the position were otherwise to become vacant, his son would have the right of first refusal to the appointment. Satisfied, Catherine signed with a flourish, dated it and sealed it, to give to Mr. Stuart who was expected very soon. Rising, she left the room and started for the drawing room. Checking, Catherine turned and ran lightly up the stairs to her own suite. As she rang for Jane, she quickly removed her earbobs and struggled out of her gown. By the time Jane arrived, she had washed her face and hands, and laid out a deep brown silk with her ivory lace cap. "Jane, pray brush and pin up my hair again. I will wear the brown silk with my pearl drops." Jane brushed out her soft brown hair, pinned it into a knot high on her head with a beautifully carved ivory comb, picking out a few curls to fall around her earls and forehead. Pinning the trifle of ivory lace on her head, Catherine nodded and smiled. "Jane, you never cease to amaze me. Thank you." The pearls glowed softly in her ears, and they, with the rich brown silk, flattered her creamy complexion. Satisfied, Catherine swept out of the door, and back downstairs to the drawing room.

Chapter 38

Catherine entered the drawing room, smiling brightly. "Good evening, my dears. Why, Lord Ridley, how delightful to see you among us! I hope my mother and my aunt have made you acquainted with Viscount Stanton and his wife?" James replied gravely, "Indeed yes, my lady. How satisfying it must be to have your family circle enlarged so…unexceptionably. My apologies for arriving so unexpectedly. I have been out of England for a time, and decided to come straight on. As you see, I got here faster than a written reply would have done." Looking at him directly for the first time, Catherine saw the twinkle lurking in his eyes. For a split second, she wavered between boxing his ears, and laughing. Rosalie broke in, "James, you are abominable!" Catherine relaxed and smiled, "Indeed, you are abominable, sir, but we'll say no more about it. This is a time of celebration, after all." James turned to Mary, and bowed gracefully. "Most definitely, a celebration. May I say, ma'am, you look excellently well. Obviously, your engagement agrees with you." Mary blushed and smiled. "Indeed it does, Lord Ridley. Happiness is the finest cosmetic, as they say. Did you come direct from town, sir? Pray, tell us who is still there." Smiling, James took his seat beside Mary, and began to regale her with the latest *on dits*. Catherine sat down next to Rosalie and John, across from her cousin. She was able to hear the viscount's low-voiced expostulations to Alethea. "Such cheek! If this were not my cousin's drawing room, I should take him to task." Alethea murmured soothingly, patting the flustered viscount's arm. Just then, Howard came in with refreshments. "Some brandy, my lord?" asked Catherine, demurely. "I believe it is in order." Viscount Stanton smiled grudgingly. "Thank you, cousin." The little bustle of sherry being served to the ladies, and brandy to the gentlemen lightened the mood, and the conversation became more general.

When Howard announced dinner, Catherine rose and led the party to the dining room, a bubble of mirth within her. She could hardly look Baron Ridley in the face. Every pomposity, every verbal brick hurled by Viscount Stanton had been deflected with bland indifference by Baron Ridley. The viscount viewed Baron Ridley with distaste, but there was no sign of choler or outrage. "However does he manage it?" she wondered. Aloud, Catherine said, "We must have some music after dinner, Mother, Aunt Mary! Mayhap, we can play some of those new pieces we bought in London. I know you have been practicing on your harp, Mother." Rosemary eagerly agreed, "That would be delightful. We might even try some duets!" Catherine did not dare look at the baron, but smiled at Alethea. "And you, Alethea, do you play or sing? We are fortunate in having both a piano-forte, and a harp." With composure, Alethea replied, "Why, yes, I do enjoy playing the piano-forte. A little music will be just the thing." Her eyes twinkled back at Catherine. The meal proceeded through the delicious courses, enlivened with lighthearted conversation about music. The ladies retired to the drawing room, where Mathilde seated herself at her harp. Plucking idly at the strings, she made sure it was properly in tune, and then played a simple, rippling air to warm up her fingers while Catherine, Mary and Alethea sat chatting by the fire. They were joined almost immediately by the three gentlemen. Howard brought a tray with tea, brandy and sherry, and bowed his way out of the room.

Rosalie and John sat with Catherine, conversing quietly. Alethea calmly disposed herself at the piano-forte to play a duet with Mathilde. Per force, the viscount took his place next to his wife, to turn the pages of her music. James devoted himself to Mary, asking when her intended was expected to join them. "He is finishing some last minute business. He wants to leave all in order so that we can have a little space of time together to celebrate," said Mary with a smile. "I hope he will be here tomorrow or the next day. The wedding is so close at hand." James returned her smile, and replied, "I'm sure he is all eagerness. We all know how devoted he is to you, and how fond of Lady Heyerwood and the Dowager Viscountess." Just the, the duet ended and Alethea rose from the piano-forte. "Catherine, will you not honor us with a piece? I would love to hear you and your mother playing together." Catherine excused herself from the cozy group by the fire. The viscount bowed her to her seat, and prepared to render the same page-turning services for her. "Thank you, cousin, but you need not stand.

My mother and I will play from memory. Shall we not, Mama? That little duet from my childhood would be delightful." As Catherine and Mathilde began to play, the viscount wandered around the room. James watched Catherine from his seat by the fire, as she played, oblivious to his regard.

Later in the evening, Catherine found James sitting next to her. James said earnestly, "Indeed, I am sorry not to have written. I found myself called away on urgent business, and was not sure I would be free to come until I was released a few days ago. It seemed better to be on my way, and get here while I could. I hope I have not inconvenienced you?" Catherine looked at him, and said neutrally, "It must have been most urgent, to have required such effort?" James replied, "Unfortunately, as it was not my own business, I am not able to discuss it. I can tell you that it required a great deal of travel, and I am thankful that it is concluded at last." Reluctantly, Catherine smiled and said, "We, too, must be glad you are able to join us." Just then, there was a bustle of arrival, and Howard announced that Mr. Stuart had arrived. "Just in time for some champagne!" exclaimed Catherine. "Howard, pray, show Mr. Stuart in, and have a footman see to his baggage. The yellow rooms are ready for him." She smiled conspiratorially at Rosalie, "He does not yet know about the other arrangements." Just then, Mr. Stuart walked in, rubbing his hands together. "How delightful it is by the fire! Spring has not quite yet penetrated to the evenings, and it is still cold on the roads." He shook hands with James, John and the viscount, then kissed all the ladies. Viscount Stanton was inclined to stand on his dignity, but, when he discovered that no one else regarded it, unbent sufficiently, to join the conversation.

A few days later, on a bright morning, Mary and Miles went to the church to be wed. John, who was to be best man, and Miles went over before the ceremony to have a few words with the vicar. Mary and Mathilde, who was attending her, went to the vicarage to get ready. As the rest of the party were getting into the carriages to ride to the church, Catherine took Howard aside and reminded him to have Mrs. Davis arrange to have all of Miles and Mary's belongings moved into their suite. "I know this puts a bit of strain on the final preparations for the luncheon, but I so wanted this to be a surprise, and there was no way to do it earlier. I'm sure Jane and Miss Potter will assist with Aunt Mary's things, if needed. I know that everything possible will be done beautifully. At, least the books I purchased for Uncle Miles' study are already unpacked!" Howard bowed slightly, and replied, "My lady, Mrs. Davis has preparations already underway. Miss Potter and Miss Thomas have already done the flowers, and have begun moving Madam St. Clair's personal items. Most of Mr. Stuart's things were moved to the suite last night. The empty cases were left in the yellow rooms, with his night gear and garments for this morning's festivities. I venture to state that all will be in readiness long before the party returns."

"Howard, as always, I can only think you for your efficiency and your care of us all. Pray, tell Mrs. Davis and the entire household how pleased and grateful I am," Catherine responded.

The ceremony itself seemed to take only moments. Cather remembered the long look exchanged by Miles and Mary as they said their vows, and the smile they exchanged when the vicar introduced the new husband and wife to their family and friends. She also remembered the steady gaze of James, fixed on her face during the ceremony. She returned his look fleetingly, flustered by his steady, sober regard. After the ceremony, Catherine made sure she was seated in the carriage next to Mathilde, and opposite Rosalie for the ride back to Heyerwood, to avoid any more unsettling glances.

Luncheon was a gay affair. The vicar and Mrs. Lamb were seated on Catherine's right and left, with Uncle Miles at the head of the table, and Aunt Mary as hostess at the foot. Each course proved more delicious than the last, concluding with a huge, beautifully decorated cake. Mary blushed as she sliced the cake, while the footman served. Champagne was passed, and they all stood for the toast offered by John. Laughter and conversation rang out. Finally, they rose from the table to change and rest for the afternoon. Catherine smiled, and said, "Aunt Mary, Uncle Miles, please go with Howard. There is something needing your attention." Mystified, Mary and Miles left the room, following the butler. Catherine turned to her other guests and said, "Pray, stand on no ceremony. We are all family. These evening, we will be having more celebration with music, and, if anyone wishes, dancing. I did not wish to fill the next few hours with too much activity. If anyone wishes to ride, the stables are nearby. The gardens are not yet at their best, but there are some pleasant walks. My library is at your disposal if you would like to read or if you have correspondence to attend to. Please, make yourselves truly at home. I will rejoin you momentarily, after I have changed." She hurried up the stairs, just in time to see the newly-weds reaction to their new rooms.

"Catherine, my dear girl, how lovely and how thoughtful! These rooms are perfect, too much for us! However can we thank..." Catherine hugged her aunt gently. "Aunt Mary, it is I who want to than you and Uncle Miles to have a family at long last. I want you both to feel that Heyerwood is your home, too." "The fire screen is especially lovely, the embroidery and the carved frame so perfect. You made that, I know." "Indeed, I did, Aunt. A wedding gift for you." Miles came in from the small library, through the cozy sitting room. "Wedding gift, indeed, my dear. You are too extravagant…but we love it. How can I tell you my appreciation? The library is complete to a shade. You may never be rid of me!" Catherine ran to hug him, smiling mischievously. "My dear sir, you guessed! That is exactly my plan. I wanted you to be comfortable, and knew the thing was impossible without a library for you to bury yourself in at will. I planned no formal entertainments until this evening. We are a family party, after all, so we need not stand on ceremony. I am going to change my gown and see who will join me in a stroll around the garden. I feel the need of some exercise."

Once Catherine was in her own rooms, Jane helped her carefully out of her gown and into a dressing gown. Catherine sat down by the window, and smiled with pleasure as she recalled the expressions on her aunt's and uncle's faces as they surveyed their new rooms. Her surprise was a complete success. Even though Mary had known about the rooms, she had not seen them decorated and finished. Impulsively, she chose the sea green wool gown, with soft black half-boots. After she was gowned, she picked up the green and rose shawl, left her rooms and ran down the stairs. Entering the drawing room, she looked around and saw no one but Rosalie and Alethea. "Where are the others?" asked Catherine. Rosalie replied, "John and James decided to walk over to the stables, and Viscount Stanton decided to accompany them. Your mother decided to go to her room to rest for a while. Alethea and I were just chatting." Catherine said, "I would like to take a stroll around the garden to see how the roses are coming along. I need some exercise dreadfully. Would you care to accompany me?" Both ladies agreed, and hurried away to put on half-boots and get their shawls.

The three ladies strolled through the gardens, stopping where they chose. The afternoon was clear and sunny, but with a cool breeze, reminding them that winter's chill was not that long ago. Trees were showing the delicate pale green mist of new leaves, and spring flowers were nodding in the breeze. Conversation was desultory, and confined mostly to idle comments about the state of the gardens, the beauty of the day, and reminiscences of the ceremony held earlier in the day. Finally entering the shelter of a small walled garden some distance from the house, Catherine suggested sitting down on the rustic seat in the shade of a large tree. Rosalie sighed with pleasure as she wriggled her toes in the snug half-boots. "It's a lovely walk, but it does feel good to sit down. This garden is delightful. The wall blocks the worst of that chilly wind. The plants in here seem much further advanced, in this sheltered spot. You see, Catherine, I do believe that that rose is about to bud." Pointing to a thriving bush, she looked around the sunny spot, and continued. "This is an idea I will take home to Ridley Manor. I have just the spot in mind for a walled garden. Being a bit further north, it seems to stay cool longer. A walled garden would be a perfect place to take the baby for an airing..." Catherine agreed with her. "It's a delightful spot to bring a book or sewing and sit for an hour or so. I get a great deal of pleasure from it." Alethea chimed in. "I wonder if I could do something similar at the London house? If I removed the shrubbery, there would be more light and room, and I believe a few rose bushes and some other plantings would make a beautiful small garden." Catherine's thoughts flashed to the dark, gloomy shrubbery chosen by her father, and said, "I think that would be wonderful, Alethea. It would be so much more cheerful and pleasant." Rising, by mutual consent, the ladies decided to return to the house to rest for the evening's festivities.

Chapter 39

Catherine awoke early in the morning a few days later. Sitting on her balcony in her dressing gown, she marveled at how quickly the time had passed. From the wedding service to dinner the previous evening, everything had gone smoothly. The party had quickly melded into a relaxed, convivial unit. Even Viscount Stanton had relaxed and shown a willingness to be pleased. The musicians from Taunton performed excellently. Catherine remembered the waltz she had had with James the evening of the wedding… The quartet from Taunton played delightfully, and dancing had begun almost immediately. Mary and Miles led off, followed by John and Rosalie, and Martin and Alethea. Catherine felt James' presence before he spoke, and turned her head to look up at him. Without saying a word, he took her hand and led her into the dance. The four couples glided and twirled around the drawing room effortlessly as the music swirled around them. For a moment, Catherine almost felt as if she were being swept along by a powerful current. When the dance ended, she and James were standing near John and Rosalie. The two couples fell into a cheerful conversation, discussing the excellence of the music, and the delightful dinner that preceded it. Miles and Mary were standing by the fire, hand-locked, smiling bemusedly at each other. Martin and Alethea found themselves engaged in conversation with Mathilde. As the laughter and chatter rose, James bent his head and spoke softly, directly into Catherine's ear. "May I beg a moment alone, Lady Heyerwood? I have something of a…personal nature to say to you, and would prefer somewhere less public." Catherine turned startled eyes on him and said, "What could you have to say to me in private, sir? I don't think…" Gripping her hand painfully, he looked into her eyes, and replied, "We have a conversation to finish, do we not?" Blushing slightly, Catherine glanced toward her mother. Feeling flustered and annoyed simultaneously, she was tempted to break away, but decided to hear him out. "As you will," she said, with a shrug. "The library is available for this...conversation you seek." Quietly, they left the room as the musicians struck up another waltz.

James courteously opened the door, and Catherine passed into the library before him. Crossing the room, she seated herself in her favorite chair by the fire, and waved him into the chair across from her. "What would you say to me, sir?" she asked, coolly. James looked amused, and replied, "I am set down, indeed! Can it be that you have forgotten, madam, that I told you I wished to pay my addresses to you?" Completely taken aback, Catherine stammered, "Pay your addresses...? You mean to discuss this *now*? With guests in the house, and so much going on, it hardly seems the time..." James leaned forward to grasp her hand. "On the contrary, to me, it seems the perfect time. A wedding, the house filled with romance and happy couples, how could it be better?" She looked at him in disbelief, and saw the calm confidence of his attitude, the mischief in his eyes. Withdrawing her hand, she snapped, "Of all the arrogant...! I think this is quite premature, sir! I am not so easily swept into an engagement. Do you really think I am so desperate for a husband that I would rush blindly to bind myself to another man I scarcely know? You have indeed missed your mark, sir, if you think I am so easily cozened! If ever I engage myself to marry again, it will be to someone I have come to know and trust, as well as for whom I have a romantic *tendre*. I had hoped we could become better acquainted, learn to know each other's minds more gradually, before we had this 'conversation'! Instead, you must needs rush into this, as if you only had to crook your finger. Well, sir, this conversation is over before ever it began." She rose from her chair and strode to the door. Catherine could hear him behind her. He took her arm to halt her progress, and she froze immediately. Icily, she looked him in the eye, and said, with disdain, "Have the goodness, Lord Ridley, to remove your hand from my arm. Or do you plan to restrain me against my will?"

James immediately released her, and said quietly, "I have indeed expressed myself badly, as well as too boldly. I was foolish to hope after our promising beginning in London...." "After which I heard nothing from you, until you appeared here without a word of warning! How could you approach me in this way? I am not an inexperienced child, to be swept off her feet." James flushed deeply. "Indeed, Lady Heyerwood, I sincerely apologize. Have you considered that I was swept off *my* feet? That it has been many years since I enjoyed the warmth, and romance, of such a party as this? You have been on my mind these last months, and I allowed myself to hope.... Indeed, if I have been too precipitate, I can only apologize and withdraw. I can remove myself tomorrow...." Catherine interrupted him, "Your apology is sufficient, sir. I would not embarrass you, or my other guests, by such an untimely departure on your part." Guiltily, she smiled slightly. "Indeed, sir, I have thought of you as well, and hoped for the opportunity to cultivate your friendship, if only as a close connection of my cousin Rosalie. Can we not start again?" James bowed, and replied, "That you are willing for me to stay is more than I deserve. I am grateful for the opportunity to prove that there is something more than...friendship between us." "Then, sir, let us return to the drawing room and our friends. I have my heart set on another waltz before I retire."

They arrived back in the drawing room just as a stately minuet was ending, with Mary and Miles, and Viscount Stanton and his wife taking their final bows. Mathilde was chatting happily with Rosalie and John by the fire. It appeared that their brief absence had raised no eyebrows. Just then, Howard and a footman appeared with trays of refreshments: champagne, some delicate sandwiches and tiny cakes. Catherine paused to speak to Mary, while James joined his brother and sister-in-law in conversation with Mathilde. After a moment, Catherine glanced toward the group by the fire, and did not know whether to be pleased or offended that James appeared deeply engrossed in what her mother was saying. Resolutely, she focused her attention on the newly married couple. Howard offered champagne; she sipped a glass gratefully, enjoying the sparkle of the festive beverage. As the opening strains of a country dance were heard, Miles bowed before Catherine, and the viscount to Mary. James and Mathilde, with John and Alethea joined them on the floor, and they took their places. After that lively dance, the evening flew by. Mathilde had retired by the time the last dance, which was another waltz, began.

Miles asked Catherine to dance, which she gratefully accepted. She asked him if he were enjoying the house party. "Indeed, yes, my dear! Such a delightful party. Even Viscount Stanton has relaxed and allowed himself to be pleased. Your aunt and I are completely comfortable and at home in our beautiful rooms, and have been able to enjoy every aspect of these last weeks." She replied, "I am so glad. I wanted everything to be perfect for you and Aunt Mary." They danced in silence for a few moments. "Are you troubled, my dear? I saw you come back into the room with Baron Ridley, and you seemed a bit...agitated," he asked. Catherine replied,

"The baron and I had an unsettling conversation, but nothing is amiss." "I'm glad," Miles responded. "He seems a personable man, and one who could be relied on." Startled, Catherine looked up at Miles. "Rely? What do you mean, Uncle Miles?" "Nothing, my dear. It just seems that, based on my own observation and the information we had gathered earlier, he seems an unexceptional gentleman of probity. Always a good thing in a family relationship." "Probity? Possibly. However, he is a man in a hurry, uncle. Let us speak of something else, if you please." Miles smiled. "As you wish, my dear." He led the conversation into general matters as they swirled around the room.

Catherine also remembered waking unaccountably early the next day. The sun was rising on what promised to be another beautiful spring day. After splashing her face with water, she tied her hair back with a ribbon and slipped into a simple, old gown and half boots. Picking up a shawl, she slipped out of her room and down the stairs. Deciding to take a walk around the garden, she went out a side door and, after a moment of indecision, took the path to the walled garden. It would be delightful to enjoy the early morning in peace sitting in that sheltered spot. She was very surprised to see her cousin Rosalie, there before her, sitting on the bench in the sun. "Good morning, cousin! I did not expect anyone else to be about so very early." Rosalie smiled. "Good morning, indeed, my dear. I thought everyone else was still recovering from last night's festivities. I don't know why, but I woke early and just could not bring myself to lie a-bed." Catherine smiled and replied, "I understand completely. I, as well, felt compelled to be out." Sitting on the bench next to Rosalie, Catherine looked about the garden. "This is such a peaceful place. I've not been here in several months, between the bad weather and being in town. It's wonderful to see it coming back to life again." She and Rosalie chatted in a desultory fashion for a few moments, then lapsed into silence.

Suddenly, Rosalie spoke, "Catherine, I do envy you your relationship with your mother, and now your aunt and her husband. Such a warm, comfortable assemblage, so pleasant to be among family. I would that I could hope I could ever communicate on any level with my mother." Catherine patted her hand comfortingly. "I can understand somewhat; my mother and I had very little correspondence for several years, and I can imagine your feeling alone. You are very welcome to share my family; after all, you are a part of it. What of your father, Rosalie? Do you hear from him?" Rosalie smiled. "Yes, I do hear from my father. He has never completely cut me off, as did my mother and Michael. I wrote him a few weeks ago to tell him I was increasing, and got a long letter from him just before coming here. I believe he is finally on the way to accepting John, and our life together. If only he could bring my mother and brother around. Alas, I am afraid they will insist on shunning us. It is so distressing for my father to be thus in the middle, and for me to feel that I am such an encumbrance to him. However, I was ever close to my father before my marriage, and I would have my child's grandfather a part of his, or her, life. If my mother and brother cannot accept that, I am sorry." Catherine patted Rosalie's hand. "I am so glad your father is responding to you. I feel sure that time will ease this situation for you. I'm certain that John is relieved for you, as well." "John is very hopeful that this will gradually lead to a *rapprochement* with my whole family. As boys, he, Michael and James were fast friends, and this estrangement has been difficult for him as well." Catherine was a bit taken aback. She had remembered Michael's friendship with John, but had forgotten that James was also involved. James showed no interest in her cousin at Julia's ball. She ventured a comment. "I had forgotten James's friendship with my cousin." Rosalie laughed. "Well, John and Michael were closer in age, but the three were boon companions. However, after my marriage and Michael's washing his hands of us, James has had nothing but disdain for Michael, saying he is a grown man, capable of making his own choices." Lowering her voice, she continued, "In fact, I heard that he knocked Michael down at an assembly in Chester, because of something Michael said about me." Looking at Catherine meaningly, "James is very loyal to those he loves, and will do what ever he must to support them."

Catherine blushed again at the memory of Rosalie's look and words. Rosalie went on to say, "John and I are both aware of James's ... interest in you. Needless to say, we are both delighted, not only by the prospect of James's happiness, but by the prospect of an even closer relationship with you. I can think of no one I would rather have as a sister, or who could make James so happy. However, I feel a ... tension between you since last night. Is there anything I can do to help, any question I may answer?" Catherine was now scarlet and tongue-tied. "I do not mean to push or interfere. Certainly, you will be my cousin and friend, whatever may occur between you and James," concluded Rosalie, earnestly. Catherine managed to reply, "It is so good of you to be concerned. I hardly know ...." Rising from the bench, Catherine walked across the small garden and back, as Rosalie watched quietly. "How can I make you understand? I hardly understand myself. It is true that James has spoken of an interest in me.

I, too, have…feelings for him. But marriage is such a huge undertaking, such a change. I have thought of it many times, especially in relation to the estate. However, I am not sure for <u>myself</u>." Rosalie was perplexed. "What do you mean? How could a happy marriage be aught than good for you?" Catherine sighed. "How to make you understand me? At this present, I am in complete control of every aspect of my life, my money, my person. I am free to choose, to go and do as I wish. Marriage would, of necessity, change that. Unless a husband agrees, and signs documents agreeing, a wife's person and goods become his to use as he chooses." She swung around to face Rosalie squarely, colour heightened. "I have done what I can to minimize the possibilities, setting up an entail, and a trust tying funds to the estate, and putting a portion aside in a separate trust I can use regardless of my circumstances."

Catherine swallowed and went on. "I was not but a possession to my father, traded into marriage against my will. To my husband, I was a token of respectability, useful to his estate. Although my husband apparently became somewhat…fond…of me, and went to great lengths to make generous provision for me, I can never be sure that my welfare was as much a consideration as jeering at my father and the polite world. I have become accustomed to making my own decisions, having the freedom to order my own life. Can you not understand how reluctant I am to put myself into a different situation? None of the usual issues regarding matrimony, position, fortune, inheritance, apply to me. Before I can make such a commitment, I must know the man well, be certain that I am more than a chattel or a bank account! I don't HAVE to marry. James is most attractive, but we hardly know each other. It will take time, and he seems to be very much in a hurry." She looked at Rosalie apologetically. "This must sound intolerably self-centered." She sighed and sat down on the bench again.

Rosalie shook her head emphatically. "No, Catherine, I think you are wise to be cautious, and fortunate to be able to choose. I made my own choice, after all, and would not change it in spite of everything. I would tell you that, with James, some of your fears are needless. However, until you know him sufficiently well yourself, nothing anyone could say would really relieve your concerns." She paused. "Would you have me express any of this to James, if he were to broach the subject to me? I can appreciate your dilemma, and would not violate your confidence for the world. If, however, he were to invite my counsel, I could endeavor to convey some of your fears. This could smooth matters for you somewhat. However, if you prefer not, I will say nothing of any of this." Catherine pondered the question. Her first instinct was an unequivocal, "No!' However, it would help clear the air between her and James, and would give James the opportunity to consider the realities of the situation without awkwardness. Slowly, she replied, "If you can avoid bring up the subject, if he asks you about these matters, I see no harm. After all I would tell him myself, if he ever gave me the opportunity." Catherine smiled ruefully. "Had I met him a few years ago, I would have been much more open to being swept off my feet, especially as my father would doubtless have disapproved." The cousins laughed and decided to return to the house.

Looking back at it, the rest of that morning flew by. Back in her room, Jane helped Catherine out of the old gown, through a hurried bathe, and into the plum wood day dress. Jane brushed her hair hard, and braided it into a coronet on top of her head, with black velvet ribbon matching the ribbons trimming her dress. Soft black slippers and small pearl earbobs completed her *ensemble*. "Thank you, Jane. This will do nicely," she said as she left her rooms. Breakfast, the riding party, tea, and dressing for dinner sped past. That evening, the party gathered in the drawing room after dinner. As Mathilde strummed her harp idly, the others engaged in general conversation. As Catherine rose from her seat by the fire, John approached her and said with a smile, "May I have a word, please, cousin?" Catherine returned his smile, and replied, "As many as you wish, to be sure, sir!" As the strolled to the window, John said quietly, "You have made our stay here so delightful. It is wonderful to be part of a family party. However, we must make our departure, and I believe we must take advantage of the clear weather to leave tomorrow afternoon." Catherine's eyes flew to meet his in shock, as she echoed, "Tomorrow…?" Earnestly, he replied, "Please, cousin, do not be concerned. We are sorry to have to depart at all. However, the weather is fine, Rosalie is feeling well, and I want to make a start while things are in good order. I have business to conduct in a week or so, and, by leaving tomorrow, we can take our time, giving Rosalie plenty of opportunity to rest and conserve her strength." He met her anxious gaze with a twinkle, and added, "You must not be thinking that this has anything to do with my brother. You must have no concerns on that score." Relieved, she smiled back, and said, "I hate to see you go, but understand completely. I do hope we will see you again before too very long." John laughed, and said, "Indeed, you will! You must come to us. Rosalie has set her heart on your being godmother to our child." Catherine beamed and hugged him. "I would be honored and delighted! To be sure, I will be with your for that event!"

Catherine blushed again, as she thought about the next morning, and the Ridley's departure. Somehow, she was not surprised to see James's carriage and luggage being readied to leave as well. Rosalie and Catherine embraced warmly, and made plans for Catherine's visit to Ridley in Flint County for the christening. John bowed, then kissed Catherine's cheek, as he made his goodbyes, then turned to help Rosalie into the carriage. James remained, looking at her enigmatically. Catherine's brows lifted, and she extended her hand formally. "I thank you, sir, for joining our party. I look forward to our next meeting." His eyes twinkled irrepressibly as he bowed, equally formally, over her hand. "As do I look forward. I will remember my sojourn here with great fondness, and hope you will do the same." As he turned to get into his own carriage, he looked back at her, he said, "Farewell, Lady Heyerwood." Catherine remembered all of this and mulled over the turn of events, as she sat on her balcony that morning, hoping she would hear from Rosalie soon. Just then, Jane came in to help her dress for breakfast.

Chapter 40

After the departure of the Ridleys, there was a certain flatness to the party. It must be said that the only person who seemed pleased was Viscount Stanton, as if he somehow had vanquished the baron by staying longer. As much as Catherine enjoyed the company of her mother, aunt and new uncle, and valued the new viscountess, she had to admit that the viscount did not improve upon acquaintance. The next several days passed with a sameness, and she noted no eagerness on the part of the viscount to return to his new estates, or to take up his new responsibilities. Fortunately, her fondness for Alethea went some way to balancing her increasing desire to see the back of his lordship. She and Alethea fell into the habit of walking each morning, and spending time in the little walled garden. Although Catherine preferred to bring a book or some handwork with her, Alethea brought her sketchbook, and proved to be quite accomplished. As they sat, the two ladies chatted about many things, but always came back to the subject of the school. Alethea considered Catherine's plan to open a school in the village an excellent one, and wanted to hear all of the details. As they worked and exchanged ideas, Catherine discovered that Alethea had had an unusually thorough education as a girl, and, had she not married, might have established a school herself.

As the days went by, Catherine finally received a message from the vicar and decided to call on him, to discuss matters related to the schoolmaster and –mistress, and making some decisions. She dispatched a note, asking if she could call the next day, and invited Alethea to accompany her. That evening at dinner, Catherine mentioned that she and Alethea were planning to call on the vicar and discuss plans for the school. To her surprise, and dismay, Viscount Stanton immediately offered his services as escort. Catherine smiled, and replied, "Thank you, Cousin Martin, but it is not far, and we will be adequately served by the coachman and groom, who will drive us. You need not disturb yourself. Unfortunately, the viscount was driven by his evil genius to persist. "It is, of course, my pleasure to escort two such charming ladies. I also feel it is my duty to accompany you, so that I might advise you on these matters. Ladies, such as yourselves, could hardly comprehend the pitfalls and ramifications of such a project. As your nearest male relative, I feel it my responsibility…." Catherine smoothly cut him off, with forced good humor. "I do understand your concern, but it is misplaced, I assure you. We are working out the final details with the vicar, and I believe we can resolve any issues that might arise, without troubling you." "As to that," the viscount said patronizingly, "we all know these parsons are more interested in feathering their own nests before anything else. I wager the fellow spends more time in London or on the hunting field than in nurturing his flock. My business sense is needed to prevent a … shall we say 'imprudence?' on your part." Catherine stared at him in disbelief, while Alethea kept her eyes on her plate, in an agony of embarrassment. That he could say such things after her previous set-downs! And to think her mother worried that she was too harsh! She coolly replied, "It does not become you to make such insinuations about a person you barely have met. I will add that I have always found our vicar to be an excellent steward of the resources at his disposal, and a faithful shepherd to his flock as well. Your concern is unnecessary, sir."

Before either combatant could say more, Alethea broke in, "My dear cousin, I so appreciate your including me, but I have remembered that I have some letters to write and cannot accompany you. I need to advise the housekeeper to prepare the London house for our arrival, and have my maid begin looking over my things for packing. We have trespassed on our cousin's hospitality for too long, have we not, my lord?" She looked her husband in the eye, expressionlessly. Caught off balance, Viscount Stanton could only stammer his agreement with his wife's statement. Alethea continued smoothly, "Pray forgive me, cousin, but I think it is best if, while you are taking care of your business with the vicar, my lord and I prepare ourselves to go back to London to start our necessary changes. If you will let me know before you leave, I will come down to see you off. You can tell me about your decisions when you return." Catherine could only hide her disappointment as she agreed with Alethea's conclusion. Before conversation could return, Mathilde and Mary rose and invited Catherine and Alethea to join them in the drawing room, leaving Miles and the viscount to their port. As the ladies seated themselves near the fire, and waited for Howard to bring in the tea tray, Catherine said, "Alethea, Mother, Aunt Mary, I must apologize for my behavior at dinner. There is no excuse for my rudeness. I should never have brought up the subject of the school in the first place; business is not suited to the dinner table." Mathilde responded gravely, "I am happy to hear you say that, my daughter, as I was quite shocked at the tone the conversation took." Before she could continue, Alethea said in a low tone, "Pray, do not say any more on the subject. If there was a fault, it was equally shared by the participants. I regret that my husband sometimes allows his...concerns to outrun his thoughts, and he says more than he intends. It causes great distress, which is not the intent. Please let us say no more on the subject." Mary went to the piano-forte, seated herself and began a Mozart concerto, and urged, "My dears, let us enjoy these last evenings while we are together. It is unfortunate, but we all say things we regret, and it is best to simply let it go. We will have some music, which always soothes the mind, and then we can have a more pleasant conversation." Mathilde patted Catherine's hand. "Indeed, there is no reason to say anything more." In a low tone, she said to Catherine, "I will own that the provocation was ... extreme." She turned to Alethea and said, "Catherine tells me you are quite an accomplished artist. Might we see some of your sketches?" Gratefully, Alethea whisked out of the drawing room and up the stairs to bring her sketchbook down.

As Mathilde exclaimed over the beauty of Alethea's sketches, Catherine sat near the fire, mulling over the upcoming visit to the vicar. She was determined not to mention it again, and to maintain at least superficial cordiality toward the hapless Viscount Stanton. Mentally, she checked off several points: her bailiff confirmed that the cottage was ready for occupancy by the schoolmaster and his wife; the one-room building taken over for the school had been repaired, cleaned and whitewashed and fitted with benches for the students, a large desk for the instructors to use, and a large cupboard already stocked with supplies. A bookcase was also ready for use. "All is in readiness, down to the globes on the desk," she thought. "Once they arrive, take a few days to get settled, and see what is where, then we can set up a meeting with the village residents, and we will see where we are. I do hope we have at least a few students!" She was so engrossed with her thoughts that Miles' and the viscount's entrance escaped her, until Miles exclaimed, "Mozart! My dear, you remembered my favorite." Mary looked up and smiled demurely, "Mine as well, dear sir. Will you not join me?" As Miles joined his bride at the piano-forte, the viscount, per force, joined the rest of the party by the fire. Before he could speak, Mathilde exclaimed, "Martin, why did you not tell us your wife was so accomplished an artist? Her sketches, indeed, are out of the common." Taken by surprise, he forgot his usual patronizing air, and exclaimed eagerly, "She is, indeed, quite gifted! In our gallery at home, I have a delightful series of water colours she painted on our travels in the Lake District. There is also a small drawing of my late mother, that is very like, which I have hung in my dressing room, where I can see it daily." He positively beamed with pride. Catherine swiftly joined in the conversation. "Her sketches in the garden were excellent as well. She has such delicacy of touch, and a distinct point of view." As Alethea blushed under all the attention, the viscount responded pleasantly to Catherine's olive branch. To everyone's relief, the rest of the evening passed swiftly with music and free-flowing conversation.

After breakfast the following morning, Catherine excused herself to her guests without comment, put on her bonnet and shawl, and got into the carriage. To her surprise, Alethea was there before her, waiting. "My dear cousin, I did not expect…. Is this wise?" she asked. Alethea smiled, and replied, "I told Martin I would be occupied for the next few hours. He did not enquire, nor did I offer more information. He and your uncle Miles have made some plans for this morning, so I doubt I will be missed. I was not going to forgo this visit. It is an opportunity not to be missed, and I plan to take as much information as possible to apply on our own estates." The ladies whiled away the brief drive in conversation about the school and education, particularly for girls. Mr. Lamb welcomed them to the vicarage, where Mrs. Lamb was waiting with tea. As Mrs. Lamb poured out, Mr. Lamb took out the letter he had received from Mr. Berkley. "Excellent news!" he proclaimed. "Both he and Mrs. Berkley should be arriving Wednesday next, and are eagerly anticipating their new situations. Among their household goods, he mentioned that they are bringing some books he used in his previous school, and Mrs. Berkley has some books from her own school years, as well as sewing and netting supplies. Both are full of plans. I believe your ideas are going to bear fruit, Lady Catherine." Catherine beamed. "I am so glad they are receptive and interested. We have a chance to reach a wider group this way. I understand the cottage and school buildings are ready?" Mr. Lamb replied, "Indeed they are. Would you ladies care for a tour? "It is only a step." Mrs. Lamb interjected, "I've tried to prepare the cottage, and you may have some ideas to make it more comfortable."

They first visited the school building. Very plain, but immaculately clean, with smooth benches for the students, and a plain sturdy desk and furniture for the instructors' use. "The stone floor should be easily maintained, and the large fireplace sufficient to keep the worst chill off the room on the coldest day," commented Alethea. "I have engaged the bailiff to make sure the school is always supplied with firewood," put in Catherine. Next door was the cottage. Larger than Catherine expected, the main floor included a small study, a comfortable sitting room and a dining room with table, chairs and sideboard. The kitchen was at the back. Upstairs were several small but comfortable chambers. Furnishings were sparse but adequate. "We were not sure what would be needed. The Berkleys are bringing their own things, of course, but we are not exactly certain of what might be required," said Mrs. Lamb. Looking around the pleasant rooms, Catherine responded, "I think you have done excellently well. There is enough for them to be comfortable while they unpack. If there is excess, the unnecessary pieces can be stored in the attic or removed. As they get settled, any needed adjustments can be made. Have my people brought over the kitchen and stillroom supplies? I ordered some basics, such as flour, salt, some tea and coffee, some preserves, and so on." "Indeed they have, Lady Heyerwood, and they are already put away in the kitchen. The beds will be made up Tuesday, so the Berkleys will be able to just step into their home," replied Mrs. Lamb. "They will stop by the vicarage for the keys, and we will accompany them to introduce them to their new situation." Catherine exchanged glances with Alethea. "Mrs. Lamb, I do not see how your arrangements could be improved," said Catherine. Alethea added, "Mr. and Mrs. Berkley should be most pleased. Every attention has been paid to their comfort." Mrs. Lamb beamed with pleasure.

As Catherine and Alethea drove back to Heyerwood, Alethea said thoughtfully, "It has been most helpful to see how this has come together. There have been many issues I would not have considered, especially supplies for the school itself, and the details of housing the schoolmaster. I had thought to leave many of those decisions to the schoolmaster, but I can see the advantage of having materials in place. I am most impressed with your arrangements, Catherine. You seem to have thought of everything." Catherine blushed, and replied, "Not I, cousin. Mr. and Mrs. Lamb have been completely involved from the beginning. It was important to have Mr. Lamb's input, as he will be conducting the Bible and catechism classes at the school, in an effort to gain parents' support for sending their children, and, mayhap, some older students as well." They continued their discussion until they arrived at the house. As they entered, Catherine casually asked Howard about the rest of the party. "The dowager Lady Stanton and Mrs. Stuart are changing. The gentlemen have not yet returned." Exchanging glances of mild congratulation, Catherine and Alethea hurried upstairs to change as well.

That evening at dinner, conversation positively sparkled. By common consent, no mention was made of the school. Instead, Miles and Viscount Stanton regaled the ladies with the details of their day. Viscount Stanton, clearly feeling expansive, had nothing but praise for the horses, and the grounds that he and Mr. Stuart had explored that day. Miles told Catherine about the additional plantings in the apple and pear orchards, and that the new presses had been installed in the cider house. He and Catherine discussed the idea of increasing the dairy herd for more cheese production. The viscount voiced his approval of these plans, and explained some of his own improvements on his home estates. Mathilde, Mary and Alethea carried on a separate conversation about handwork, until the ladies adjourned to the drawing room to enjoy some tea as they settled comfortably near the fire. They were joined by the gentlemen very shortly, who requested some music. Catherine seated herself at the piano-forte, and allowed her fingers to drift over the keyboard, playing some ballads, flowing from one song to the next, to provide a pleasant background for the conversation by the fire.

Chapter 41

Catherine and the viscount managed to maintain polite relations over the next few days. After further consideration, Viscount and Viscountess Stanton decided to return to their northern estates for a few months, before visiting the newly-acquired country estate and the London property. The viscount wanted to look over his home property and talk to his bailiff about some additional improvements. He also wanted some privacy in familiar surrounding, to consider taking his seat in Parliament, and preparing a first address. Privately, Alethea told Catherine that this would give her an opportunity to talk to the rector of their parish about the possibility of a school of some sort. "I have some ideas, based on your plans here, but am not sure how he might feel. We may have to begin slowly, with a Sunday school, perhaps," said Alethea. "I will write to you, to let you know how we go on. You will have the benefit of our experiences. I look forward to receiving letters from you, as well. I have so enjoyed getting to know you!" replied Catherine. Later, as the viscount and viscountess were preparing to get into their carriage to depart, she and the viscount exchanged formal farewells. As he turned away to take his leave of Mathilde and the Stuarts, Catherine and Alethea exchanged hugs and good wishes.

Later that evening, as Catherine, Mathilde, Mary and Miles sat in the drawing room after dinner, it was very quiet, no sound but the ripple of Mathilde's harp as she played. Catherine smiled at Mary and Miles and said, "It seems so very quiet with just ourselves, does it not?" Mary responded, "Indeed it does, but it is rather pleasant not to *have* to make conversation, or make sure others are entertained. As enjoyable as it is to have guests, it requires so much planning, effort and attention." "Especially when one has to be prepared to step into the breech at any moment," interjected Miles with a twinkle. Catherine flushed with embarrassment, but laughed in spite of herself. "We did have a few awkward moments, did we not?" she acknowledged. "However, I think it passed very well. Your wedding was delightful, and having Rosalie and John with it made it even more special. I own, I was surprised that my cousin Martin arrived so very...promptly after receiving the invitation. However, it was an excellent opportunity to learn to know Aletha. She is definitely a welcome addition to our family circle." Mary was quick to agree. The conversation continued comfortably, in a pleasantly reminiscent fashion. No one mentioned James, and Catherine refused to think of him.

A few days later, Catherine was going through the correspondence brought to her by the footman. Letters from Caroline and Julia appeared, as well as a note from the vicar. To her surprise, the post also included a letter from her former school friend, Maria. She had not heard from Baroness Fortescue directly since the icy note received upon arriving in London, and was mystified as to the baroness's purpose in writing. (She disregarded their meeting while shopping; it was too brief to signify.) Opening Maria's letter first, she was amused to read that she was suddenly become Maria's dearest friend. Catherine's brows knit in puzzlement as she read Maria's personal news, but cleared as she got to the crux of the matter: Maria was wondering when she planned to return to London, and if she planned to open her London home for the Season. Maria had so enjoyed her encounter with Catherine at Julia's ball, and delighted to see her dear friend so warmly greeted by Lady Castlereagh. Enlightenment dawned, and Catherine realized that Maria wanted Catherine to introduce her to Lady Castlereagh. Doubtless vouchers for Almack's for Maria's fubsy-faced daughter were the root of the matter! Catherine tossed the letter aside, not bothering to finish. She would have to reply, of course, but not right now. Caroline's and Julia's letters were so much more entertaining, and heartwarming in the affection for her that ran through each. Caroline's preparations for her child were almost complete; the materials they had purchased together were all made up into the layette. Her health was excellent, and (other than looking like she had swallowed a bolster!) she was progressing well.

Julia's letter was full of news about Juliana and Jean-Paul, and how much they were enjoying country life. Her parents were coming for a visit later in the summer, and her mother was staying for the birth of the child. (That Jean-Paul's mother would also be joining them, was Julia's only mention of her.) Other than to say she was well enough, Julia did not mention her condition. Catherine immediately got out pen, ink and paper and responded to Caroline's and Julia's letters, regaling them with the details of her aunt's wedding, her further trials with her cousin Martin, and the unexpected pleasure of her friendship with Martin's wife. She also told them a bit about her activities on her estate, especially about the school. Aware that neither was particularly interested in or involved with these aspects of their homes, being more the province of their respective husbands, she wanted to share with them her pleasure at being able to make these decisions and innovations, and her hopes for the possible improved futures of the people for whom she was planning. Setting aside her letters for the post, she opened the vicar's note.

She was pleased to read that Mr. and Mrs. Berkley were safely arrived, and settled into their new home. Mr. Lamb reported that they were vastly pleased with the cottage; there was exactly enough furnishing and their own bits and pieces filled out the arrangements perfectly. They had already visited the school house, filled the bookcase with the books they had brought with them. Mrs. Berkley had even arranged all of the handwork supplies in the cupboard, ready for use. Mr. Lamb was extending an invitation for Catherine to call the next day in the afternoon, for a little reception for the Berkleys. Her mother, aunt and uncle were, of course, invited as well. Checking hastily with Mathilde and the Stuarts, Catherine dashed off a note of acceptance for all of them. Giving the note and the letters to the footman, she went upstairs to wash and change for dinner.

As they were driving to the vicarage the next day, Catherine told her companions what the vicar had told her about the Berkleys. "From everything he said, they are very pleased with the cottage and school, and eagerly anticipate the opening of the school. Mr. Lamb was quite delighted with them, and I know Mrs. Lamb must have been relieved and gratified at their satisfaction with her arrangements. She had made every effort for their comfort." Mathilde expressed her pleasure at meeting new people. Miles said, "If you can succeed in getting some pupils and opening your school soon, your chances of success will increase rapidly. It may be difficult in the beginning; people are not easily persuaded to change their ways. I am very proud of the way you have set about this project. In time, if you have interested pupils, I will see about helping you find apprenticeships, clerk positions and so forth for those who qualify." Catherine grasped his hand with pleasure, and said, "Uncle Miles, that is exactly what I prayed for. Having a prospect to use their new abilities will give students a reason to persevere. Once we see our way, if I see enough interest, I am planning to help place students in various positions in town or on other estates, as they acquire their skills. Those who prefer to remain here will still be better able to manage their homes and farms, even possibly to establish local businesses."

Everyone gathered in the vicar's small parlor. Mrs. Lamb had ordered tea, sherry and ratafia, and there was a definite party atmosphere. Mr. Lamb introduced the Berkleys to the company. "Ladies and gentlemen, it is my pleasure to introduce Mr. Stephen Berkley and his wife Anne, late of Birmingham." As everyone circulated, each tried to make conversation with the new couple. Chatting with Mr. Berkley, Catherine noted that he was at ease with the company, and very well spoken. He was a tall, sturdily built man, with an energetic air. Upon inquiry, he told her that he had been educated at Oxford. He told her how pleased he was with the school building and its supplies. "I cannot tell you how much it means to have a pleasant, clean, fully-equipped location, ready to begin. With my last school, there was nothing like this. My wife and I found ourselves providing most of the materials ourselves, which was quite difficult at times."

Circulating around the room, Catherine found herself next to Anne Berkley. Roughly the same age as Catherine, Anne was tall and straight-backed, with thick dark hair in a knot low on her neck. She looked Catherine in the eye as she curtsied, and said, "I have been wanting to thank you. It was so very agreeable to walk into the house and brew some tea, *before* unpacking! You and Mrs. Lamb were so thoughtful of our comfort." Catherine smiled, and replied, "I am so happy that you are comfortable in your new home. We are so pleased to have you and your husband here, and wanted you to feel welcome." As they chatted, Catherine discovered that Anne had attended a young ladies' seminary in Tunbridge Wells, and had become a governess after her father's death. "I taught in two households, before I married Mr. Berkley. I found teaching to be most enjoyable, but did not...relish the other duties than were required. Being a governess is so very awkward. I had planned to find a position in a school, but it is difficult to find such as a married woman. Mr. Berkley and I were delighted by this opportunity. To be able to start a school together, and under such circumstances is truly a dream come true. We are both educationists, you see, and have many ideas that we are eager to try." The two ladies discovered a similar taste in music, and Anne mentioned that she had had her piano-forte shipped. "If there is interest, I had thought to give lessons, but I enjoy playing myself so very much, and it had been one of the few pieces I kept from my childhood home, so I could not bear to part with it." The reception continued for some time, with everyone enjoying the conversation and Mrs. Lamb's carefully chosen refreshments.

As they drove home, Uncle Miles was very enthused. "Mr. Berkley took two firsts at Oxford, in history and in philosophy. He will be an excellent instructor, and I think his students will respect him." Mathilde was equally pleased with Mrs. Berkley. "We talked of music for some time. Our tastes are very similar, and we discussed the possibility of practicing some duets together." "She also mentioned that she draws. I was telling her about Alethea's sketches, and she was most interested. She hopes to offer some sketching classes to female students," interjected Mary. Struck, Catherine though, "We could provide a thorough education, fit a young woman to be a governess or a lady's maid, help a young man prepare for an apprenticeship or clerk's position. We could find ourselves taking boarding students eventually." When she voiced her thought aloud, Miles cautiously said, "It is certainly a possibility for the future, but you do not want to lose sight of your original intent, which was to provide basic education to the local children in the village and on the farms. We have not yet approached the local families or started classes. A boarding situation such as you describe could completely change the nature of the school you have planned. My advice is to go slowly, and concentrate on getting and keeping local students here. Time will show if expansion is possible." Somewhat dashed, Catherine replied, "I know you are right, Uncle Miles."

Chapter 42

After giving her Uncle Miles' comments regarding the school some earnest thought, and discussing the matter with her mother and aunt, Catherine felt that she needed to give Mr. and Mrs. Lamb, with Mr. and Mrs. Berkley, more license to work with the families and plan the courses of studies, without her direct involvement. "I do not want this to smack of a charitable concern, nor to come 'the lady of the manor' into the situation. I will keep my participation discreet, I think, and only make an appearance if it seems useful." Accordingly, a few days after the departure of the viscount and viscountess, Catherine sent a note to the vicar asking him to keep her abreast of the events concerning the school, and to let her know of any needs that might arise. She sent a similar note to Mr. and Mrs. Berkley. She was careful to explain that her interest was still engaged, but that she felt she could be a distraction or even a burden to them in recruiting students from her tenants and the villagers. She also asked Mr. and Mrs. Berkley to let her know a convenient afternoon to call. "I certainly don't want them to think I have lost interest, or do not want to work with them. I simply don't want to be a distraction or an encumbrance. Mr. and Mrs. Lamb know the people much better than I, and Mr. and Mrs. Berkley are experienced educationists. It makes much more sense for them to take the lead, and for me to remain in the background," she thought.

Catherine was sitting in the drawing room later that afternoon when, to her surprise, Howard announced, "Mrs. Berkley is calling, Lady Heyerwood, and asks if you are at home." "Indeed, yes, Howard. Pray, have Mrs. Davis request a tea tray." Howard bowed, and, shortly, Mrs. Berkley came into the room. "I hope you don't think I am pushing, my lady, but, after receiving your note, I did not want to delay speaking with you," said Mrs. Berkley warmly. Catherine rose, and extended her hand. "I am delighted that you have called, Mrs. Berkley. By all means, come sit by the fire. It is still chilly in the wind, even though spring is finally upon us," responded Catherine, equally warmly. "My husband and I wanted you to know how very much we appreciated your giving us such a free hand with the school, Lady Heyerwood. I know that it is difficult to step back from such a project," Anne Berkley said directly. Catherine blushed and smiled. "You should rather thank my uncle, Mrs. Berkley. I was starting run before even trying to walk, and he halted me before I could confuse things. I do want the school to be a success, and my first priority must be the children and young people here. I want to do everything possible for this to begin successfully, and I really believe that letting you and your husband and the Lambs be the leaders will allow that to happen. I will be pleased to make an appearance when you feel it will be useful, and, of course, want to be part of the planning. As supplies are needed, I also expect you to let me know, at least until such time as the school is generating sufficient funds to cover such expenses." Mrs. Berkley laughed, and said, "My dear Lady Heyerwood, I do not think we would fare well without your input. Your suggestions and ideas have been very sound. I know Mr. Lamb has been most impressed with your forethought. He is planning to address the congregation at church on Sunday, asking anyone interested to stay afterwards. This first meeting should, I think, be as informal as possible, but I know that, when the school opens, your presence will be essential for the opening ceremony." The air thoroughly cleared in regards to the school, the conversation turned to other topics.

"My aunt tells us that you are interested in drawing. Do you enjoy sketching, Mrs. Berkley?" asked Catherine. "Indeed, I do enjoy sketching. I drew every day as we travelled from Birmingham to Somerset County. However, I much prefer painting. Are you artistic, Lady Heyerwood?" Anne replied. "I'm afraid not," replied Catherine, regretfully. "Our drawing master did his best, but I was very bad at sketching and painting. I am able to draw out designs for embroidery, and gowns, but never achieved a good eye for artistic composition. I am able to appreciate the skills of others, however. My cousin, Viscountess Stanton, draws delightfully. What subjects do you prefer, Mrs. Berkley?" "Landscapes are always enjoyable, but my favorite subject matter is portraiture. Capturing a face is so much more challenging, I think," responded Anne. Impressed, Catherine asked, "Have you painted many portraits?" "For pleasure, yes. I have done many sketches of faces seen in passing, and painted a few as portraits simply because I found the faces so interesting. At my last place, my employer commissioned a portrait of the youngest child, who had died. I had done several sketches of all of the children, and was able to capture a very tolerable likeness. They were most pleased with it. I also painted a miniature of the oldest daughter, for her fiancé who was travelling. It was well received as well." "I would love to see your work, Mrs. Berkley," said Catherine. "Certainly, you may, Lady Heyerwood. You will be welcome in our home any time," replied Anne. "You said you draw your own embroidery designs? I would consider that an artistic endeavor, especially if you complete the embroideries. I have never acquired the skills of a needlewoman, and embroidery is far beyond me. I can barely mend my stockings! Mayhap I could see *your* work?" Both ladies laughed. "I can see we have much in common, Mrs. Berkley," chuckled Catherine. "It is a great pleasure to have you in the neighborhood."

Anne rose to take her leave shortly thereafter, after inviting Catherine to call Sunday afternoon, to hear the results of the vicar's announcement about the school. Catherine walked her out, and the ladies parted, both pleased with each other and looking forward to future conversations. Catherine went upstairs to her private sitting room, and sat before her embroidery frame, studying her current project with new eyes. "Artistic, indeed!" she thought. "I never thought of myself as artistic." She worked with a new enthusiasm and, when Jane came to help her dress for dinner, looked at the work completed with satisfaction. Catherine decided to wear the violet velvet she had designed some months ago, with the jet and amethyst beading on the bodice. She chose to wear her pearl and amethyst brooch on a black velvet ribbon around her throat, and amethyst drops in her ears. "Almost appropriate for half-mourning," she thought somewhat guiltily. Jane pulled her hair back into a coil with more black velvet ribbons entwined. Soft black silk slippers completed her *ensemble*. "Thank you, Jane," said Catherine. "This is a new look, is it not?" Jane said anxiously, "I saw something similar in the fashion pages, my lady. Are you not pleased? I can change it…" "Indeed, I am most pleased, Jane. You keep me up to snuff, and I am always amazed. Thank you very much." Jane curtsied, and, pink with pleasure, said, "Thank *you*, Lady Heyerwood. I am very glad to give satisfaction."

At dinner that night, Catherine mentioned Mrs. Berkley's interest in art, especially portraiture. Miles seemed struck, and said, "I would like to see her work. I have been considering having a small portrait of Mary for my business rooms in London. It would be interesting to see Mrs. Berkley's view point and skills." "She invited me to call Sunday afternoon, to discuss the results of the vicar's announcement regarding the school. I will send her a note to see if you may accompany me," replied Catherine. "After all, you have had a great deal of involvement with the business end of the school, so would have an interest in the outcome. Mrs. Berkley knows I am interested in seeing her work, so it would be an excellent opportunity for us both. She may well be interested in such a commission; I know she has painted for others before." Mathilde interjected, "When you write, please invite Mr. and Mrs. Berkley for dinner one evening soon. I would so enjoy getting to know them both better. They seem so conversable. We could consider a small party, with them and Mr. and Mrs. Lamb. Possibly, later in the week?" "An excellent idea, Mother! I will write after dinner, and have the notes delivered in the morning!" exclaimed Catherine. The next afternoon, Catherine received replies to her missives. The Lambs accepted her invitation to dine; Mrs. Berkley also accepted for herself and her husband, and warmly welcomed Miles' companioning Catherine for the Sunday afternoon call.

Sunday dawned grey and cloudy. As the party from Heyerwood got into the carriage to go to church, a misty rain began. "Oh, dear," said Catherine anxiously, "I do hope this is not an ill omen for our venture." Miles, Mary, Catherine and Mathilde barely made it into the narthex of the church before the rain got heavier. They quietly made their way to the family pew, and sat down. As the church slowly filled, the acolytes lit the candles, while the smell of wet wool threatened to overpower the slight fragrance of incense lingering. After the bells were rung, the services began, and the congregation rose, knelt, and sang when appropriate. Finally, the end of the morning service came, and Catherine and her family quietly rose and departed. She could hear the vicar ask the rest of the congregation to stay for a meeting as she entered the porch. The weather cleared as they drove home, promising a beautiful afternoon. When they arrived back at Heyerwood, the ladies went up to their rooms, to shed the heavier wraps of the morning, freshen up, and to put on shoes appropriate to a stroll in the gardens before breakfast.

Later that afternoon, Catherine and Miles got back in the carriage to ride to the schoolmaster's cottage. As they rode along, they engaged in desultory conversation about the improved weather, and the possible outcome of Mr. Lamb's announcement and meeting about the school. After being admitted by a neatly-garbed young maid, Mrs. Berkley welcomed them warmly. "Please step into the parlor, and be seated, Lady Heyerwood, Mr. Stuart. Mr. Berkley is with Mr. Lamb in the study; they will join us in a moment." As Catherine sat down on the settee before the fire, a quick glance around the room discovered several changes. Mrs. Berkley's piano-forte had been placed in the far corner of the room, and the settee had been augmented by two Queen Anne wingbacked chairs. Over the mantel, Catherine noted an oval portrait of an older woman clad in blue, seated on a bench under a tree. The artist captured her kindly glance, and a hint of a smile. It was as if the subject knew and liked the artist. "What a lovely portrait! Is that your work, Mrs. Berkley?" asked Catherine, most impressed. Mrs. Berkley glanced up, smiled and replied, "Yes, it is. I painted it some years ago, of my mother before she died. My father considered it very like." Miles was also impressed. "Do you have other examples of your work?" he asked. Mrs. Berkley gestured to a small picture on another wall. "I painted that last summer. It is of a corner of our garden in Birmingham," she replied. The canvas showed a low wall with roses and flower beds in bloom in the foreground, with a view of a meadow and distant trees behind the wall. Miles rose and walked over to see the picture more closely. "A delightful view," he commented.

On either side of the fireplace, Mrs. Berkley had placed a small bookcase. Each was filled with volumes of poetry, some novels and some history. Catherine was pleased to recognize several of her own favorites. "I see you have read *Marmion*. Did you enjoy it?" she asked. "I own, I am fond of Walter Scott's works." Mrs. Berkley said, "Although I am not fond of poetry in general, I did enjoy *Marmion* very much. I confess to being more a reader of novels than of poetry, I'm afraid." Catherine responded eagerly, "I, too, enjoy novels. I have so enjoyed *Sense and Sensibility*, and have started another by the same author titled *Pride and Prejudice*. I could not help but notice that you also have a copy of *Sense and Sensibility*. What did you think of it?" "After reading Mrs. Radcliffe's and Mrs. Burney's works, I own I found it quite different to what I expected. However, I did enjoy it. The author was able to bring her characters so clearly to the reader, and she wrote of circumstances, experiences and feelings familiar to all of us. I confess that I have never wandered in a ruin at midnight!" Miles and the two ladies laughed. Miles said, with mock severity, "I myself have little time for novels. Such frivolity is not suited to a man of business!" He went on, "However, I did enjoy Southey's *Life of Nelson*. Well worth reading, I do assure you!" "As to that, Mr. Stuart, you will find my husband's well-worn copy of that noble work in the other bookcase!" replied Mrs. Berkley. "Dare I confess that I, too, read and enjoyed that work?" commented Catherine. "I do not believe that a liking for novels precludes the capacity to enjoy more serious works." "Indeed, I agree with you, Lady Heyerwood. I found Mr. Southey's work most interesting, and enjoy reading books about history and notable people as keenly as any novel," responded Mrs. Berkley. Catherine was pleased to note more shared tastes, and the ladies smiled at each other. Just then, Mr. Berkley and Mr. Lamb entered the room.

Mr. Lamb immediately took charge. "Lady Heyerwood, Mr. Stuart, I am delighted to see you both. Mr. Berkley and I were just discussing our situation regarding the school, and I would like to let you know how it stands at this present." Eagerly, Catherine leaned forward. "How was the announcement received, Mr. Lamb?" she asked. Mr. Lamb sighed and shook his head. "Not what I am hoped, I fear. Several of the parents were quite vocal in their objections, not least their fears that their children would become dissatisfied with their place in life and look down on their parents." He brightened, "However, there was considerable interest in the Bible and catechism classes, and there were some girls and women interested in the needlework classes. There were also a few families who will give serious consideration to allowing their sons to attend school after the spring planting. Some of the younger tenant farmers could see the advantage of increased skill in reading and figures."

Mrs. Berkley said, bracingly, "Well, sir, it sounds a promising beginning. We have some students to start immediately, and the promise of more in just a few weeks. Mr. Berkley and I will be happy to assist with the Bible classes, while you conduct the catechism classes, if you approve." Gratefully, Mr. Lamb said, "I thank you. That would be kind indeed. My wife also plans to help with those classes, so you and she can plan them out together." Catherine put in, "I will order some Bibles and some prayer books. The lessons may mean more if the students have their own books to keep and from which to study." Miles added, "Some objections were only to be expected. Recall that Hannah Moore and her sister encountered great difficulty establishing their schools a few years ago. We can make a small beginning now, and see growth over time." Catherine added, "Vicar, I hope you will consider having the catechism and Bible classes in the schoolhouse, instead of the church or your office. As people become accustomed to being in the building, seeing it used, mayhap they will feel more comfortable with the *idea* of it." She looked at Mrs. Berkley. "The needlework classes should also be conducted there, don't you agree? I understand that you brought some materials with you; I hope you will let me know if more are needed." Mrs. Berkley nodded briskly, and replied, "Indeed, I shall. I think it would be well to have these classes on Sunday afternoons, at least to start. We can keep them to a length that will not interfere with the dinner hour. If more time is wanted, we can add additional time during the week. Then, when we start regular lessons after the spring planting, the school will have lost some of its newness, and simply be a part of the village." Mrs. Berkley, Catherine and the gentlemen smiled at each other with an air almost of relief. They chatted briefly, then Catherine and Miles rose to take their leave. As she put on her bonnet and shawl, Catherine said, "I look forward to seeing you all at dinner later this week. Perhaps we can have some music after we dine?" Mr. Lamb and the Berkleys assented. As they drove off, Catherine commented, "Uncle Miles, Mr. Berkley said nothing, and it seems his skills will not be call upon for some weeks yet, except for the Bible classes. I hope he is not too cast down." Thoughtfully, Miles replied, "I got no sense of disappointment. I feel certain that he will assist with the Bible classes with enthusiasm, especially if any men or boys participate. He can use this time to learn to know the people hereabouts, and lay his plans for future classes. No, my dear, I'm sure his time will be occupied usefully."

Chapter 43

The next morning, immediately after breakfast, Catherine went to her desk in the library, and wrote a letter to Hatchard's, ordering twenty copies of the Book of Common Prayer, and twenty Bibles, to be delivered directly to the vicarage as soon as may be. She gave it to a footman with instructions to send it Express. She was reading a letter from Caroline when Howard entered quietly. In some apparent distress, Howard say, "Pray, pardon me, my lady." He held out a letter and added, "This letter, my lady, came two days ago. A footman set it down and forgot it until today. I deeply regret the error, my lady." Catherine took the letter, and said, "Howard, please do not upset yourself. I am sure it was simply an oversight, and am certain it won't happen again." Grimly, Howard said, "Of that you can be certain, Lady Heyerwood. I have made the young man fully aware." He bowed, and went on his way, brooding darkly on the breakdown of his system. Smiling, Catherine opened the letter, glancing down for the signature. Stunned, she realized the letter was from James. Her thoughts in a whirl, Catherine sat for a moment, the letter in her lap. He had not asked permission to write to her, had not mentioned the possibility of such a correspondence. She shook her head, a reluctant smile coming to her lips. "How typical of him!" she thought. "Always he goes his own way, regardless of convention."

She picked up the letter and began to read. He began with a formal, conventional expression of thanks for her hospitality, and then wrote of the journey back to Ridley Manor, Rosalie's health, and other items of general interest. "I should have asked if I could write to you," he wrote, "but it did not occur to me until I was *en route*. I hope you are not offended by my taking this liberty." Wryly, she thought, "As if it were an

209

unusual or a shocking event!" He then told her how much he had enjoyed learning to know her family. "I had hoped you and I could spend more time together, but had not reckoned the time required for your other responsibilities. I must tell you, however, seeing you in your home, with your family, made me even more appreciative of your quality. I was all admiration when I learned of your scheme for a school for the local people. The intimacy of the atmosphere, the air of romance lent by your aunt's wedding, the existing depth of my esteem for you, caused me to move too fast, to push too hard. My hope is that my conduct has not given you a disgust of me, and that we can come to know each other better through exchanging letters." He then continued with a discussion of business that awaited him at Ridley Manor, and of plans he had made regarding his estate with John. He concluded almost formally, indicating that he was hers respectfully. Catherine felt conflicting emotions about the letter. "So many contradictions! One moment, occupied with mundane remarks; then preoccupied with romance; finally back to business. I don't know how to answer such a letter. I am not even certain that I want to answer." She read the letter again, blushing slightly as she read of his admiration and esteem. Putting the letter carefully into her reticule, she hurried upstairs to her sitting room. Glancing through the contents once more, Catherine thought deeply, then gave a nod of decision. She put the letter carefully into a drawer in her dainty writing desk, locked the drawer, and then sat down to write.

Catherine got out ink and paper, and began to mend her pen as she thought about what to say. "Lord Ridley," she began formally, "I received your letter with some surprise, and read it with interest." She went on to acknowledge his thanks, and to express her appreciation for his news, especially regarding Rosalie's health. She pondered deeply, and then continued. She thanked him for his thoughts of her. "You are most kind to think of me so generously. I would enjoy improving our acquaintance, and the distance between our homes would make correspondence practical. However, I would that we start this correspondence strictly as acquaintances and marriage relatives, which we are. I will make no promises at this present, and intend to keep these messages on a strictly friendly footing. If you can write to me on this basis, I look forward to an interesting exchange. To anything more than this, I cannot agree. As it is, we are stretching the limits of propriety. I write plainly, as you see, for I would have no misunderstanding between us." She continued with a brief description of the current plans for the new school, and signed her letter cordially. Catherine read over her response, feeling dissatisfied with the temperate nature of her letter, half-tempted to tear it up. Finally, she folded and sealed it, and wrote his direction, setting it aside to take down for a footman to put it on the Mail the next day. Briefly, she considered discussing it with her mother or aunt, but decided to follow her own instinct on this issue. "I own that I find him attractive. He and Rosalie both say he has feelings for me. Although it may seem improper, a correspondence seems an opportunity to deepen our acquaintance, get to know each other's minds, without risk. I have so little experience, and must confess that I am afraid of being disappointed and of being hurt."

The next several days flew by. Catherine, her mother and Aunt Mary spent more time in the garden as the spring days lengthened. Their music was enhanced by occasional calls paid by Mrs. Berkley for the purpose of practicing with them. As they played, the four ladies found time to chat. Their subjects ranged from music to books to art. Anne Berkley had seen Madame Vigee LeBrun's portrait of Lady Hamilton, and had the privilege of watching Madame paint while she was visiting London some years ago. "She was commissioned to paint the Prince of Wales, and Society could not get enough of her," recalled Anne. "She was a lovely woman, and her paintings were immensely popular. So fresh, and gracefully rendered, and her colours were so natural and lively. She inspired me to spend more time working on my sketching and painting, and with my drawing master." She laughed. "I had never thought of a woman being a serious artist, you see." Impressed, Catherine asked, "Did Madame LeBrun's work inspire you to paint portraits?" Thoughtfully, Anne replied, "In a way. You see, my governess and drawing master focused on landscape, flowers, nature. My drawing master told me of a theory that, because women's brains were smaller, females did not have the intelligence to master complicated ideas. He felt that the subtleties of expression, colour and features involved with portraiture would perhaps be too taxing for a young female. After seeing Madame LeBrun's work, he was willing to consider giving me additional instruction." With an impish smile, she added, "I believe you may say she inspired us both."

Mary took Anne up to her suite, to show her the firescreen Catherine had embroidered. "What exquisite work!" exclaimed Anne. "The design is so graceful and balanced, and the colours so well chosen. Your niece is quite talented." Looking more closely, she exclaimed, "The frame is quite remarkable as well. You can tell it was created especially for this embroidery; it compliments it so well. Who made this? Was it done in

London? I would love to speak with the craftsman who made it." Mary replied, "The vicar told Catherine about him. He is the son of a local farmer, a very young man. He made some frames for some paintings for the vicar, and Catherine commissioned this when she completed the stitching. He is indeed very talented, is he not?" They went back downstairs, just in time to join the others in a cup of tea. After a couple of hours, Anne Berkley returned home, while the ladies of Heyerwood retired to their rooms to rest and change for dinner.

In her own suite, Catherine sat on her private balcony, looking over the rose garden. Absently, she admired the glossy leaves and the flowers just beginning, thinking of a design for a chair cover. Feeling a bit chilled, she went to her room and lay down on a *chaise longue* before the fire, with a novel to read. She read a few pages, then fell into a doze, from which she did not awaken until Jane came in to help her dress for dinner. Catherine sat up with a start. "My goodness, Jane, I must hurry. I did not mean to fall asleep!" she exclaimed. "The blue velvet will be fine." Hastily, she stepped out of her dress, washed, and seated herself before the mirror. As Jane took down her hair, brushed it hard, and coiled it into a soft knot low on her neck, Catherine put pearl drops into her ears and clasped a single strand of pearls around her neck. Hurriedly, she stepped into the blue velvet and turned around for Jane to fasten it. "Thank you, Jane! I don't know what I would do without you."

Catherine ran down the stairs to the drawing room, only to find she was the first one down. Stepping over to the library, she sat down at the desk, took out a sheet of paper and a pencil, and drew a quick sketch of her idea for an embroidered chair cover, with a few notes regarding colours. Setting it aside, she returned to the drawing room to find Mathilde and Mary seated before the fire, sipping a glass of ratafia and conversing idly. Sitting down in her favorite chair, Catherine asked for a glass of sherry and, after she was served, turned her attention to the conversation at hand. It appeared that Uncle Miles was upstairs, changing for dinner. He was delayed due to a letter from London, and, it appeared, he would have to return to town for some important business matter, and wished for Mary to accompany him. Catherine responded quickly, "Of course, you must go with him! I will send an Express to Morrow tomorrow to let him know you are coming, so that your rooms will be ready, and the housekeeper prepared. We, of course, will miss you but this is still your honeymoon! Just think, in town, you can see a play or go to a concert, shop and see some acquaintances. You and Uncle Miles can enjoy yourselves when he is not engaged with work." Mary blushed and smiled, saying, "Thank you, my dear, I do want to accompany him. It seems that some of his colleagues wish to give a dinner for him, in honor of our marriage, and he would like me to accompany him, to meet his associates' wives, as well as some of his clients. He also indicated that he would like to talk to you, dear niece, before we go about some sort of business matter."

Just then, Miles entered the room. Howard followed, and announced that dinner was served. Miles escorted the three ladies to the dining room. The foursome discussed again the wedding, the festivities afterwards, the pleasures of company, and the peacefulness after company departs. Casually, Mathilde turned to Catherine and asked, "Have you heard from your cousin Rosalie since she departed?" Catherine flushed slightly, but replied steadily, "Not from Rosalie herself, but I did get a letter from Lord Ridley. He thanked me for our hospitality, and informed me about Rosalie's health. It sounds as though she is blooming." Mathilde raised her eyebrows, and said, "Lord Ridley, you say? That seems a bit … forward, do you not think?" Catherine stiffened a bit, and said pleasantly, "I think not, Mother. He is a marriage relative, after all. I see nothing inappropriate about a friendly correspondence with my cousin's brother-in-law." Mathilde and Mary exchanged glances, while Miles replied, "Of course you are right, my dear Catherine. All in the family, you may say. Did he mention John? He and John were dealing with some interesting cases; John serves as Justice of the Peace for that area, but Lord Ridley, of course, has input as well." Catherine turned to her uncle and smiled, in some relief, saying, "Lord Ridley did not mention any details, only that John was well and anxious about Rosalie. I will be happy to give you his direction, if you do not have it." "Thank you, my dear, I would be grateful. However, I do expect to see him in London. I'm sure Mary told you that I must go to town for some business matters quite soon. I have some clients with legal affairs that require my attention, but Lord Ridley and I are also engaged in some business as well." Catherine was surprised by this response, but only murmured that she would be happy to furnish the information to her uncle after dinner.

Chapter 44

Catherine and Mrs. Davis finalized the menu and plans for that evening's dinner. Mr. and Mrs. Lamb and Mr. and Mrs. Berkley were coming to dine. Since Aunt Mary and Uncle Miles would be departing for London within a very few days, Catherine wanted the evening to be as festive as possible. She planned a larger meal than customary, each with several removes, and an elaborate dessert. She also carefully discussed the wines to be served with Howard. Going to the drawing room, she sat down, mulling over her wardrobe. She decided to wear the chocolate pattern-silk, over the ivory underdress, with pearls as her ornaments. Getting up, she wandered over to the window, looked out at the garden, then sat down at the piano-forte. Deciding to practice, Catherine played for over an hour, drifting from one melody to the next without stopping. Finally closing the instrument, she got up, and hesitated for a moment, uncertain what to do next. She went to the library and found her hasty sketch on the desk. Catherine picked it up, looked at it critically, and decided to work on the design some more. She ran upstairs to her sitting room, and sat down at her writing desk. As she studied the design, she decided to add more detail, and began to sketch.

Catherine worked on until Jane quietly entered the room. Looking up, Catherine said, "Good morning, Jane. I hope you are having a pleasant day." "Indeed, yes, my lady. It is well into the afternoon, and Lady Stanton was almost ready to go downstairs for a nuncheon. Would you like to change and join her, Lady Heyerwood?" "I completely lost track of time, Jane. Thank you for reminding me. I must hurry," she said, catching sight of the clock. "The brown sarcenet will do." Jane unfastened Catherine's morning gown; Catherine stepped out of it, and sat down at her dressing table. She hooked in her topaz earbobs, and sat thinking while Jane brushed and braided her hair into a coronet. Jane fastened the sherry brown day dress, but, as she went to pin the ecru lace cap on Catherine's head, Catherine halted her. "No, Jane, I don't feel like wearing it today and, since there are none to be offended except my family, I will do without it. Thank you."

Catherine hurried down the stairs, and toward the drawing room. Just as she approached the door, a footman approached her and bowed. "The post, my lady," he said as he presented a small tray with several letters neatly stacked upon it. "Thank you," she said with a smile. He bowed again, and held the drawing room door for her as she entered. Her mother and aunt were just sitting down before the fire, while Howard was arranging a small table. She went through the letters, and found two for her mother, one from Lady Castlereagh and another from the Earl of Aldersey. She greeted Mary and Mathilde affectionately, handed Mathilde her letters, and sat down to read her own. As she sorted, she found one from Rosalie, another from Caroline, and a third letter from Baron Ridley. Hastily, she folded the letter from the baron and put it into her reticule to read later. As she opened the letter from Caroline, her mother exclaimed, "Oh, no! How terribly sad!" Looking up, she said, "What has happened, Mother?" Her mother glanced at Catherine, then back to her letter. "I have received a letter from my cousin Maria's husband, the Earl of Aldersey. It appears she has been taken very ill. Indeed, she has had a stroke!" Catherine's thoughts flew to Rosalie, then to Michael. "Does he mention Rosalie or Michael, Mother?" she asked. "Lord Aldersey says that Michael, of course, is there with him and his wife; he does not mention Rosalie in this letter." "How sad if her mother were to die before Rosalie's child is born!" exclaimed Catherine. Mathilde looked up at Catherine. "It would indeed be a sorrow, my dear. However, unless things have changed, she is still living and may recover. We must hope for the best, my dear. Mayhap her illness will soften Maria's heart toward her daughter. In any event, I must write to him immediately and offer what comfort I can." "Please, Mother, enclose my best wishes, as well," said Catherine. As Mathilde hurried from the room, Catherine looked at Mary and said, "Pray, Aunt, excuse me, but I must have some time alone." James's letter seemed to be burning a hole in her reticule, and she did not want to read it before company. She then looked at Howard and said, "Please let Mrs. Davis know that my mother and I will each have a small tray in our rooms, and my aunt would like some tea here in the drawing room." Howard bowed, and left the room, while Catherine hurried upstairs.

Left alone with her thoughts, Catherine could not help thinking of Rosalie. How sad Rosalie would be if her mother passed away, unreconciled to her daughter's marriage. Of course, Rosalie's father and brother would then be free to associate with Rosalie and her husband. It was, truly, a difficult situation. She picked up Rosalie's letter and began to read. "Cousin Catherine, I hope this finds you well. I am in good health, and receiving the tenderest care possible from John and my whole household. If not for one circumstance, I would be the most contented woman in the world. My father has written to me, advising that my mother is gravely ill following a stroke, and cautioned me not to try to visit or to write to her, for fear of aggravating her condition. He did not tell me what circumstances surround her stroke. I am dreadfully worried that I have somehow caused this situation. John tells me I am foolish to feel this way, but it does weigh on me." The letter continued with details of her preparations for the coming child, plans for her garden, and other items of domestic interest. Laying Rosalie's letter aside, Catherine opened the letter from James next, curious to see if it contained more information about Rosalie's mother.

James wrote more formally than in his previous letter, which both pleased and annoyed her. He wrote of estate business, improvements he was making, and certain matters relating to issues John was handling as Justice of the Peace. Only towards the end did he mention Rosalie's mother. "As you may know, Lady Aldersey is gravely ill. Rosalie feels it deeply. Her father did write to her; however, she has heard nothing from her brother, and is not permitted to visit or write to her mother." James continued, "I wonder if you are aware how much the *rosa centifolia* reminds me of you? I noticed it growing in your walled garden, and have had one planted near my study window. I think of you constantly." That was all. The letter ended as formally as it began. Catherine gazed absently out of the window, lost in thought. "That letter could have been written to anyone," she thought crossly, taking a sip of tea, "except for the last two or three lines. No indication of his thoughts or opinions about anything." She put James's letter aside as well, intending to answer his and Rosalie's letters later. She had almost a feeling of relief as she read Caroline's letter. Caroline's letter was full of her happiness, and carried only good news of their mutual acquaintances. That one she could respond to immediately. She wrote a quick letter, letting Caroline know of her own activities, and Mary and Miles impending return to town. She was just fixing the seal on her reply, when Jane came to help her bathe and change for dinner. Catherine then recalled her virtually untouched tea tray.

That evening, as the party gathered in the drawing room, a festive atmosphere prevailed. Mr. and Mrs. Lamb arrived with Mr. and Mrs. Berkley. Neither Mathilde nor Catherine mentioned Rosalie's mother to the company at large. All of the conversation focused on Mary's and Miles' departure for town, music, plans for the school and other cheerful subjects. "Catherine, you must give me a list for any shopping you would like me to do," said Mary. "I can order things to be delivered directly to Heyerwood, or take them with me to the town house to await your convenience." Her eyes sparkled. "You must know I am delighted to have an excuse to shop!" Catherine's eyes twinkled back at her aunt. "I will write out a list this very evening! Shall you mind a visit to Hatchard's? You can have them send the books I want here directly; they have done so several times. I will write out an order that you may give them. If you chance to visit Grafton's or the Pantheon, I would like some silk in a soft, deep plum or violet. I have an overdress in mind, something I can wear over either my gold or the ivory underdress ... Oh, I will indeed make a list! I do thank you, Aunt Mary!" Mathilde mentioned some new music, some embroidery silk, and some Gowland's lotion. Mary laughed, and said, "A list! I will never be able to remember everything." Catherine agreed to make a list for the household.

Mathilde then asked Miles about the business requiring his presence in London. "I am afraid I can give very little information, so much of my work being confidential. I am assisting a barrister on a rather complicated case, requiring some discussion. I am also working with another client on a will, with some entail questions," he replied. "Both of these matters have been under consideration for some little time, and need to be completed. I am also needed to consult with a different client about some estate business." Smiling at Catherine, he said with a twinkle, "You are not my only client, my dear." Catherine laughed. "Not? I am utterly cast down, indeed!" She turned to Mr. Berkley. "What news of the school, sir? Have the Bible classes begun?" Mr. Berkley beamed. "We have, indeed begun the Bible classes, Lady Heyerwood. We have several children, and even a few adults. In fact, after the first class, when we gave the students their Bibles, one of the men asked about getting his children into regular classes. 'I want them to be able to read,' he said, 'I just did not think I would be able to get a book for them.' They will be starting next week, in the evening, after their work is done. I foresee a rapid growth from this beginning."

Mrs. Berkley added, "We have also started a handwork class, with a few of the girls, in embroidery and netting. I was wondering, Lady Heyerwood, if you could design a very simple sampler for them to work?" "I would be delighted to do that, and to supply the linen and threads. Would you prefer the alphabet or a verse?" Mrs. Berkley replied thoughtfully, "An alphabet would be best, I believe. It is practical, for marking linen, and most of the girls have not yet learned their letters. We can work in some reading lessons painlessly, as we sew." Catherine agreed. "In time, maybe they will consider joining the regular classes." She turned to include Mr. and Mrs. Lamb, and Mr. Berkley. "Ladies and gentlemen, now that we have had a promising start, it is not too soon to consider results. Would it be possible, within a few months, to assess progress, maybe award some prizes of some sort? Mayhap a sewing basket for one of the girls in the handwork class, a book for one of the regular students, a prayer book for a Bible student? I think it important to reward achievement, and to provide some incentive. Please give this some thought. If you will let me know what is appropriate, and when you wish to present them, I will be happy to provide the awards and attend the ceremony. Maybe there could be recitations? At any rate, please advise me what you would like, and I will attend to it."

At that point, Catherine rose, and the ladies withdrew to the drawing room. Mary and Mathilde sat down by the fire with Mrs. Lamb, while Anne Berkley joined Catherine at the piano-forte. As they began to play a duet they had practiced, Anne said, "Mr. Stuart has approached me about painting his wife's portrait, but I understand they are going to London soon. Have you any idea how long they may be gone? I can start it and work with some drawings, but would need to have her sit to me at some point. It is awkward to start, then to have to set the work aside for an indefinite period." "I believe they go for a few weeks only. I know my uncle has business to conduct. My aunt will be shopping for our household. If you like, I can ask if they have considered a return as yet," replied Catherine. "What a lovely idea, to have her portrait taken! Have you any idea for the composition?" Anne looked at Mary appraisingly. "I had thought to use a garden setting, but her current position in that high-backed chair, by the fire, is perfect, as is her black lace gown. If only I had my drawing paper!" Catherine said with a twinkle, "I use drawing paper for my designs. I would be happy for you to use some, if you wish to start tonight. Of course, we did not invite you here this evening to make you work!" "That would be wonderful! I can at least make some preliminary sketches." Catherine fetched the paper and pencils, and Anne began to draw. Catherine resumed playing some of her favorite melodies, while watching Anne's rapid strokes. Mary, unaware, continued her conversation with Mathilde and Mrs. Lamb, entirely natural. Catherine was intrigued to see several remarkably-detailed sketches of her aunt appear, smiling, looking thoughtful, full-face, head turned. Anne also made copious notes, regarding colours, skin tone, and so forth.

The gentlemen appeared, having finished their port. The conversation at the fireside became more general. Catherine continued playing softly, and Anne did more swift sketches. Just then, Mathilde asked Miles, "Do you plan to return to Heyerwood soon, or will you be fixed in town, Miles?" Catherine listened alertly, as Miles responded, "I expect all of my business to be concluded in a week or two; however I may have to go on to Exeter. If that is the case, I will come here first to leave Mary and her boxes, then continue on. Otherwise, we will both return together. Eventually, we will spend more time in London, but, just now, it is so very pleasant here, in the country." Catherine glanced at Anne just in time to see her make a note of Miles' comment regarding Mary's return.

Chapter 45

The next several days passed in a blur, and suddenly Mary and Miles were gone in a flurry of hugs and kisses. Mary had tucked a voluminous shopping list into her reticule, recklessly promising to procure every item. After waving farewell, Catherine and Mathilde returned to the house. Hesitating in the hall, Catherine impulsively suggested that she and her mother have some tea in the walled garden. Mathilde agreed with pleasure, and hurried upstairs for a sunshade, while Catherine went to look for Mrs. Davis. After giving Mrs. Davis' her instructions for the day and for tea, Catherine went out to the garden to join her mother. She found Mathilde on a bench, under the spreading branches of an oak in the corner. She looked around with pleasure. "In another few weeks, Mother, I believe we will have a profusion of flowers," said Catherine. "Already there is a great deal of colour for so early in the spring, especially considering how bitterly cold the winter had been." Mathilde agreed, "The weather is truly delightful today, my dear. It is such a pleasure to be out here, sheltered as it is, and see such loveliness." Both ladies fell silent as they basked in the filtered sunlight. A footman carried out a small table, which he set up before them, while a maid carried out a tray with tea and some small cakes. Catherine dismissed them with a smile and thanks, then poured her mother and herself each a cup.

Leisurely sipping, they engaged in idle chat. Mathilde rose and strolled across the soft grass. "It is a real joy to be able to step out of one's door into such a beautiful place, my love. I did so dislike the gloomy shrubbery that Stanton insisted on planting. I hope the new viscount and his wife make changes." Drily, Catherine replied, "I do not think you need concern yourself, Mama. My cousin Martin has every intention of making the

London house and the country estate completely his own. I dare swear we shan't recognize either place when next we see them." Brightening, she added, "I have every confidence in Cousin Alethea's taste, and her ability to handle Cousin Martin. I'm sure the town house, especially, will be much more pleasant and comfortable when it is finished, than it was in our time there."

Catherine and Mathilde spent a restful few hours in the garden, then decided to make their way back to the house. They were walking slowly up the path, when they met Howard, on his way to find them. "You have a caller, Lady Heyerwood," he said, looking perturbed. "I told him that I did not know if you were at home. Viscount Chatellerault is waiting in the drawing room. Are you at home, my lady?" Remembering the acrimony of their last meeting, Catherine could feel only dismay. Gently, Mathilde reminded her, "He may be here to inform us of a change in my cousin Maria's health." Catherine replied, "Very true, Mother. I will endeavor to meet Michael cordially." Turning to the butler, Catherine added, "Howard, you may tell the viscount that I will join him in the drawing room shortly. Please have a footman take some refreshments to the drawing room for his lordship, and advised Mrs. Davis that my mother enjoyed greatly enjoyed our tea in the garden. She can have the maid clear up. Thank you, very much, Howard." Turning back to Mathilde, she said, "Pray excuse me, Mother. If I am going to meet my cousin, I must tidy myself." She entered the house through a side door, and went upstairs to her room, where she rang for Jane.

Desiring Jane to get out her burgundy crepe day dress, Catherine removed her half-boots and took down her hair. After Jane helped her out of her gown, Catherine washed quickly, then slipped on the burgundy dress. Jane swiftly fastened the dress, then brushed Catherine's hair into a soft knot high on the crown of her head, leaving a few shining, brown curls about her face and ears. Catherine slipped her garnet earbobs into her lobes, and pushed her feet into soft black slippers. Taking a deep breath, she ran down the stairs, crossed the hall and entered the drawing room. As she stopped near the door, Catherine saw the viscount standing by the window, staring out across the lawn.

Alerted by the rustle of her skirt, Michael turned and bowed stiffly. "Good afternoon, Lady Heyerwood," he said unsmilingly. "I apologize for calling unexpectedly. My father, the Earl of Aldersey, desired me to detour this way on my return to Cheshire, to advise my mother's cousin of her current state." Raising her brows slightly, Catherine sketched a curtsey, and said, "Good afternoon, my lord. You are welcome. Pray be seated and have some refreshment. A beautiful day, is it not?" She seated herself in her favorite chair by the fire. Tight-lipped with annoyance, Michael crossed the room, took a seat facing her and accepted the glass of brandy she extended to him. "Thank you, my lady," he responded. Catherine rang the bell and, when Howard presented himself, said, "Howard, please request my mother to join us in the drawing room when she is ready. The viscount has news regarding her cousin." Howard bowed, said, "Very well, my lady," and left the room.

Left to themselves, Michael and Catherine sat by the fire, saying nothing. As the silence stretched between them, Catherine sat at her ease, and noticed her cousin's increasing irritation. Finally, she said, "We appreciated his lordship's letter, and were so sorry to read of your mother's illness. I hope your father is well?" Unbendingly, he replied, "The earl is enjoying his customary good health, apart from his anxiety about his wife, my lady. I thank you for asking." Exasperated, Catherine looked at him and snapped, "My lord, this is outside of enough. You came here; I did not invite you. If you cannot be civil to me in my own home, you are welcome to leave." For a split second, Catherine thought he was going to respond furiously; then, a reluctant smile crossed his face. "It is foolish, I suppose, to stand on ceremony," he said. Just then, Mathilde entered the room. "My dear Michael!" she exclaimed, "how does your poor mother?" As Mathilde held out her hand, Michael rose, took it, and led Mathilde to the settee. Catherine said, "Cousin Michael, have you made arrangements for a meal or for a room for the night?" Sheepishly, he replied, "Well, I had hoped…" Catherine rose, shaking her head. "You two may talk while I speak to Mrs. Davis about preparing a room for you, and adding a guest for dinner." Mathilde looked pleased, and Michael embarrassed, as she left the room.

Catherine paused in the hall, wanting to stamp her foot with vexation. She had no inclination to have Michael as a guest in her home, especially after their conflict the last time they met. "What could I do?" she asked herself. "There is no suitable inn for at least ten miles, and it is already late in the afternoon. How I dislike having my hand forced, especially if he is disposed to be disagreeable!" She spoke to Mrs. Davis about preparing a room, assigning someone to wait on the viscount, and rearranging dinner plans to accommodate an unexpected guest. In response to Mrs. Davis' enquiry, Catherine responded, "I expect the viscount to take his leave tomorrow. He merely broke his journey to give my mother some news. You may recall that he prefers an early breakfast." Returning to the drawing room, Catherine found Michael and Mathilde chatting comfortably, and said, "My lord, your baggage has been removed to your room, and your horse taken to the stables. Dinner will be at six o'clock; you know we keep country hours here. When you are ready, please advise Howard so he can have you shown to your room." Catherine turned to leave the room, planning to escape to her library, when Michael rose, and said, "Thank you for your hospitality, Lady Heyerwood." She nodded, and left the room without further speech.

Catherine seated herself at her desk, and began to look over some letters. A note from Anne, advising that some preliminary sketches for her aunt's portrait were ready to see, prompted an immediate response. A brief note from the vicar, letting her know that each day more students were enrolling in Bible classes or the regular classes, resulted in her sending a note asking if more Bibles were needed. As she broke the seal on the last letter, she looked up as her cousin said, "Lady Heyerwood, -er, Catherine, may I trouble you for a moment?" Surprised that he had entered without announcing himself, Catherine refrained from saying, "You already have." She replied instead, "It is no trouble, my lord. Please tell me how I may assist you." "Your mother has retired to her rooms to rest, and I wanted to speak with you for a moment." "By all means, sir. Pray, how is your mother?" Michael went to the window, and stood looking out. "She appears to be recovering, albeit very slowly. She is much calmer, and no longer tries to leave her bed without assistance. Although it appears she understands when someone speaks to her, she does not yet try to talk. She sleeps a great deal." Gently Catherine said, "Surely, sir, these are positive changes, are they not? Calmness, the ability to comprehend, getting plenty of rest are all indicators of improvement, I would think." "We are trying to be hopeful, but, until she speaks to us, we just do not know." Turning back to face her, he said, "Thank you for your cheerful words, Cousin. I was wondering if I could borrow a book to read later." Catherine rose, came around her desk, and went to the shelves. "Of course you may, Cousin. I have Southey's *LIFE OF NELSON*, some histories here, or a novel if you prefer..." She turned to face him, and found he was standing near her desk. Easily, he replied, "A novel would be excellent, madam. What would you suggest?" Mechanically, she suggested any of several of Mrs. Edgeworth's or Mrs. Radcliffe's novels, gesturing towards the shelves where the volumes were located. As he moved to the bookshelves, her eyes flew to the desk. Nothing appeared different, except that the letter she had not yet read appeared slightly askew. This put her in a quandary, as she had not seen Michael touch it. However, Catherine, remembering the disorder she found in her desk during his previous visit, had an odd feeling....

Without haste, Michael selected his book. In passing, she noted it was a volume of one of Ann Radcliffe's novels. Thanking her, Michael indicated that he wanted to retire to his room, to rest before dinner. Stiltedly, she replied, "By all means, sir. I will have you called in time to dress for dinner." He bowed and left the room. Catherine sat back down at the desk, and picked up her letter. Unfolding it, she noticed it was from James, and began to read. "My dear Lady Heyerwood," the letter began, "I hope this letter finds you well, and your school prospering. I know that is a project dear to your heart. Rosalie is well, thank goodness, though John gets more nervous each day." He went on to discuss several estate matters, giving his opinions of the correctness of decisions made in certain situations, and suggestions he had made to facilitate matters. "At last," she thought, "I begin to see something of his thoughts and opinions!" She read on. He mentioned a case John had heard as justice of the peace, and the debate he and John had had over the correct resolution. He continued on a second sheet. Again, he waited until the very end of the letter to tell her how frequently he thought of her, and how much he looked forward to seeing her again. A half-smile playing about her lips, Catherine sat for several moments, remembering his tall frame and deep blue eyes, as well as his calm assumption of authority and irritating tendency to sweep all before him. She felt like she was actually getting to know him. Folding the letter, she put it into her reticule and went upstairs.

Tapping at Mathilde's door, Catherine went in and found Mathilde reclining on a *chaise longue* near the fire with a volume of poetry. "Come in, Catherine," said Mathilde with a warm smile. Saying she did not want to disturb her mother, Catherine seated herself. She asked Mathilde about her cousin. The information Mathilde provided basically matched what Michael had told her. Excusing herself, Catherine went on to her own rooms, where she found Jane tidying up. Jane helped her out of her dress and into her warm velvet robe and slippers. She put her letter from James in the small writing desk in her sitting room, and sat down in a comfortable chair. "Jane," she asked slowly, "Could you stay near my rooms as much as possible for the next day or two?" Surprised, Jane replied, "Certainly, Lady Heyerwood, if that is your wish. Is anything wrong?" "Not that I know of, Jane; I just don't want my rooms left unattended at this present." "I have some mending I could do in your dressing room, my lady. May I suggest that you have Mrs. Davis assign a footman to remain on this floor as well? That way, you may feel easier in your mind." "An excellent thought, Jane. Please pass that instruction to Mrs. Davis, when you go down to your dinner. Thank you!" Jane curtsied and left the room, intending to give Mrs. Davis the instruction regarding the footman right away. As she opened the main door from Catherine's suite to the hallway, she was startled to find the viscount near the door.

Startled, Jane bobbed a quick curtsey, and asked, "May I assist you, my lord?" Discomfited, Michael said, "No, no, I was just reacquainting myself with the house. Is Lady Heyerwood resting?" "Yes, my lord, she is. May I give her a message for you, sir?" "No need to disturb my cousin," he said easily, "when I will see her at dinner." Turning he strode rapidly down the hall. Looking after him thoughtfully, Jane thought, "I see why my lady feels uncomfortable. I will offer to sleep in her dressing room tonight as well." She hastened down the stairs, and found Mrs. Davis with the cook. Passing on her mistress's request for a footman on her floor, she managed to imply a sense of urgency, which resulted in Mrs. Davis immediately stationing a footman to remain in the hall, moving from one area to another as often as necessary to make sure everything was properly maintained. She also arranged for another to take over when the household retired, to be available during the night. Satisfied, Jane returned to her own room to gather the mending, her nightrail, and a book.

Catherine was a relaxed and cheerful hostess, made much more comfortable by having the faithful Jane in her rooms and a footman keeping an eye on the floor. Mathilde was also very pleased to be entertaining her cousin's son. Only Michael showed signs of constraint, even appearing ill at ease at times. Catherine and Mathilde maintained a pleasant conversation, while Michael sat silently, pushing his food around his plate. Finally, he looked at Catherine from under frowning brows and said, "Cousin, I must know... Are you corresponding with Rosalie or either of the Ridley men?" Shocked at the interruption, and the impertinent nature of the question, Catherine looked at him in silence for a moment, and then replied coolly, "I can hardly believe that you have any interest in my correspondence, sir. In any event, it is none of your business or concern with whom I choose to correspond." He was obviously irritated by her response, and opened his mouth to respond hotly, when he caught Mathilde's shocked gaze, and subsided. Catherine and her mother continued their conversation, as if Michael's rude interjection had never occurred, through both courses, then both rose to adjourn to the drawing room. "We will leave you to your port, my lord," said Catherine with a forced smile. "I hope you enjoy it."

The two ladies took their seats just as a maid brought in a tray of tea. Catherine asked the girl to provide some sherry and some glasses. "At this moment, I would like something with a little more...presence than tea, Mother," she said to Mathilde. "I understand, my dear. I was quite appalled at Michael's rudeness. However, I would vastly prefer a cup of tea, myself." Catherine poured out her mother's tea, and then accepted a glass of sherry presented by Howard. "Thank you, Howard." She and her mother engaged in idle chat for a moment, then, unable to settle, Catherine took her glass and sat down at the piano-forte. She idly played a few melodies as Mathilde tranquilly sipped her tea. Just then, Michael appeared in the drawing room door. Composedly, Catherine said, "We were just discussing how much more forward the roses are in the walled garden, my lord. In the main garden, there are very few blooms." Michael stalked in and bowed awkwardly, before taking a seat opposite Mathilde. Tersely, he said, "I know little of flowers. The gardens in Cheshire are still bare, so far as I've noticed." Mathilde calmly poured a cup of tea, and passed it to Michael. Per force, he had to unbend enough to thank her and accept the cup. The three fell silent, and Mathilde and Michael sipped their tea while Catherine played a little more. The silence fell more and more heavily, and Catherine thanked heaven that she at least could occupy herself at the piano-forte. "Mother," she suggested, "Would you care to joint me in our little duet before we retire?" With alacrity, Mathilde rose and went over to her harp. "Indeed, yes, my dear," she replied. "I do enjoy playing with you." As Mathilde was adjusting her harp, Michael rose, bowed, and said, "Pray, excuse me, ladies, I believe I shall retire to my room. I am rather... worn this evening." Concerned, Mathilde asked if he were feeling ill. "No, madam, I am in health. Just rather tired." Turning on his heel, he abruptly left the drawing room. Immediately, the tension relaxed and the two ladies enjoyed their music.

Chapter 46

Late that night, Catherine was awakened by a loud crash of thunder. Blinking sleepily, she got up, went to the window and pulled open a heavy drapery. In the flash of lightening, she could see rain streaming down. "Oh, no," she thought with dismay. "The roads will be a sea of mud if this keeps up." Drearily, she lit her candle and returned to her bed. Now wide awake, she picked up a novel and began to read, quickly losing herself in the story. As she read, her dressing room door opened and Jane peeked in, yawning. "My lady, are you ill?" asked Jane in concern. "No, indeed, Jane. The thunder woke me and I could not get back to sleep. This is a dreadful storm, is it not?" "Yes, Lady Heyerwood, it is indeed, and, in the kitchen, they were saying that the signs indicate that it will rain for at least a few days." Aghast, Catherine looked at her maid. "A few days! The roads will be in a dreadful state." The two looked at each other. Catherine dropped her eyes back to her book. "Jane, please get your rest. There is no need to stay up with me." Jane sketched a curtsey, and said, "Of course, my lady. Thank you. Oh, by the way, Lady Heyerwood, I locked the door to the main hallway after you retired. I thought you should know." Catherine looked up. "Ah, yes, Jane, I appreciate that. By chance, did anyone approach my rooms yesterday, apart from household staff?" Jane looked at her impassively, "Only the viscount, Lady Heyerwood. He was near the door as I was going to leave. He said he was reacquainting himself with the house. I stayed in your rooms until dinner was served, then went to Mrs. Davis with your instructions. I saw no one else. I hope I did right, my lady." Catherine said warmly, "Indeed, Jane, you did perfectly. Now go finish your rest." "Good night, my lady." Catherine read a little longer, then decided to get what rest she could and blew out her candle.

The next morning, the rain was still coming down hard. Catherine could see it streaming down the windows and splashing heavily on the balcony. Looking further, all she could see was a dark grey blur outside. "In common decency, I will have to ask Michael to stay," she thought despondently. "I could not turn a dog out in this weather. How we are going to get through this without a quarrel, I do not know, unless he decides to let be." Impulsively, she called for Jane, remembering just in time that Jane was in the dressing room. "Jane," she requested, "please have Mrs. Davis order breakfast in everyone's rooms today. I cannot face a company breakfast in the dining room this morning. I know my mother prefers a tray anyway. I believe it is still early enough to prevent them setting up in the dining room." Fortunately, Jane was already dressed and her usual tidy self. "I will go down immediately, Lady Heyerwood," replied Jane, and she left the room. Catherine pulled her warm velvet robe over her night rail, pushed her feet into slippers, and went to the hall door. Peeking out, she saw a footman standing near the stairs. Closing the door softly, she went to her sitting room and made herself comfortable before the fire on the chaise longue with her novel.

Early in the afternoon, after enjoying a leisurely breakfast, Catherine went down stairs. Her plum wool day dress kept the damp chill at bay, as she crossed the hall and entered the library. Seating herself at her desk, she started looking for her correspondence. Finding nothing, she rang for Howard. "Howard, did I receive no letters today?" she asked. "Indeed, yes, Lady Heyerwood, I have them here for you," he replied, and presented some letters on a tray. Surprised, she glanced up at Howard as she took her letters. "Mrs. Davis told me of your concerns and the instructions you sent through Miss Jane," murmured Howard. "I ventured to have all post brought directly to me for this present, so that I could hold yours until you ring for it, my lady." Catherine thanked him with a smile, and said, "That arrangement will do nicely, for the time being." Howard bowed and left the room, as Catherine broke the seal on the first letter. A brief note from Julia, telling Catherine how much she, Jean-Paul and Juliana were enjoying their time in the country. "The weather is not yet really suitable for spending time outside yet, but we are reading by the fire, playing nursery games, and having splendid times. Juliana has grown so, you would hardly recognize her. She and her papa have grown amazingly close, which delights me, as you may imagine." Catherine dashed off a short letter to Julia, telling her how well the school was progressing, how forward the walled garden flowers had been, and her fears that the storm in the small hours had damaged the plants. "The wind was howling, and the rain beating down in torrents. I cannot bear to think of how torn up the gardens may be, and I have been told we may have a few days of it!" She did not mention her cousin's visit. Opening the next letter, she found a brief missive from her aunt, advising her that they were safely arrived at the town house, and that all was in perfect order. "Your uncle has gone to his place of business this morning, but I am resting today, before starting the shopping. Even though the coach is well-sprung, by the second day, I feel stiff in every limb."

The last letter Catherine opened was another letter from James. Surprised to receive another letter so soon, she immediately began to read. "My dear Lady Heyerwood, I am on the point of leaving London for Ridley Manor, business here having been satisfactorily concluded. I have been offered an appointment which I must discuss with my brother. There are also a few estate matters that I must manage myself." He then went on to tell her some society information about acquaintances. "I dined with Lord and Lady Castlereagh a few nights ago. Both are well, and Lady Castlereagh requested that I give your mother, and you, her best wishes." A few more lines about other matters, and then, "I find that I would like to discuss several things with you in person, and hope that you will forgive my presumption in planning my journey so that I may stop at Heyerwood on my way home. If it is inconvenient or too impertinent, you have only to say the word and I will continue on. However, I did not want to wait for a reply and, dare I say? I hoped that you would not be so hard-hearted to exclude me if I appeared at your door." His letter concluded, Catherine fell back in her chair, feeling that her cup was now full. Pouring rain, her cousin Michael here in a foul mood, and now James about to pop up on her doorstep like the demon king in a pantomime! Helplessly, she pictured the look that would appear on Michael's face as James entered the drawing room, and couldn't refrain from shuddering. "There isn't even a hope of stopping him, and, of course, if it's raining, I couldn't refuse admittance." All of a sudden, Catherine thought of the years she had been here alone, and now her house was being overrun! She began to giggle at the absurdity of the situation. Putting James' letter in her reticule, she picked up the letter she had written to take to the hall for the post, and left the library, still chuckling.

Going back through the hall, she asked Howard, "Do you know where my mother is, Howard?" "I believe, my lady, that she went up to her own rooms a short while ago," he replied. "Thank you," she said, and ran lightly up the stairs. Tapping at her mother's door, she waited impatiently in the hall. To her surprise, her mother called, "Come in." "I was expecting Miss Potter, Mama," she said as she entered. "Are you alone?" "Yes, my dear, I am. I did not tell Potter that I was retiring after dinner, and she is still belowstairs. Sometimes, I do enjoy a little time alone." "I can come back later," offered Catherine, turning back toward the door. "No, indeed, my dear. I am always glad to see you." Catherine went in and sat down in a chair by the fire, near Mathilde. "Mother, I wanted to warn you what was happening. The weather is so dreadful that I cannot, in good conscience, suggest that Michael be on his way. You may recall that I have been corresponding with Baron Ridley since Aunt Mary and Uncle Miles married. He wrote, just before leaving town, expressing an intention of stopping here on his way back to Ridley Manor. Unfortunately, he and Michael are very angry at each other, and may not be able to be civil. It is too late to intercept Lord Ridley, and, unless the weather improves drastically, it will be impossible to refuse him shelter. What do you suggest?" Mathilde, sitting straight-backed in her chair as always, looked at her daughter in amazement for several moments. Then she said briskly, "Well, daughter, have them both shown to the ballroom, and let them deal with it. Either or both could well afford to take care of any damages…." Stunned, Catherine looked at her mother, saying, "Are you serious, Mother?" Mathilde burst out laughing, "My dear, this whole situation has an element of comedy, do not you agree? So ridiculous for Michael to behave like a sulky boy; let him address his grievances to Lord Ridley, who is, after all, the most proper person for him to approach, as the head of Rosalie's family at this present. As long as they manage to behave in company, they will have to resolve their own difficulties. You cannot hope to reconcile them yourself, and, unfortunately, it does not appear that there is any way to avoid their meeting here. While I do not completely approve of your correspondence with Lord Ridley, he *is* a marriage relative and you are both independent. Michael really has no right or reason to object whomever you choose to receive, and should, per force, behave like the gentleman he was bred to be. If Michael can behave with control, my limited exposure to Lord Ridley indicates that he will as well."

Completely surprised at Mathilde's calm response, Catherine sat in silence for several moments. As she caught her mother's eye, the twinkle she saw stirred a response, and she laughed out loud. "It *is* a ludicrous situation, is it not? When I think of all my years of solitary existence, and this to occur now, it is impossible not to laugh. It shall be as you suggest, my dear. I will treat James' arrival, if it occurs, as the merest commonplace; if either shows hackle, I will request Howard to have a footman escort the gentleman to the ballroom. It is to be hoped that they, too, will be able to see the farcical quality of the situation before they become embroiled." The two ladies enjoyed a hearty laugh, then discussed meeting for a nuncheon shortly. "I really cannot leave Michael on his own the entire day, Mama, and do not hope to avoid him indefinitely. I will tidy myself, and meet with Mrs. Davis. I shall order a nuncheon for this afternoon, and let her know that we may have another guest." Catherine kissed her mother fondly, and thanked her for her advice.

A few hours later, Catherine was sitting in the drawing room when Michael entered. She was working on her embroidery, the floral design of the chair cover just becoming evident. "Good afternoon, Michael," she said pleasantly. "As you see, I am profitably engaged this stormy afternoon. I hope you have not been dreadfully bored." Michael bowed, and said, "Good afternoon, cousin. I, too, have been busy. I received a letter from my father, requiring a reply, and went out for a walk. As you may expect, the drive is mired." Taken somewhat aback, Catherine said, "A message from your father? What news, sir, of your mother?" Michael replied, "He wrote to tell me that my mother is much improved. She is speaking now." Sympathetically, Catherine replied, "I am so pleased to hear that. You must be quite relieved." "Naturally, it is a great relief. Now it must be our concern to see to it that she does not relapse," returned Michael. Catherine looked at him questioningly. "Relapse, sir? Surely, safe in your home in Cheshire, her surroundings can be kept as peaceful and soothing as need be. Monitoring her activities to ensure that she does not unwisely tax her strength should not be difficult, I would think." Michael returned her gaze meaningly, "Do not fence with me, cousin. You know to what, or rather, to whom, I am referring."

Most unexpectedly, Catherine began to laugh. "My dear sir, I must give you full marks for determination. You are a veritable bull-dog with a bone. Nothing seems to discourage you, or put you off." Sobering, Catherine said firmly, "It is unfortunate that you cannot find a more worthy object for your determination. While I have all respect for your father and mother, the Earl and Countess of Aldersey, there is nothing wrong or dishonorable in Rosalie's marriage or situation that warrants my refusing to see her. Added to that, I hold her in great affection, and find her husband and his family to be unexceptionable. While their degrees may be different, at the end of the day, a gentleman's daughter married a gentleman, and lives in comfort. You seem to forget that you were all strangers to me until some months ago. As I have told you, I am not an inexperienced chit in the schoolroom. I am an independent adult, accustomed to thinking for myself. Please do not importune me on this matter again. Besides, there is no reason for your mother to know aught of my friendship with Rosalie, unless you take it upon yourself to inform her. I cannot think of single reason why you should do so." Catherine took a few more stitches while Michael strode to the window and back. Looking up, she said, "How was your walk, my lord? It seems a very difficult day to get the full benefit of such exercise." Reluctantly, Michael replied civilly, "It was a challenge to keep my feet at times, between the wind and the heavy rain. However, I must say that it was quite exhilarating. Of course, I was completely soaked by the time I returned to the house." Mathilde came in, wrapped in a warm shawl, and went straight to her favorite seat by the fire. "I was so certain that spring had arrived," she said with a shiver. "The damp chill seems to just creep into my bones whenever I am near the windows." Michael gave her the news about his mother's improvement, which Mathilde received with unfeigned joy. Her reminiscences of her debut with Maria were only interrupted when a tray of tea appeared.

The rain contined to pour, and the wind to howl, all evening. The three sat down to dinner, with Mathilde and Catherine dressed in warm velvet gowns, by a roaring fire. The heavy velvet drapes had been pulled tightly to block the drafts and the sound of the rain. Conversation was desultory at best. Catherine and Mathilde rose to go to the drawing room, leaving Michel in solitary state. As they crossed the hall, Catherine asked Howard to bring sherry and brandy. She and Mathilde took seats either side of the fire and sipped their sherry silently. Catherine was suddenly overtaken by a yawn, and said, "Please excuse me, Mother. I am suddenly exhausted. It must be this dreadful weather. I think I will retire early." Mathilde replied, "I, too, am quite tired and would relish an early night. However, I do think we should wait for Michael, so that we can bid him good night." Both ladies sat on by the fire, battling increasing drowsiness. Howard came in, and said, "Lady Heyerwood, Viscountess Stanton, Viscount Chatellerault wished me to extend his compliments and his apologies for deserting you so early. He has retired for the evening." Catherine looked at her mother, brows lifted. She rose and said, "Thank you, Howard, I believe we shall do the same. Good night." Turning to Mathilde, she said, "Mother, I will walk up with you." Mathilde stood up, bade Howard a dignified good night, and the two made their way upstairs. As Catherine paused at Mathilde's door, Mathilde remarked, "Well, that was definitely *not* the thing; I am surprised at Michael showing such a lack of breeding. Maria was always a very high stickler." "It did seem odd, Mama. However, he may not have felt entirely well," replied Catherine. "Sleep well, my dear."

Catherine went on her way to her own rooms. Pleased to see a footman in the corridor, she paused to say good night. The young man blushed and said, "Thank you, my lady. I hope his lordship found his rooms all right, my lady. I gave him directions, and offered to escort him, but he said that he could manage. I hope I did right, my lady." Catherine responded, "You did excellently well. I appreciate your thoughtfulness." She passed on into her suite, to be greeted by Jane, who curtsied and said, "Good evening, Lady Heyerwood. The weather shows no improvement, I'm afraid. An early night seems to be in order." "Indeed, yes, Jane. I think we would all benefit from it." "By the way, my lady, you had asked me earlier about anyone approaching your rooms. As I was returning to the dressing room after my dinner, I saw the viscount in the main hall, near your door again. The footman on duty helped him find his rooms. He seems to be having difficulty with learning his way about." "Thank you, Jane. I appreciate your letting me know." Once Catherine was disrobed, Jane took her candle and retired to the dressing room again. Catherine sat before the fire in her bedroom, pondering her cousin's wanderings. "I feel certain he is trying to find my personal correspondence. But why? He surely knows I am corresponding with Rosalie; what more does he want to know?" She got into bed, and blew out her candle, thinking, "At least, Lord Ridley did not put in an appearance today."

Early the next morning, she awakened earlier than usual, and was disheartened to see the rain still falling. "It does not seem as heavy, nor the sky so dark as yesterday. Maybe the storm will at least lessen today," she thought hopefully. She put on the golden brown wool crepe, her topaz earrings, and her topaz betrothal ring, hoping the warm golden colour would brighten the day. Going downstairs, Catherine crossed the hall to the library. She opened the door to the library just in time to see Michael sitting at her desk, rummaging through the drawers. She closed the door behind her, and said, "May I help you find something, Michael? I would love to know what you are looking for." Michael looked frozen in place. She could see from the disorder of the open drawers that he had been searching frantically, and was curious to see what excuse he could give for such a breach of her hospitality. He rose hastily, "Cousin, I was wishful to write a letter…" Approaching, she picked up paper and a pen from the floor. "Come, sir, you should be able to do better than that. You have been prowling near my rooms, now I find you rifling the contents of my desk. Obviously, you are searching for something specific. What do you expect to find?"

Crimson with embarrassed frustration, Michael responded, "Answers to my questions! You refuse to tell me if you are corresponding with my sister or others in her circle. I have the right to know what they are saying, what they are planning. If you will not tell me…" Cutting him off, Catherine said, "Sir, I can only believe that you have taken leave of your senses. You have no right to question me about my correspondence. To search my desk, to attempt to read my personal correspondence without my permission, is a complete violation of my hospitality, and is a despicable act. For someone who prates of his sister's dishonorable conduct, you, sir, are in no position to throw stones!"

The two stood for timeless seconds, glaring at each other across the desk, when a footman entered the library, and said, "Lady Heyerwood, Lord Ridley is here, and requests to know if you are at home. What answer may I give him, my lady?" Semi-hysterically, Catherine thought to herself, "It needed only this!" Still meeting her cousin's eyes squarely, Catherine answered, "By all means, inform him that I am at home and show him into the drawing room. I shall be there shortly." When the door shut behind the footman, Catherine said to Michael, "Sir, these matters are closed between us. You will not ask me about my correspondence again. I hope I make myself very clear on this point. Now, if you will excuse me, I will join my other guest in the drawing room." With raised eyebrows, she looked from her disordered desk back to her cousin, and said ironically, "By all means, sir, write any letters you need. As you see, there is plenty of paper and ink." Turning, she swept from the room, leaving the red-faced viscount standing alone by the desk.

Chapter 47

Catherine paused in the hall, struggling to regain her composure. Stepping over to the window to cool her flushed cheeks, she stared sightlessly out at the pouring rain. Giving herself a mental shake, she scolded herself, saying, "Come now, I must be in control of myself. This is awkward enough, without letting my cousin's bad conduct put me into a flame." Smoothing her skirt, she straightened her back and went into the drawing room. James was standing by the fire, warming his hands. She went to him, hand extended her hand. "My Lord Ridley, we have been expecting you. I do hope the trip was not too dreadful, in this horrible rain." He took her hand warmly and said, with a grimace, "No worse than could have been expected, certainly. We were mired to the axles twice. I blessed my good fortune when we turned into Heyerwood's drive, I do assure you!" Gesturing him to take a seat, Catherine sat down near the fire. "May I offer you some refreshment, sir? Some brandy or …." "Frankly, after the drive I have had this morning, a cup of tea would be delightful," he said. Surprised, she said, "Why, certainly, my lord. I believe I could do with a cup of tea myself." Summoning the footman, she requested a tray of tea. "How was town, my lord? Has this dreary weather made its way south?" James smiled, and said, "London so far has been spared your floods and torrents, my lady. The spring was advancing beautifully. Indeed, the sun was shining, and spring flowers were to be seen in all of the gardens." Catherine smiled back. "The contrast is almost too much to bear, is it not, sir? And yet, just a few days ago, my mother and I had tea in the walled garden and were commenting on the beautiful weather." A footman entered with a laden tray, which he set before the fire, and Catherine poured Lord Ridley a cup of tea, and another for herself.

The two sat across from each other, sipping their tea in silence. Catherine was rather surprised to note that she felt no awkwardness in Lord Ridley's company. She looked up to find him gazing back at her, a twinkle lurking in his blue eyes. She smiled again, and said, "It is a pleasure to see you again, my lord. I have rooms prepared for you so that you will not need to go further tonight. However, I must make you aware that you are not our only guest." James put up a brow and said, "Indeed, my lady, I would never presume…." Interrupting, Catherine continued, "Indeed, sir, I realize that you would not presume. However, our other guest is my cousin, the Viscount Chatellerault. I know that matters are … difficult between you, and would not have you overset by meeting him unawares." In no way discomposed, James took another sip of tea. "I thank you for your concern, my lady. However, I believe I can undertake to meet his lordship with civility under your roof. Our difficulties are not of my making or my desire, and I have no personal quarrel with him. If he can maintain ordinary courtesy, there will be no reason for concern." Catherine looked at him in some perplexity, and James continued. "Of course, if he cannot control himself, the situation will be resolved speedily enough." "How do you mean, sir?" He looked at her with twinkling eyes, and said, "Why, my lady, the nearest window will suffice. If a few minutes outside in this rain cannot cool the most furious temper, I will be most amazed."

Catherine, taken completely by surprise, giggled. Just then, the drawing room door burst open, and Michael strode furiously into the room. Taking one look at the couple by the fire, he exploded, "YOU here! By God, this is outside of enough, sirrah! I have a mind to…" Without bothering to rise, James said urbanely, "You have a mind to remember where you are, sir, I would hope." Caught in mid-tirade, Michael nearly choked on his wrath and sputtered. James turned to Catherine and smiled. "My lady, might I suggest that your cousin and I speak in private? Maybe we can finally put to rest this … quarrel." Catherine looked back at him gravely, but with a twinkle deep in her green eyes. "Of course, my lord. My mother suggested the ballroom as a suitable place for a conversation." "The ballroom?" he responded blankly. Then, unbelievably, he grinned. "Oh, I see. Plenty of room for action without distressing the household. Please, make your mother my compliments." Catherine rose, and said, "I shall have a footman to escort you, gentleman. I do hope you are able to resolve your differences suitably." Catherine pulled the bell pull, gave her instructions to the footman who answered, and resumed her seat by the fire, as the gentlemen left the room. When Howard came in to remove the tray, she said, "Howard, I would appreciate a fresh pot of tea, and, if you will have someone request my mother to join me, I would be grateful." Howard bowed, and said "Certainly, Lady Heyerwood," before picking up the tray and vanishing. She was sitting there, staring into the fire, not daring to contemplate what might be happening in the ballroom, when Mathilde hurried in, saying, "My dear Catherine, whatever is going on? Howard tells me that Michael and Lord Ridley are actually in the *ballroom*? Why on earth...?" Catherine laughed, and said, "Why, Mama, the farce has well and truly begun! Lord Ridley bade me make you his compliments, by the way."

"His compliments?" responded Mathilde, perplexed. "Indeed, yes, my dear. I told him that the ballroom was your idea." Sinking into her seat opposite Catherine, Mathilde said weakly, "My idea.... My love, it was a jest! Surely, you don't believe...." Catherine replied soothingly, "Certainly not, Mother. However, it does seem to have answered. James took Michael off, so they could try to resolve this in private. This pointless rancor has been allowed to go on far too long, separating Rosalie from her family, and causing entirely too much distress. I own, I do most fervently wish it were happening anywhere but here. Michael's behavior has been so ungentleman-like and ill-bred, that I am almost relieved to think he can vent his spleen on a suitable opponent!" Catherine went on with rather more enthusiasm, "I could wish you had been here to meet James, and see how calmly he handled the whole matter, Mother. You would have found it completely distressing, I know, and I am glad you were spared, but James was so imposing and, yet, able to see humor in the situation. Michael seemed an ill-mannered child in a tantrum." Mathilde looked at Catherine thoughtfully, and remarked, "I am astonished to hear you comment on the *humor* of the situation, daughter. Most women of my acquaintance would have been horrified by such behavior in their drawing rooms." Ruefully, Catherine replied, "My dear, I believe my sensibilities have been sadly blunted by Michael's sulks and temper spurts. I am afraid that, by the time, Michael came into the room and saw James, I was delighted at the possibility of giving him the opportunity to take his passions out on the proper target. A sad hostess, am I not?"

Meanwhile, in the ballroom, James invited Michael to tell him all. "Rather than subjecting your female relations, with whom you are barely acquainted, to your ill temper, tell me what is troubling you. Are you concerned with John's treatment of Rosalie? I can assure you that she wants for nothing and is very happy. Are you worried about having to pay the rest of her dowry? You can be certain that John cares nothing for that. What has been ailing you all these years, that you snap and snarl like a cur when we meet, and treat your sister like a pariah?" "You know why, my lord! All my life, it seems that you and your brother have gone your way without thinking of anyone else. I thought you were my friends; instead, you encouraged my sister to disobedience, allowing your brother to continue his courtship, helping him obtain the special license. *You* were free to travel, to do as you chose, while I must needs dance attendance on my mother, living the life my parents have laid out for me, regardless of my preferences. And now, I have to sit by while my father sends letters to my sister, mourning his favorite child, while my mother is ill from the stroke caused by that child's conduct! Even here, you turn up, corrupting my cousin, interfering….!" Lip curling in contempt, James looked at him.

"You blind fool, you could have done what you chose at any time. What would your parents have done to stop you? I remember very well; your father agreed to your University course and your tour. He took you to a Drawing Room, to make your bow to the king. He never put an obstacle in your way. You have an independent income, and the estate is entailed to you. *You* were the one who chose to let your mother bullock you into going back to Cheshire and staying there, to say 'Yes' and 'Amen' to whatever she told you. You have ever resented Rosalie for having the strength of character to stand by her own choice, and you have chosen to blame her, my brother and myself for your inability to free yourself from your mother's apron strings. I am sorry for her illness, but you know very well that she has not been entirely well for years, and that her condition is brought on by her own spleen, her unbridled lust to control and dominate everyone around her. My father was your father's oldest friend; as boys, we were constantly together. Do you honestly believe that either John or myself ever deliberately set out to thwart you in any way? If you do, you are as delusional as your mother. What do you want to do with your life? What has been denied you? I am sorry for you, you poor thing. If you want to live your own life, it is up to you to decide what you want, and to go after it, not blame your mother and others because you don't have what you think you might want." White-faced, Michael stood there looking at him, lashed by his contempt.

Suddenly, James couldn't stand to look at him any longer. Instead of seeing an equal, an adversary, he suddenly saw an uncertain, quarrelsome boy, despite their similar ages. He went to the window and looked out, leaving Michael standing in the middle of the ballroom floor with clenched fists. Minutes went by with no sound. Michael suddenly heaved a shuddering sigh, and strode the other way across the floor. Turning around, he said, through gritted teeth, "That I should hear this from you! My God, if I had a gun, I would shoot you like a dog!" Striding back, he glared at James; then, he laughed mirthlessly and said, "The really sad thing about it is this; much of what you say is true. That is probably why I have hated you all for so long; I haven't had the courage to face my own inability to make a decision or to act." James looked at him temperately, and replied, "Well, having come this far, maybe you will think about it now. You are a man; act like one. You have been a boy far too long." Michael grimaced and said, "Indeed, I have no choice but to think on it, have I? You've flung it in my face." James said, with some compassion, "You have time, you know. And you have family waiting to support you...." Michael turned on him and said, through clenched teeth, "Do I detect pity in your voice? I want no support from you and yours, my lord. I may have to acknowledge the truth in your words, but nothing, *nothing*, can undo our estrangement. I have hated you for too long." Turning on his heel, Michael strode to the door of the ballroom, where he paused. "Pray, give her ladyship my thanks for her *hospitality*," he said with a sneer. "I will have my bags packed, and will leave at first light, regardless of the weather. I would appreciate a tray in my room for dinner. Somehow, I feel certain that my presence in the dining room could not be other than awkward." So saying, he disappeared into the hall and down the stairs.

Feeling desperately sorry for his former opponent, James stayed by the window for some moments, trying to reconcile his boyhood friend with the troubled, vitiated man who had just left. Finally, he shrugged, and went back down to the drawing room.

Mathilde and Catherine were still sitting by the fire, saying very little. As James quietly entered the room, both ladies swung around to gaze at him, eyes wide. Reluctantly, James smiled and said, "Good evening, ladies, I hope I see you well?" Catherine replied, indignantly, "James, whatever happened? We are agog with curiosity and most concerned...!" Wearily, James sat down. "Your cousin is well, as am I. We had words, and finally got out in the open what has been poisoning the air between us for years now. I wish I could say that there was relief, but I am afraid his feelings are unchanged. However, we have faced it out, and he is planning to resume his journey tomorrow. He is having his belongings packed and requested a meal on a tray this evening. I believe he plans to leave at first light." Mathilde said, with compassion, "Poor Michael, he has been sorely troubled, I know. Should I look in on him, do you think?" "Lady Stanton, your kind heart does you credit, but I think it would be best if you leave him to himself this evening, as he himself has requested," replied James. He went on to tell them the gist of their discussion. Mathilde and Catherine, shocked, were unable to comment for several moments. "Poor Michael, how much he must have hated acknowledging the truth of your words," observed Catherine. "Indeed, I believe that to be the final straw," acknowledged James. Mathilde rose quietly, and excused herself. "I believe I shall go lie down in my room until it is time to dress for dinner. It is so distressing, to have this bad feeling in the family." James and Catherine rose, and Catherine kissed her mother tenderly. "I am sorry, Mother. Maybe this will pass, and things improve with time." Mathilde pressed her hand, and nodded to James. "I will see you both at dinner, my dears."

Catherine and James resumed their seats by the fire. Catherine looked at him, and asked, "May I pour you another cup of tea, my lord?" With the ghost of a smile, James said, "I believe, at this moment, I would prefer a glass of brandy." Catherine rang the bell and, when Howard came in, she said, "Howard, pray have the tea tray removed and bring some brandy and some sherry. Viscount Chatellerault is planning to leave early in the morning. Please be sure that he receives all assistance in packing, and a dinner tray in his room this evening. Please be sure that an early breakfast is offered, also. I would not have him leave on an empty stomach." Howard bowed, and said, "I will see to your refreshments immediately, my lady. One of the footmen is already assisting the viscount's man with the packing, and his carriage has been ordered for first light. Mrs. Davis has already taken the liberty of bespeaking breakfast for his lordship, and a good dinner will be sent up to his lordship's room." Fervently, Catherine said, "Howard, I do not know what we would do without you and Mrs. Davis." Bowing, Howard picked up the tray and left the room, only to return shortly with the brandy, sherry and glasses.

Catherine poured a glass of brandy and offered it to James. Pouring herself a sherry, Catherine looked at James and said, "Well, sir, this has to have been a singularly exhausting and unpleasant day for you." James took a mouthful of brandy and swallowed gratefully, "Indeed, I cannot remember another as trying. While airing our differences was desirable, I fear it brought the viscount little relief. It seems his rancor is like a festering wound, where the poison has gone so deep that lancing can no longer release it." Shuddering slightly, Catherine said, "What an evocative picture, my lord. Unfortunately, it seems sadly accurate. Each time he flew into a passion, he seemed to get angrier; yet the cause seemed to be so inadequate for the amount of temper he displayed." Sitting in silence, they finished their drinks. Catherine looked at him and said, "My lord, I would like thank you for helping me with this situation, and yet feel I must apologize to you as well. It was no desire of mine to have you confronted in such a fashion under my roof." James nodded gravely. "I appreciate your feelings, my lady," he acknowledged, and rose. "My lady, would it be possible for me to retire for a rest before dinner? Like your mother, I suddenly feel the need to be alone." Catherine rose also, and replied, "I will have a footman show you to your room. I, too, would like to rest for a while. It has been a most enervating afternoon."

Dinner that night was pleasant but not festive. With Michael's lurking presence in the house, a dark cloud fell over everyone's spirit. Even the weather contributed to the rather gloomy atmosphere, with thunder and lightening crashing and rain pouring down. The ladies retired to the drawing room, and tried to lighten the mood with music. James joined them almost immediately, and listened courteously while Catherine and Mathilde played several airs. However, by common consent the party adjourned early, and all retired to their rooms. As Catherine closed the door to her suite, she leaned against it with a sigh, then hurried down the hall to her sitting room. Relaxing onto the *chaise longue*, she stared into the fire and listened to the pouring rain. "I will certainly be glad when Michael takes his leave. I do hope the weather clears by morning. I really could not bear for him to stay, but could not wish for anyone to travel in such horrible weather," she thought. "Poor Rosalie, I had so hoped some sort of resolution would be possible, so that she could regain her relationship with her brother. It is so sad that Michael is determined to hold on to his grievance and anger. I cannot even write to her about this; I will have to leave it to James to tell John and Rosalie about this afternoon as he sees fit." She rose and went to her bedroom, where Jane was waiting to help her get ready for bed. With Jane in the dressing room, Catherine snuggled in her bed in the darkness and fell asleep listening to the storm.

The next morning, Catherine woke to bright spring sunshine. Sitting up with a jerk, she realized that it was much later than she intended. "Jane," she called, "I am late! Please bring me water and help me get dressed, quickly." Faster than she thought possible, Catherine was gowned and presentable, and hurried down the stairs. Entering the dining room, she saw only her mother and James, enjoying their breakfast. "I am so sorry to be late. I fear I slept longer than I intended," she said, as she sat down. The footman presented a few dishes, from which she helped herself at random, and poured some coffee. As soon as the footman left the room, Catherine looked at Mathilde, and said, "Mother, I am so embarrassed. I meant to at least try to bid Michael farewell…." Mathilde smiled affectionately, and said, "Frankly, dear, it is better that you were not there. I rose early and sat with him at his breakfast, and saw him off very early indeed. I do not think he would have wanted to see you today. He seemed very tired, and wanted only to take his leave. He did say that he hoped I would continue to write to his mother, so I can at least retain that connection. Poor young man, I fear he has a long road ahead of him today." Catherine said, "I am glad that you will be able to continue corresponding with your cousin; I know that is important to you." Turning to James, she said, "I hope the storm did not disturb your rest, sir." James replied, "My lady, it would have taken more than some thunder and rain to keep me awake last night. I was most comfortable."

Chapter 48

The day passed pleasantly enough. James went out to check on his horses, and to take a ride around the estate. Catherine dealt with some correspondence and spoke to Mrs. Davis about some deliveries from London, clarifying which items were for the estate and which for the school. Later in the afternoon, she and Mathilde went out to the gardens, to see how much damage the storm had done. Both ladies wore sturdy half boots and plain gowns, as it was very muddy. The gardener and his assistants were hard at work, cleaning up broken limbs, blown leaves, and other debris. Looking about with some dismay, Catherine said, "Oh, dear, I was afraid the storm had wreaked havoc, but was not prepared for this!" Overhearing, the gardener said, "Begging your pardon, my lady. It looks worse than it is. We will get it cleaned up today. You will be surprised what a few days of sun and gentle weather will do." Smiling her appreciation, Catherine led Mathilde down the path to the walled garden. To her relief, although there was some debris, the damage was far less noticeable here. "The walls sheltered the plants and bushes from the worst of the wind. I believe that, once it has dried up, this area at least will be all right." It was too wet to sit down, so the ladies contented themselves with looking about them, and shortly thereafter returned to the house.

James had not yet returned from his ride, so Mathilde and Catherine enjoyed a nuncheon in the drawing room, then returned to their rooms. Mathilde lay down to rest, as was her custom in the afternoon. Catherine sat in her sitting room, and worked on her embroidery. The chair seat was taking shape now, the colours rich and glowing against the neutral background. Absorbed, she continued working until she noticed the changing light. Just then, Jane came in with warm water with which to wash. "What would you wear to dine, my lady?" Jane asked. Catherine replied, "The dark green silk over the ivory underdress, I believe, Jane. I shall wear the emerald pendant and earbobs as well." Somewhat startled, Jane said, "The dark green...? Is that not more formal than usual for a family dinner in the country, my lady?" Catherine laughed and said, "It is, indeed, Jane, but I feel more festive tonight than I have since my aunt and uncle left, and would like to dress up." Jane smiled, and said, "I will get the gown and underdress, while you bathe, my lady." Catherine lingered in her bath, feeling like a dark cloud had been lifted. "It isn't just that the rain has finally stopped," she thought, "it is such relief to know that Michael is gone. I should feel sorry that he left in such anger and haste, but I cannot. It is sad, but I hope that much time passes before I see him again." Her hair swept up in a braided coronet threaded with a golden chain, she clasped the pendant around her neck and slipped the hooks of the earbobs into her ears. "I am ready. What do you think, Jane?" Looking at herself in the mirror, Catherine was pleased. The ivory underdress shimmered slightly under the deep green silk, and the emeralds matched Catherine's eyes. Sincerely, Jane said, "My lady, I do not think I have seen you look so becoming since the night of the ball in London. The ivory underdress is a bit less formal than the golden *crepe lisse*. You look lovely, my lady." Catherine blushed, and thanked Jane. As she made for the door, she stopped and looked over her shoulder. "Jane, you may return to your own room tonight. Thank you for staying with me; I'm sure it was uncomfortable for you. Now that my cousin has resumed his journey, we may go back to our accustomed arrangements." Somewhat relieved, Jane curtsied and said, "Thank you, my lady."

Catherine joined her mother and the baron in the drawing room. Mathilde was also looking her very best, in silver lace over black silk, with diamonds in her ears and at her throat. The baron was elegantly clad as well, in formal evening clothes. "Well, my dear," said Mathilde, "You look quite lovely. It seems we are all in a festive mood this evening." Frankly, Catherine said, "I feel as if I have been given a reprieve, Mother. Celebration is definitely in order, I think." The baron bowed over her hand. "Lady Heyerwood, I must agree with your mother. You are indeed in looks this evening. I hope you do not mind, but I have taken the liberty to ask Howard to bring champagne this evening. As heavy as last evening was, I thought we needed the bright sparkle of champagne to lift our mood tonight. May I pour you a glass?" Catherine smiled in response, and said gaily, "Champagne is just the thing! Mother, may we tempt you to a glass?"

Mathilde, in her favorite seat by the fire, chuckled and replied, "Indeed you may! I have always felt champagne was the perfect accompaniment for any celebration, and a certain mood lifter when needed." The frothy golden wine was poured into delicate crystal, and the glasses handed round. James lifted his glass and said, "To your good health, ladies, and to happier days." Catherine and Mathilde lifted their glasses in return, and they all sipped the cool, sparkling wine. Howard came in and announced that dinner was served, so they all went in to dine.

Feeling the celebratory mood, the cook had outdone herself. Each course was delicious, perfectly prepared, and just enough. The dessert was a very special concoction of whipped cream, fruit and wine, and the champagne flowed throughout the meal. Catherine, Mathilde and James engaged in light-hearted conversation, ranging from music and art, to gardens, to travel. The baron held the ladies spellbound with tales of his travels to foreign places. "I had no idea that you were so well-travelled, my lord," said Catherine. "My work has required a great deal of travel, Lady Heyerwood. I had hoped that, once Napoleon was halted, I would not be required to be out of England as much as I had been, but it had not worked out as I had hoped." "Napoleon?" echoed Catherine. "Do you work for our government in some capacity?" "Let us say that I did my part, as did many others. I have been useful in some respects, if only as a courier," said James, urbanely. "I finished what I hope will be my last errand just before I arrived for your aunt's wedding. It was that which delayed me." Turning the conversation, he told them something of Ridley Manor and the estate which he shared with John and their brother Charles. "Charles is currently on the continent, but talks of selling out. He hopes to return to Ridley in the fall. His house is being readied for him, and he expects to be married then. He has been betrothed for two years now, to an unexceptionable young woman."

The conversation turned again to less personal matters, until Catherine and Mathilde rose to return to the drawing room. They had barely seated themselves, when James appeared. "I can hardly sit in solitary splendor in the dining room, when two such charming ladies are in here," he said gallantly. The threesome laughed and chatted, as they sipped champagne. Mathilde played a few airs on her harp; then Catherine took her seat at the piano-forte. They played a duet, then Mathilde returned to her seat by the fire. Catherine continued to play, her fingers drifting from melody to melody, while James stood near by. They carried on a desultory conversation for a while. Catherine glanced over at her mother, and noticed she was dozing in her chair. Turning to James with a smile, she said, low-toned, "My mother has found it quite exhausting, trying to keep my cousin and me on a civil basis. Poor darling, she is worn out." James said feelingly, "I have no difficulty imagining what a strain it must have been for you all. After I retired last night, I felt like I had been beaten. It was all I could do to rise at my usual time this morning." Curious, Catherine asked, "Did you see my cousin off, sir?" "Not exactly. I could not feel that my presence would be welcomed, but wanted to be at hand if there were any difficulties. Viscount Chatellerault was all that was polite to your staff and to Viscountess Stanton. In fact, their parting was quite calm and friendly. After he departed, I joined your mother in the dining room for breakfast. I do not think she suspected that I had been lurking on the landing, my lady." Catherine chuckled, saying, "I can hardly see you *lurking*, sir. I'm sure she would have appreciated your support. I know I certainly do."

Catherine rose from the piano-forte and started back toward the fire, when James put his hand out. "Stay a moment, Lady Heyerwood. Could I tempt you to take a turn on the terrace? It is cool, but dry. I checked it before I changed for dinner. The sun did its work magnificently this afternoon." Looking up at him, Catherine murmured something about getting a wrap, and hurried away. Coming back with a black silk shawl, Catherine took James' arm, and they stepped out of the drawing room through the long window to the terrace. Silently, they strolled along the stone floor, looking up at the stars and enjoying the fresh scents of spring. The air was cool and crisp. "It almost sparkles, like our champagne," said Catherine, as they strolled. "This was a delightful idea, my lord." They admired the stars shining above, and paused to look across the lawn and the gardens. The pauses in their conversation grew longer, as they stopped and strolled and stopped again. Finally, James swung Catherine around, to look straight into her eyes. "I know our correspondence has been short," he said, "and I know that I rushed my fences again, when I wrote you that I wanted to break my journey here. However, the events of the last couple of days seem to have changed things between us. What do you think, my lady?" Catherine stared up into his eyes for a long moment. Turning away, she said, "I do feel that things are different, my lord. We have seen each other through a situation fraught with strain and strong emotions. It is not often that one has the opportunity to see how another will deal with a moment of personal crisis. It gives one a depth of insight that is not easily achieved in a more casual situation." Smiling down at her, James responded, "I, too, feel that I have gained insight into your character as well. Your refusal to accept his overbearing manner, and your ability to see the humor in the situation were both remarkable."

Catherine looked back at him. "I must confess that I marveled at your restraint, sir. When the two of you left for the ballroom, I made certain that, at the very least, there would be blows, if not a duel out right. You both seemed pushed to the very limits of control, and yet managed to walk away from it." Deliberately, James said, "I worked very hard to resolve matters peaceably, not only for your sake, but for Rosalie, and for myself. In our youth, Michael was like another brother to me, and it was painful to incur his enmity. I have long hoped that I could salvage something of friendship with him. I have given my best effort to discovering the reason for his anger and to find a way to clear it. I know now that the remedy rests solely with him, and can let it go." He took a step toward her and said, "I would like to talk, Catherine. I have told you how I think of you, that you are always in my mind. Is it still too soon to speak of courtship to you? In our few meetings, I feel that I have come to know you well. I know how reluctant you are to give up your freedom. However, I must tell you that I value your independence of spirit, your ability to think for yourself, to face a challenge. I am not looking for a girl to cosset and protect. I am looking for a woman to share my life, an intelligent woman capable of making decisions, able to manage for herself when necessary, willing to discuss and find a compromise at times. Are you still unwilling to consider the possibility of marriage?"

Catherine took a few steps away, and said, "My lord, had you asked me this a week ago, I would have told you again that it was too soon. The events of the last few days have shown me that I would have regretted that answer. It is true that I am not yet ready to commit to another marriage." She turned back to face him with a roguish smile in her eyes. "But to consider the possibility? I have come to realize that one must always consider one's possibilities. Why, I have never enjoyed a real courtship." Impetuously, James took two long strides to close the gap between them. Taking her hands in his, he looked deeply into her eyes and said, smiling, "If it is courtship you want, you shall have it. Would it be premature of me to plan for a happy ending?" Gazing up at his face, she smiled back and said softly, "I would prefer to think of a new beginning."

About the Author

LAUREN GILBERT has a Bachelor of Arts degree in English, with a minor in Art History. She has continued her education with classes, work shops and independent study. An avid reader, she is a member of the Jane Austen Society of North America, and has presented several programs to JASNA chapters. She lives in Florida, with her husband, Ed.

CPSIA information can be obtained at www.ICGtesting.com
Printed in the USA
LVOW062058090312

272365LV00002B/230/P

9 781463 402518